Malay Chatterjee was born in the shadow of the Taj Mahal in 1947—a midnight's child. He attended eight different schools while growing up, studying Architecture in Delhi and later City and Regional Planning at Harvard and M.I.T. Over the seven years spent in the U.S. he worked as an architect, taught ballroom dancing, and sold encyclopaedias door-to-door.

At different points in his varied history he studied European languages, philosophy, drama and classical music. He has been an actor, a tourist guide, and a founding member of the Conservation Society of Delhi. From 1979 to 2009 he was a professor at Delhi's School of Planning and Architecture.

Chatterjee's many academic/non-fiction publications have covered complex issues concerning architectural conservation and heritage management. He is considered an authority on the planning and design history of New Delhi.

The Drunk Bird Chronicles

MALAY CHATTERJEE

SPEAKING TIGER

SPEAKING TIGER BOOKS LLP
4381/4, Ansari Road, Daryaganj
New Delhi 110002

First published in paperback by Speaking Tiger Books 2019

ISBN: 978-93-89231-87-8
eISBN: 978-93-89231-88-5

10 9 8 7 6 5 4 3 2 1

Typeset in Sabon Roman by SÜRYA, New Delhi
Printed at Sanat Printers, Kundli, Haryana

For Meera

Contents

Prologue

Allegro, the great white raven, did not know how he would survive now that his master Gareth Armstrong had died (aged one hundred). With whom would he discuss politics? Who would laugh at his jokes? Who would give him his nightly shot of brandy? As his tears began to fall, young Julio tried to comfort him, 'Oh, Allegro, don't be so sad. I promise to look after you now.'

Allegro perked up. He was very fond of the young lad, and quite touched by this sentiment. 'Yes, we shall be good friends, Julio. Your great-grandfather wanted *me* to look after *you*. He wanted you to be an inventor like him. I shall show you his sketches and notepads. Here, take the keys to his trunks, full of wondrous things.'

'Tell me again about your travels with Grand-Grandpa Gareth,' implored Julio, settling down cross-legged on the floor. And so the brisk-talking bird, perched in the veranda of the Braganza's flat in Delhi's Connaught Place, narrated the long, complicated journeys from London to Calcutta and further East. Wistful regret crept in as he recounted the time he had left Gareth for the dark forests beyond Shillong. 'That was where I was born, Julio, but I felt like an outsider there. The black ravens abused me; they considered me an undesirable alien to be scorned and chased out. All my life, through hundreds of years, I had thought *that* would be the place where I belonged. But really my home was with Gareth, wherever he went.'

After Gareth's cremation, Julio, Allegro and the other Braganzas drove to the Ridge to scatter Gareth's ashes. Allegro looked around and noticed that the birds in this forest were a friendlier lot—mynahs, pigeons and koels that were small and sang sweetly. Were even the vultures a little afraid of him—an oddity, a freak of nature? And in that moment he felt his deep fears begin to fall away and he was reconciled to his uniqueness; after all, he did talk a dozen or so bird and human languages, and he had once outwitted even the brilliant Karl Marx.

He whispered to Julio now: 'Just as I tried to reclaim my roots, Julio, you may do so too someday...'

1

The Lazy Duck

New Year's Day, 1877. In far-away Delhi, the Viceroy, Lord Lytton, proclaimed that Queen Victoria was now also Empress of India. On that same day in London, strange sounds were heard in a brothel on Lemon Tart Lane: SPLASH!...THUD!

Mrs Lena Armstrong looked up from her knitting. She called out to one of the maids.

'Lucy! Go and see what the Master is up to—hurry! And don't go tripping over your new skirt. Cost me a pound, it did.' Lucy ran up the stairs, her skirts held high above her knees. Mrs Armstrong heard her scream, and then sob as she tumbled back into the parlour.

'Oh Mamlena, the Master—he be drownded in the bathtub!'

Except for her husband Gareth, everybody at The Lazy Duck and the adjacent brothel called her by the short form. With a bored expression, Mamlena dragged herself up the stairs to the bathroom to see for herself. Drownded? Really, that Lucy made a drama out of everything.

But sure enough, Mr Gareth Armstrong, the almost-famous inventor, was lying face-down in the overflowing tub, a few bubbles rising to the surface. Mamlena was sure he was unconscious. She hauled him out of the tub with Lucy's help and laid him out on the floor. A sorry sight.

'Go fetch the Captain. Mind how you wake him. Knock gently on his door. Only *gentle* knocks. You know damn well he's usually dead asleep in the morning. He'll be crotchety. Tell him it's an emergency. I can't shut the wretched taps off. The house will be ruined with all this water. Now go!...Oh, there's another thing. After you've spoken to the Captain, hop over to The Black Bull and wash out all the rubbers and dip them in petroleum jelly for the next use. Becky's taken ill, so you'll have to assume some of her duties...And, oh, send the boys up! The Master will have to be carried to his bedroom. Go now! What are you staring at?'

Mr Armstrong's latest project was to design and fabricate the plumbing for a fully-automated bathtub. One dial to set the desired temperature, one dial to indicate body-weight: the idea was to ensure no water was wasted, using an intricate system of level indicators, valves, taps and thermostats. With six bathrooms and three kitchens between them, The Lazy Duck and The Black Bull consumed enormous quantities of water. Some of the girls even insisted on bathing between clients. And some clients insisted on bathing afterwards.

The Black Bull featured a pub at street level and a flourishing brothel on the upper floors. The Lazy Duck—which shared a much-punctured party wall with the brothel—housed the servants on the upper floors, the living quarters of the Armstrongs, a large reading room for the poor, and a cluttered laboratory and workshop in the cellar.

Captain Jack Crusoe scratched himself awake. He got dressed leisurely and made his way to the Armstrong bathroom. A big rat scurried ahead of him. The blessed catorat wasn't doing her job. The Captain was used to so-called emergencies: fights in the pub, violence in the brothel, botched abortions, murders on Lemon Tart Lane...

'What exactly did you hear, Mamlena?' She told him about the splash and the thud. Lucy gasped with excitement and chipped in with, 'The Master, he say summat like "Bap-bap-Baptist"...'

'He's had a bad concussion. Happened all the time on my ships. See that lump on the back of his skull? Slipped, fell, and knocked his head on the rim of the bathtub, most likely. Better send for Doctor Pecksniffer—though I don't completely trust that German. In Hamburg he used to roam the docks. The sailors called him Peckersniffer...Lucy, send that brother of yours to fetch him. This is a real fucking emergency. The Master might cop it any moment.'

Mamlena was tense about something else. 'Captain,' she said, 'get the water to stop, or else the whole house will be flooded. Cost a fortune to repair. Do something!'

The Captain reached behind the tub and found three valves. He turned all three this way and that way. The water—now scalding hot—stopped flowing presently, and the tub began to drain. Mr Armstrong stirred, opened one eye and yelled out, 'I AM A BAPTIST!' then returned to a state of unconsciousness.

Mamlena had often heard Mr Armstrong shout out silly things while pottering about his laboratory in the cellar—mainly blessing the memory of great scientists, dead and gone. So she was not particularly concerned about this Baptist business. She knew her husband and her daughter Rachel had been fascinated for some time by the doings of London's countless Evangelicals and had often attended their meetings. They loved all the singing and dancing.

Doctor Pecksniffer's arrival caused a flutter among the servants, who trooped into the crowded bathroom to gawk and gasp. His advice was practical: get dry clothes on Armstrong to avoid pneumonia, take him to his bedroom, have him lie on his stomach—no pressure on the lump at the back of his head, wave smelling salts under his nose every half-hour. As the doctor was about to leave, Mamlena led him to her parlour to have a word in private. Rachel would be returning from the Bakersfield cemetery any time soon. She would want to know the prognosis. She was utterly devoted to her father. Mamlena lowered her voice.

'Doctor, I now have a vexing dilemma. My father in Ireland is likely to pass on any day. He has sent for me, his most devoted daughter. I am due to leave the day after tomorrow. See, I've been rushing to complete knitting this brown pullover for him. Brown, his favourite colour. And now there's this problem with Mr Armstrong. Do I stay or do I go? What should I do? Here there are the Captain, Rachel—who is a mature eighteen—and all the servants to take care of him. The pub and the business won't suffer if I'm away for a fortnight. Rachel can keep an eye on things. I have gone away before, each time Father was sickly... What do you think, Doctor, medically speaking?'

The versatile doctor assured her that all would be well and dandy soon enough. He promised to visit the patient once a day and if there were complications he would telegraph her promptly. Besides, Rachel was a sensitive, caring daughter who could be trusted to nurse her father. And the Captain was loyal and competent.

Rachel returned home at about five. It was already pitch dark. She had been to a distant cemetery—taken the train there and back—on the lookout for beautiful inscriptions on graves. She made rubbings of gravestones that caught her fancy. This was a hobby started long ago, when she was a little girl. She used to accompany Mr Charles Dickens on his search for unusual names on tombstones. He was practically blind and all of his many children were mortally afraid of cemeteries. The distinguished novelist and the Armstrong girl were thus a familiar sight in London's cemeteries on Saturday afternoons. Rachel served as his eyes.

That evening she leaned over her father's head. 'It's me, Rachel, Father...Father? Say something please...' Mr Armstrong remained inert. Mamlena told her the doctor's advice. She reminded her daughter about the urgent trip she had to make to Ireland to see Grandfather before he passed on. Rachel, stroking her father's hand, was reassuring.

'Of course you must stick to your plans, Mother. I'll be here, and promise not to leave the house until he recovers. I'll arrange for one of the boys to be in Father's room whenever I have to step out for necessities.'

Mamlena sighed with relief. All the arrangements were in place. Two days later she left for Ireland after briefing the Captain and the staff and the girls on their duties. She told Rachel not to visit The Black Bull unless it was strictly necessary. Most brothel issues could be handled by the Captain.

~

Mr Armstrong made a miraculous recovery four days after the mishap. Rachel and the Captain were in his room when he sat up suddenly and shouted, 'I am a Baptist. A BAPTIST!' Rachel was astonished by this piece of nonsense. The Captain feared the Master had not fully recovered.

What followed over the next couple of days can best be described as a series of heated confabulations involving the Captain, Rachel and Mr Armstrong. The inventor repeatedly maintained he'd had enough of the undemocratic Catholic Church and its dogmas.

'I have long admired the Protestants—particularly the Baptists. Their theology is so straightforward and simple. Their preachers actually depend on the Bible and don't have to answer to the tyrant in Rome. Rachel, don't you find Mass boring? An unending, repetitive litany, week after week. Even your devout mother usually nods off to sleep. I've seen you nudge her awake on countless occasions...Now that I'm a Baptist, my conscience does not permit me to be the owner of a brothel.'

Rachel was intrigued by this turn of events. Eventually she found herself agreeing with her father. He was quite adamant that he wished to become a Baptist missionary. A lay missionary in some distant corner of the Empire. Rachel gradually warmed to the idea and said she would accompany him. She'd had enough of Lemon Tart Lane where she was constantly being mistaken for one of 'Mamlena's Girls.' A long journey was just what she needed. Her career options in London were limited anyway. She had trained to be a typist but was reluctant to sit in a gloomy office all day. She now thought that running away with her father would be a grand adventure. With due ceremony, Mr Gareth Armstrong baptized Miss Rachel in the same delinquent bathtub. The Captain was the only witness.

Preparations followed. The Captain was sworn to secrecy. Father and daughter had decided to sail to India where, the Baptist Head Office informed them, they would be very welcome. The Captain was dispatched to Mr Armstrong's bankers on Lombard Street to arrange for the withdrawal of a colossal sum of six thousand pounds in bank drafts, bank notes and gold sovereigns. The laboratory and workshop were tidied up, and certain critical instruments and scientific notebooks were packed carefully into a large steel trunk which sat unobtrusively in a dark corner. Rachel was put in charge of packing summer clothes for both of them. She added a generous supply of art materials because she assumed India would be a large graveyard of Christian men, women and children who had perished due to the extreme climate.

Meanwhile, a lengthy telegram arrived from Mamlena. The old man was much better now and wore the brown pullover constantly. But Mamlena's sister Sheila had asked her to stay on for a week to see her through a difficult confinement. The midwife anticipated trouble during the imminent birth of Sheila's twelfth child. This proved a welcome reprieve for Mr Armstrong and daughter. The Captain had booked berths on the Bombay-bound *Eastern Star*. Its departure had been postponed by six days.

~

Why Bombay? Well, her Majesty had just been proclaimed Empress of India. The arts and crafts manufactures of India had generated wide interest through the Great Exhibition of 1851. The Baptist headquarters in London put out frequent advertisements calling for men and women of all ages, in good health, to sign up as missionaries and sail away to the jewel in the crown. Mr Armstrong had been keeping track of the notices in the newspapers for some time (he had made it a habit to spend at least an hour each morning in his reading room for the poor and newly-literate, whom he charged a modest tuppence an hour).

The notion of India had interested him ever since the Great Exhibition. His first scientific achievement came about when he was working in the glass factory patronized by Joseph Paxton, the designer of the original gigantic pavilion that housed the exhibition. The pavilion had burnt down. Paxton now wanted to make a superstructure that was as light as possible. He mentioned this in young Armstrong's hearing. Working on a hunch, the experimenter added certain chemicals to molten glass and discovered that large, tough panes could be manufactured in this way. Paxton was delighted, and gave the eager inventor from Glasgow five pounds—a fortune for Gareth in those days. And this was how the sparkling new Crystal Palace came to be erected. The special glass was the only Armstrong invention that was fully realized through manufacturing. Most others were just ideas, visions, models, or sketches in his notebooks.

~

Two days before the Armstrongs were to leave, a major hitch occurred in their travel arrangements. The Captain had gone over to the *Eastern Star* to inspect the cabin he had reserved for them, make final payments, and so on. He returned to The Lazy Duck in a foul mood.

'Master, the ship has a very strict policy of not allowing pets on board. Not even birds. So what do we do about Allegro? I threatened to cancel your bookings but that had no effect.'

'That's a great disappointment. We will have to leave him behind,' said Rachel.

'We can't do that to him,' said Mr Armstrong. 'I promised I would take him back to his birthplace. Let me write the shipping company a note.' He made several points in the note:

> *Allegro, a giant white raven, was reputed to be at least two hundred years old. No one knew how this garrulous creature came to be named Allegro. He had outlived a dozen successive owners. And there was also the India connection. Allegro could talk in English, Sanskrit, French, Khasi and some other Indian languages. He was born in the Khasi Hills in north-eastern India, and was sold into slavery because of his enormous size, unusual colour and phenomenal memory. He could recite all the psalms and the Bhagavad Gita by heart. All on board would find him extremely entertaining. A special exemption*

should be made for this extraordinary bird who was actually a personage, an intellectual.

There were other details which Mr Armstrong thought it best not to mention. That Allegro was headquartered in the pub at The Black Bull and had become an alcoholic on account of the fumes generated by the heavy drinking all around him. That he was very sociable: every passing woman was greeted with 'Oooh, you Delectable Slut,' and male customers were hailed with, 'O-ho, you Handsome Bugger.' Allegro in his large cage was very popular.

The Captain carried Mr Armstrong's note back to the ship. Its eloquent words carried no weight. The answer was still a terse 'No Pets.' Allegro was most disheartened at this development. He spoke in an agitated whisper.

'Pet? I'm no pet! I have been your friend and companion for exactly twenty-six years, five months and seventeen days. I was here when Rachel was born twenty-five years, three months, six days and seven hours ago. I wish Mamlena did not keep telling people Rachel is eighteen to make herself seem younger...Pet? Who did you bounce your scientific ideas off of? Who gave you constructive suggestions on your engineering sketches?'

Allegro now lost his poise and raised his voice. He was determined to make Mr Armstrong feel guilty and wretched. 'I gave you sound advice on how to handle your cousin Alexander Bell. But you didn't follow it, and now he is going to earn a fortune with your ideas for a teletalker...Pet? How dare anyone call me a pet? Who gave you the idea of a watch that men and women could wear on their wrists and which required no winding? A watch so accurate that it would never need correcting. And you went and lost the sketches on your journey to Geneva!...Master, Master, Master, will you ever take me back to the forest where I was born?'

Mr Armstrong put his arms around Allegro's neck and asked for forgiveness and patience. He promised he would send for him once he and Rachel settled down in India. He made Allegro swear not to divulge their destination to anyone, particularly not to Mamlena. To underscore the need for secrecy he read out the letter he had written to her. Mr Armstrong assumed a very formal tone:

> *Dear Mrs Armstrong,*
>
> *Rachel and I have left on a long journey whose destination is uncertain. We go, trusting in the Lord, with an ardent desire to serve as Baptist missionaries. Do not, under any circumstances, attempt to track us down. Our minds are made up and we look forward to a life of joy in the service of others.*
>
> *I have the funds to travel around the world. We are considering Buenos Aires, Johannesburg, Sydney or Auckland as the first port of call. Wherever white people have interacted with and abused native populations.*
>
> *I leave The Lazy Duck and The Black Bull in the safe hands of you and the Captain. Financial and legal matters will be handled by my solicitor and our bankers once we have a fixed address.*
>
> *Do not forget to send Professor Karl Marx five pounds every month. He is always hard up and, as you know, I am an enthusiastic supporter of his writings.*
>
> *Take good care of Allegro. Remember he can't sleep without a large thimbleful of brandy every night. The servants at The Black Bull know what he has for his meals. Remember he is allergic to rum and beef.*
>
> *Yours very sincerely,*
> *Gareth Armstrong*

And then it was Sunday morning at last. Father and daughter left The Lazy Duck at ten o'clock. It was the day off for all employees. They were expected to go to Mass and to visit London's famous parks. A carriage had been engaged by Captain Crusoe. No one except him was aware of the secretive departure. At the docks, the Captain assisted with boarding the *Eastern Star*. He wondered, not for the first time, how he'd got involved in the Armstrong controversy. Nevertheless, he was privately glad to have Mr Armstrong off the scene. Now he would have Mamlena all to himself. He had a soft spot for her.

The Black Bull–Lazy Duck establishment was conveniently located five minutes' walk from Waterloo Station. Its original owner, Robert Armstrong, had set up a pub and brothel to take advantage of the proximity of his property to the busy railway terminus. The clients were mostly clerks and small-time businessmen who periodically 'worked late'. The girls and other women employed at The Black Bull were from Ireland, France, Belgium and Holland. Ten to twelve at any given time. These charmers were categorized into four classes: Princess (two pounds), Duchess (one pound), Baroness (ten shillings, six pence), Countess (five shillings). Something to suit every purse, and a system that gave every girl a future to aspire to. It was not unheard of for a Countess to be promoted to a Duchess in five years. The Countess class was the entry level, and these young women had only to demonstrate skill, versatility, charm and loyalty to become much in demand. Some of the girls got married and migrated to distant suburbs where they could conceal their past. Some moved to Granby Street where the pickings were richer than in Lemon Tart Lane. Some of the senior women had children, and sent them out to work when they were as young as six. The Evangelicals maintained that London had at least eighty thousand prostitutes. A very Victorian phenomenon.

A word is in order about the Captain. He had been dismissed from Her Majesty's Service for gross insubordination. He was later employed by Robert Armstrong to act as his Man Friday, Bouncer, Pimp, and Chief of Staff. Robert Armstrong's young wife Lena was put in charge of 'the girls.' She took care of their health, hygiene, clothing, discipline, and other assorted womanly needs.

The Black Bull was a flourishing enterprise, run on cooperative lines: fifty per cent of the net profits went to Armstrong, twenty-five per cent to Lena, and twenty-five to the Captain. After 'the Admiral' died suddenly of a stroke in the pub one evening, it was found that a considerable fortune was at stake. Robert had left his property and share of investments to his younger brother, Gareth, who promptly moved in and took over Robert's responsibilities, including his wife.

A few months later, Lena gave birth to a daughter. But she was never quite sure who the father was. Robert? Gareth? The Captain? She did not dwell too much on this matter for, in her line of business, it was best to remain discreet. Thus, it was universally taken for granted that Gareth was the father of the beautiful girl. They named her Rachel.

Running the pub had been Robert's chief occupation. He spent hours there, drinking too much along with the regulars. Gareth, on the other hand, had little interest in alcohol. He spent a significant proportion of his time walking about the streets of a London that was changing fast: large-scale demolitions, slum clearance, new road names, dirt, begging and hunger on the streets. The coming of the railways had affected almost every facet of urban life. A million of the poor were displaced.

Gareth Armstrong also befriended many notable scholars during the long hours he spent studying books and journals on biology, chemistry, physics and mechanical engineering in the reading room of the British Museum. His closest friends were Professor Karl Marx, Mr Charles Darwin, and the half-blind Mr Charles Dickens. Through whispered snatches of conversation with Professor Marx he developed an abiding compassion for the working classes. Hence the tuppence-an-hour reading room at The Lazy Duck. From Mr Darwin he gained insights into evolutionary biology. This led him to 'invent' the catorat, a cross between cats and rats. It took him eight years of genetic experiments. Catorats could hunt down and devour common rats in sewers and drain pipes. He bred a large number of them and sold them at a tidy profit. Mr Brown at the Palace had arranged to buy two dozen, and Her Majesty was quite pleased with the dramatic decrease in the rat population there. But, by some quirk of nature which neither Gareth nor Charles Darwin could understand, the catorats became infertile beyond the third generation. By the time of Gareth's 'Immersion' there was only one left, Katerina. She followed Mamlena around The Lazy Duck like a puppy, squealing, 'I want a husband, make me a husband.'

~

The Captain congratulated himself on how well the great escape had been accomplished. Not a soul had witnessed the manner of Gareth and Rachel's departure from The Lazy Duck. There was no sign of Mamlena returning from Ireland. The Captain was now solely in charge. He was lying in his bed luxuriating in his late morning nap when there was a timid knock on the door.

'Who is it? Don't disturb me now. I'll be down in a couple of hours.'

'It's me, Lucy. I needs to aks you summat. Won't take a jiffy.'

Captain Crusoe drew the blanket up to his chin and asked her to enter his bedroom. Lucy got to the point immediately.

'I saw you take the Master and Miss Rachel in a carrij yesterday. I want to know where you took 'em. Mamlena will aks me when she comes home. I stayed away from Mass coz I had a heddick. I was the only one to see you go.'

The Captain was dismayed. He had made such careful plans and here was this chit of a girl on the brink of exposing him. 'On no account must you tell Mamlena I was involved in the Master's departure. Let it be a secret between you and me. After some time, I'll ask Mamlena to increase your wages for good behaviour.'

Lucy tried hard to think why the Captain wished to keep such an ordinary thing so secret. She immediately saw an opportunity to try a little blackmail.

'I'll keep mum if that's what you want, Sir. But I want summat in return. I want to be a Countess. Housemaid's not good enough. I know the girls at The Black Bull very well. They say the first time hurts. After that it's as easy as shelling peas. I've been learning to talk propah for some time. You must convince Mamlena to send me to The Black Bull.'

The Captain did not know what to make of Lucy's demand. 'But you know nothing of the business. You are a virgin. Mamlena has a policy not to employ virgins. She takes on only experienced girls...And then, Lucy, you're not much to look at. No flesh on you at all.'

'As for the virgin part, Sir, you can fix that in a jiffy. I'll take me clothes off and get under your blanket, and you can make me virginity vanish.'

The Captain realized he was in a lot of trouble. If he turned down Lucy's impulsive offer she'd go babbling to Mamlena who, in turn, would force him to reveal that Gareth and Rachel had taken a ship to India. She had powerful clients who might order the ship to return to London. Or she might have the police arrest them at the next port of call.

Between the Captain's lack of enthusiasm and Lucy's inexperience, it took a long spell of strenuous effort to get the deed done. Lucy shed a few tears of gratitude and made the Captain promise to put in a word on her behalf to Mamlena. On her part, she vowed not to utter a word to anyone about what she had seen that Sunday.

~

When Mamlena returned from her father's house, she was devastated at the turn of events at The Lazy Duck. The Captain tried to console her.

'The Master's mind was quite made up. And Miss Rachel's too. I tried to dissuade them as best I could...'

'But you must have collaborated in this holy mess! They've been gone three days. If I knew what ship they're on, I'd follow them and drag them back. Or *you* could do at least that for me.'

The Captain raised his voice. 'Saturday night is always busy. I slept late on Sunday. All the girls and the staff were away to Mass and the parks. I didn't notice a thing. The Master and Miss Rachel chose to escape some time on Sunday morning when they knew no one was around to spy on them.' The Captain sneezed and blew his nose. Mamlena started sobbing.

'Why Rachel?' she asked. 'She was so happy here. Would go to Mass regularly, unlike Mr Gareth...I gave him almost thirty years of my life, put up with his erratic ways. I gave him moral support in his unsuccessful career as an inventor. Put up with his high-brow friends who were incapable of speaking plain English...Wherever they go, people will assume Rachel is his mistress! Oh, the shame of it!' Mamlena wiped her tears and looked quite ferocious. 'Did Mr Armstrong not give even a hint of where they were going? His note to me lists many possibilities. It's as if he was trying to throw me off the scent.'

'They'll be alright, Mamlena. The Master is carrying six thousand pounds with him and—'

'Six thousand! That's the sum total of our savings! He promised to renovate our establishment and add ten rooms to The Black Bull! And said he would give the rest of his share away. My share is earmarked for Rachel's wedding—whenever that happens—and for buying her a nice spacious house in the country. I've been robbed, Captain! Of my money and my daughter...Did he ever borrow money from you?'

'No, never,' the Captain lied. Gareth Armstrong frequently borrowed small sums whenever he felt low on cash, or was too lazy to go to the bank. He usually repaid these debts promptly. Mamlena pursued her trend of thought.

'You must have squirreled away a great fortune by now, Captain. Tell me, how much do you have?'

The Captain evaded the question and changed the subject. 'You should call me "Jack". Then I would be relaxed in your company. Like I used to be when the Admiral died. Think of the good times we had. Everything has become so formal now.'

'That was another era, Captain. Technically you are an employee of The Black Bull. So *you* must continue to call *me* "Mamlena". The old days don't count. I was quite confused then.'

'I am a partner, not an employee,' said the Captain. 'This was the understanding with Mr Robert and later with the Master... Oh, by the way, I find my room at The Black Bull very noisy. The

Irish girls quarrel and squeal so. I've put up with it all these years. Could I move into the Master's bedroom?'

'Next you will want to climb into my bed! No, Captain, we shouldn't look back. I was so young and vulnerable and unhappy then. As I said, I was confused. Now to business. You are going to help track down where those two are. I'm not going to let Mr Gareth get away with it.'

The Captain knew only that the conspirators had sailed to Bombay, not that they then planned to take the train to Calcutta. He had to keep his piece of intelligence strictly to himself. So he talked vaguely of the West Indies, possibly Nigeria, Tanganyika, Australia and other outposts of the far-flung British Empire. He was sure, he said, that they would go to a place where some English was spoken. So he ruled out South America.

Mamlena soon sent off letters to these countries, addressed to Governors and Governors-General, enquiring if a certain Mr Gareth Armstrong and his daughter, Miss Rachel Armstrong, had reached their shores. Of course, this effort proved futile. She got only one reply from some District Commissioner in Tanganyika: there was an Armstrong family, tea planters for three generations, who lived in the Highlands. They had no knowledge of the fugitives.

Mamlena also accompanied the Captain to check the passenger manifests of some fifteen ships that had sailed out of London that crucial week. Mr Armstrong had anticipated she might do this and had instructed the Captain to book their berths under assumed names.

~

Two years passed and still no word. Mamlena began to think that her husband and daughter were lost at sea, or had been devoured by cannibals on some remote island. She pined for Rachel and even missed her husband from time to time. Life with him had seen many ups and downs. It had nevertheless been interesting. The rascal had been quite a charmer.

Lucy was now a Countess. A very successful one, much

in demand by those who could not afford more than five shillings a go. Freed from the strenuous exertions of being a housemaid, she had put on a good bit of weight and was now quite attractive.

Given her closeness to Mamlena—she had been a maid at The Lazy Duck for six years—she acted as Mamlena's eyes and ears in the brothel. In the afternoons, while waiting for the first clients to arrive, she spent some time with Allegro, who taught her a little French to help her climb further up the ladder.

Allegro talked very little now. He refused to let the maids at The Black Bull clean his cage: 'Get your dirty paws out of my house, you Slut.' Mamlena and Lucy found themselves catering to all the bird's requirements. Allegro now demanded not one but two thimbles-full of the finest cognac as his nightcap. The inmates of The Black Bull—with the exception of Lucy—stopped attempting to have conversations with him and often suggested he be sold off to a circus or menagerie. They placed bets amongst themselves on how much he would fetch. Their estimates ranged from a low seventy-five pounds to a high two hundred. The Captain was inclined to agree that Allegro should be got rid of, but kept his mouth shut on this sensitive issue. Another year passed.

~

Then, at last, a letter arrived from Mr Armstrong. Mamlena was disinclined to open it. She stared at it for three days, dreading what it might contain. The Captain couldn't bear the suspense. He offered to open it and read out its contents. Mamlena kept her smelling salts handy.

> *'Dear Mrs Armstrong,*
>
> *Rachel joins me in sending our affectionate greetings from India. We have spent the best part of three years in Serampore, across the river from Calcutta, the capital of this marvellous country. Serampore has a fine*

theological college, a huge library, and a sizeable Baptist community.

Most of our time in Serampore was taken up in Bible study, learning local languages, and working as volunteers in the printing press. In fact, Rachel has become quite an expert in typewriting and typesetting. She and I are glad to be out of London with its pollution and its transformation into a city of many sins—'

'What does he mean by "a city of sins?" Didn't he profit from them? He's made off with the money made here,' said Mamlena.

'Please, Mamlena, don't interrupt! I'll lose my place.'

'I write this from Calcutta. Rachel is now working at the Baptist Mission Press on Lower Circular Road, and I am teaching the Bible and some science to the children of unfortunate prostitutes in Chitpur. I am handicapped in the teaching of science as I haven't access to my instruments and notebooks. These, as you will know by now, are in the large steel trunk in the cellar. I carried the keys with me.

I miss Allegro. He must be miserable in London's climate. Calcutta is, by and large, a clean and charming city, but the climate here is very trying. I have made suggestions to the local government that I could help them design an electric tram system. This would enable citizens to travel in comfort and speed at twenty miles per hour. Again, I would need my notebooks. So I have decided to send for the above-mentioned articles, along with Allegro. For years he has longed to return to the Khasi Hills. You know this. Allegro claims he was born—hatched—there.

Rachel and I now live on Free School Street, some distance from Chitpur but fairly close to her place of work. Below us is a music shop, Arthur Tomlinson & Brothers. Mr Arthur is quite aged. He came to Calcutta sixty years ago and has no children. His brothers died a long time ago, thanks to the humidity and malaria. Mr Tomlinson is now in the process of selling his piano rental business to a Mr Antonio Braganza from Bandel. The long and short of all these tiresome details is that I learned that Mr Braganza's son, Emilio Braganza, has spent the past year in London, training to be a piano tuner and repairer. He is due to return to Calcutta in February and will be accompanying the shipment of four grand pianos ordered by His Highness the Nawab of Ibrahimpur. Emilio's father, Antonio, thinks the young man could be persuaded to bring Allegro and my things back with him. Allegro would require special care on the long journey, though the distance has been reduced somewhat with the opening of the Suez Canal.

I trust this letter reaches you well before February. I gather young Emilio is currently staying at Mrs Barker's Lodging House on Hanover Street, near Covent Garden. I wonder if this is the same Mrs Barker who ran a school Rachel attended when she was a little girl. Anyway, please send the Captain over with a note introducing yourself. Invite Emilio for tea or some other convenient meal. I authorize you to offer him a generous compensation for his troubles. Emilio's father has already written to him in London, spelling out the plan.

Send me a cable when you receive this and have made contact with Emilio. Send the cable to Rachel's work address: The Baptist Mission Press, Calcutta. And now a line or two from Rachel.

My Darling Mama,

Father has given you all our news. Don't fret about me. I am exceedingly happy in the Lord's work. Someday you may decide to forgive us and travel here to stay a while. The winters here are quite pleasant. Give the Captain our regards. I'm looking forward to seeing Allegro again. Read out this letter to him. It will cheer him up.

Your loving daughter,
Rachel

Your devoted husband,
Gareth'

The effect of this letter on Mamlena was predictable. She read it for herself twice over, and said bitterly, 'Mr Armstrong must have forced Rachel to write those words. It would be just like him to do so...And now they are missionaries, are they?!'

'Well, Mamlena, at least we now know where they are. We can communicate at last,' said the Captain.

'The unhappy Allegro and the trunk he speaks of *are* his property after all,' said Mamlena. 'I'll be glad to see the last of that troublesome bird. You have no idea how finicky he's become. We'd better contact this Emilio chap...Do you remember Mrs Barker? She ran a school for young ladies. Remember, Rachel attended it for a year when she was fourteen? I didn't know Amy Barker was reduced to running a boarding house! She was always such a pain in the arse. And a snob, to boot!'

'The trouble with you, Mamlena, if I may say so, is that you always think the worst of people—everyone, including members of your own family. Let us be grateful that the letter has reached us in time. There are a large number of letters sent to the Master at this address, accumulated over the past three years. I have stored them safely in my room. We could send them as well to Calcutta...I have an idea. Why not invite Emilio Braganza for luncheon next Sunday? That way the girls will be off the scene. We can ask one of the maids and the cook to stay and see to the meal. And Emilio can return to Hanover Street while it's still daylight. We should introduce him to Allegro and show him the trunk in the cellar.'

Mamlena accepted the Captain's suggestions, and sent off a note to Emilio at Mrs Barker's. She had quickly formulated a plan of her own. She was determined to be exceedingly hospitable, courteous and charming in the company of Emilio. She would also hint—just a slight hint—that she had been abandoned and, had it not been for the friendship of the Captain, she would have taken her own life ages ago. The idea was to evoke some pity in Mr Armstrong, some remorse, and a measure of jealousy. A lot would depend on the impression she made on Emilio Braganza.

Then she waited for Sunday to come around. She requested Countess Lucy to take time off from entertaining clients and spend Saturday—normally very busy for the girls—cleaning up Allegro's cage and giving the bird a thorough bath.

'He won't let anyone else touch him. You've got to do this for me. Allegro had his last bath a year or so ago. He's filthy and smells like a crate of chickens. We don't want Emilio Braganza to form a poor opinion of us all.'

Lucy, who had grown quite fond of the feathered giant, agreed, provided she was compensated one pound for her loss of earnings, and provided she had the assistance of the Captain. (She'd had a dream in which the Captain, who had deflowered her, eventually asked her to be his lawfully-wedded wife.)

The weather deteriorated on Saturday night. There was much rain and it even began to snow. The roads were in a mess, with horse-dung all over the place. It was so unpleasant that the entire household decided to skip Mass. Some of the girls went back to bed. It was bitterly cold on Sunday morning. A blizzard was raging. Carriage traffic came to a standstill.

Mamlena had taken considerable trouble, ordering special dishes for Mr Braganza's meal. She was dressed entirely in black, not a speck of powder on her cheeks. The Captain commiserated with her. He thought the young man couldn't possibly venture out in this unseasonal storm. Twelve noon, the appointed hour, came and went. One o'clock, then two o'clock, and then, when all hope had been lost—and Mamlena was undressing in her bedroom—the front doorbell rang. A quarter to three.

Mamlena hurriedly dressed in her mourning clothes once again, pinched her cheeks, and arranged her shapely form on a velvet armchair in the parlour. 'Rosy,' she called out, 'see who is at the front door. If it's Mr Braganza you are to say, "Madam is at home and is expecting you, Sir." Then you are to show him in here.'

Rosy hurried to the hallway and opened the heavy oak door. She had taken over Lucy's duties two years ago and was generally unflappable. But now she got the fright of her life. She quickly closed the door, leaning against the storm, and rushed back to where Mamlena waited anxiously.

'Holy Mother of God, Mamlena! There be a stark-naked savage at the door. Should I say you are not at home, like you taught me?'

Mamlena moved briskly. She opened the front door to the sorry sight of a dark oriental gentleman turned purple in the cold. He was as naked as a new-born babe. Except for the hat he held against his crown jewels. Mamlena frowned and averted her eyes. 'Mr Braganza, I presume? Please do come in.'

Emilio nodded unhappily, his teeth chattering, his entire body trembling, his bare head matted with snow. Mamlena led him to the fireplace and wrapped her black shawl around his shoulders. Then she handed him over to the Captain, while she went upstairs to fetch some old clothes from Mr Armstrong's room. Her husband had been slim and muscular once upon a time. He'd hung on to all his old clothes thinking he might lose weight someday or his clothes would come back into fashion again, and anyway he was too busy to deal with the Salvation Army or some other charity.

The Captain refrained from asking Emilio questions, as the young man had to be revived first. He sent Rosy to The Black Bull to fetch a bottle of the finest Scotch whiskey. Mamlena had been a teetotaller ever since Mr Armstrong's disappearance and kept no spirits at The Lazy Duck. In due course she reappeared with some clothes. 'While you help him get dressed, I'll go and see about some hot soup. The undergarments may be somewhat loose but the rest should fit Mr Braganza perfectly.'

Emilio stopped shivering in a couple of hours. Sensation returned to his extremities. He opened his eyes. His breathing became more regular and he lost some of his haunted look.

Warmed by the whiskey and the soup, he watched Mamlena at her knitting—her father in Ireland was still alive—and the Captain at his solitary game of cards. When Mamlena judged Emilio had recovered sufficiently, she looked across to the Captain, who nodded. They then sat forward in their chairs and almost simultaneously asked, 'What on earth happened?'

Emilio found it difficult to talk and began to speak reluctantly. He paused frequently and it was hard at times to make sense of his incomplete sentences.

Mamlena and the Captain learned that Emilio was attending early morning Mass when the blizzard began. After the service, he searched high and low to find a carriage to bring him to Lemon Tart Lane. Failing to find one, he decided to walk but soon lost his way. It was quite dark and his eyes were blinded by sleet. Mrs Barker's instructions proved little use. Emilio came across a very tall man who told him of a short-cut through various back-alleys. The stranger offered to show him the way. Suddenly, Emilio was attacked by three ruffians who dragged him into a secluded portico. They stripped him of everything including twelve shillings, the last of his money. Shoes, clothes, undergarments, everything, except his socks and hat. Emilio struggled and cried out for help. He was made to lie face down in a gutter and, in that position, was brutally sodomized by all four men and left for dead.

Mamlena was horrified. 'You were...you were...er... violated?' She saw then that a pool of blood had congealed around his socks. 'We'll send for the Doctor.'

'You mean raped, Mrs Armstrong? I'm...but...well, yes... I'm so ashamed...My fault for talking to a stranger in those circumstances. May God forgive me...I see it has stopped snowing. I must get back to Mrs Barker's. My father wrote to me about Mr Armstrong and Miss Rachel and the bird. I'll come again another day...Could you get me a carriage? I'll have to borrow a pound or two. This is very embarrassing. Mrs Barker will be worried. She was expecting me back by five.'

Mamlena protested. Emilio must rest and spend the night at The Lazy Duck. Besides, he had developed a high fever. So she sent for Dr Pecksniffer, apologizing for the lateness of the hour. Lucy's fourteen-year old brother, Thomas, trudged across the snow to the Doctor's house, a mile away. He brought back a message to say the elderly doctor would not step out in this weather. He promised to come on Monday morning.

The Captain, along with two of the other boys, Richard and Harold, carried Emilio up to Mr Armstrong's old room. The Captain undressed him, applied iodine to the young man's various injuries, supplied him with a clean, fresh nightgown, and instructed young Thomas to watch over him throughout the night.

The next morning, Dr Pecksniffer pronounced that Emilio was on the verge of developing a bad case of pneumonia, required four stitches in his arse, and should on no account be shifted elsewhere. The painful stitching-up procedure followed. The Doctor advised a strictly liquid diet. Clear chicken broth. He charged Mamlena six shillings for the house visit and surgical procedure.

At about noon, a messenger arrived with a note from Mrs Barker, Emilio's stern landlady.

Dear Lena Armstrong,

My Indian lodger, Emilio Braganza, left for your brothel yesterday morning and has not yet returned. I demand you send him back in a carriage. What have you done with him? Is he in the arms of one of your pox-ridden tarts? I warn you he has no money. He owes me for three weeks lodging, apart from the twelve shillings he borrowed yesterday. He says repeatedly that he is expecting his father to transfer funds to him any day.

Send Jack Crusoe (that despicable if competent pimp of yours) with Emilio to make sure there is no further trouble.

With regards,
Cordially yours,
Elizabeth Barker

Mamlena showed the Captain the note. He was furious. 'I've a good mind to go to Hanover Street and pay off that old bitch. I can sort it out...And I will bring back all of Emilio's effects. I'll take our own carriage—the horses have not been exercised for two days. Thomas! Richard! Harold!' The Captain was yelling now. When the boys shuffled into the parlour they were instructed to get the horses and carriage ready. 'We'll leave at three, after I have fed Mr Emilio.'

Mamlena was not entirely comfortable with the Captain's initiative. What if Mrs Barker was reluctant to part with Emilio's effects, particularly his piano-tuning tools and instruments? What if she blamed Mamlena for the loss of a lodger, a very handsome one at that? What if she went to the police?

All went well, though. Emilio—lying on his stomach—had scrawled out a list of his belongings and calculated what he owed Mrs Barker, hoping fervently that he would not have to face her again. The Captain could not help delivering a parting shot as he left Mrs Barker's house: 'You know why Miss Rachel left your school for young ladies? She found you sarcastic, abusive and overbearing. She used to say you were no lady. Would a lady have sent a note such as you did to Mamlena? Full of in-in-uendos. Unjustified suspicions. Now you've got your money. That's all you really care about, isn't it? The young man's injuries do not concern you, do they?'

~

Mamlena, the Captain, Rosy and Thomas went to great lengths to make Emilio comfortable. Rosy felt herself falling in love with the exotic young man. They learned he was just twenty-four, and was booked to sail back to India in exactly ten days. His chief anxiety was about the money his father was due to send him. It should have arrived a month ago.

Mamlena was reassuring. 'Don't worry about the money from your father. I plan to give you two hundred pounds for your expenses: the cost of transporting Allegro and Mr Armstrong's trunk, and so on. I also want you to buy a new suit and shoes.

You told the Captain that the cost of shipping the four pianos has already been paid for in Calcutta. You must tell me if two hundred pounds is enough.' Emilio could not find words to thank her. There were tears of gratitude in his eyes.

The Captain drew Mamlena aside one evening. 'Do you realize that Emilio now knows we run a brothel here? I think young Thomas told him by way of explaining why I sleep till noon every day...Anyway, damn it, he will come to know when we take him across to meet Allegro. We'll do that as soon as Emilio can manage the stairs.'

With just four days to go for the embarkation, Emilio was finally fit enough to go downstairs to Mamlena's parlour. She had dressed in black throughout his stay at The Lazy Duck. They sat opposite each other and Mamlena picked up her knitting. She proceeded to tell him all she knew about the extraordinary Allegro and also about the difficulties of being an unsuccessful inventor's wife.

Emilio's gaze wandered around the room as she spoke and came to rest on each of several framed photographs of a striking young girl who—through the pictures—he saw had grown to be a beautiful young woman with luxuriant auburn hair. Several photographs were hand-tinted.

Mamlena noticed that Emilio was distracted by the images of her daughter. She got up and took him around the room. 'Those of the young lady are of my daughter Rachel; then there's my father; and that's Mr Robert Armstrong, my late first husband who was my current husband's elder brother. And that is Gareth Armstrong, the delinquent inventor who has carried my daughter off to Calcutta, of all places...People say Rachel has my looks and her father's straight back.'

Emilio, with a pronounced lack of tact, asked Mamlena how old Rachel was now. Mamlena blushed and was evasive. 'I have lost the birth certificate and our church burned down, so I can't be sure. She must be close to twenty...She was a wonderful child. So attached to her parents. She must be much younger than you.'

Emilio thought it best to change the subject. 'When do I get to see the pet raven? Can he really talk? In India some parrots and mynah birds are trained to talk, tell fortunes and sing songs, but they rarely live beyond twenty-five years.'

'I'll take you across to The Black Bull where he is billeted. I gather young Thomas has told you about the brothel we run there. It's a clean, well-managed business, and my girls are ever so nice and refined. Ours is a necessary profession. Most married women are so shy about sex these days. Where are the men expected to go to fulfil their natural urges? The demand for the services of my girls is very high. I take good care of them. We form a kind of sisterhood. I care for each girl as if she were my own daughter. The Captain manages the business end of things. You need a real man for that...Oh, Rachel has never had anything to do with The Black Bull. She is as pure as fresh snow...With the man of the house gone, it has been difficult to manage all the servants. There are twelve of them including the three boys...Now don't be put off by Allegro's rude manners. He's really a dear old thing.'

~

Allegro was reciting the 'Song of Solomon' in his 'house,' as he called the very large collapsible cage Mr Armstrong had fashioned for him. When Mamlena and Emilio walked into The Black Bull, Allegro opened his eyes wide. 'Ooh, you Handsome Bugger—or is it Buggered? Lucy told me about you. All the girls and the Captain are still asleep. I'm in charge. So what is it to be today? A Countess? You have enough money for a Princess?...Speak up, speak up, lad. You have a funny accent. I'd almost forgotten what a Calcutta gentleman sounds like—I was there over a century ago...Do you speak Bengali?'

Mamlena cut him short. 'This is Mr Braganza. He's here to take you back to India, to Mr Armstrong and Rachel. Be polite to him and he'll take good care of you on the long journey.'

Allegro flapped his wings with joy. 'Remember, my needs are quite simple, given my age. A piece of toast with marmalade for breakfast, a large apple for lunch, two poached eggs for dinner at six, and a nightcap before I retire. A balanced diet. I drink only brandy. Good brandy. The cheap stuff people drink these days only upsets my stomach.'

Emilio was dismayed by the bird's requirements. How would he arrange for this peculiar diet on board ship? Mamlena reassured him, 'You'll manage somehow. Make friends with the chef and the stewards. Slip them a pound now and again. You will have ample funds...Now take over the complete care of Allegro for the next three days so that you learn what is involved. You two must grow to like and trust each other.'

Next, Mamlena took Emilio down to the cellar to inspect Mr Armstrong's laboratory and workshop. She had the three boys carry Mr Armstrong's heavy trunk up to the hallway. The Captain joined them at this point. He felt the trunk looked too battered. So the boys gave it a fresh coat of green paint, and it looked as good as new. Quite respectable.

The last couple of days witnessed a flurry of activity. The balance of the money was handed over to Emilio with strict instructions to conceal it in a belt worn around his waist. New clothes and shoes were bought. Dr Pecksniffer removed Emilio's stitches and pronounced him fit to travel. Emilio was to continue the liquid diet for another ten days.

On the day before departure, the four pianos were carefully crated and lowered into the hold of the *Caledonia*. The Captain and Emilio supervised every bit of the operation. Thanks to the Captain's forceful personality, a suitable spot was earmarked for Allegro's 'house.' There were two portholes adjacent to it so he could view the oceans, the clouds and the occasional shoreline. He would thus be able to tell night from day.

Then the momentous morning arrived. Two large carriages were ordered. Mamlena, Lucy, the Captain and the three boys accompanied Emilio to the docks for an emotional farewell. The trunk was taken aboard first. Then Allegro's cage was hoisted up and lowered by a crane. It swayed gently from side to side, and Allegro shouted out, 'Goodbye, you Sluts and Buggers! This is going to be fun.'

Mamlena embraced Emilio and shed a few tears. True to her resolve, she was dressed in black. Her last words to him were, 'Will I ever see Rachel again? It's all up to you.'

2

Calcutta

What Gareth Armstrong omitted from his letter to Mamlena were the circumstances under which he was compelled to leave Serampore College. The work on this missionary campus was concerned mainly with translating the Bible into various Indian languages. It struck Gareth that the effort of translation would be infinitely more straightforward if the Gospels were to be rewritten first in simple, everyday English. And this he set about doing, secretly.

His idea was to write about Christ in one running narrative, omitting all the repetitions contained in the four Gospels, reconciling the inconsistencies and contradictions, and removing all the inconsequential genealogical details—the 'begats'—that cluttered the texts. While his colleagues at the college were scholars of Hebrew, Aramaic, Greek and Latin, Gareth was totally ignorant of these languages and relied on the King James Version in English. Thus he could not be mistaken for a genuine Bible scholar and, as far as his day job went, he was assigned purely administrative duties. He was, after all, a mere volunteer. He was put in charge of maintaining accounts, supervising the gardeners, and conducting stock verifications of the extensive library. The secret Bible project was taken up after dinner in the privacy of his own room.

Rachel soon learnt what he was up to and advised caution. 'Father, I know the Gospels were written several decades after Christ lived and are probably based on hearsay and failing memories, but that does not justify what you are doing. Imagine the scandal if it came to be known that you were rewriting the Bible! You'd be burnt at the stake!'

'My version will be a transcreation,' said Gareth. 'That's a word I've invented and I'm rather proud of it. It will be simple to read—direct and inspirational. Even children will find it full of adventure and excitement. When the time comes, I'll ask you to fill the little book with drawings. That will give it flesh and blood. You are such a good artist! It's a pity you are stuck all day at the printing press. I think thirty drawings should do it. I've revised the opening. I'll read it out for you—

> 'Once upon a time, when Herod was King of a small country named Judea, there was a plump temple priest named Zacharias. He had a long beard. His wife Elizabeth, a good cook, was equally plump, but they had no children. They were both middle-aged, which means they were over forty years old. They were much in awe of God. They were devout Jews and prayed day and night for the birth of a son...'

'Stop, Father!' Rachel begged. 'You are taking too many liberties. If Reverend Beecham were to find out, there'd be hell to pay.'

Reverend Beecham did find out. He had left standing instructions with all the sweepers to bring him every scrap of paper from the waste-baskets in the scholars' rooms. He would examine these to check on the progress of each scholar. He often found that the rough drafts of their writings contained valuable ideas and brilliant insights. The Reverend thought this form of monitoring was a pious duty as scholars often threw away bits of writing out of a misplaced sense of modesty. He summoned Gareth.

'Mr Armstrong, I have come to know of your secretive and deplorable endeavours. No man has the right to tamper with the Word of God. In our translations we do our best to preserve the beauty and majesty of the King James Version. And you have wilfully attempted to rob the Bible of these very qualities...Your lack of progress on other fronts is equally disappointing. I've been informed that you yawn throughout your Bible Study classes. Your knowledge of Bengali is weak, to say the least. You've made some progress with the Khasi tongue but your vocabulary is extremely limited. You have much to be embarrassed about...I think the time has come for us to part ways. You have private means and could settle down to a comfortable life in Calcutta.' A brief pause, and then in an attempt to mollify Gareth, he added, 'Miss Rachel, on the other hand, is a model of virtue. She may continue to work here as she has become quite an expert at operating that new-fangled machine they call the typewriter. Or I could recommend her for a salaried post at our Mission Press on Lower Circular Road in Calcutta. The choice should be hers, and hers alone. At her age she should be self-sufficient.' The Reverend pursed his lips and straightened his collar. 'Well?' he asked.

Gareth frowned and attempted to defend himself. 'Reverend Beecham, do you mean to say that I am prohibited from simplifying the New Testament? I am a scientist. I've explanations for all the miracles. Most of them have clear medical or scientific causes. They need to be demystified. This is possible now because of two thousand years of scientific advancement. We mustn't forget the Apostles wrote largely from hearsay. Any physical phenomenon they could not fathom was called a miracle...If I am no longer welcome at the College, I shall carry on my work in Calcutta.'

After these developments, Gareth and his dutiful daughter felt obliged to leave Serampore. He tipped the many servants handsomely. He donated a thousand rupees to the college to sweeten his departure. He wanted to be thought of well.

In Calcutta, the pair found lodgings on Free School Street. Rachel was engaged by the Baptist Mission Press on the strength of Reverend Beecham's recommendation and Gareth cast around for ideas of what to do next. He was not ordained and had no theological degree. The Calcutta Baptists were not exactly welcoming as news of his 'tinkering' with the Word of God had preceded him. He lost interest in rewriting the Bible. He confided in Rachel one evening.

'No one would publish such a thing. It would be too revolutionary, too scandalous, too scientific. I could of course pay to have it printed at my cost, but how would I distribute the books? I would have liked children to read it, but how would I get it into their hands without their parents getting wind of the matter?'

'Oh, Father!' Rachel exclaimed. 'Don't you see it was not meant to be? Reverend Beecham did you a favour by asking us to leave the college. Serampore is too small a place for a gentleman of your wide interests. In Calcutta there is greater scope for your talents. You could have a scientific career here.'

~

Gareth found it impossible to resume his scientific pursuits without the notebooks and instruments he had left behind in the basement of The Lazy Duck. He finally hit upon the idea of opening a small school for the children of prostitutes. This was a subject he knew a lot about, having spent decades in the company of such women. In Calcutta their unfortunate children were denied admission to all regular schools. Even the various mission schools that had sprung up shunned them.

Gareth came to an understanding with Ushalata, a retired courtesan who was left a wealthy widow when her English lover expired in her arms one December evening. Ushalata provided Gareth with three large rooms on the ground floor of her mansion on Chitpur Road, not far from Sonagachi, the location of numerous low-class brothels. This was in the Black Town, some distance from the northern edge of White Town where Gareth and Rachel lived above a piano shop.

Gareth engaged a young man and a slightly older woman to help him teach the children. They both had a smattering of English, and Gareth, of Bengali. Gareth himself taught English, Bible Study, and General Science. The young man taught Mathematics, Civics, and Geography. The older lady was in charge of Bengali, Writing, and Art. The entire expenses of running the school—utilities, salaries, supplies, textbooks and exercise books for the children—were borne by Gareth. He even provided free lunches. Sixty children worshipped him as a god, and their mothers were made to swear they would make the children attend school six days a week, come hell or high water.

~

Transportation to and from Chitpur meant negotiating crowded bazaars and teeming throngs of undisciplined pedestrians. One had a choice of small carriages or of palanquins. Women preferred the shuttered palanquins for the privacy they provided. Gareth felt a keen sympathy for the bearers of such heavy burdens. He had seen an illustration of a hand-drawn Chinese rickshaw in a magazine. He did some sketches of it, enlarging the diameter of the two wheels to give added clearance, and he thought of a new axle system with ball-bearings. The larger wheels would turn smoothly and the axle would make for light work. Gareth built three successive prototypes in the courtyard of Ushalata's mansion.

Everyone who saw the 'Garethgari' marvelled at it. A delegation of Calcutta-based Chinese entrepreneurs arrived one morning when Gareth was in the middle of explaining how Christ walked on water. The Chinese gentlemen bought the rights to the innovative rickshaw for five hundred rupees, cash down, and in a few months they had mass-produced a large number and hired Chinese coolies to ply them in the streets of North Calcutta. These rickshaws had the great advantage of keeping passengers' feet dry during the frequent monsoon floods. They also had collapsible hoods. The inventor became a minor celebrity. After a couple of months, Gareth was invited to join the Royal Asiatic Society. Recognition at last!

At his first Royal Asiatic Society meeting, he described the various inventions he had executed when he was in London. He now proposed an electric tram system for the rapidly expanding city of Calcutta. The meeting was attended by seven members of the society, all of whom were highly impressed and, though ignorant of engineering matters, they asked to see his drawings, construction details, and formulae. He promised to send for these from England. And then he remembered, with a stab of guilt, his promise to Allegro: that he would arrange for his dear friend to return to the Khasi Hills. The great bird had yearned to go home. This is why Gareth had attempted to learn something of the Khasi language at Serampore. Khasi had no script of its own and the missionaries used the Roman script for their translations. He consulted his feeble landlord, Mr Tomlinson.

Mr Tomlinson introduced Gareth to Mr Antonio Braganza who was about to become his new landlord. The Braganzas were buying Mr Tomlinson's piano-rental business, along with its large commercial building. The piano shop and the furniture shop presented a long, imposing frontage along Free School Street. Two spacious flats occupied the upper floor. The Armstrongs rented one of them. The Braganzas planned to move into the larger flat. The Braganzas also bought out the furniture business, thinking the space would be needed once their son, Emilio, returned from England and business expanded.

Mr Tomlinson fretted constantly about the complicated demands made on him by His Highness the Nawab of Ibrahimpur. The Nawab wanted to import four new grand pianos for his palace. A huge Bösendorfer for himself and three smaller Steinways for his three impatient Begums. The Bösendorfer should be gold in colour, the three Steinways white. The pianos, made to order, would be shipped from Hamburg to London and then sent to India under expert supervision. It was the supervision stipulation that worried Mr Tomlinson the most. Then he learned of Emilio's impending return from London. Things began to fall into place. Emilio would accompany the pianos. Mr Tomlinson handed over implementation of the plan to Antonio Braganza, signed the sale deeds, disposed of his non-essential belongings, and caught the first train to Allahabad. He changed for Bombay and then sailed back to England to live there with his niece in Bournemouth.

The Braganza family settled in promptly. A huge signboard was erected above the shop: Braganza & Sons. Antonio made the acquaintance of the many customers to whom Mr Tomlinson had rented pianos: the European missionaries, the churches and chapels, schools, the anglicized Bengali babus, the Calcutta-based zamindars, and the Indo-Anglians (who now preferred to be known as Anglo-Indians). In his twilight years Mr Tomlinson had been unsure how many pianos he had rented out. His record-keeping had been abysmally poor and his income uncertain. After his two younger brothers died, there had been no one to tune the pianos on a regular basis. In his last days in Calcutta, he consoled himself that young Emilio would return shortly to take good care of the beloved instruments.

~

Rachel Armstrong had very little time to spare. She worked full-time at the Baptist Mission Press, six days a week. On Sunday mornings she dragged her father to the old Baptist Church next to the press. If truth be told, Gareth was fast losing faith as a Christian. The Sunday visits to church were motivated more by the cup of tea and delicious ginger biscuits served afterwards than by the ritual of the holy services.

After church, Rachel came home to cook lunch and dinner. In the afternoons she went to different cemeteries to make her stone-rubbings. Her father refused to have any servants around on Sundays—it was a day of rest and quiet for all.

Gareth spent these Sunday afternoons with Antonio Braganza, his stern wife Flavia, and their two minor daughters, who were constantly quarrelling. The girls, Rose and Iris, adored their elder brother Emilio, who would on occasion tell them ghost stories about Claude Martin, who had founded their school La Martiniere for Girls. With Antonio as his guide, Gareth took a keen interest in the inner workings of pianos—the hammers, the weights, the pegs, the strings, the sounding board, the keyboards, and the miraculous combination of many materials: ivory, wood, felt, steel, brass, copper, lead, iron and wax-polish.

The Braganzas and the Armstrongs waited for Emilio's return with growing concern. There had been a telegram from Aden:

Engine room of ship caught fire. Sails used to drift to Aden. Have to change ships. Berths difficult to find. Bringing the bird posing problems. Will probably leave for Bombay after a fortnight. From there to Calcutta by train. Anticipate delays at every stage. Will let you know latest position from Bombay. Cargo safe. I check on the pianos every two days. Tell Mr Armstrong Allegro not too well. Am doing my best by him.

Antonio made a rapid calculation. His son would probably not return before the first week of May. Gareth hoped fervently that Allegro would hold out until he reached Calcutta, and that the trunkful of scientific apparatus would not get knocked around needlessly.

~

Some evenings the Braganzas and the Armstrongs got together on the large balcony overlooking busy Free School Street. On one occasion, Antonio and Flavia began to talk of their former house in Bandel, a Portuguese colony some fifty miles north of Calcutta. It was a small port town on the river Hooghly. Antonio was quite sentimental. Gareth just listened.

'Ours was an old family who migrated from Saligao in Goa almost two centuries ago. Because of the Inquisition there, my father's ancestor Claudio left in a hurry. He sold off our huge house for a pittance, and joined up with six other Goan families to establish an exclusive Portuguese enclave in Bandel…'

Flavia broke in: 'Don't forget to mention that *my* family owned vast mango orchards and four houses. Calcutta was then little more than a collection of villages. My family used to travel by carriage to British India to shop. Mainly for shoes and soap. We spoke English—mostly, and a little Konkani at home—unlike some of the other families who spoke only Portuguese or only Konkani. Of course, we all had to learn some Bengali to get by.'

Rachel brought in a tray with four large cups of 'native tea.' She liked the Braganzas. But Flavia had a poor sense of humour. Rachel sat down and Antonio continued. 'Bandel grew as the trading activities of the Portuguese picked up. The Goans were not discriminated against. Far from what Flavia would lead you to believe, we were the clerks, accountants, policemen and builders the Portuguese masters needed. The Braganzas even constructed the great big church you see there today. There were several harpsichords and primitive pianos in the colony. Claudio's son, Cristiano, had an exceptionally fine ear for music, and taught himself how to tune all sorts of musical instruments. He was also a gifted guitarist. He established Braganza & Sons. The signboard was in English. Gold on black.'

'We intermarried,' said Flavia. 'The Goans of Bandel maintain family trees that show we are all related to one another. I'm a Britto. Antonio's great-grandfather was also a Britto. See what I mean? It's interesting, isn't it? I hope Emilio will carry on the tradition. I have my eye on a DaCosta girl in Bandel whom everyone says sings like an angel and plays the church organ. Emilio is twenty-five now. With our move to Calcutta a bright future awaits him. We have arranged everything for him. All he needs now is a wife.'

Antonio got up from his chair, stretched and sat down again. 'I'll have my whiskey now, if you don't mind. Why don't you join me? You missionaries don't know what you are missing. Where was I? Flavia keeps interrupting. I lose my thread...Oh, yes. We changed the spelling of our name from "Bragança" with a c-cedila to "Braganza" with a zed. In this way our branch of the Braganças stood out. Braganza & Sons were also building contractors—a fact Flavia tends to suppress. But that's where the bulk of the income came from. There were no qualified architects or engineers worth the name in Bandel in those days; contractors did everything—'

'—Now the young people come here to Calcutta,' Flavia cut in. 'It has become huge: the second city of the British Empire! Hundreds of shoe shops. Bandel is no longer a charming place. Bazaars, garbage, pigs and stray dogs all over the place. There is not enough work. Emilio would have no future there. That's why we sold our extensive orchards and properties in our home town. We sent Emilio to London to be properly trained as a piano tuner and restorer. I told Antonio that our new signboard should read "Braganza & Sons, London-trained." He does not agree. Said he would include London on Emilio's visiting cards if our son wishes.'

Just then Antonio's daughters rushed on to the balcony, shouting that a telegram had been delivered. It was from Bombay. The girls screeched with excitement. 'What does it say? What is Emilio's news?' Antonio put on his reading glasses.

> Will arrive on eleventh May Howrah Station twelve noon. Please arrange appropriate transportation for pianos to be taken directly to Nawab's palace. A barge then elephants? Consult His Highness. Allegro a bit more cheerful. We are longing to see you all.

The Nawab, the Armstrongs, the Braganzas and a dozen coolies, all went to the railway station to receive Emilio. Formalities for releasing the freight took an age to complete. Allegro cawed happily. In his excitement he had momentarily lost his power of human speech. When they were all safely on the barge for the river-crossing, Allegro calmed down and began whistling catchy tunes. Then he began to speak.

'I remember this river. Before Fort William was built. Only a few fishing boats here and there...It's so bloody hot now. Your Highness will join us for a glass of champagne? It won't be chilled though. Mr Emilio has been saving it for this moment.'

The Nawab could scarcely believe his ears. He was astonished. 'A talking crow? It's so enormous. It's a freak of nature. I must have it! I *must* own it. My Begums will be so amused and excited. Mr Armstrong, I will pay you anything you want for this marvellous creature. Ten thousand rupees!'

Allegro bubbled with laughter. 'Only ten thousand? The price of a medium quality piano, I'm told. I'm not for sale, Your Lowness. I'm a member of Mr Gareth Armstrong's family, not a pigeon you can buy in the bazaar. I withdraw my offer of a drink of champagne.' The Nawab was horrified by Allegro's rudeness but said nothing.

After the river-crossing there was a fork in the road. Turn left, the long road to Ibrahimpur. Turn right, it was three miles to Free School Street. The waiting elephants were loaded and Emilio sounded a note of caution.

'Your Highness, please see personally to the unloading of the piano crates. I've guarded them with my life for three months...I have a high fever now. I haven't slept for five days, so forgive me for not coming with you right away. I'll come first thing next week and unpack the crates and set the pianos singing.'

But Emilio had contracted malaria, possibly in Aden. He was often delirious. His mother, Flavia, and his sisters wanted to know all about London. Rachel, who popped across the landing now and then, was full of questions about her mother, the Captain, Lucy and The Lazy Duck. Emilio was lucid most of the time and didn't mind the questions. He had questions of his own. Emilio asked Rachel why she had left England. Was it just to keep Mr Armstrong company?

'I left London suddenly. After Father baptized me, I couldn't possibly have continued living in The Lazy Duck. It was filled with ten different types of sin. I thought the life of a Baptist missionary would be pure, filled with hope and doing good for others...Mother would never have understood this. Her idea of goodness was to get girls off the streets and into her brothel. I expect we must give her some credit for that.'

Emilio would gaze into Rachel's eyes as she spoke. He thought she was even better looking in person than in the photographs he'd seen at The Lazy Duck. He came to admire the way she moved, the clarity of her speech and the beauty of her slender hands. He looked forward to her visits to the Braganza household. When his fever subsided, he told her in detail about his stay at The Lazy Duck, omitting certain painful particulars. He told her of the long, troublesome journey home. Allegro hardly ate anything due to sea-sickness but demanded brandy three times a day. The ship's crew wanted him to sing music-hall songs on demand. Allegro had a store of these, learned when he was installed in the pub at The Black Bull. He sang sadly but was very popular all the same.

One morning Emilio felt well enough to convey Mamlena Armstrong's various messages to her daughter, the long and the short of which were that Rachel should return to London and help out with the family business. Rachel was distressed that her mother wished her to give up her calm life in Calcutta and return to sinful Lemon Tart Lane.

Emilio tried another approach: the strict truth. Mamlena grieved over the loss of her only child. She shed many tears over Rachel (but not over Gareth.) Mamlena dressed only in black and had told Emilio she had saved a considerable sum of money to buy Rachel a grand house in the country after she was married to a suitable gentleman. Rachel was amused and smiled a broad smile.

'I will never be tempted by a large house in the country. My life and work are here in Calcutta. I've got used to the climate. The cemeteries are very interesting. I'll take you there when you recover fully. The gravestones are works of art.'

Emilio thought it was time to change the subject. He'd done his duty by Mamlena. There wasn't anything further by way of messages to convey. Emilio was secretly relieved by Rachel's reaction. He asked about her work and her friends.

'The British families I've come to know here are rather stuffy. Practically all of them High Church. They tend to look down on Baptists and other non-conformists...The Mission Press, though, is a wonderful place to work. I actually enjoy the sound of well-oiled machinery and the click-clack of my typewriter. I love the smell of fresh paper and printing ink. I look forward to taking you there. And stop calling me "Miss Armstrong." If I can call you "Emilio," why can't you call me "Rachel?" We are neighbours. No need to be so formal.'

~

The Nawab was impatient. He sent a message to Antonio. There had been some early monsoon showers and it was very humid in

Ibrahimpur. The piano crates lay stretched out beneath a large tent that was not exactly waterproof. He sent a second message:

> *Kindly come and unpack the crates so that we can move the pianos inside to the safety of the Durbar Hall. I understand they have to be assembled before they can be tuned. Your son can come up for that when he has recovered. My Begums are very anxious to see the instruments. I will make sure they do not touch them. I have a message for Mr Armstrong: his rude bird needs to be taught some manners.*

Emilio was not quite sure his father was up to the task. He felt much better now and his strength had returned. He had in his possession a set of instructions which set out precisely the procedures to be followed when unpacking, assembling and tuning the pianos. Although these instructions were in German, he'd had enough experience in London of similar challenges. And Rachel had studied German during her year at Mrs Barker's. It was decided that Antonio, Emilio and Rachel would combine forces and go up to Ibrahimpur together. Rachel obtained seven days leave from the Press. Antonio informed the Nawab that they would travel on the first of June.

Flavia Braganza helped her husband and son get ready. She had her doubts about Emilio's fitness to undertake heavy work so soon. Atypically she kept these doubts to herself. She promised to keep an eye on the piano shop below. Antonio's two assistants would handle routine matters.

Antonio and Emilio packed their tools carefully. Among these were the latest implements from London. Rachel borrowed a German-to-English dictionary from Mr Ellis at the Press. And then they were off, riding in a grand carriage sent by the Nawab. It had his coat-of-arms emblazoned on each door and was accompanied by six bodyguards riding magnificent Arabian horses. All this for a journey of a mere fourteen miles that took a little over an hour to complete.

The Nawab and his courtiers gave the father, son and Rachel a rousing welcome and a grand lunch. They were shown to their rooms in the luxurious State Guest House. Emilio and Rachel proceeded to decipher the instructions. Sensing the Nawab's anxiety, Antonio decided to see to the Bösendorfer first. The Nawab was keen to see it unpacked and moved into the Durbar Hall as quickly as possible for fear that it might rain. It was nearly three o'clock and His Highness couldn't stop chattering away.

'I have waited for this moment for over a year. My own Bösendorfer! The King of Pianos! I will hold concerts here, inviting great pianists to give recitals before distinguished guests. My aristocratic audiences will have their first experience of a Bösendorfer, the only instrument of its kind in all of India! Your predecessor, Mr Tomlinson, assured me it would be a great novelty. I will learn to play it. I could start with "Twinkle, twinkle, little star"—it's by Mo-sart, no? My Begums will play their Steinways. There will be healthy competition all round.'

Antonio and Emilio set to work, together with some helpers from the palace. With Rachel translating the instructions, they managed to unpack all the bits and pieces by six in the evening. The sun was setting. The various piano parts were moved carefully indoors. Throughout the afternoon the court photographer documented the procedure, step by step. All concerned were asked periodically to stand quite still to enable him to do his work. Emilio and his father were exhausted. Rachel withdrew to her room to study the dictionary.

The next day the visitors decided that Antonio would unpack the Steinways, now that he had got the hang of it with the Bösendorfer. Rachel and Emilio were to work in the Durbar Hall, assembling and tuning. When they walked into the hall, they were confronted by a sea of eager faces. There was much noise. Most of the crowd did not know what a piano was. Some thought a new golden throne was being erected. Others thought it was a new kind of dining table sent by Queen Victoria. Yet others thought it was some kind of royal bed.

Emilio had to request the Nawab to clear the hall of all

onlookers before he could start the delicate work of tuning. The Bösendorfer took over two days to tune. When it was finally done, the Nawab was invited to sit on his throne and listen to the rich sound. Emilio played the first movements of Beethoven's 'Moonlight Sonata' and 'The Apassionata.' The Nawab had tears in his eyes.

The next day, Rachel was introduced to the three Begums. One of them, the youngest, knew a smattering of English. They were all in purdah. Complicated arrangements had to be made. As each had her own sumptuous quarters and reception hall, the pianos had to be assembled in different parts of the Zenana Mahal. Each Begum had been gifted with her own white Steinway, all three identical. Rachel warned them that it would take a minimum of two days to set up each piano. And as several strange men would be involved, their Highnesses would have to retire to the inner recesses of the Zenana Mahal. The senior Begum insisted that her piano be the first to be commissioned. The three Begums were hardly on talking terms.

Each evening after the day's work was done, Rachel and Emilio went for a walk in the vast palace gardens. This was when the Nawab and Antonio would sip brandy and soda in secret. The young couple discussed piano technicalities, Calcutta, and their recollections of London. Emilio told Rachel that in London he had been taught how to read music and had learned twenty piano pieces as part of his training. When each piano was tuned he was to play three or four classical tunes for his clients, thus inculcating appreciation and respect for his skills and, as importantly, respect and love for the instrument. Emilio said, 'You have no idea, Rachel, how badly pianos are treated. Thump, thump, thump... bang, bang, BANG!! It's disgraceful! As far as the Nawab's new instruments are concerned, they will be tuned to respond to a light touch. Everyone must appreciate this.' Emilio, it could be seen, treated each of his pianos with infinite tenderness.

The next day Rachel decided to send a message to Mr Ellis: she would be detained at Ibrahimpur for another three days. She needn't have prolonged her stay. The Nawab would have been happy to send her back to Free School Street, now that the tuning work was underway and further translations from German were not strictly required. But Rachel enjoyed Emilio's company and treasured their walks together. Besides, she was now fascinated by the piano business.

That evening, Emilio could not restrain himself. During a lull in their conversation, he reached quietly for Rachel's hand. She did not withdraw it and gave his hand a gentle squeeze. They both sensed that something of immense importance had just occurred. They were quite oblivious that they were being observed by someone from the palace windows. They stopped talking as they approached a vine-covered pergola. They came to a halt under the canopy of leaves and kissed passionately. Then they sat down on a bench and looked into each other's eyes.

Just then, a palace functionary approached them hurriedly. 'Wild leopards often wander in after dark...His Highness beckons you for dinner.'

Their last two days together were very busy. The Nawab had decided he needed a piano teacher in residence. She would have to be a lady with unbounded patience because all three Begums were slow and lazy. The teacher should be above fifty, single and plain-looking. The Begums should not become jealous of her for she would have to teach the Nawab as well. Antonio enquired what kind of salary the Nawab had in mind. The Nawab knew the value of a rupee and made an offer no one could refuse.

'Well, Mr Braganza, she would also be required to teach my Begums some English and some etiquette. So it's actually two jobs rolled into one,' he said. 'Would seventy-five rupees a month suffice? She would have no expenses. We would provide her with a spacious apartment in the Zenana and she would dine with my Begums.'

Antonio was impressed by the Nawab's generosity. He thought of Teresa D'Souza, a music teacher who had just retired from La Martiniere School for Girls. This is where his two daughters studied. Mrs D'Souza was a widow and a stern taskmaster from all he had heard. The Nawab was most grateful for this recommendation and shot off an offer of employment to her, care of La Martiniere.

The last task concerning the commissioning of the pianos was the wax-polishing. Antonio supervised the work with growing satisfaction. The instruments soon gleamed. Meanwhile Emilio and Rachel did the rounds. He played Chopin, Scarlatti and Bach for each of the Begums, and Beethoven's 'Waldstein Sonata' for the excited Nawab. His Highness sent urgent word to the British Resident: His Excellency may like to inspect the new acquisitions and help the Nawab plan a grand soiree after the monsoons. The Resident, H.E. Mr Rose, was curious. He arrived that very afternoon, just as Rachel and the Braganzas were about to leave for Calcutta. Introductions were made. Mr Rose was outwardly full of compliments for the Nawab. He was impressed by the sheer audacity of His Highness. Inwardly he seethed at the squandering of public funds.

On the way back to Calcutta, Antonio had his face buried in a newspaper. Emilio and Rachel held hands discreetly.

~

As the weeks and months went by, the senior Braganzas suspected nothing of the romance blossoming under their noses. On Sunday afternoons, Rachel and Emilio would visit various cemeteries in Calcutta. Everyone conceded she needed an escort. Gareth Armstrong insisted on it. She would make her rubbings and Emilio would wonder at all the artistry that went into the engravings and statuary on tombstones. By three or four o'clock, other visitors would drift off and the lovers would have the cemetery all to themselves. They would embrace and kiss and fondle, whispering endearments into each other's ears. The future was not discussed until one dreary Sunday when Rachel blurted out that she could not tolerate the situation any longer.

'We can't carry on like this. Though we live across the landing from each other, we can't meet regularly or in privacy. Our work keeps us busy all day. We have to come to cemeteries to make love...Something has to change. Oh, Emilio, though we belong to different churches, will you marry me?'

Emilio stared at the setting sun for a few long moments. He reached for her hand, kissed it and said very simply, 'Yes, Rachel.'

The pairing was quite unconventional. Emilio was a Catholic but was not self-conscious about it. Rachel was originally also a Catholic but was now some kind of Baptist missionary. There was the age difference and the difference in skin colour. He was quite dark and good-looking. She was fair and just short of stunningly beautiful. Emilio had grown up in Bandel, a very small town, while Rachel was raised in the largest city in the world. There were differences in food habits too. Yet this unlikely duo was deeply in love. They prayed their parents would raise no objections when the time came. They decided to concentrate on their jobs. Another year passed.

~

Emilio's services were much in demand. The Nawab of Ibrahimpur had recommended him to several of his friends, piano-owning aristocrats in Calcutta, British and Bengali. Many zamindar families owned upright pianos in addition to harmoniums and pedal organs. A few Englishmen even owned grand pianos. There was a clamour for the London-trained tuner. Depending on how out-of-tune the instruments were, Emilio could tune at most one or two a day. He always advised his clients to have their pianos tuned at least three times a year. The humid climate of Calcutta required nothing less.

Emilio's visiting card now said 'London-trained.' Flavia was very proud of this. She persuaded Antonio to buy Emilio a carriage for his exclusive use. The two horses were stabled in the yard behind Braganza & Sons. Allegro was the only one to sense what was going on between Rachel and Emilio. He held his tongue. He thought very highly of Rachel and was confident that the young lady could take care of herself, and Emilio was a true gentleman.

Our handsome hero reasoned to himself that Rachel would eventually be persuaded to return to the true Church. Rachel, for her part, had no reservations about Emilio's Catholicism.

Although she did miss the chant of the Latin Mass at times, she did not miss having the Holy Father dictate what she should believe or not believe. She had no desire to convert Emilio into a Baptist; she unreservedly accepted him the way he was.

Her work at the Baptist Press was going so well that Mr Ellis gave her Saturdays off in addition to Sundays. Rachel now spent most Saturdays drawing plans for her father's latest invention, the 'Pedalgari.' This was the cycle-rickshaw that would eventually become famous all over Asia. The Asiatic Society of Bengal was very supportive.

The idea was simplicity itself: attach half a bicycle to the 'Garethgari' to get a fast-moving tricycle. Gareth had by then shown the Society members his notebooks and they showered him with praise. To tell the truth, not a single one of the members really understood his diagrams. They were largely antiquarians, linguists, archaeologists and botanists. Praising Gareth made them feel virtuous, broad-minded and progressive. They wanted to be seen as encouraging Science and Engineering. One of them, an amateur historian by the name of Sir Barton Reed, even promised to put in a word to the Viceroy. Gareth had several brilliant ideas that would benefit Calcutta but he needed powerful patronage. Sir Barton was a retired High Court Judge and the only member of the Society to have actually ridden in a Garethgari and—like Gareth—he felt manual rickshaw-pulling was a cruel, back-breaking form of labour. The Viceroy needed to be informed that the cycle-rickshaw would alleviate much of the pain and drudgery of such work. Sir Barton approached the Viceroy, who promptly gave instructions for five hundred licenses to be issued for Gareth's revolutionary 'Pedalgari.'

~

Gareth's school was doing very well. Now, on any given day, it had approximately one hundred and thirty children, several of whom were girls. Their mothers did not wish them to follow in 'the Profession.' He recalled how difficult it had been to shield Rachel from the sordid dimensions of life at The Lazy Duck and

The Black Bull. She had thus grown up with a strong practical streak and, at twenty, had gone to work in a bank. There she developed a fine handwriting and a good head for numbers. Gareth's dear friend, Professor Karl Marx, had been quite fond of her and advised her to remain independent of men. Even the ageing courtesan, Ushalata, held somewhat parallel views.

'Garethbabu, women like me entice foolish men to be dependent on us. It is *we* who exploit *them*, not the other way around. But you are a different kind of gentleman. I've grown to respect you and am even a little bit in love with you...Look, I'll be direct. At our age there's no time to waste on sweet nothings. I want you to come up to my rooms after school ends at five. Spend half an hour with me each evening. I long to be held in your arms. I miss the scent of an Englishman.'

~

Several missionaries came to visit Gareth's school. They were grudging in their admiration for the work being done there. The Baptists among them decided to let bygones be bygones, and promised they would recommend that the school be given official recognition and a generous grant by the government. But a Reverend Wood made a disturbing suggestion: 'A separate establishment must be started for girls and young women. This will encourage the enrolment of girls from better-class families.'

Gareth argued back: 'The so-called better-class families will have nothing to do with the daughters of whores. They are prejudiced. That is the social reality.'

Ushalata raised a strong objection as well. 'Girls and boys must study together as this will encourage greater mutual respect. Our school is the most progressive one in Calcutta. See how you people are coming to admire it! Mr Gareth and I have designed the perfect syllabus. We don't need advice from you...' She adjusted her saree and smiled at the gentlemen sweetly. Then, lowering her voice, she said, 'My servants have laid out glasses of sharbat for you on the veranda. You must be thirsty after all your discussions.' Subdued, the missionaries downed the sharbat hastily.

The petition for government aid got stuck in the bureaucracy for several months and then Gareth was informed that it had been rejected. The government could not be seen to be encouraging prostitution, either directly or indirectly. Gareth Armstrong's school was a private, charitable initiative, run by someone who was not an official missionary and who had no formal qualifications in the field of education.

'Garethbabu?' said Ushalata, as she lay in his arms one evening. 'Why are you so keen to get government recognition for our school?'

'The reason is simple. When our children complete their studies with us, they will need to do their matric exams. Without passing the matriculate, they can never hope to get proper government jobs. Without a government job, they will be reduced to being paupers and coolies,' said Gareth. Ushalata contradicted him.

'What is so special about a government job? Becoming clerks for the British? Our children have grown up in the streets. They'll earn their living one way or another. I have no doubt of that.'

~

Five years after they first met, Rachel and Emilio finally decided that they would dispense with formalities and simply declare their intention to get married. They did this one Sunday evening when the elders were sitting on the balcony. Antonio and Flavia held glasses of whiskey. Gareth was sipping his lemonade.

Rachel looked directly at Flavia. 'We have some wonderful news to share with you. Emilio and I are getting married as soon as arrangements can be made. Isn't that so, Emilio?...It will be a Catholic ceremony, have no fear. This will please both you and my mother in London...Say something, Emilio! I should not be doing all the talking.'

'This is something we have wanted for a long while. Ever since our trip to Ibrahimpur...I love your daughter, Mr Armstrong. Give us your blessings. Mother, if you fear a scandal, we can move out of this place and open a new establishment on Park

Street. I now have money of my own. We could easily rent a shop and a flat nearby. You would never have to see us again.'

The elders fell silent. Moments passed. Flavia had never quite approved of Rachel. She was too independent for her liking. And now this not-so-young woman had snared her only son. Antonio foresaw endless difficulties arising from the difference in religious affiliation. Gareth wondered about the age difference, but was otherwise accepting. Allegro had been listening attentively from his cage in Gareth's parlour next door. He was the first to speak. He yelled, 'Hurrah! Hurrah! Bravo, my girl! Emilio will take good care of you. You make a handsome couple.' Flavia got up from her chair and raised her voice. She was very cross. 'Mind your own business, Allegro. This has nothing to do with you. Don't interfere!' She returned to her chair and gulped down her glass of whiskey. Allegro was offended. He raised his voice, 'Madame, I have known Rachel since the day she was born. Her future is definitely my business.'

At that moment, Emilio's adolescent sisters rushed up to Allegro and asked him what was happening. He lowered his voice. He told them their brother was getting married very soon and that they would be bridesmaids dressed in pink. The girls ran on to the balcony screaming in excitement.

'A wedding, a wedding! Will our Bandel cousins be invited? Will royalty be there? You know so many rajas and nawabs, Emilio. Will there be a grand wedding cake?'

Flavia was quite vexed. 'Be off with you. Our neighbours will hear you. Keep quiet for heaven's sake. Nothing has been finalized. Finish your homework for school tomorrow. Clear off now, or I'll slap you both!'

The matter was, in fact, finalized swiftly. The progressive parish priest, Father O'Donnell, made Rachel give an undertaking that all the children born of the union would be raised as Catholics. Reverend Pocklington of the Baptist Church made Emilio promise he would not coerce Rachel into reverting back to Catholicism. A date was fixed in December. Flavia moped around her flat, still disturbed by Emilio's threat to move out to

Park Street. She was also worried about what her son would eat after he married Rachel. Boiled potatoes? Bland English food? Rachel must be taught to cook good Goan fare, particularly pork sarpatel and mutton vindaloo, his favourites. It would be simpler if Rachel moved across the landing to the Braganza flat.

~

Gareth wrote to Mamlena in London once the arrangements were firm.

> *Dear Mrs Armstrong,*
>
> *You will be happy to know that Rachel and young Emilio Braganza are to be married on the twentieth of December. A Catholic ceremony. I have given my consent, and wish them every happiness.*
>
> *Rachel's work at the Baptist Mission Press is widely appreciated. My little school for children of fallen women has become quite well known, and we receive many visitors who shower us with praise for our dedicated work.*
>
> *Allegro has slowed down somewhat. He wishes me to take him to the Khasi Hills, the land of his birth. But what with school, my scientific work and Rachel's courtship, I haven't had the time to undertake such a long journey.*
>
> *My regards to the Captain.*
>
> *Yours, etcetera,*
> *Gareth Armstrong*

Mamlena was scandalized by Gareth's letter. She shot off an angry telegram, unaware that many eyes would read it before it reached Free School Street.

> Mr Armstrong,
>
> You are aware of my plans for Rachel. I have already bought a lovely house for her in Greenwich. It's now

> on lease to a Member of Parliament. He has a most distinguished son, educated at Winchester and Oxford. Ideal for Rachel.
>
> More importantly, the time has come for me to reveal that Rachel is not your daughter. I am now sure that the Captain is her biological father. You have thus NO rights over her and would be well-advised to send her back to England forthwith. Should you fail to do so, I shall take legal steps. You are a kidnapper.
>
> Lena Armstrong

Gareth was somewhat shaken by the telegram. He went over to Reverend Pocklington's house and asked him how, as a Christian, he should react to the disturbing news. The Reverend considered the situation carefully.

'You must forgive Mrs Armstrong. Forgiveness frees the forgiver. You are the only father Rachel has ever known. She is a mature woman now. I will explain things to her and advise her to forgive her mother too...And you must pray, Mr Armstrong. In prayer lies our salvation.'

But Gareth told Rachel the devastating news himself. He explained that he and Lena were never legally married. She was thus his common-law wife and therefore Rachel was technically a bastard. In the early days of his liaison with Lena—after his brother Robert had died—Gareth was dimly aware that Captain Jack Crusoe and Lena were unusually friendly, but he did not suspect a physical relationship. He had put the matter out of his mind. Rachel should reveal all this to Emilio, otherwise they would be guilty of misrepresentation. Rachel did so and Emilio was horrified.

'But she was so kind to me in London and I, in turn, treated her with great affection and respect. I thought she had developed a healthy liking for me. Even regard. What on earth does she hold against me now? That I am brown and do not have a British accent? That I was raped and so, in her eyes, am no longer a virgin? That I have little formal education? It is not as if you were marrying a complete stranger...I too can buy you a grand house—in the posh suburb of Alipore.'

Rachel did her best to calm him down. 'You're not to blame, my love. Mother was always a hysterical person. She is right to suspect that after our marriage I will never forsake you and return to The Lazy Duck...But what is this about "rape," Emilio?'

Emilio was silent for a while. 'I never told you about it because it would have upset you. It was part of the assault on me the evening I visited your mother for the first time. It was a horrible experience. I used to have terrible nightmares about it. I saw myself wandering all over London naked and bleeding, looking for the Lazy Duck. I don't care to talk about it anymore... Are you sure Mrs Armstrong has nothing against me personally?'

'No, no, it's Father she's attacking. She'll never forgive him... Somewhere down the road—after you've trained a capable substitute—we could take a trip to London and be with her for a few weeks...I would not like to move to a grand house in Alipore! Remember, I grew up in one of the most crowded parts of London. I like crowds. Life is so interesting along Free School Street. My work is not far off. And you, my darling, can nip upstairs for lunch or a cup of tea.'

~

Flavia was not at all enthusiastic about the wedding, a fortnight away. But she was quite afraid of her son. What if he and Rachel decided to move out of the Free School Street flat and what if he abandoned the business? His time in London had also made him too independent, in her view. He even had arguments with his father over new-fangled ideas for the care and repair of pianos.

The invitations went out: to Bandel, to Serampore, to friends in the old Baptist Church, to Ushalata and her colleagues, to Rachel's friends and superiors at the Press, to assorted royalty and piano owners, and to members of the Asiatic Society of Bengal. Gareth was determined that no expense would be spared.

When the wedding ceremony was about to start, Gareth had to make hasty arrangements for extra chairs, borrowing them from here and there. This caused a delay of an hour. Ushalata had not only invited her 'professional' colleagues—mothers of children at the school—but also a good number of the children themselves. At the open-air reception afterwards, tea, coffee, sandwiches and a three-tiered cake were consumed with great relish. The girls among the school children flocked around Emilio's sisters, touching their splendid dresses and conversing in broken English. The Braganza girls responded in fluent Bengali. Flavia smiled apologetically at her relatives from Bandel, and Antonio, quite overcome by the activities, longed for a drink.

That night, Gareth suggested to the Braganzas that Emilio move into the Armstrongs' flat—they had plenty of room. Flavia objected noisily. She had just imbibed two glasses of whiskey neat. The only thing she looked forward to from this marriage was Rachel's presence in the Braganza flat. This would permit her to delegate several household duties. Rachel could also supervise her daughters who were quite a handful.

For the sake of peace, Rachel moved into the Braganzas' flat. Emilio had rather looked forward to the privacy of Gareth's flat and to resuming his conversations with Allegro. But he felt he had to humour his mother or she would harass him continually. Rachel reminded him again that she was used to crowding. It didn't matter where they slept as long as they were together. Allegro had taken to singing a music-hall ditty each time he saw Rachel or Emilio: 'Daisy, Daisy, give me your answer do...' It would have been more appropriate if he had sung it before the wedding.

~

After two years of married life, Rachel declared one day that she was 'with child' (the word 'pregnant' was not used in polite society). The Braganzas were delighted and Gareth was relieved that Rachel could conceive at her age.

But Allegro was depressed. 'While all of you are busy making babies—such a long, drawn-out business—you have broken your promise to me. To take me to the Khasi Hills. My native place. I may not live much longer. Take me back, Master. I beg of you. I do not have the strength to go by myself, and I do not know the way...'

Gareth thought deeply about Allegro's predicament. He consulted Reverend Pocklington, who told him about Shillong, the newly-designated headquarters of the Khasi region. The Baptist Mission there was losing out to the Catholics, Methodists and Presbyterians. The Baptist pastor in Shillong, Reverend Bell, was ailing. His wife, a qualified nurse, had died, leaving the old man helpless and grieving. The much-needed Mission dispensary, once run by his wife, had shut down. A new pastor had to be found. Would Gareth be interested in going up there to assist Reverend Bell until an appropriate missionary was appointed to take the old man's place? It would be a noble act of charity and would facilitate taking the troubled bird home. There would be a modest stipend.

Gareth asked when the new man could be expected to join. Reverend Pocklington assured him that the paperwork was moving briskly. Six months at the outside. Six months: Gareth calculated that he could be back in Calcutta in time for the birth of his grandchild. The Reverend Pocklington reckoned that Gareth could bring the old preacher back to Calcutta. Then, health permitting, Reverend Bell could be sent back to England in the care of some missionary family going home on furlough.

Gareth made preparations for the journey to the hills with mounting excitement. He put Ushalata in charge of the school after transferring a generous amount to keep it solvent for six months. He found an educated widow—Mrs Biswas—to take his place as the English and Bible Study teacher. The study of science could wait. He told his friends in the Asiatic Society of his plans. They asked him to scout the Shillong region for coal and other valuable minerals and bring back samples of what he found. Also, copies of the meteorological records for Cherrapunji. It was reputed to be the wettest spot on earth but this had yet to be proven. He was warned that it could get quite cold in Shillong—he should take appropriate clothing. Sir Barton Reed even provided Gareth with a letter of introduction to the Provincial Governor.

Ushalata was not enthusiastic about Gareth's expedition. 'We will miss you, Garethbabu. Especially me. Let us spend your last night in Calcutta together. I'll sing, even dance, for you. And after this we will make love...No? You know I can be quite charming and versatile. I'll do whatever you like. I know all the English positions. I need some memories of love to keep me going while you are away.'

~

What to do with the servants? Rachel was living with the Braganzas. Gareth would be in Shillong, so his flat would be empty. He decided he would pay the servants six months' salary and send them home to their villages to spend the unexpected holidays with their wives and children. Rachel advanced a further sum of fifty rupees to each of them on the condition that they bring back five examples of folk art—paintings, carvings, textiles and pottery. She had begun collecting such artefacts because she had growing doubts about the so-called superiority of European art.

Allegro preened his feathers thoroughly. He wanted to look his best, and wondered what the journey would be like. He insisted that Gareth take ample quantities of brandy with them. Reverend Pocklington was shocked by Allegro's demand.

'Reverend Bell would not approve of brandy in his manse. It's a strong drink and leads men to sin. When you reach the Khasi Hills, you will find more innocent beverages. I was telling you about the organ you will be taking up for us. It's brand new and thus sturdy enough to withstand the journey. It's being donated by our Circular Road church and, once installed in the Baptist chapel in Shillong, will draw much admiration. You will be praised for carrying it to the hills. Church attendance is bound to go up, and some non-believers may become believers...God works in wondrous ways.'

Gareth felt somewhat put upon. He frowned when the Reverend also requested him to carry up a large number of Khasi-language hymn books. God was demanding a lot from him.

Gareth spent his last night in Ushalata's arms. This is what she wanted. A troupe of musicians accompanied her while she danced and sang for two hours. Then she sank to the floor with a graceful movement and waved the musicians away. She lit candles around her bedroom and gently removed Gareth's clothing. They made love. Both were rather clumsy and panted heavily. Ushalata then sent for her private palanquin, waking the bearers in the wee hours of the morning. Gareth felt somewhat embarrassed to be riding in a palanquin but he urged the bearers to hurry, for he had to be home before dawn. He needed to nap for a couple of hours.

The next morning, when the luggage was crated and secured, Allegro asked to see Rachel and the entire Braganza family. He gave them an assortment of unsolicited advice—on babies, cooking, pianos and tombstones. He ended with, 'I will not say just "Au revoir." Goodbye Forever.'

3

Scotland of the East

The weather was hot and humid. The deck of the steamer was cluttered with various items of freight, including the crated pedal organ and Allegro's large cage. There were ten cabins on the boat, seven of them occupied by military personnel who were friendly enough. Two cabins housed a team of four civilians bound for Dacca. They held themselves aloof and ate at separate times in the small dining space. They ignored Gareth. It was quite apparent they held missionaries and army men in contempt. Gareth befriended the army chaps.

He briefed Allegro on the journey on which they had embarked. 'First, the steamer will travel downstream on the Hooghly to meet the Bay of Bengal in the south…' Allegro asked why they didn't go by train: 'Trains are much faster and I would have a proper roof over my head instead of a leaking sheet of canvas.'

'Allegro, there are no trains where we are going. River transport is considered much cheaper, and the government gives greater priority to laying down railway lines in the north of Bengal rather than the east. There are far too many rivers to be crossed in East Bengal; the railways would go bankrupt building a hundred bridges…Next, from the sea we will steer left and go upstream quite a long way—for a week, I'm told—to Dacca. Then we will change boats frequently on our way to Sylhet. Stretches will be done by carriage or bullock-cart.'

Allegro looked alarmed. 'Where did you get all this information, Master?'

'From Captain Ward, one of the officers travelling with us. He's returning to Shillong after home leave...As I was saying, after Sylhet our problems will really begin. It's a steep climb up to the Khasi Hills. Pack mules, palanquins, elephants—I do not know what awaits us. Our luggage is most peculiar. Captain Ward thinks elephants would be suitable. He told me that military equipment was usually disassembled and carried up on the backs of sturdy mules. But Emilio has warned me not to take the organ apart en route. So as I said earlier, it will be elephants for us... Cheer up, Allegro, riding on the back of an elephant could be no worse than a choppy sea journey.'

~

Dacca proved to be a city of innumerable mosques and small gardens. The snooty civil servants disembarked there and Gareth was glad to see the back of them. His new-found military friends also said their fond goodbyes over glasses of strong rum and much back-slapping. All except Captain Ward who would accompany Gareth and Allegro all the way to Shillong.

Allegro was particular about his daily exercise. Gareth would let him out of the cage and the great bird would walk up and down the deck, flapping his wings. He hoped to gradually regain the strength to fly. This would be essential if he was to enjoy the freedom of the forest where he was born. (He never used the word 'hatched.')

The travellers met many natives on their journey up to Sylhet. Each time they changed a boat, there would be a fresh crew of fascinated men who made a big fuss over Allegro. His size did not surprise them: there had been several rumoured sightings of giant birds in the province. It was Allegro's ability to speak several languages—including some Bengali—that held them spellbound.

As expected, the elephant ride up to Shillong was difficult. There were three elephants: Roopmati, Chameli and Raja. Raja and Chameli carried masses of fodder—leafy branches, straw and sugarcane. Chameli also carried the organ and assorted smaller crates. Raja carried a larger load of fodder, tents, cooking utensils, and the personal belongings of the mahouts and their helpers. Gareth, Allegro and Captain Ward rode on the smallest elephant, Roopmati. The procession could not cover more than twenty miles a day, about five hours' journey. Then it would halt, the elephants would be relieved of their burdens, the search for fresh fodder would take a couple of hours, the elephants would be bathed sometimes, the night meal cooked, and then the company would retire to the tents. Each long day was very much like the last.

Allegro was nauseous most of the time but he made considerable progress learning to fly again. He would fly to a point ahead of the procession, rest on the branch of a tree and, when his companions caught up, he would re-enter his cage, lodged between Gareth and Captain Ward. He followed this drill several times a day.

When Gareth and the entourage reached the Khasi plateau, they found that the landscape was dramatically different: low rolling hillocks, downs, fresh-water streams, a thousand species of wildflowers, fruit trees, and oak and rhododendron forests. The environs reminded Gareth of the Scottish highlands. Captain Ward confirmed that the plateau was often referred to as the 'Scotland of the East.' The military surveyors had computed its altitude as an average of 5,000 feet above sea level. When the provincial headquarters of Assam were shifted from Cherrapunji to Shillong in 1864, this was mainly because of the much lower humidity in Shillong, and because of the paucity of buildable land in Cherrapunji.

Allegro was beside himself with excitement. Much to the annoyance of Roopmati's mahout, Allegro had taken to sitting on the elephant's forehead and chattering away in a strange dialect of the Khasi language. It was all coming back—the language, the scents and the sights. At journey's end he spotted Shillong Peak which towered over the adjoining hills.

When they reached the fledgling cantonment in Upper Shillong, Captain Ward invited Gareth to spend the night in his quarters. The Captain's batman would ensure that Gareth was served a decent dinner and had a good night's rest. Allegro said he would spend the night among the pine trees. He had to get used to this sooner or later. But that night there was an accident. Allegro fell off his perch on the tallest of the pines, crashed to the ground and fractured both his feet. In agony he lay in the mud for hours. When morning came he dragged himself into the kitchen to announce to the astonished cook that he wanted some breakfast: two scrambled eggs, a piece of toast and an orange. Allegro was lucky that the batman had a smattering of English. He was used to the strange things white men ate for breakfast.

The plan was to unpack and pay off the mahouts in the morning. Elephants were not allowed in Lower Shillong because of the prodigious quantities of dung they produced. Captain Ward kindly arranged for two horse-carts to carry Gareth, Allegro (groaning in pain) and their luggage to the manse in the Baptist Mission compound. Gareth tied splints to Allegro's injured feet, assuring him that all would be well in a few weeks. Allegro begged to be allowed three measures of brandy to ease his pain. It was a two-mile journey to the manse.

~

Reverend Bell's ancient khansama, Abdul, was pulling out carrots in the kitchen garden of the manse when the carriages drew up to the portico. He rubbed his hands on his apron and shuffled up to Gareth. Abdul had impeccable manners. 'Huzoor, Sir, who shall I say is calling?...I shall see if the Reverend Sahib is at home...Is he expecting you?...My name is Abdul Peter Khan. I have been here in the Mission for more than sixty years, ever since I was fifteen. I hail from Dacca. My ancestors were Moghuls. I am the first Muslim convert in the Khasi Hills...I will go now and see if the Reverend Sahib is free to see you.'

The Reverend was dozing in his bed. Abdul woke him up with news of the visitors and helped him get dressed—always a slow and painful process. The old gentleman was too feeble to show much excitement. He had to be supported as he shuffled into the parlour. When he saw Gareth he managed a faint smile.

'God be praised! Mr Armstrong! That's your name, isn't it?...I am now a man of few words. Delighted to welcome you to God's work in Shillong...Abdul, show Mr Armstrong to Memsahib's old bedroom. That's where my late lamented wife would rest after her arduous labours in the dispensary...Do you know anything of medicine, Mr Armstrong? You don't have to answer my questions right away. There'll be plenty of time for that...And Abdul, see what you can produce for lunch. Carrot and onion soup will do. You see, Mr Armstrong, I have a very delicate constitution. Abdul and I eat only what we can grow in the garden. I hope you don't mind. There are simply no funds for more elaborate fare.'

The Reverend was quite exhausted by his long speech. He sat back in his armchair, quite out of breath. He closed his eyes for a full minute, then peered about him. 'What is that monstrous bird in the cage? Is it for eating? We are vegetarians here. Abdul has a dozen chickens in the backyard. We sell the eggs for an anna each. There's a small bazaar down the road.'

Gareth had a lot of explaining to do. At the end of it he realized that the Reverend had slept his way through much of the account. But he woke up with a start when Allegro shouted, 'Praise the Lord, the end is near.'

The Reverend continued, '...funds. Yes, funds. We have no funds to speak of. The dispensary which my late wife Rebecca used to run brought in a little something by way of gifts from grateful patients. But all that is over. The collections in church used to bring in a couple of rupees each Sunday, but I am now too weak to conduct regular services. The Mission headquarters in London has no idea of the conditions here. The authorities promised me a replacement ages ago. When I can summon the strength, I preach to an almost empty chapel—there are just eleven baptized members in attendance. There have been no fresh converts for three years. You and I must think of a strategy to increase church attendance. Our rivals, the Welsh Presbyterians, are making rapid strides. The Roman Catholics are buying up the choicest sites in Shillong. What we need is a pastor in robust health. I'm too old for the challenges ahead.'

Gareth was quite depressed by the Reverend's negative report. He had a clear notion, though, that a beginning had to be made somewhere. He installed the new organ in the chapel and taught himself to pick out the tunes of the more popular hymns. Captain Ward appreciated his diligence and communicated an interesting piece of information: the new organ was the only instrument of its kind in working order in Shillong. An earlier organ owned by the Presbyterians had succumbed to dampness after nine years of fitful performance.

Soon church attendance at the Baptist Mission went up by fifty per cent, from eleven to seventeen souls. The new Khasi hymnals were much appreciated, but Gareth found the verses were only literal translations from the English and the tunes had to be the standard British ones. The small congregation, however, loved to sing—the Khasis were a musical lot and Gareth found himself both organist and choirmaster.

~

Captain Ward then made a generous proposal. He would be willing to bring across medical supplies from the cantonment hospital if Gareth would undertake to re-open the Mission dispensary. The Captain felt that as Gareth was a man of science, he should find no difficulty in dispensing simple remedies. If found out, the Captain would explain away the depletion of the cantonment stocks as a sympathetic gesture to the local population: its goodwill towards the army had to be maintained at any cost. The inhabitants of Lower Shillong were already resentful that the best land in the upper reaches had been taken over by the army. Certain inhabitants had also complained that the soldiers were polluting the small river that flowed down to Lower Shillong. It was the only source of fresh water for both the upper and lower parts of the town. The situation was tense.

Gareth agreed to the Captain's plan but one thing puzzled him: 'How do you propose to remove the medicines without being discovered? It would be nothing short of stealing.'

'Don't worry—may I call you "Gareth" from now on?—my

batman and the ward boy in the hospital are distant cousins. I have only to fill an indent; the two boys will do the rest. Don't worry, Gareth. My conscience is clear. It's not as if we are profiting personally from the arrangement.'

~

The Civil Lines in Lower Shillong consisted of a few government offices, a grand mansion for the Chief Commissioner, and assorted bungalows for various categories of officers and staff. On one occasion Gareth and the Captain rode six miles on horseback to the top of Shillong Peak. A grand view was to be had of the town and the hillocks, forests and downs all around. Gareth turned to the Captain.

'Why is the settlement not more compact?' he asked.

'Nobody gets along with anybody else,' the Captain replied. 'Each Christian mission wants its own vast compound. Your Baptist Mission has twenty acres and just one failing missionary! The civilian officers have large orchards and gardens attached to their bungalows. There is no proper market—just a few shops here and there, strung along the dirt roads. The locals call them "bazaars". The Bengali migrants call them "haats".'

Gareth's eyes swept across the vistas and he noticed an oddity. 'What is that wooded patch to your left? Why has that not been developed? It is centrally located. Observe the hill slopes around it. A sizeable lake could be created with those contours.'

'That is the property of Ka Lasubon and her family. They are very rich and have no need to sell. Besides, Lasubon is the youngest daughter and, according to the inheritance codes of the Khasis, she has a duty to protect the wealth of her clan. If she were married and had children, the properties would be passed on to *her* youngest daughter. I have simplified the laws considerably... Miss Lasubon is very particular and has not yet met a man who lived up to her expectations.'

'That's very interesting,' said Gareth. 'How old is she? How much land does she control?'

'Why are you interested in this, Gareth?...She must be in

her mid-thirties—I could be wrong...As to the land she owns, I'd say about two hundred acres. To the best of my knowledge, it has never been properly surveyed...Miss Lasubon has recently converted to Presbyterianism...The army has its eyes on her land. It is becoming increasingly important to have an army contingent located near the seat of civilian authority as a security measure. Miss Lasubon's land is right in the middle of the Civil Lines and would be ideal for constructing a large parade ground, barracks and sundry office buildings. But she has turned down several generous offers. My commanding officer has even threatened compulsory land acquisition on grounds of the Empire's security. She just ignores him.'

~

One evening Gareth was rummaging through various items at the bottom of his trunk. He was looking for his slim notebook on hydraulics. He felt he could draw up plans for creating a beautiful lake below the Chief Commissioner's residence. Surveying instruments could be borrowed from Captain Ward. He came upon an envelope on which was written:

> *Dear Father: To be opened only when you have settled down in Shillong. Forgive my subterfuge. Enclosed is a letter to me from Mother with disturbing news. I do not know what to make of it. Your loving daughter, Rachel.*

Mamlena's handwriting was an untidy scrawl at the best of times. The letter Gareth held in his hand had obviously been written when she was in a highly emotional state.

> *Dear Rachel,*
>
> *You are by now fully aware of my views on the unfortunate conduct of you and your so-called 'father.' I feel totally abandoned and pray the Almighty will forgive you. I see nothing but misery on the path the two of you have taken.*

Under the circumstances, you will understand why Captain Jack and I decided to get married last month. We had our qualms but our priest concluded that, as neither Jack nor I were currently married (technically I was Robert Armstrong's widow), there could be no objection to our union.

I now have my own lawyer. We are contemplating legal action against your 'father.' Meanwhile, your real father and I are thinking of selling out the business and moving to the house in Greenwich.

As to your own marriage, I heard of it from Mrs Barker, your old teacher. She has a handsome nephew in the army, posted in Calcutta. Had I known earlier, I would have put the two of you in touch. At any rate, he's white and English. Your husband, Emilio, is polite, but ever so dark. Now I feel I have lost you forever. Mark my words, you will turn native. As to what Gareth Armstrong is up to, I can only guess—he must have a Hindoo mistress by now.

Your Mother

P.S. I trust Mr Armstrong has a good lawyer. Our lawyer here is the best money can buy.

Gareth guessed that Rachel must have secreted the letter among his belongings while helping him pack in Calcutta. But why such furtiveness? Had she shown him the letter in Free School Street, he would have had the opportunity to obtain legal advice. Even to arrange for an injunction against any sale of his property in London. He was the sole legal owner of The Lazy Duck and The Black Bull.

As for news of Lena's marriage, Gareth was quite indifferent. He had always suspected that his 'wife' and Captain Jack were well-suited to each other. And perhaps her marriage to him would cure her of her obsession with Rachel...Rachel's secretiveness could have been because she feared that the Braganzas would come to know of her sordid background. Gareth was aware that she had told Emilio some things, but she had understandably drawn a veil over certain other matters. Flavia would have been horrified to learn that her daughter-in-law was the illegitimate offspring of a brothel-keeper. The situation was worrying, but Gareth was certain he could do nothing about it until his return to Calcutta, where he would have access to the telegraph. So he returned to the study of hydraulics.

~

Over the following six months Reverend Bell's health deteriorated steadily to the point that he was completely bedridden. Gareth engaged two young men, Paila and Lurshai, to help Abdul care for the patient. But not much could be done. Reverend Bell sank rapidly.

There was no sign of a replacement. Gareth found himself carrying out the duties of a minister (births, marriages, deaths), organist, choirmaster, and dispenser of purloined medicines. Yet despite his fatigue he spent the late evening hours pursuing various scientific and engineering pre-occupations: the proposed lake, how to save the potato crop which had been ruined in recent years, devising precautions against a recurrence of the plague, and so on.

One morning the manse—which smelled strongly of disinfectant—received two surprise visitors. Gareth knew of them through Captain Ward. The wealthy Ka Lasubon and her elder sister, Ka Paleimon, called to enquire about the Reverend's health. They had fond memories of the late Sister Rebecca Bell. She had treated the entire family in the early days, when the only remotely medically-qualified person was the horse doctor in Cherrapunji. Gareth was touched by their concern.

Gareth had practically refurbished the entire manse at his own expense. The parlour was quite respectable now. He chatted with the ladies, who were full of compliments about the improvements.

It was close to noon when Paila, one of the new boys, ran into the parlour with the sad news that the Reverend had breathed his last. The ladies started sobbing. They recalled what a good man he had been, a tower of strength to his wife. He would journey fifty miles on horseback to Cherrapunji to stock up on medical supplies once a month. But he was not charismatic: his small Baptist flock had drifted away.

Ka Lasubon was very pretty, a fine figure of a woman, and, when all was said and done, Gareth was a fine figure of a man. Each was acutely aware of this as they made arrangements for the funeral to be held later that afternoon. There was no time to be lost as the weather was quite warm. Decomposition would set in if there were delays. Nobody felt like eating lunch. Abdul and the boys were despatched to the houses of various parishioners to give notice of the service and burial to be held at six that very evening. There was no time to arrange a proper coffin. While the ladies laid out the body, Gareth knocked together a crude rectangular box with odds and ends of timber left over from the refurbishing of the manse.

Twenty-six Baptists attended the funeral. Gareth read out the service and hymns were sung, ending with the immortal 'Abide with Me' as the sun set. Reverend Bell was buried beside his late wife Rebecca in the mission compound. Paila and Lurshai had been the gravediggers. Ka Lasubon and her sister offered their condolences to all present. They were hungry by now and went into the manse to eat some fresh fruit.

It was fairly dark when the moment arrived for the ladies to say goodbye to Gareth. He took Lasubon's hand and held it for a whole minute while reviewing the unfortunate happenings of the day. His conclusion was sad.

'This has been a most stressful day for me. I expected that the Reverend would hold out until his replacement arrived. It has already been a year since I came to Shillong. Many matters await my attention in Calcutta. Yet I must admit I have fallen in love with this place. I realize that there is much good to be done here by someone with my interests and abilities. I have always tried to serve God through the medium of science and engineering.'

Ka Lasubon saw an opening. 'Medicine depends on scientific

knowledge. You have been running the dispensary single-handed. Would you like me to help you out three mornings a week? The Khasi women would be grateful to have a lady present. And the men would then encourage their women-folk to seek treatment. You could leave minor matters to me and also teach me about the appropriate medicines for more serious maladies. As things stand, I know only a bit about traditional Khasi remedies...'

Gareth jumped at the offer. His heart throbbed with excitement. 'That would be most charitable of you. When could you start? Are you sure your Presbyterian elders will not object to your volunteering for this work in a Baptist Mission compound? They tend to look down on Baptists...'

Ka Lasubon shrugged and waived his comment away. 'Mr Armstrong, do remember I was a Baptist till not long ago! Besides, medicine has no religion—don't you agree? I'm quite lonely in my ancestral house. My older siblings—with the exception of one sister—have all married and moved away. Only Ka Paleimon remains. There are no children and I love children. My nephews and nieces are all grown up...So, Mr Armstrong, beginning next week: Mondays, Wednesdays and Fridays?'

Gareth smiled and nodded in agreement. He and the boys accompanied the two palanquins to the compound gate and waved their goodbyes. Gareth could not sleep that night for he had much on his mind: Reverend Bell's death, the matter of his replacement, Rachel's secreted letter, Mamlena's threats, his romantic interest in Lasubon...Most of all, he thought about Lasubon. He liked to think he was in her thoughts as well.

The next day he hiked to the cantonment to meet Captain Ward. The busy officer apologized for not being able to come to the funeral. He then embraced Gareth warmly and half-shouted, 'Congratulations! You are now grandfather to two bonny boys!' A message had come via telegraph from Calcutta to the cantonment at Sylhet, and from Sylhet to Shillong by horseback.

Gareth was surprised, and relieved that Rachel's earlier miscarriage had not caused lasting damage. He asked the Captain to send Rachel a short message (misusing the Army Signals network): 'Delighted with news. Tell Reverend Pocklington that Reverend Bell expired yesterday. I await instructions.'

~

The next several months passed blissfully for Gareth and Lasubon. He learnt her name meant 'a flower' and he began referring to her as his little flower. She was thirty-eight years old and he was almost sixty, an age when most men have retired. Yet Gareth had retained a fine physique and had a good head of black hair. Lasubon insisted he didn't look a day over forty-five and that he had better not divulge his true age to anyone else.

Gradually Lasubon introduced him to members of her extended family who, without exception, took a great liking to him. Some, however, had recently converted to Presbyterianism and had reservations about his Baptist faith. It began to be assumed by all, though, that the couple would marry sooner rather than later. Lasubon must give birth to children before she was too old to do so. She must have a daughter to carry on the Khasi traditions.

The mornings Gareth spent with her in the dispensary were amongst the happiest of his life. He found a tactful way of telling her about his life in London and his various entanglements there. He had to tell Lasubon about Mamlena and Rachel's dubious parentage. He had to convince his little flower that there was no substantial impediment to their marriage.

Lasubon fell into a mild depression. Yet a week later she snapped out of it and accepted Gareth's marriage proposal. She and her sister Paleimon then considered what to do about Gareth's religion. Lasubon's family were now enthusiastic Presbyterians as they saw no future for the Baptists in the Khasi Hills. The beautiful All Saints' Church, built by the Presbyterians over fifteen years ago, was a marvel of colonial architecture. The Baptists only had a tiny dark chapel in their Mission compound...And the whole town knew about the ineffective Reverend Bell, may his soul rest in peace. He was single-handedly responsible for the decline in Baptist fortunes. Lasubon put the case for conversion rather well.

Long ago William Carey had left the Church of England to become a Baptist. Lasubon's family had converted. All around them, conversions were taking place to Catholicism, to Methodism...There was no shame attached to conversion. And didn't Gareth himself leave the Catholic Church? Lasubon was quite persuasive.

One morning Lasubon confided in Gareth that she simply must have children soon. One of them had to be a daughter. Gareth should convert right away so that they could start a family. He was startled by the directness of her approach. Lying awake at night Gareth had often wondered whether it would be wise to begin fathering children at his age. Yet the notion tickled him. He had happy memories of Rachel as a toddler. Maybe he still had it in him.

Gareth thought long and hard. If he converted to marry Lasubon, what would his status be in the Baptist Mission? He couldn't just abandon his work there. At least not before a replacement arrived for Reverend Bell. On the other hand, he almost hoped that a replacement would never come. He enjoyed his various activities. He had now mastered the organ, become proficient in the dispensary, and was diligent in his 'pastoral' duties. The numbers attending church had started to increase each week. He had put Lurshai and Paila to work on the compound grounds, planting fruit trees and extending the kitchen garden tenfold. He preached a simple, straightforward religion. He had little patience with 'High Church' rituals.

~

Gareth worried a lot about the marriage. The details were complex. He proposed an arrangement to Lasubon. He reminded her that he had not been baptized by a minister.

'My immersion in London took place by accident. Technically I am just a lapsed Catholic. I'm not even a certified missionary. My work here is entirely voluntary and I am completely self-supporting.'

'Gareth, what's your point? I know all this and admire your

sense of charity. The dispensary is doing quite well. Church attendance is up. My family members joke about Paleimon and me. They call us the "sisters of charity," a good Catholic term. I don't understand what you are trying to say.'

'I know I'm a bit confused,' Gareth admitted, 'but I am trying to put together an agenda for our married life. Your Khasi customs are such that I could continue my work in the mission compound by day and come to your house at night. That way I would not get in the way of Paleimon and other relatives. As for our wedding ceremony, we could try the All Saints' Church—you are now a Presbyterian. If that fails, we could be married by the Anglican chaplain in Cherrapunji—he is a dear old soul and would not insist on ticklish formalities. And, ah, yes, I have decided that our children would be brought up as Presbyterians.'

Lasubon noted that there had been no talk of conversion. Gareth was wary of anything that smelled of 'High Church.' It seemed he preferred to remain in a state of religious limbo. Lasubon and her relatives accepted this rather convoluted reasoning with some reluctance. At least they were assured that the children would be raised as Presbyterians.

A date was fixed. Lasubon glowed with happiness. Gareth looked forward to intimacy. His arrangement with Ushalata didn't count and Mamlena was a distant memory. Through the never-failing courtesy of Captain Ward, he sent Rachel news of his impending marriage and enquired after her twins.

All this while Allegro grew stronger and stronger. His foot fractures had taken over six months to mend to the point where he could walk about in the manse. After another year and a half—which he spent perfecting the Khasi language—he started to fly from bush to bush in the compound. Then the day came when he could fly fearlessly from tree to tree in the twenty-acre grounds. Gareth had successfully weaned him off his nightly dose of brandy. Allegro would bring various berries to Gareth and ask him to pronounce whether they were fit to eat. Other birds in the compound flew away whenever they saw Allegro approaching. He would call out to them in Khasi—they were scared of his fluency in the language of humans. Allegro knew little of the language of birds.

He reminded Gareth that it was time he returned to his ancestral forest in Mawphlong. The magnificent creature felt fully acclimatized. So Gareth borrowed a horse-cart from Captain Ward and drove the long distance to Mawphlong. On the way there they stopped in Upper Shillong, where the Captain had arranged for an army photographer to take several photographs of them. At Mawphlong, Gareth had tears in his eyes. At the edge of the dense oak forest, Allegro and Gareth wished each other every happiness. Allegro flew off into the dark interior of the forest without so much as a backward glance.

On his way back to Shillong with Allegro's empty cage, Gareth thought of how this brilliant bird had been the cause of much that had happened to him over the past several years. He was going to miss him dearly. Allegro had been the best of companions. Gareth was quite depressed for a week. He told Lasubon what he knew of Allegro's long, miraculous history. He was a bird for all seasons, a rarity of evolutionary biology.

There was no time to continue fretting over Allegro. The wedding day arrived and unusual arrangements had been made. The ceremony was conducted in a large clearing in one of Lasubon's forest groves, not far from her house. The Cherrapunji chaplain officiated.

Lasubon's relatives numbered over one hundred, Gareth's staff of three were in attendance, and Captain Ward came with one of his army friends and a piano accordion to provide the music. All present remarked that holding a wedding ceremony in the open air, washed with the scent of pine trees, was a brilliant idea. They also maintained a discreet silence over the fact that permission to hold the service in All Saints' Church had been denied.

Rachel's good wishes reached a month later, along with the news that the twins had been christened Orlando and Bartholomew. The senior Braganzas were now certain that Emilio would be succeeded by sons and the family business would not die out. Rachel had taken a year's leave from the Mission Press to care for her infants. The Ellis brothers, her employers, were full of sympathy because the junior Mr Ellis's wife, Peggy, had given birth to a daughter at around the same time. Mrs Peggy Ellis and Rachel therefore had much in common. Rachel's letter continued:

> *...Emilio and I have moved into your vacant flat. Flavia was constantly interfering with the babies. An endless stream of advice, morning, noon and night. Emilio's sisters were also a nuisance—constantly waking up the twins with their rowdy behaviour. The old servants ensure we are well cared for. One of them—remember Anthony?—has a wife who helps me with the delicate aspects of motherhood. She lost her own baby to malaria a couple of months ago, so she is also our wet nurse. Nursing twins is no joke, as you can imagine. Sorry to burden you with all these intimate details.*
>
> *The big news is that I have my own business now. I design tombstones and Emilio has them fabricated in a stone-mason's yard next to Howrah Station. The hundreds of stone-rubbings I have collected over the past twenty years or so are a rich source of lettering formats, and my sketchbooks are a source of beautiful ideas for ornamental statuary. I am quite an expert now in the various kinds of sandstone and marble to be had in India. I try my best to give my clients designs that perfectly reflect their sentiments.*
>
> *Emilio's work keeps him frightfully busy. He is now considered the finest piano tuner in Calcutta. He enjoys the patronage of the Viceroy, High Court judges, and the many English-medium schools in the city. The piano shop now sells a large selection of music scores, a novelty for Calcutta. He orders them from England and Germany and sells them for a handsome profit here. The shop also deals extensively in second-hand pianos. My father-in-*

law sees to the rental activities. Branganza & Sons now has thirty pianos for rent and Emilio has to tune each one of them every six months. He is hopelessly overworked.

Everyone looks forward to meeting your wife. But Reverend Pocklington cannot seem to find a replacement for you. He had hopes of a young minister, Reverend Hunter, but Mrs Hunter fell seriously ill and was advised against coming out to the tropics. The Baptist missionaries in Calcutta are disinclined to serve in Shillong, which they consider a one-horse town, to use an American phrase. They would miss the creature comforts of this wonderful metropolis.

Mother has not been in touch for several months, even though I write to her every two months. She will be upset about your marriage, I expect. What a troubled family history we Armstrongs have! But you will always remain my darling father. Give Allegro my love. He taught me many useful phrases in six different languages which come in handy from time to time.

As always,
Your daughter Rachel

P.S. Your friend Bibi Ushalata is worried about the school's finances. She visited the other day and asked if I could advance a thousand rupees to enable her to continue running the school. I told her she should write to you directly, and that I had no power of attorney to operate your bank accounts. I have given her your address. She is a beautiful woman and ever so courteous.

Gareth was grateful for Rachel's letter. It had taken only three weeks to arrive, which represented significant progress in communications. But first things first. He wrote off to his bankers to transfer enough funds to run the school for another year. That should relieve Ushalata. Then Rachel's reference to Mamlena brought on a surge of anxiety.

Gareth had thought long and hard about what to do with his property in London. There was no point in being an ostrich. His only real friend in Shillong was Captain Ward, who now asked to be called by his Christian name, Horatio. Gareth and Horatio spent several evenings discussing Gareth's problems.

'If I were in London the matter could have been disposed of smoothly,' Gareth said. 'I have no wish to return to Lemon Tart Lane. Or to England for that matter. The properties left to me by my brother would have to be sold sooner or later.'

Horatio said, 'From what you say, they would fetch an astronomical sum. Upwards of fifty thousand pounds, I should guess. Well, perhaps not fifty thousand but several thousand, for sure. What will you do with all that money?'

'That is precisely my dilemma,' said Gareth. 'I suppose I owe Mamlena and Jack Crusoe some of it. There is Rachel to consider, though she really does not want for anything just now. Then there is Lasubon and any children we may have. I would also like to endow a co-educational school for children of coolies here in Shillong. I must not forget the school I started in Calcutta. I have just arranged to transfer funds to meet a year's expenses. Horatio, do you see how many obligations I have? I pay for half the upkeep of the Baptist Mission, the day to day expenses of the dispensary, staff salaries...It goes on and on.'

'Gareth, the inheritance issues can be sorted out later. The first step is to get competent lawyers in Calcutta and London. Authorize a quick sale. I shall be going to Calcutta next month and would be happy to act on your behalf. The army has a large roster of lawyers specializing in property matters. As you know, the army owns vast tracts of land all over the Empire and there are frequent disputes with the local population.'

'Mamlena has said she has good lawyers in London. She may be reluctant to give vacant possession,' said Gareth.

'She will not resist if you make a generous offer,' Horatio suggested. 'How much of a share would you be willing to give her?'

'Half the sale price? After all, she *is* my brother Robert's widow, and she and Jack are thus, in all fairness, entitled to half the proceeds of a sale. How long do you think it would take to sell, given that I am in Shillong and the property is in London?'

'There's no knowing till we have spoken to the lawyers,' said Horatio.

'I left London ages ago. I'm completely out of touch with property prices. My best friends have passed on. We'll have to trust the lawyers. I'll give you a power of attorney and some letters to carry to Calcutta. It's very kind of you to help out. The gossip here in the town is that you will soon be promoted to the rank of Major—is there any truth to this?'

'It's a certainty, I believe. A bit overdue but a welcome development all the same. Keep this to yourself, Gareth: I expect I shall be appointed Commanding Officer of our cantonment here. Then, after some experience in that post, I'll be posted to headquarters in Sylhet. My career till now has been one of slow advancement.'

'Horatio, you are an outstanding officer. And generous to a fault...There's another matter we should discuss. I have calculated that a huge reservoir could be created by damming up the Umiam River. A hydroelectric station there could provide electricity to the entire town, including Upper Shillong. I need some up-to-date items of surveying equipment though. If you can't get them through the army, I'd be happy to pay for them myself.'

'Give me the specifications,' Horatio requested, 'I'll see what I can do. I agree with you that our equipment is fifty bloody years out of date. It's time we modernized...It's a clear afternoon. Shall we ride up to Shillong Peak?'

This was a favourite pastime for Gareth and Horatio. They would take in the views of Shillong, some fifteen hundred feet below, and daydream about making the small town into a great city through the healthy collaboration of the army, the civil authorities, and the various Christian missions. There was too much distrust among these groups as things stood.

~

Meanwhile, Lasubon was determined to have a child as soon as possible. Gareth was somewhat exhausted by her constant demands for love-making: twice a day, seven days a week. Her persistence paid off. She soon declared she would give birth that very year. Khasi superstitions die hard: she went to a traditional diviner who assured her that the child would be a daughter.

The day the child was born, Allegro returned from the forest in a miserable condition. He had lost a large number of feathers. His left eye was partially damaged and scarred all around. He looked quite scrawny. When he limped into the kitchen of the manse, Abdul received the shock of his life. He called out to Lurshai.

'Go, quick, fast, to Ka Lasubon's house. Tell the Master Allegro has returned and needs urgent doctoring!'

Lurshai ran all the way to Lasubon's house where all concerned with the birth were enjoying fresh lemonade. The Presbyterian minister had just chanted prayers of thanksgiving, and Gareth was rather proud that he had managed to father a child at his age. Lurshai's news startled him. He was torn between hurrying to Allegro's aid and staying with Lasubon and her cheerful relatives. He decided to stay as those gathered were discussing an appropriate name for the baby. After a couple of hours of debate, they settled on 'Kerdalin' or 'one who protects and maintains.'

Gareth left Lasubon's house as soon as it was polite to do so. He hurried to Allegro's side, only to find the bird unconscious. He fetched some smelling salts from the dispensary and waved the bottle under Allegro's nostrils. Gareth stroked the inert bird until he began to stir. Allegro opened his good eye and began to speak feebly.

'I have given up on the forest. My life was in constant danger there. The black ravens ostracized me from the very beginning. I was attacked almost every day...'

'Allegro, just rest now. You can tell me all later. I'm sure it's a horrible story,' Gareth reassured him.

'No, Master, I want to get it off my chest. There was a family of black ravens who enjoyed swooping down on me each time I tried to perch in the trees along the edge of the forest. Those thuggish birds had carved out separate territories. I was exiled from all of them and had to sleep on the damp mouldy ground. I could only help myself to the rotten berries that had fallen down. The worst part was that we had no language in common. To the birds of Mawphlong I was an ugly monster...Forgive me, Master, for insisting on going there in the first place. I left you as a sentimental idealist; I return completely disillusioned. Totally defeated. Forgive me, Master.'

Gareth was upset to learn of Allegro's misadventures. He offered to give him a bath as he was now a dirty brown colour. Allegro declined the offer and waited to hear what Gareth had to say. He hoped he would be welcome to join the household once again.

'You should have returned long ago,' said Gareth. 'Or at least learned some of the local bird language. Once the black ravens knew of your distinguished history and travels, they might even have elected you to be their chief...The fundamental problem appears to have been a lack of communication...Anyway, I'm so glad you are back. I must confess I wept a little when I saw you off in the forest. You are one of my dearest friends.'

'Master, the birds of Mawphlong have no skill of abstraction or conceptualization. They have no sense of history, poetry, religion or art. Even if we had been able to converse, what would we have talked about? Berries, trees, weather and mating rituals? Master, I haven't eaten for three days. That's how long it took me to find my way back. At one point some army men aimed their rifles at me and shot off my tail feathers. They were as uncouth as the wretched black ravens! Do you think Abdul could make me an omelette and some toast? It would be just like the old days. The past year has been a nightmare.'

~

The seasons came and went. Lurshai, Paila and Allegro formed a close bond. The boys learned English from Allegro. Abdul remained his grumpy self. There was no sign of a replacement for the late Reverend Bell. Gareth was kept busy in the dispensary in the mornings, and in the afternoons he oversaw the surveyors working on the Umiam Reservoir project. Major Ward was now Commandant of the cantonment and thus a very important man. Gareth feared the day that another promotion for Horatio would take him away to a posting in the plains.

When Gareth's daughter was two years old, Lasubon resumed her volunteer work in the dispensary, leaving the child in the care of her sister, Paleimon. Major Ward took to personally delivering stocks of appropriated medicines to Lasubon's house at times when he knew she would be away at the dispensary. He would linger a while, chatting with Paleimon, and soon began to show an ardent interest in her. Paleimon was somewhat embarrassed by Horatio's attentions but responded in keeping with her name, which meant 'sober and patient.' When the matter came to Lasubon's attention, she pointed out that the Major was four years' Paleimon's junior. And if she was thinking of marriage, could she bear the thought—the terrible thought—of living in a succession of identical cantonments in the hot plains of India? Paleimon shrugged and said, 'We shall see.'

~

The project to construct an ornamental lake below the Chief Commissioner's residence was completed with the help of army engineers working under the direct supervision of Major Ward. The Chief Commissioner, Sir William Ward, and Horatio shared a common surname, which was a source of occasional confusion. Chief Commissioner Ward insisted—in a benign gesture to the army—that the lake be named after Major Ward; and the latter—for courtesy's sake—insisted that it be named 'William Ward Lake.' A colonel who had come up from Sylhet for the inauguration suggested a way out. Instead of 'Ward's Lake' it could be known as 'Wards' Lake.' Gareth welcomed the solution and hoped it would herald a new era of cooperation between the civilian and military authorities.

By this time Shillong was connected to Calcutta by telegraph. Gareth had resolved his property issues, getting a good price. Mamlena and Jack Crusoe were more than satisfied with their half-share, which amounted to the very respectable sum of thirty-two thousand pounds. Three sets of lawyers had to be paid their fees and, finally, all Gareth's financial assets were transferred to his bank in Calcutta. He was very embarrassed by the sheer size of his fortune. He kept putting off the making of a will, much to Horatio's disapproval.

On one occasion he made a rough tabulation of all the entities he wished to remember in his will when he got around to making one: Rachel and her sons, Orlando and Bartholomew; Ushalata and the school in Calcutta; the Asiatic Society of Bengal; the Baptist Missions in Serampore and Calcutta; an endowment to set up the school for coolies' children in Shillong; an endowment to construct a large church in the Baptist Mission compound in Shillong; his wife Lasubon and their daughter; Abdul, Lurshai and Paila in Shillong; and Major Horatio Ward in appreciation of his friendship and unbounded kindness.

Horatio looked over the list and made a stern observation. 'Gareth, do you know how much it would cost to build a sizeable church? Every single building material—except limestone and wood—would have to be brought up from the plains. Be realistic, my friend. And, as for me, I don't deserve a legacy.'

~

Gareth's daughter Kerdalin loved to go out horse-riding with her father. Lasubon cautioned Gareth to hold on to the little girl with utmost care. The two of them would frequently ride around Wards' Lake or visit Horatio in the cantonment. Horatio was enchanted by the child. Trips to Shillong Peak and the Umiam River were too far, so Gareth would make up little stories about the magical creatures who lived there.

It was a warm day in mid-June of 1897 and Gareth and his little girl were returning home from Upper Shillong when, suddenly, there was a loud, rumbling sound. The hillsides began to crack open. The road disappeared before their eyes. There were sounds of buildings collapsing. Trees were felled. Telegraph poles keeled over. There was a lot of dust in the air. Birds fell silent. Gareth's horse reared up in terror. The quake went on for several minutes. When a deathly silence prevailed, Gareth calmed the horse and carefully picked his way to Lasubon's house. It had collapsed. A faint voice could be heard calling for help from a small timber outhouse. Gareth forced the door open and found Paleimon trapped under several wooden rafters that had fallen. Kerdalin wailed loudly when she saw her aunt. Gareth extricated his sister-in-law as best he could. Except for a couple of minor fractures, she was not too badly hurt. Gareth looked desperately through the rubble of the house. He could not find Lasubon. He handed his water flask to Paleimon and said he would hurry over to the Mission dispensary. He left his daughter in her care. Inwardly, Gareth cried, 'Lasubon...Lasubon...'

As he rode to the compound, Gareth noticed that all buildings made of stone masonry were either completely destroyed or severely damaged. In contrast, the majority of timber-framed houses—and these were few in Shillong—were still standing and had suffered only minor damage. At the manse the destruction was complete. Only the small chapel still stood as it was largely constructed of timber. Abdul was dead—he'd been in the kitchen preparing lunch. Allegro, Lurshai and Paila survived as they had all been in the vegetable gardens when the quake struck. Lasubon's badly-bruised and lifeless body was found in the rubble of the dispensary.

The week that followed was a nightmare. First Gareth arranged for a palanquin to bring Paleimon and Kerdalin to the chapel in the Mission. Then he housed another twenty people in the little chapel. First-aid materials were salvaged from the ruins of the dispensary. A makeshift kitchen was set up in one corner of the chapel. Fortunately the extensive vegetable gardens provided a steady supply of food. There were ample stocks of coal for cooking. Allegro dispensed expert advice to all who would listen. He claimed he had experienced over seven major earthquakes in his long life. He warned there would be severe aftershocks. He was right. Fresh tremors were felt as far away as Calcutta, Dacca and Rangoon.

Horatio's cantonment experienced some, but not extensive, damage. On the fifth day after the quake, several troops arrived from Sylhet to assist what remained of the civil authorities. Their first priority was to repair the telegraph lines. Then they erected a large tent city on the parade ground for surviving civilians, and arranged for supplies of fresh water by clearing the local river of boulders and rubble. Major Ward, who escaped unhurt, undertook to organize the speedy burial of a hundred and twenty-eight bodies, without dwelling on denominational affiliations. There were four small cemeteries in Shillong: the Baptist, Presbyterian, Catholic and Anglican. The Baptist one in the Mission compound had, understandably, the most space. Lasubon and Abdul were buried there along with sixty others. No services were held.

Gareth felt quite demoralized by the disaster. His life of amateur missionary service, and his affection for his wife and daughter were the anchors of his existence. Only six Baptists survived. The one great project with which he had been closely associated—Wards' Lake—was now a vast empty crater littered with dead and rotting fish. The earthen embankment had given way and a deluge of water had gushed out, causing extensive destruction downstream. Repair and reconstruction work would have to wait. There were other priorities. The whole town had to be rebuilt.

~

Gareth's only consolation was that his daughter and her aunt got along very well. Paleimon had a deep love for the little girl. Kerdalin had always assumed she had two mothers so she did not grieve long for Lasubon. Most little children have short memories.

Horatio's large timber-framed bungalow had four bedrooms. He invited Paleimon and Gareth and his daughter to stay with him until alternative arrangements could be made. Gareth repaired Allegro's cage with tools borrowed from the army. Kerdalin loved to stand in the veranda of the bungalow and watch the marching bands go by and the horses being exercised. She also took to hiding in Allegro's cage along with some dolls and toys. Horatio and Gareth wore themselves out directing the soldiers in relief operations. The surviving residents of the town were anxious to salvage what they could from the rubble of their homes: clothes, important documents, utensils, furniture, old photographs. Gareth was able to rescue his scientific notebooks, documents related to his finances, the notes and sketches relating to the Umiam Reservoir project, and some of his scientific instruments. It rained off and on, which greatly hampered salvage operations.

A large number of villagers had poured into Shillong in search of shelter, food and work. Horatio accommodated them in the tent city—fifteen to a tent—and paid them daily wages for clearing rubble, repairing roads, and unblocking drains, streams and waterfalls.

~

Rachel and Gareth were in frequent touch through the restored telegraph system. That is how Gareth learned of Reverend Miller. After many years of fruitless search, the Baptist Mission headquarters had at last identified an energetic young missionary, keen to serve in the Khasi Hills. So keen, in fact, that news of the devastating earthquake only spurred him further. Rachel had met him three times in Calcutta and briefed him on what she knew of her father's exertions over the many years he had spent in Shillong.

Reverend Miller, tall and athletic, reached Shillong at the end of July. He felt the disaster presented an ideal opportunity to convert men and women who were still grieving over the loss of dear ones. The message of Christ would be a great comfort. The Reverend played the organ very well and soon proper services were being held in the small chapel. Potential converts came for the music, not the teachings of Christ. The Reverend organized the erection of painted wooden crosses in the cemetery. The majority merely said 'R.I.P.' as the names of the dead were rarely known. Lurshai and Paila quickly transferred their allegiance to Reverend Miller. They found him brimming with energy and new ideas.

Gareth convinced himself that the time had come to wind up his affairs in Shillong. He was now sixty-seven years old, and did not have the physical stamina to engage in the tremendous tasks that lay ahead. He and Allegro would return to Calcutta where Gareth could engage in scientific pursuits more conveniently. Horatio was aghast at the idea.

'Shillong has never needed you more than now! Your continued work on the reservoir and dam will bring us a modern water-supply system and electricity. Wards' Lake has to be rebuilt. Government buildings need to be erected. You have an instinct for engineering matters...And then there's your daughter, Kerdalin. How will she bear the loss of both mother and father in such quick succession?...You will be my guest in this house for as long as I'm posted here...And Gareth, I have some happy news at last. If you have no objection, I'm going to propose to Paleimon this Sunday. We get along very well. She is—like her name—sober and patient. She has no desire to quarrel with her male relatives for a share in Lasubon's property.'

But Gareth had made up his mind to leave. After some soul-searching he welcomed Horatio's plan to marry Paleimon. In fact, it would solve two pressing problems. His sister-in-law would gain a secure roof over her head and Kerdalin would gain a devoted 'father' and 'mother.' Gareth shared these perceptions with Horatio, who reacted sensibly.

'Perhaps you are right, Gareth. I will raise your daughter as if she were my own flesh and blood. Paleimon is probably past child-bearing age so your little girl will bring laughter and joy into our lives. When she is older, I promise, she will receive the best possible education, including in mathematics and science...'

Gareth said that as soon as he got his affairs in order, he would set up a separate trust fund for Kerdalin and one each for Rachel's sons. He also planned to gift the sum of six thousand pounds to Reverend Miller for new construction in the Mission compound: a manse, a dispensary, extensions to the chapel, and a school for the children of coolies. The money would be sent immediately. Disbursements were to be handled by Horatio.

Horatio and Paleimon's wedding ceremony was a military affair. It was conducted on the parade ground and a few of the military band survivors were in attendance: one drummer, two trumpet players and one flautist. Even Horatio later remarked that they sounded pretty awful. The ceremonies were conducted by a Presbyterian minister whose entire left leg was in a cast. The newly-weds heaved sighs of relief when it was all over.

~

Allegro was initially not too enthusiastic about returning to the beastly climate of Calcutta. For a while he toyed with the idea of requesting Horatio to allow him to join his household on a long-term basis. He even thought of learning bird language so that he could have another try at settling down in the Mawphlong forest. Hadn't Gareth once said it was all a matter of learning to communicate? Then he remembered the thousands of stimulating conversations he had enjoyed with Gareth and Rachel. After an intense inner struggle, he resolved to stay loyal to his master. Besides, his damaged feathers had not grown much again.

In mid-September, on the day before his departure when the worst of the rains was over and many farewells had been said, Gareth drew the Reverend Miller aside.

'Remember, young man, you can't be too aggressive in your proselytizing. You will only drive potential converts to the other churches or to the Seng Khasi, the new movement promoting pride in traditional customs and rituals. In fact, you can learn a lot from members of the Seng Khasi. Our churches in India must indigenize sooner or later. Start with the hymns...And you simply must learn the language. We can't rely on English any more...So, young man, I wish your Mission every success.'

The next day Allegro and Gareth, with their meagre luggage and the cage, started back on the arduous journey to Sylhet and Calcutta. It had been difficult to get Kerdalin to vacate Allegro's cage.

4

The Queen is Dead ...

Gareth spent most of his days sitting on the balcony overlooking Free School Street. He rarely spoke and, if he did, it was only to say 'Yes' or 'No.' He was thoroughly depressed. The only time he stirred himself, a year ago, was to attend Ushalata's funeral, where he was surrounded by prostitutes of all classes. A young man called Ashok introduced himself to Gareth. He maintained he was the old courtesan's only son and had come to take possession of her property. Gareth had never heard of him and was quite shocked. The young man delivered an ultimatum. The school Ushalata ran had fallen into disrepair over the years the big Sahib was in Shillong. Ushalata's 'son' wanted Gareth to vacate the premises right away, or he would call in the police.

Gareth was beside himself with frustration. 'Mr Ashok, you have to produce some proof of identity, and proof that your alleged mother wanted you to inherit the property. She told me on more than one occasion that the entire mansion was to be turned over to the school.'

'You were her last white babu. Show me her will. I have searched her quarters. Her jewellery is also missing...' said Ashok.

The truth of the matter was that one afternoon Ushalata was hurrying across a road, carrying important legal documents to her lawyers' chambers. It was a wet day. A large, empty, speeding carriage hit her. The horses panicked and trampled all over Ushalata. She died on the spot of a brain contusion. Her documents were scattered in the rain, and nobody thought to rescue them. They had included a will naming the school as beneficiary of her property and wealth, with Gareth as the sole trustee.

So Gareth could produce no will and, in a fit of despair, he decided to wind up the school. The other teachers were most disheartened; the younger children were rather glad they didn't have to attend school any more. Gareth was saddened by the ingratitude. The fight had gone out of him. He stopped speaking. The loss of his wife Lasubon in a few moments of terrestrial turmoil had left him feeling utterly defeated. And now there were the deaths of Ushalata and the school.

Another matter hurt him deeply. His daughter, who was named Kerdalin by Lasubon, had a lovely Khasi name—one that was poetic and rich in symbolism. But Gareth's good friend Horatio insisted that the little girl's name was too cumbersome and called her 'Lynne.' This, too, saddened Gareth. Telegrams from Shillong arrived every month, and each one mentioned how happy Lynne was. He gathered that she was quite the little lady. Gareth felt somewhat jealous that Paleimon and Horatio commanded all the child's affections.

Gareth conceded to himself that he had failed as a missionary. His various acts of charity had not transformed him into a man of God. Whenever he had tried to prepare a sermon in Shillong, he ran out of theological ideas beyond the first few paragraphs. He thus found himself giving lectures on evolution and on the economic ideas of his late friend Professor Marx. He would slyly hint that all the miracles, including Christ's Resurrection, had scientific explanations. Now, back in Calcutta, he had completely lost all faith in himself and in God. Allegro tried to cheer up his master with smutty music-hall ditties, but to no effect.

Then, one January afternoon in 1901, Rachel walked briskly on to the large balcony. She bent low over the motionless figure of her father and whispered, 'Her Majesty is dead. There's to be a prayer meeting in the Baptist Church in a couple of hours. I told the Reverend that you would come.' Gareth said his usual 'No.'

'Come on, Father. It will be good to get out for a while. You have sat here, staring into space, for three years. There is so much to be done in this city. So much that would interest you...'

Then Gareth spoke his first words in a long time: 'I'm not well enough to go.'

'But you are, Father, you are. You have lost weight and are quite trim. You don't overeat; you do your exercises in your room...'

'I don't believe any more in prayer,' Gareth muttered. 'The day scientists invent a direct telephone connection to God, I will start speaking to him...'

'You are saying these things to provoke me, Father. The old Queen took a keen interest in her Indian Empire...'

'She had a long innings, Rachel. Why grieve for her? She's been Queen ever since I was seven years old. Had far too many children...Nine, was it? Now we'll get Edward. A real rotter, if ever there was one...Would I have to wear a black suit? I don't have one in reasonable repair. So there! I can't go, even if I wanted to.'

'Oh, Father, don't make excuses! I'll borrow one from Emilio. You're about the same size now. Go have a bath—and please shave. I'll be back with a suit in a jiffy. You'll see, the outing will do you a lot of good. I thank God you are speaking now. Please don't go into a slump again.' Gareth looked straight into Rachel's eyes and said, 'We'll see what happens.'

The outing to the church brought some colour back to Gareth's cheeks. While the various eulogies were being read, his mind was elsewhere. The new century would be one that was powered by science in every field of human endeavour. The awesome forces of nature would be shackled for the benefit of all mankind.

Some measure of hope returned to Gareth's heart. Inexplicably, the old Queen's death cheered him up. He began perusing his many scientific notebooks. He also started going on walks again to get some strength back in his legs. Allegro was thrilled by the turn of events.

~

Sir Barton Reed, Gareth's colleague in the Asiatic Society of Bengal, was now a venerable man in his nineties. He came to visit Gareth at Rachel's invitation one day. After an exchange of pleasantries, Sir Barton gave Gareth the happy news that the electric tram system was to be commissioned any day. Its engineering was based entirely on the ideas Gareth had presented to the Society many years ago. The Viceroy was very enthusiastic and, according to Sir Barton, there was hushed talk of a Knighthood for Gareth 'for services rendered in the field of transportation to the great city of Calcutta.' Sir Barton insisted that Gareth resume attending the Society's meetings. Gareth did so with steadily increasing enthusiasm.

~

Reverend Peter Miller, Gareth's energetic replacement in Shillong, would visit Calcutta in the cold season every year. He brought nice photographs of the various new structures in the Baptist Mission compound: the enlarged chapel, the manse, the dispensary, living quarters for Lurshai and Paila, and a seven-foot-high boundary wall enclosing the entire complex to keep little boys out of the flourishing fruit orchards. On his most recent visit to Calcutta, Reverend Miller announced that the congregation now numbered fifty or so. He had introduced a system of tithes and, thus, the Mission now had a regular source of supplementary income: on average, two hundred rupees a month.

'We always remember you in our prayers,' the Reverend told Gareth. 'You have been a most generous benefactor. In Shillong you are a legend. Major Ward and Ka Paleimon bring your lovely daughter to visit us off and on. She is fluent in Khasi, English and Bengali, and likes looking at the photograph of you that is hanging over the mantle in our parlour. Paleimon has given her to understand that you are her uncle in Calcutta. I don't think this is wise but have learnt to keep my own counsel in such matters.'

Gareth was taken aback by the designation 'uncle.' He felt hurt but decided it was no use taking up the issue with the Reverend. The Ward family were about to be transferred to Dacca. Major

Horatio would be promoted to Lieutenant Colonel. Gareth's remaining link to Shillong would be Reverend Miller's messages and his visits to Calcutta in the winters. There was now a pukka road connecting Shillong to Sylhet and the journey had become more bearable. Still no sign of a rail link from Calcutta to Sylhet though. Gareth turned his attention to problems concerning Calcutta and the miserable condition of the roads.

The Viceroy, Lord Curzon, was a man of boundless energy and an all-consuming appetite for administrative reforms. According to members of the Society, Curzon interfered in every government department. He had a grand vision of the Empire and how it should be governed. Gareth was glad that Curzon took such an interest in good governance, but he feared the Viceroy was partial to extreme measures and hurried decision-making.

The great man announced one day that a grand memorial would be built to Victoria, the late Empress of India, on a vast piece of land in what the natives called 'the Maidan.' It was to be financed through public subscription. Shortly after this announcement, Curzon got busy arranging a great Coronation Durbar in Delhi. It was a splendid event and enhanced Curzon's reputation for meticulous planning and implementation. Many thousands attended.

On his return to Calcutta, Lord Curzon and his American wife decided to have the five old grand pianos in Government House repaired and tuned. They made enquiries as to who the best piano tuner in Calcutta was. Government sources told the Viceroy that the only qualified tuner was the 'London-trained' Emilio Braganza of Braganza & Sons on Free School Street. Curzon sent a message to Emilio to show up at Government House the following week. He had been informed by his secretary that it would take a minimum of five days to tune the five grand pianos. They had not been played for some time as none of Curzon's predecessors had an ear for music. Their children and grandchildren had ruined them by thumping away.

Rachel begged Emilio to allow her to accompany him to Government House. She wanted a word with the Viceroy and could pass herself off as Emilio's assistant. Emilio was doubtful whether the ruse would work. He nevertheless agreed, and on the following Monday morning the two of them presented themselves at Government House at precisely nine o'clock. Rachel had a large portfolio of artwork tucked under her arm. The Principal Secretary to His Excellency had made the necessary arrangements: sequence and location of pianos to be tuned, where luncheon would be served, and so on. Emilio set to work. From time to time he asked Rachel to hand him a particular tool to keep up the pretense that she was his assistant.

Lady Curzon dropped in periodically to check that all was well with the tuners. She arranged for tea to be served every couple of hours. There was no sign of the Viceroy on the first day. The next day the great man appeared and took a keen interest in the proceedings for a full twenty minutes. Then he noticed Rachel's portfolio and, ever curious, enquired as to its contents. This was the moment she had been waiting for.

'I would like to show Your Excellency some drawings, engravings and paintings I have collected over the years. These are a few examples. Look at these monuments. They show the ruinous condition of gems of Indian architecture. These engravings were prepared by the Daniells, uncle and nephew...'

Rachel continued, showing the Viceroy some originals of what she called 'Company drawings' for want of a better term. These were done by native artists for British customers. Next, the appreciative Viceroy was shown some pat-paintings and bat-tala etchings, all the work of traditional artists.

'The point, Your Excellency, is that the native artists need training and protection against cheap imports of mass-produced etchings and prints. The great architectural heritage of India needs to be thoroughly documented, repaired and conserved. I thought it appropriate to bring the situation to your notice.'

Lord Curzon was impressed by Rachel's advocacy of matters to which he had given little thought until that day. He prided himself on his appreciation of beauty but had been too busy to pursue this interest. He and Rachel discussed what could be done for the arts of India. Curzon then looked at his pocket watch and rose to leave.

'I'm rather tied up this week with political matters, but promise to have draft legislation for the protection of ancient monuments and remains ready by the end of next week. As for the visual arts—I love that new term, "visual arts"—I'll talk to the heads of the Calcutta Art School and the Indian Museum. We'll work out an appropriate curriculum for the art course, and I'll issue instructions that the museum should henceforth also display the finest examples of native art in all media, not just sculpture. As it is, the large museum building is half-empty; such a new display will endear us to all citizens…I'm late for a meeting, Mrs Braganza. Before I forget, I have a message for Mr Gareth Armstrong—I'm told he is your father and that he lives with you? I should be very happy to receive him at Government House. I gather he is a gentleman with a remarkable scientific career. He understands this city better than I do. I wish to consult him on transportation issues. Would nine o'clock tomorrow morning be convenient for him? My secretary has just informed me that it is the only free spot for several days…Was there anything else you wished to discuss, Mrs Braganza?'

Rachel was nervous and cleared her throat. 'Well, yes, Your Excellency. It's a matter dear to my heart. I'd like to donate my extensive collection of Indian art to the museum. This would start off matters, I think. If you consider it appropriate, I'd be happy to advise the museum on further acquisitions. I am familiar with the names of several fine artists, and have made a beginning in classifying various workshops and schools of native painting…'

'Done, Mrs Braganza! You have performed a most valuable service by bringing all this to my attention. Now, I look forward to meeting your illustrious father tomorrow. He has a record of exemplary public service, I'm told. I'll take your leave now.'

Meanwhile Emilio was having some problems with one of the pianos. The sounding board had rotted away, so the bulky instrument would have to be moved to Free School Street for extensive repairs. That night Emilio described the piano's condition to his father. Antonio was dead set against moving it.

'It will never sound the same if we replace or repair the sounding board. Their Excellencies will be disappointed and Braganza & Sons will get a bad name. No, son, better to confess that the piano in question is beyond repair. The Viceroy will appreciate your candour.'

Rachel gave Gareth her news over dinner. She was bubbling over with excitement. After their meal, Gareth began sketching furiously in preparation for the appointment with the Viceroy. He had straightforward views on town-planning: roads should be wide enough to cater to future volumes of traffic, thatched roofs should be strictly banned to avoid fires, clean water supply and sanitation should be priorities, and large public buildings should be built to last at least two hundred years. This implied that such buildings should be of stone and not of brick and crumbling plaster.

Gareth shared these and other views with the Viceroy the next day. Lord Curzon was most interested in the road widening proposals, the suggestions for developing a new city on the eastern edge of Calcutta where salt marshes predominated, and new ideas for extending the suburbs to the south. Gareth also proposed new roads linking north and south Calcutta. He predicted that motorcars and motor-driven buses would soon overtake all forms of horse-drawn vehicles on the streets. To prevent future congestion, he advised the new electric tram system should be extended to all corners of the city and its suburbs...Lord Curzon was amazed by the comprehensiveness of Gareth's thinking. He promised to set up a Town Planning Committee the following week, and Gareth agreed to serve as a non-official member.

Emilio's work on the Government House pianos took three days longer than anticipated. Now four of them were in perfect tune. Lady Curzon suggested that he take the derelict fifth away to Free School Street where he might be able to cannibalize it for parts. The Principal Secretary insisted that Emilio pay a token sum of two hundred rupees for it. It was government property after all, and the Vicereine could not be seen to be giving this away. A sale was in order.

Lord Curzon lived up to his commitments: appropriate draft legislation for the protection of monuments was readied in a fortnight; the Principal of the Art School and the Director of the Museum received terse written instructions; and a Town Planning Committee was constituted with Gareth as one of three non-official members.

~

Things started looking up for the Braganza household. The piano business was flourishing. There was talk of buying a car. Rachel's objection was over-ruled—she felt that the cars on the streets were noisy, slow, and emitted clouds of smoke. The twins, Orlando and Bartholomew, were now fifteen, and the former was doing rather well at school. Orlando was the musical one. His brother—Grandmother Flavia's favourite—was, however, quite different. He took early to pinching money from Flavia's chest of drawers and spending it on cigarettes, toffees and rum. Several complaints were received about him from La Martiniere School for Boys. His nickname at school, and latterly at home, was Blotto. He was rather tickled by how his name sounded: 'Blotto Braganza.' Blotto refused to go to church but he took an interest in Rachel's work with gravestones.

The Viceroy would leave Calcutta for Simla, the summer capital, every year. Half the government would move with him. There were several pianos in the picturesque hill town and they required tuning. At last count there were about thirty and their number was increasing year by year. Emilio was persuaded by Lord Curzon to spend a couple of months up in the hills each year. The last time these pianos had been tuned was when a half-blind English tuner had come up from Lahore. That was four years ago and now the Englishman had died.

On one occasion, when Emilio was up at the Viceregal Lodge in Simla, he overheard a troubling argument between the Viceroy and his lady.

'My mind is made up. Bengal has to be partitioned into two provinces. Today it is too large and far-flung for effective government. The eastern half will be predominantly Muslim. The western half Hindu...'

'But, my beloved,' the Vicereine interjected, 'that is playing with fire. There will be violent protests. Calcutta may be placed under siege...'

Lord Curzon walked to an open window and looked out at the manicured lawns of the Viceregal Lodge. He turned to his wife and muttered, 'Good governance is more important than religious sentiment...No, I'm sure I'm doing the right thing. Besides, I'll have the blessings of London. The nationalists here need to be taught a lesson. Troublemakers, the lot of them...'

'What about transferring the capital to Delhi?' Lady Curzon asked. 'Your Principal Secretary mumbled something to that effect the other day. Sounds like a crazy idea—'

'Why are you quizzing me on matters that must be kept strictly confidential? Do please confine yourself to your charity work, Madame. The move to Delhi is an old idea. I'm afraid a decision has been taken. London is just waiting for an appropriate moment to announce the transfer. I'm dead set against it. It would entail huge administrative disruptions, an expensive new city would have to be built and, mark my words, Calcutta would decline into a mofussil town. I have conveyed these reservations to Whitehall. There now, don't fret about such matters. You Americans are far too curious. Let's go for a walk in the gardens. I'd like to visit the aviary and see how the white peacocks are doing.'

Emilio was astonished by what he had heard. When he returned to Calcutta (via Delhi) he called a family conference with Antonio, Flavia, Gareth and Rachel. None of them had ever been to Delhi or Simla. What Emilio wanted to know was whether the time was ripe to open a branch of Braganza & Sons in Delhi. Property prices would shoot up once the decision on the transfer was announced officially. Antonio raised the first difficulty.

'You can't be here and there at the same time. Your mother and I have sacrificed so much to build up the business here in Calcutta. We could never abandon all this and move to the harsh climate of the Punjab where, I hear, the winters and summers are both unbearable.'

'But the trains are so swift these days,' said Emilio. 'Delhi is a little over two days' journey away. I could divide my time equally between Delhi, Simla and Calcutta. I have been thinking of promoting my two assistants anyway. I'd leave one in charge of tuning here in Calcutta and post the other one to Delhi. They are good Anglo-Indian chaps and thoroughly dependable. I could rent a large house up in Simla and we could all go up there for the summers...'

Rachel was torn. She felt Gareth would never move out of Calcutta. He was too involved in his work with the Town Planning Committee. Allegro was probably too infirm to undertake frequent journeys. Her own business relied on the respectably high mortality rate among Christians in Calcutta. Her sons had to finish school and her in-laws had to be within easy reach of numerous relatives in Bandel. Yet Rachel could not bear the thought of being separated from Emilio for long periods of time. The family would fall apart.

Flavia, who was concentrating on knitting a sock, simply said, 'What nonsense is this? A bird in hand is worth two in the bush, no? I will stay here even if the rest of you abandon our city. If I wanted to escape the heat in summers I'd go up to Darjeeling, not to far-away Simla. If you go to Delhi, you'd have to build a new business there from scratch. It's not worth it, not worth it, son. I'll pray that God grants you wisdom.'

Gareth was intrigued. The first eight meetings of the Town Planning Committee had not gone off too well. The Committee, it seemed to him, was packed with obstructionists. Whenever Gareth came up with new ideas, other members shot them down mercilessly. He was beginning to realize he was neither a good committee man nor a competent politician.

Now Emilio had offered an opportunity to move to Delhi to witness the birth of a new capital cradled in the ruins of other ancient capitals. Calcutta was in turmoil over Lord Curzon's partition of Bengal. The nationalists were setting off bombs in the streets. The Viceroy's memorial to the late Queen had not made much progress, and now Curzon had left and a new Viceroy was in place. Gareth had no hopes of support from this new man. The only comfort was that his suggestions on town planning had been recorded in the minutes of committee meetings, and they might come in handy at a later date when wiser heads were in charge. Gareth took a deep breath and spoke. 'I think it is an excellent idea. Calcutta has no worthwhile town planning. The quality of life here is bound to deteriorate further in no time. Up north, the building of a new Delhi will signal a future era in city planning. The finest minds will be applied to the task. Of course, your proposal will entail the expense of maintaining three establishments—in Simla, Delhi and Calcutta. But we have no shortage of funds. Those of us who wish to remain here may do so. The others can now undertake a grand new adventure.'

Over the next couple of years, the family worked out the details regarding the move in slow, often painful, steps. Gareth, Allegro, Emilio and Orlando would move permanently to Delhi. Orlando had declared he wished to be a piano tuner like his father and would value serving as an apprentice under Emilio. Rachel, Blotto and the senior Braganzas would remain in Calcutta. Blotto wished to join Rachel's gravestone business and branch out into supplying high quality sandstone and marble to the city. Neither of the twins had the remotest interest in attending Presidency College where Gareth had made some friends among the brilliant science teachers. Gareth was disappointed by this.

~

Two shops down the way from Braganza & Sons there was a large chemist's shop named Bagchi & Sons. The Bagchis had been in the apothecary business since the early nineteenth century and had branches in Kanpur, Lahore, Lucknow, Patna, Calcutta, Dacca and Delhi. The Bagchi clan was packed with uncles, brothers, cousins and in-laws, all of whom had shares in the medical empire. The patriarch, Bipin Behari Bagchi, ruled from Calcutta. At ninety-five, the old man never missed a day at the chemists on Free School Street. A grandson, Benoy Behari Bagchi, had set up shop in Delhi, where he was reputed to be doing quite well in the walled city. He had bought up a number of properties in and around Kashmere Gate in an era when prices had yet to recover from the 1857 Mutiny. The multi-purpose shop in Kashmere Gate was popularly known as 'BBB & Sons.'

Emilio caught up with Benoy Behari on one of the latter's biannual visits to Calcutta. He arranged to lease—sight unseen—a spacious shop in Delhi next to BBB & Sons. It had a wide frontage and extensive storage space behind. Emilio also arranged to rent—again, sight unseen—a large second-storey residential flat in a building overlooking the city walls and Nicholson Cemetery. The rentals were ridiculously low compared to those in Calcutta. Emilio still hoped Rachel would change her mind about going to Delhi. The Christian population would increase rapidly after the capital was transferred. The demand for gravestones would therefore also rise. Blotto could set himself up as a supplier of building materials for the construction of the new city. At least this way Emilio's immediate family would remain intact.

Benoybabu was full of praise for Delhi. 'It's a clean city, Mr Emilio. The Civil Lines are a delight. Many shady trees. Not too many missionaries, but they all have pianos. Compact, sir, compact. You can walk anywhere. Good water supply and proper sanitation. I even have a motorcar—for picnics to the outlying villages and their beautiful monuments. Business is good. I stock the latest in allopathic, ayurvedic and homeopathic medicines... Please call me Benoybabu, not Mr Bagchi. It will also ease our friendship if I can call you Emilio. We are neighbours on Free School Street, and will be neighbours in Delhi.'

~

None of the Braganzas nor the Armstrongs nor Allegro had divulged news of the impending transfer to anyone. Only a very small number of bureaucrats in London were aware of what was afoot. After the uneventful five-year tenure of the Earl of Minto, Lord Curzon's successor as Viceroy, Lord Hardinge, took over in

November 1910. He was kept very busy making arrangements for yet another grand Durbar to be held in Delhi in December 1911. King George and Queen Mary planned to attend, and all the Princes of India would be 'invited' to pay homage to the royal couple. Fearing an all-round escalation in prices, Emilio and Gareth decided to make the move to Delhi in February 1911.

Orlando was quite excited, and Allegro declared, 'I'll go wherever and whenever you go. It's my turn to make sacrifices. Presumably the railway services have improved since I last journeyed on them twenty years ago. Or was it nineteen years? My short-term memory is unreliable these days. Though I still remember every word of the conversations I had with Raja Ram Mohan Roy, Mr Darwin, Mr Dickens and Professor Marx. I reckon the company in Calcutta has not been stimulating enough. In Delhi I hope you will make more interesting friends...I gather there are famous doctors in that city—hakims—who have cures for arthritis, atrophied muscles and poor digestion. I am old now and may need frequent medical attention. Allopathic medicines do not suit me anymore. Benoybabu must know all the best hakims...I like him. He is a man of medical science.'

Gareth had hoped Allegro would opt to stay behind with Rachel in Calcutta. But Allegro could not bear to be parted from his master. Like most elderly humans, he had developed a strict regime for mealtimes, defecation and brandy. He had resumed drinking alcohol. He grew quite cross if there were any disruptions. Gareth was the only person who understood and catered to his fastidious needs.

The journey to Delhi was uneventful. The gentle rocking of the train put Gareth to sleep a good part of the way. When the men were not playing cards, Gareth kept wondering if he had packed all of his scientific notebooks and instruments. When the party reached Delhi, they were met at the Gothic-style railway station by Benoybabu. Allegro had to be extricated from the brake van. He declared he had a headache. There had been hundreds of filthy chickens travelling with him. Ten to a cramped cage. And ever so noisy. They stank to high heaven. Allegro was nauseous and decided he needed a bath as soon as possible. The chickens would be slaughtered in the big poultry market next to the biggest mosque in the walled city. Allegro was torn between pity and disgust.

Benoybabu had hired a truck to transport his friends to their lodgings on Nicholson Road. Emilio, Gareth and Orlando found a pleasant surprise awaiting them. Their flat was directly above the one occupied by Benoybabu and his family, and their gracious landlord had partially furnished their flat and engaged the services of a cook. A hot meal was soon produced. After the men had bathed and changed into fresh clothes, they stepped on to a wide balcony overlooking Nicholson cemetery.

Orlando noticed that a comely young lady was drying her hair on the corresponding balcony of the building adjacent to theirs. Benoybabu followed the young man's gaze and said, 'That's Verna Pinto. A Goan family. Her father works in the Railways.'

The next three weeks were spent furnishing the shop and the flat. A green and gold signboard was painted, larger than any other in the Kashmere Gate market. 'Braganza & Sons. By Appointment to His Excellency the Viceroy.' A large shipment of fifteen used uprights arrived from Calcutta. They would form the nucleus of piano rentals. Emilio soon found that a surprising number of Britishers and Indians had a need for the services of a piano tuner.

Emilio saw largely to the grand pianos which, according to rumours, numbered around twenty in the city. In May he was summoned to Simla and began what would become a biannual round of professional visits to Viceregal Lodge and the mansions of important personages: high-ranking officials, judges, top army brass, various rajas and, of course, missionaries. Emilio was quite an expert and could tune two pianos a day. He rented a spacious house, Dunloe, near Scandal Point on the Ridge. He collapsed each night from sheer exhaustion. He opened a bank account at Grindlay's and soon felt quite settled.

Emilio had trained Orlando fairly well. His son was adept now at tuning uprights and had his own set of tools and instruments. Practice would give him confidence. In Delhi he was a slow worker, a bit unsure of himself. 'Grandpa, I know what the pianos should sound like but I'm never quite sure how to get there. I seem to have forgotten some important steps that Father taught me. He'd be quite cross. I find myself impatient and only too ready to replace obstinate strings. The missionaries are usually unwilling to pay for new parts or incur expenditure on re-felting...I need coaching in customer relations. I'm just not persuasive enough.'

'You're young, Orlando, you'll learn soon enough. In Calcutta pianos have been around for over two hundred years. They are part of the local culture. Even many gentrified Indians, the Babus, own them. They rarely know enough to play them well but they know what a piano tuner's duties are! It's different in Delhi. Pianos have probably been around here for only sixty years. Now—hush—when the new capital gets going, every respectable household will want a piano. New churches will want both organs and pianos. Schools, restaurants, hotels—pianos will become symbols of European civilization.'

Gareth felt sorry for his grandson. He urged him never to take on more than one piano a day. He needed to be patient. Tuning forks never lied.

~

As a result of Gareth's advice, Orlando would be home well before sunset. If it was an easy case, even as early as three in the afternoon. Orlando spent a considerable length of time on the balcony pretending to read a book but actually hoping to catch a glimpse of next-door Verna. There was a pattern to her appearances. At four she would emerge to collect the clothes that had been put out to dry. She would glance up at Orlando and, in the beginning, would frown a bit. After about ten days she began to smile at him. Then she took to waving at him... At five or so she would emerge on Nicholson Road with a big shopping basket and head for the fresh food market at Kashmere Gate: vegetables, meat, fish and fruit. She would return home at about six, struggling to carry the heavy load. At seven she would join her parents on the balcony while they had drinks. The Pinto family's chit-chat was just out of ear-shot and Orlando found this quite frustrating. Gareth and Allegro had observed Orlando's frequent spells on the balcony. They concluded romance was in the air but decided to keep completely mum on the matter. Nature should be allowed to take its course.

~

Rachel wrote often from Calcutta. Blotto, it seemed, had hit the big time, as the Americans would have said. He had set himself up as a sub-contractor for supplying marble of all kinds for gravestones, exterior cladding, flooring and statuary. Thanks to Rachel's extensive and influential contacts in the British community, he brokered a lucrative sub-contract to provide white Makrana marble for the Victoria Memorial. The contract was too large to be in his own name so Mrs Rachel Braganza was the official awardee. All correspondence, supply orders, and so on were signed by her. The construction of the Memorial dragged on. After Lord Curzon left, activity on the sixty-four acre site came to a near halt. The scope of work kept expanding. It was to be not just a memorial to the dead Queen but also a celebration of the British Empire that she had commanded. The architect, Sir William Emerson, kept revising the floor layouts to accommodate a host of often-conflicting ideas originating in the bureaucracy. Commemorating the long reign of the late Queen was not to be such a straightforward affair. The flow of funds dried up from time to time, and donations became erratic.

~

Emilio returned to Delhi from Simla in October 1911. He found Orlando had neglected Braganza & Sons. He had managed to add only six uprights to the initial fifteen brought from Calcutta. He had been renting out the pianos for ridiculously low amounts. And he had also been tardy in importing stocks of music scores. He was lazy and rarely tuned more than four pianos a week. Sales of other musical instruments were down to a trickle. Emilio was quite cross. He had heard rumours.

'It's that girl next door, isn't it? You disappear every evening supposedly to carry her shopping bag. You hurry through your work so as to return in time for your rendezvous with her. This has got to stop, Orlando.'

Cornered, Orlando decided to make a clean breast of it. 'I can't live without being with her for a little while each evening. It's the only time I get away from the wretched pianos…'

'Wretched? Wretched! Need I remind you that *you* elected to become a piano tuner of your own accord. I left you in charge here because I felt you required some independence. I thought you would grow into the job. In future you will accompany me on my assignments. You clearly have a lot to learn about professional responsibility!'

'Father, try to understand. Verna and I plan to get married as soon as possible. I have proposed to her and her people do not seem averse to the idea. After all, they are Goans like us.'

Emilio let out a deep breath. 'Why would they be averse? You are tall, fair and good-looking. An English mother, a very rich grandfather. Businesses in Calcutta, Delhi and Simla. Verna's people must have checked all these details about us. I'm told her father is a mere clerk at the railway station. You know I'm not a snob in most matters but how do you see a girl like Verna fitting into our family? Think about it!'

'Verna is a talented pianist, Father. She is a music teacher at St Mary's Convent. So you see, we do have a lot in common. And we're the same age. We'll have talented children. Everything will be perfect…'

Emilio softened after this revelation. A musical daughter-in-law may not be such a bad proposition. He'd have to consult Rachel before taking a firm decision. He sent her a long telegram that very evening. Rachel replied the next day, wanting to see photographs of Verna.

Now that the probability of a marriage was being discussed, Orlando became less frantic about the frequency of his meetings with next-door Verna. Emilio conceded that Orlando need team up with him for just three days a week. And for three days the love-sick young man could be on his own. Orlando would return home early on such days and he and his lady-love would hurry with the food shopping before walking over to the cemetery, where they would hold hands, kiss passionately and explore other tactile possibilities.

~

All this while Gareth kept a sharp eye on the Durbar preparations. He gathered that some twenty-five square miles had been earmarked for the grand event. Thousands of enormous colourful tents were being erected, each fully furnished with all the modern amenities for gracious living. A special and extensive railway network was being finalized. Hundreds of advance parties had been dispatched to the site by some five hundred Princes of India to ensure that Their Highnesses would be comfortable. Gareth marvelled at the sheer magnitude of the spectacle being planned. He estimated that the whole thing would cost the government a million pounds at least, not counting the private expenditures incurred by the Indian royals.

On the fourth of December, barely a week before the grand Durbar was to be held, Gareth received a startling letter. Colonel Horatio Ward, his wife Paleimon, and their daughter Lynne would be arriving in Delhi on the sixth of December. This letter announcing their arrival had been posted at Dacca on the sixth of October, but had obviously gone astray. Horatio had been appointed to discharge various ceremonial duties during the visit of their Gracious Majesties, the King Emperor and Empress, on their visit to Delhi. He hoped Paleimon and Lynne could stay with Gareth for a two-week period. Horatio himself would be staying in the cantonment. Lynne was excited by the prospect of the journey to a legendary city. Paleimon had never been to Calcutta, let alone to the great cities of the northern plains. They planned to visit Agra and the Taj Mahal on the return journey to Dacca.

Gareth rushed down to Benoybabu's flat. Could the chemist

spare a bedroom for Orlando's use for a fortnight? After extracting a promise of strict confidentiality, Gareth told his friend about his years in Shillong and the inconvenient details of Lynne's parentage. Benoybabu had become Gareth's best friend in Delhi. He smiled indulgently and simply asked, 'I hope Orlando still likes fish? Or has he forgotten his Calcutta days? You know we Bengalis eat fish thrice a day. Those of us who can afford it... Oh, by the way, what is happening between your grandson and that Goan girl next door? I hear a lot of gossip. I heard they are to be married. Is this true?'

Gareth nodded, 'I'm afraid all that remains is to fix the date. I don't want to interfere. I think they are too young to be making such commitments. Allegro seems all for it though. He has been observing the pair for quite a while.'

It was decided that Gareth and Allegro would share a bedroom; Emilio would retain his room; and Paleimon (Horatio now called her Polly) and Lynne would share Orlando's bedroom. All three bedrooms opened on to the balcony. A flurry of activity could be witnessed in the vast open grounds below the fort walls. Armies of workmen could be seen trudging to the Durbar site a few miles northwest of Kashmere Gate.

Gareth went alone to the railway station to receive the Ward family. Emilio and Orlando both had appointments they could not cancel. Next-door Verna offered to accompany Gareth—after all, two ladies were involved—but he declined. Introductions at this early stage would have been too awkward. Besides, Gareth did not want to be beholden to Verna in any way. Not yet. Next-door Verna had taken an age to produce two good hand-tinted photographs of herself dressed in a green velvet gown. The pictures had been taken by a professional photographer in the walled city, against a backdrop of the Taj Mahal painted on a flimsy curtain. Emilio sent the pictures to Rachel who responded by stating the girl's looks were 'acceptable' but that Orlando could surely have done better in that department. A piano teacher would be welcome.

On the crowded railway platform, Gareth heard a young

woman's voice cry out, 'Uncle Gareth! We're here...!' Then Polly called out, 'Mr Armstrong! Gareth! We are standing next to the bookstall!'

The reunion was brief and enthusiastic. In all the din around them, Horatio managed to say a few words.

'You look very fit, my old friend. You must be eighty now? I retire next year. Stuck at a Colonel. Will never make it to Brigadier, I'm afraid...Khabardar!' Horatio called out to the clumsy porters handling their luggage. 'I say, it's awfully decent of you to put up Polly and Lynne. With all this Durbar business going on and the huge crowds, it would have been impossible to find safe hotel rooms. Their safety was my major concern.'

When the two families assembled for dinner that night, Orlando kept staring at Lynne, who was an exceedingly good-looking young lady. He kept reminding himself that she was some kind of relative and he had better watch his manners. At one point during the meal he attempted to clarify the familial bond. He leaned towards her.

'My grandfather, Gareth Armstrong, is your uncle—it's all rather simple, don't you agree?'

Lynne closed her eyes in an effort to concentrate. 'That can't be right,' she said. 'Now that I have met your grandfather, I think I recognize him. He used to take me horseback riding in Shillong—before the earthquake. I haven't thought about it for almost fifteen years—but it's all coming back...I remember calling him "Father!" If I am truly his daughter, that would make me your aunt, even though we are about the same age.'

Gareth looked across the table at the young couple seated next to each other. 'What on earth are the two of you nattering about? The prawn curry will get cold.'

Lynne blushed and blurted out, 'Oh, dear! I have just discovered something momentous. You are my true father, sir, and I am Orlando's aunt.' Pin-drop silence followed. Then Gareth ventured an apologetic explanation.

'I am indeed your father, and your Khasi name is Kerdalin. Your mother, Lasubon, was killed in the great earthquake when you were five years old...Surely you have heard this? Paleimon is your mother's sister. She and the Colonel adopted you as I was in no position to look after a little girl on my own. It seemed the best solution at the time...Look, Lynne, your story has a happy ending after all. Thanks to your adoptive parents, you have grown into a lovely and brilliant young lady. We are all proud of you.'

Lynne was puzzled and embarrassed at this revelation, and had tears in her eyes. 'But I don't know what to call you both,' she objected. 'It's not often that a girl suddenly has two fathers. Would you mind if I called you "Daddy?" And the Colonel, whom I have known all my life, will continue as my "Father." I like the sound of "Daddy." It's so modern, and now quite fashionable.'

Polly found her voice. 'The Colonel and I will continue to be your parents. You are my closest living relative. The Colonel and I plan to take you back to England where you can study at a great university like Oxford or Cambridge. We know you are keen on higher education.'

The dinner ended with all present feeling somewhat uncomfortable. If only the Colonel had been present. He would have taken command of the troubling conversation: smoothed over the rough spots, chided Lynne for her startling speculations, and changed the subject. No one slept easily that night. There was too much to think about.

Next-door Verna came calling the following day. She wished to firm up plans for the twelfth, the day of the Durbar spectacle. Gareth had decided he would not attend. All the sycophantic bowing and scraping before the Emperor and Empress would only sicken him. Benoybabu had heard that the throngs would number over half a million people. Gareth did not fancy himself navigating through such a crowd. Benoybabu offered the use of his car, for which they were most grateful. Colonel Horatio had arranged for six passes to be delivered to the flat. Emilio and Orlando felt obliged to attend in order to forestall having to make excuses when their lady clients asked, 'Where were you? We didn't see you in the pass-holders' section of the amphitheatre.'

~

The twelfth came. The Durbar was much grander than the ones in 1877 and 1903. Bands, horses, marching, trumpets, speeches, proclamations, and much bowing and scraping...And then the big surprises: the announcements that Bengal was to be re-united, and the Capital was to be shifted from Calcutta to Delhi.

The Nicholson Road party shook their heads meaningfully. The reversal of the bifurcation of Bengal would be a popular move, neutralizing the mischief caused by Lord Curzon. The decision to transfer the Capital came as no surprise to Emilio and Orlando but caused much excitement later in Delhi and Calcutta. The Emperor also announced several minor policy initiatives which left the audience spellbound. Next-door Verna handed out chicken sandwiches and passed around a flask of hot tea. Hundreds of spectators ate snacks around them. The sky was dotted with kites that swooped down in large numbers and snatched away the food. Frightened children bawled.

The details of the various ceremonial duties of the imperial couple over the next few days need not detain us. These were many and involved strict protocol. Horatio was kept on his feet almost the entire time and could manage only two hours of sleep each night. At the end of it all, the Viceroy Lord Hardinge and the Vicereine were thoroughly exhausted and slept for three days.

~

Gareth began to dream of the new capital city. He opened a fresh notebook and jotted down various ideas as they came to him. His chief concern was how to integrate the new with the old. How to avoid the creation of a 'White Town' and a 'Black Town' as had happened in Calcutta. He was pre-occupied with such thoughts when—three days before her scheduled return to Dacca—Lynne approached him cautiously.

'Daddy, I've had enough of living in Dacca. Cantonment life there is so dull. Calcutta, Oxford, Cambridge do not interest me either. When my parents retire to England next year, I have no wish to go with them...My only major talent is that I can draw and paint.'

'What are you getting at, Lynne? Where will you go? Any other young lady would jump at the opportunity to live in England. I believe your father has a substantial house in Poole. There are lovely beaches there. It's not too far from London. I heard there are now trains that take you anywhere you want.'

'...I'd like to draw the many monuments in Delhi—the ramparts of the ruined cities, the flora and the fauna. I've read about them in the guidebook loaned to me by Orlando...In the few days that I've been here I've grown quite fond of you and Allegro. We have not had a chance to be together much but I feel very comfortable in your company—'

'Lynne, I'm an elderly man,' protested Gareth. 'Get to the point before I kick the bucket!'

'Alright then. I have an important question for you. May I live with you from now on? You are, after all, my real father and I am no longer a little girl. I'd love to look after you and Allegro. And about Shillong—I've been thinking about the earthquake and realize I would have been killed along with my mother, Lasubon, had you not taken me for a horse-ride that morning. So I owe you my life twice over. I'd like to repay that debt.'

It took a lot to astonish Gareth. He was silent for a long while. Then he whispered:

'It would not be fair to Horatio and Polly. It would be a mortal blow to them—they have invested so much in your upbringing. As for me, I'm touched by your affection and concern. I don't deserve it.'

'But, Daddy, what if I had married an army officer in Dacca, and we had been posted to some distant town like Rawalpindi? My parents would have been forced to let me go. This situation is no different.'

'Have you spoken to your mother yet?' asked Gareth.

'I thought it best to clear it with you first, Daddy. Oh, do agree! I'll be self-supporting in no time. Verna told me that there's an opening for an art teacher at her convent school. There are other missionary schools I could apply to in case Verna's convent turns me down because I'm a Protestant.'

'Look, Lynne, I can't give you an answer till I know the views of your parents. Horatio, Polly and I were inseparable friends in Shillong. I wouldn't dream of offending them in any way. I don't want them to think I put you up to this.'

'So you have given me conditional assent? If my parents agree, you will accept me? I am twenty now, quite grown up. Don't worry, I'll persuade them when Father comes to collect us tomorrow. I'll talk to them together. Mother will take more persuasion. For years she's been saying she's entitled to inherit a large tract of land in Shillong—the ancestral home. Acres and acres, by her estimation. She wants me to inherit it after she goes. Something about my being the youngest daughter of a youngest daughter. It's all about Khasi inheritance laws. I have absolutely no interest in that land. What would I do with it?'

~

Horatio arrived at Nicholson Road at three in the afternoon the next day. The train to Calcutta was due to depart at seven in the evening, so Horatio decided they would leave for the station at five. That left only two hours to complete the packing and to say goodbyes. And it left just two hours for Lynne to persuade her parents she should stay with Gareth. After all, he *was* her biological father.

It was a cold but sunny afternoon. Gareth wheeled Allegro's cage on to the balcony where they chatted about the deplorable housing conditions in Bengal. Gareth's mind was actually elsewhere—the earthquake, Lasubon's death, Wards' Lake, the Umiam Reservoir...

The soon-to-be-fractured Ward family emerged after about an hour's heated discussion. Polly was in tears. Horatio looked grim. Everything had happened so suddenly. He drew up a chair next to Gareth.

'My old friend, are you sure you want the responsibility of keeping an eye on Lynne's activities? She's quite headstrong, if you haven't noticed. She now wants to draw, paint and teach. She has never discussed these matters seriously with us...And there are legal issues to sort out. So it can't be a formal adoption on your part.'

Gareth looked directly at Polly. 'Nothing will actually change. You, Horatio and I have always known the truth. Now Lynne knows it too and, if I may say so, has taken it rather well. I shall ensure that she writes to you every month. Rachel in Calcutta will be delighted she now has an officially-recognized step-sister, and my conscience will be eased somewhat. I have always felt regret at leaving Kerdalin behind in Shillong—but there was no other option, was there, Polly?'

Polly looked somewhat relieved at Gareth's confession. She had studiously avoided telling the truth to Lynne to spare her feelings and avoid confusion. Horatio turned to Lynne and spoke quite slowly. 'You must realize that we continue to be your legal parents...Yes, you will have two fathers...Now, quickly make up a list of all the things you want us to send you from Dacca. Think carefully and write neatly. Clothes, books, your old drawings, shoes and so on. I'll have them here in six weeks. Some young officer is bound to be coming to Delhi and will convey your possessions to you. Now go make that list. I'll give you half-an-hour; then we're off to the station.'

The clock was ticking away. The list was prepared hurriedly. Emilio and Orlando appeared just in time for the departure to the station. Next-door Verna made a predictable appearance. Benoybabu gave the use of his car and driver again. He looked out from his front door and thrust a large box of sweetmeats into Polly's hands, 'It's for the long journey,' he said. Horatio refused to let Gareth and Lynne accompany them to the station.

'It will be too crowded. Pickpockets and scoundrels everywhere. No place for a gentleman of your seniority...Dry your tears, Lynne. This is what you wanted, and you are a fully-grown young lady now. Be mindful of your hitherto unblemished reputation.'

And so only Emilio and Orlando accompanied Horatio and Polly to the station. The train was late in departing.

5

Monkey Mischief

When Colonel and Mrs Ward departed for Dacca, Gareth had to see how to accommodate the various branches of what had become an extended family. Lynne, Emilio and Orlando needed rooms to themselves. Gareth could not possibly share his room with any of the others. Benoybabu offered a solution. He owned several properties in the Old City.

'I own two adjacent flats a short distance down the road, next to Mori Gate. They are vacant now. First floor, top class. Three bedrooms each. Separated only by a landing—just like your Free School Street accommodation in Calcutta...uh, well, the rooms are a bit smaller...I'll let you have them at the pre-transfer price. The long balconies are six feet wide. If you are free this evening, I'll show you around...There's a good vegetable market around the corner.'

Orlando was a bit disappointed as the new place was about fifteen minutes' brisk walk away from next-door Verna's balcony. Communications would be disrupted. On the other hand, she and Orlando would have a place to stay once they were married.

The wedding had been fixed for the last week of February. Gareth and Emilio thought it best to move early in January so as to furnish the new premises suitably. Relatives were informed. Antonio and Flavia were too infirm to travel. Rachel and Blotto would come, of course. Emilio arranged for one of Antonio's assistant piano tuners, an Anglo-Indian, to accompany them. Eric O'Brien could help with all the running around involved in organizing a wedding. His father played the clarinet in various bands that performed in restaurants along Park Street. The Goans and the Anglo-Indians were often united in their love for Western music. Eric also had a good singing voice.

Gareth then thought it was time to buy a car, a large one. Benoybabu strongly recommended a six-seater Ford, the kind he had. Model S, right-hand drive. There was much excitement in the family when the car was finally delivered on the fifteenth of February, just in time for the wedding. A Muslim driver was appointed. He had accompanied the very aged Nawab of Ibrahimpur to the Durbar, and then decided he did not wish to return to the congested streets of Calcutta. Mustafa was a careful driver, punctual and immaculately dressed. His top speed was twenty miles per hour.

~

Next-door Verna's people were staunch Catholics. At any rate, Verna and her mother were. Going regularly to church, attending Mass, observing fasts, commemorating feast days. Verna's mother, Irene, even went to early morning Mass each weekday, returning to cook breakfast and wash clothes. She said her rosary several times a day. Mr Pinto, considerably less devout than his spouse, was a late riser and would rush out each morning to take a tonga to his office at the railway station. Most mornings he had a hangover on account of the half-bottle of rum he consumed each evening. Rum was the poor man's drink.

Irene Pinto was looking forward eagerly to the wedding. Orlando was an excellent catch. Attractive in every way. But Mr Pinto had mixed feelings about the marriage. With their only child gone, who would take care of them after he retired? They would need Verna's income as a music teacher to supplement his meagre pension. Irene Pinto reassured him that all would be well:

'You can begin to give English lessons. Become a private tutor. After thirty-five years as a clerk in the Railways, your language skills are next to none in the bureaucratic set-up. Just see, you will earn three hundred rupees a month! More, if you get up early in the morning. Meanwhile, I need money for the wedding. Take an advance from your Provident Fund.'

~

A weary Gareth drew Orlando aside a few days before the wedding and gave him a thick envelope full of cash. 'This is my wedding present to you. Five thousand to defray expenses and to pay for a honeymoon in a hill station of your choice. I suggest Simla. You've never been there—'

'But it's too much, Grandpa,' Orlando protested.

'It isn't, Orlando. I've always thought it unfair that the bride's parents have to fork out the major share of wedding costs. See that three thousand reaches Verna's parents today, but be tactful about it. They should not think the money is charity. You and Verna should come up with some explanation.'

Mrs Pinto was relieved. Verna told her that the money was saved from her teaching job. A lie, but understandable under the circumstances. The Pintos had been desperate, as the advance from Mr Pinto's Provident Fund had not been sanctioned.

Rachel, Blotto and Eric arrived three days before the wedding and settled into one of the flats. Eric was immediately deputed to help the Pintos with the flowers, church decorations and catering. It was all rather last-minute. Lynne and Rachel decided to share a bedroom. They had taken an instant liking to each other. Lynne was keen to discuss the fact that she and the middle-aged Rachel were actually half-sisters, but she held off on the topic. It would be up to their father to explain things. Anyway, Rachel might know the details already.

Lynne thought Blotto was even more handsome than Orlando, and part of her regretted that she was his aunt and, thus, could not be his lover. The day before the wedding, she and her so-called nephew walked across to the magnificent Red Fort, where she sketched and Blotto inspected the beauty of various red sandstones and white marbles employed in its construction. Blotto could tell her the names and locations of the various distant quarries from where the stones had come almost three hundred years earlier. Many of these quarries were still in use. Lynne looked adoringly into Blotto's eyes as he spoke.

Eric O'Brien volunteered to play the organ at the ceremony because the regular church organist was down with a severe stomach infection. Eric was quite accomplished and played several Bach pieces while the guests trickled into the church. The Delhi Goan Association was represented by forty devout souls. Another thirty came from among Mr Pinto's colleagues at the Railway Office. He had felt obliged to invite all his co-workers though he was close to only the handful of Christians among them. On the groom's side there were thirty, including employees of Braganza & Sons, a representative of Viceroy Hardinge's personal staff, Benoybabu's extended family and his employees, Gareth's new contacts among the architects and town-planners of Delhi, and a few Protestant missionaries who came unwittingly out of a sense of duty. There was also the representative of the motorcar showroom from which the new car had been ordered. Gareth did not want to take any chances, in case the car broke down on one of the many trips to and from St Mary's Church. Mustafa too supported this precaution as he was not yet familiar with the machinery of the Model S Ford. His driving career to date had been limited to the Nawab's stately Rolls Royce. As the sacred hour drew near, Orlando became quite cross with Mustafa.

'Why can't you drive a bit faster? You'll delay everything. I'll be late for my own wedding! There are three more trips to be made...Guests will have assembled in the church already. Thank God O'Brien is there to fill in the time with organ music.'

Mustafa tried his best to increase his speed but was too nervous to exceed twenty miles an hour.

Except for being forty minutes late, the ceremony started well. The bans were in order, the Latin Mass was said, the vows exchanged...And then all hell broke loose. A large troop of monkeys walked into the church through the main door which someone had neglected to close. The monkeys strolled up the carpeted aisle, baring their teeth to the right of them and to the left of them. Two baby monkeys hopped from hat to lady's hat, picking at the decorations, causing seven women to faint outright and others to shriek in fear. The leader of the rhesus delegation walked calmly up to the altar and drained the chalice, munched on the remains of the host...Ultimately, he defecated on the steps leading down from the pulpit.

It took several minutes for the men in the congregation to organize themselves. Eric O'Brien played random chords on the organ at maximum volume, thinking this would frighten the creatures. There was much shouting and throwing of hymnals and shoes before the monkeys could be persuaded to exit. The Pintos thought that they would never be able to live down this scandal. Alone in the turmoil, Father Fonseca who was presiding over the ceremonies remained calm and philosophical.

'It's happened before. The creatures enjoy special occasions. They have visited us at christenings, confirmations, weddings and funerals. Give them a few bananas and they depart peacefully. We must remember to close all the doors while the ceremonies are on. But that is not always feasible when the weather is very hot. So it's best to buy them off with fruit and slices of bread...Now, go in peace...Our Good Lord will understand. We must not forget that monkeys are God's creatures too.'

The lunch for a hundred-odd guests at the parish hall was a sober and sparsely-attended affair. Several ladies, thoroughly rattled, skipped the meal and ate only tiny slivers of wedding cake for form's sake. The Pintos, Braganzas and some close friends watched apprehensively as the monkeys regrouped and loitered in the compound, waiting for their share of the wedding feast.

The Pintos were heart-broken. Verna was so distraught that she took to her bed for two whole days. Rachel nursed her and kept insisting that Verna should not take the matter personally. Mr Pinto was the laughing-stock of his office. His Hindu colleagues joked that the Pinto wedding had been blessed by the reincarnations of the monkey god Hanuman. Orlando was acutely embarrassed. He and Emilio worked hard to make up for the loss of working days. The newly-arrived Eric O'Brien had to be shown the ropes of working at the Delhi branch of Braganza & Sons.

Gareth thought about the sacrilegious behaviour of the monkeys. The Catholic priest had shown a compassionate way to tolerance and forgiveness. Gareth suggested to the Pintos that Father Fonseca be requested to bless the young couple all over again at St Mary's Church. And, in this instance, only the close relatives should attend the ceremony. This was agreed, and done on the fifth day after the monkey fiasco. All concerned felt somewhat comforted after it.

Emilio then broached the subject of a honeymoon, a little holiday for the newly-weds. Verna and Orlando chose Simla, where a fully-furnished house and servants were available. Despite the incongruity, it was decided that Lynne and Eric would accompany them on the charming rail journey to the hills. The toy train from the foothills to Simla was a marvel of engineering. Lynne had never been to the northern hills. Once there, Eric was to make the rounds of Emilio's old clients and take bookings for the piano-tuning season which was around the corner.

~

The honeymoon was delayed by three weeks on two counts. Verna found that the Mother Superior at St Mary's Convent refused to grant her leave until she had completed her course of sixteen piano lessons for the junior classes. After that was done, she would ask Kitsy Ince, the senior music teacher, to fill in for Verna. That is, if Kitsy agreed to the increase in her workload. The other matter that caused delay was that Emilio came down with malaria. Orlando had to take over his piano-tuning appointments. Rachel and Blotto postponed their train tickets back to Calcutta so as to be at hand to nurse Emilio.

In an unexpected development, Verna refused to go to bed with her new husband, Orlando. Her reasoning was religious. There could be no intimate hanky-panky until they decided to have a baby. Verna had not fully recovered from the traumatic wedding and did not feel up to child-bearing just yet. Besides, the nuns had made it amply clear on more than one occasion that, should motherhood intervene, her music teaching job would go to someone else. (They had some candidates in mind.) Verna loved her job and hated the thought of losing it so soon.

Meanwhile, one afternoon while both Orlando and Eric were out tuning pianos, some monkeys invaded Braganza & Sons. They played havoc with the musical scores, tearing out page after page. They inspected several pianos in the showroom, banging away at the keys, lifting and dropping hinged lids, chewing leather strips off the piano stools...They climbed up the walls of the showroom and detached three violins that were displayed there. The two shop assistants were so terrified of being bitten that they raced out of the building to summon help.

It was at this point that Orlando and Eric returned to the showroom, and an old man, balancing a large basket of bananas on his head, passed by. And a ten-year-old urchin appeared from nowhere with a string of firecrackers in his hand. (Later, people wondered what the boy was doing with firecrackers at that time of the year. It was not Diwali, the usual time for firecrackers.)

The little boy drove a hard bargain. Five rupees for scaring away the monkeys with his 'patakas.' He was a professional scarer of monkeys. Orlando told the banana-seller to wait, and he and the boy ventured into Braganza & Sons. By this time the monkey brigade had discovered the display of wind instruments in several cases and were staring at themselves, mirrored in the polished brass, with great fascination.

The fearless little boy went to the centre of the showroom, lit himself a bidi, and set off a long string of crackers. Eight monkeys fled, but three of them lingered on the pavement outside as they noticed the banana-seller and decided that a dozen bananas would be in order. The old man threw four bananas to each of them, and they soon took off for unknown destinations. Orlando paid him a whole rupee.

The local papers covered the incident in great detail, itemizing the damage caused to Braganza & Sons. In fact, with each passing day, reports of monkey-mischief here and there in the city increased. The press urged the authorities to act. The experts claimed that if citizens stopped feeding the monkeys out of religious sentiment, the miscreants would go back to the forest on the Ridge, their original habitat. Devout Hindus were aghast at the suggestion and complained to the Viceroy that the authorities were trampling on their religious beliefs.

~

The journey up to Simla went smoothly. Verna and Eric had their first view of high mountains. Orlando undertook to have Dunloe—the house Emilio had rented—thoroughly cleaned and dusted. The servants were glad to have something to do. Verna insisted that each of them—she, Lynne, Orlando and Eric O'Brien—have separate bedrooms. The servants wondered what kind of honeymoon this would be, with the newlyweds sleeping in separate rooms.

It had been decided in Delhi that Orlando would steer clear of work while on his 'honeymoon.' Eric would do the rounds, checking out the pianos that required tuning. So Orlando had time on his hands and so did Lynne. Verna would go off with Eric to inspect the local pianos. She had somewhat of a professional interest in them. She'd be gone after lunch for two or three hours. Sometimes the odd couple would return only at sunset. Orlando and Lynne were thus left to their own devices.

Orlando was depressed. Lynne asked him what the problem was. He confided his troubles to her. He whispered as he brought his face close to hers: 'Verna is being so unreasonable. I'm embarrassed to tell you why. She believes that love-making is only for procreation—it's such an old-fashioned idea! Must have had it drilled into her by her overly-religious mother or the nuns in the convent. I believe there are effective means to avoid getting pregnant, aren't there?'

Lynne blushed, and did not know how to continue the conversation. She wasn't a virgin. There had been three lots of flirtations with junior army officers in Shillong and one serious liaison in Dacca. She had now become deeply attracted to Orlando. With his aquiline nose, fleshy lips and long, black eyelashes, he was beauty personified. Lynne wished she could find some way to put him out of his misery. Orlando, for his part, was enchanted by Lynne's good looks and her talents as an artist. If only she had come to Delhi before he'd got involved with Verna, and if only she were not his aunt.

One afternoon, five days after the group had arrived in Simla, Orlando and Lynne found themselves alone at Dunloe, as usual. The servants had gone down the hill to rest in their quarters. There was an atmosphere of total silence in the house. Aunt and nephew began to embrace each other passionately. Then Lynne, at her seductive best, undressed them both in slow, tantalizing stages. They were soon stark naked on Lynne's bed. She guided him into her and issued instructions. After a bout of vigorous love-making, Orlando lay back exhausted. He asked for one of Lynne's cigarettes—the ones she smoked in secret in her bathroom. They both knew that their relationship was purely transitory. They'd all be returning to Delhi in a few days. But Orlando had the satisfaction of knowing he was no longer a virgin. They repeated their tryst for the next three days.

Now Verna was not blind. She suspected something was brewing between Orlando and Lynne, something more than ordinary friendship. She had noticed her husband had stopped complaining, and that at meal times he and Lynne would look at each other coyly and blush frequently. One evening, after trudging back from distant Summerhill, she cornered Orlando just as he and Lynne were about to go for a stroll on the Mall. Verna had been thinking.

'Orlando, you seem to have forgotten that *I* am your wife. You spend all your time with Lynne. What sort of honeymoon is this? *You* should be doing the rounds with Eric. We are constantly having to explain that we are not related. Eric is deeply embarrassed. I have noticed he is not very communicative with your father's clients...I have seen all that I want of Simla. Now it's your turn. Lynne and I can explore the bazaars below Mall Road. I believe the monkeys there are not too aggressive. We'll take one of the young servants along for protection, and to carry our shopping bags. I simply must get over my fear of monkeys. I must remember Father Fonseca's advice: they are God's creatures too. Still, it's best to be prepared. This evening I want you to go to Lakkar Bazaar and buy four stout walking sticks—the kind that would make the rascals think twice before approaching us. They will come in handy in Delhi also.'

Orlando tried hard not to let his disappointment show. He grinned with a forced cheerfulness. 'Why, that's a wonderful idea! I was getting quite disheartened playing chess with Lynne—she always wins. I'll certainly accompany Eric and discover more of this enchanting town.' Orlando comforted himself again with the fact that he was now not a virgin. He would be eternally grateful to Lynne for making a complete man of him.

Lynne was relieved. Their secret was not out. She and Verna were happy enough to explore Lower Bazaar in the afternoons, rummaging through antique shops for early photographs, quaint postcards, empty scent bottles, cutlery, crockery, tattered novels and travelogues. Old gramophone records were a special delight because the shop-owners would play them for the memsahibs, scratches and all. As a town, Simla was over seventy years old. Old enough to generate its own treasure trove of cast-offs and memorabilia.

When a week remained of their holiday, Lynne received a telegram from her biological father, Gareth. It was brief but sad.

> I have just heard from Dacca that my esteemed friend Colonel Ward passed away suddenly a week ago. A seizure. He was buried in St Anthony's Presbyterian Church. Ka Paleimon has declared her intention to move back to Shillong. My deepest condolences.
>
> G. Armstrong

Lynne was stunned by the news. Horatio Ward had played the role of a loving father for fifteen years. Her aunt, Paleimon, had been more than a mother, and now would be returning to boring old Shillong. Where would she live? The family house, rebuilt after the earthquake, was occupied by various uncles, aunts, and their children. Would they welcome her back? Would they part with Paleimon's fair share of ancestral land? Lynne was deeply troubled. She stopped thinking of Orlando and turned to Verna for advice. The new bride had her own motives for making suggestions.

'You must go to Dacca right away. Your aunt will require your help in many matters. There's the gravestone to begin with. My mother-in-law Rachel can design a fine one for you. Then the army will require various formalities to be completed. The Colonel's will has to be probated...He did leave a will, didn't he? I remember all the bother my parents had when Grandfather Pinto died suddenly and left no will. He was also in the Railways. He always said he wanted to be buried in Bandel, but he died in Delhi. Imagine how difficult it all was for us. A lot of things were left to me to organize. It is not easy being an only child. You are in the same position. Orlando is lucky he has a brother.'

~

When Orlando was in Lakkar Bazaar buying the walking sticks, he met Mrs Anabelle Lisbey. She owned and managed a shop, and her fellow shop-owners in the bazaar thought she was crazy. Her 'Wood Crafts Emporium' was connected via a bridge to her house at the rear. She had lost count of the number of dogs she had. She bred them but was constantly on tenterhooks lest there be unofficial couplings. She specialized in small dogs: terriers, Pomeranians, Apsos and Pekingese. She reckoned that if things did go wrong, prospective buyers wouldn't be able to tell the difference. All the pups looked alike when they were very small.

Lisbeymadom, as she was known locally, offered Orlando a bargain price: fifteen rupees for each of the sticks. While they chattered, her dogs set up a fearful yip-yipping. Lisbeymadom exited from the backdoor of her shop and crossed over to her home. 'Shut up! Shut up, you scoundrels! I'll give you your dinner as soon as I have attended to my customer.' She turned to Orlando, 'The rascals expect their dinner at six sharp...Oh, by the way, can I interest you in an Apso pup? Black and white, and now three months old. I'll let you have him for fifty chips. He's been weaned and now eats chapatis soaked in milk. No trouble at all.'

Orlando had a sudden stroke of inspiration. He would buy the pup for Verna as a peace offering. He was beginning to feel guilty about his fling with Lynne. And perhaps rearing a pup would awaken Verna's maternal instincts. Perhaps that would lead to...And that in turn would lead to...

Orlando hid the pup—named Dorji by Lisbeymadom—in the folds of his jacket, and went straight to the servants' quarters below Dunloe. He handed the pup to the mali's wife and asked her, in his broken Hindi, to take care of it for a couple of days or so. She was to maintain complete secrecy. He would come for it at an appropriate moment. He wanted Verna Memsahib to be pleasantly surprised, and grateful for his gift. Little Dorji licked his fingers but already showed signs of missing his mother. The mali's wife asked the pups name and, when told it was 'Dorji,' was indignant.

'He should be called "Raja," or "Tiger" or "Dabboo." That's what we call our dogs in my village. I'll call him "Dabboo," for now...' She cooed over the pup, 'Dabboo, Dabboo, Dabboo... See, he likes the name...It's not a sahib-type name like "Rex." That's what the previous owner of Dunloe kothi used to call his Alsatian...The madam was a dreadful nag. Even the Alsatian didn't like her—used to bite her once a week...Go, Orlando sahib. Your secret is safe with me. But I'll have to tell some of the other servants who live in the same block of quarters.'

~

Lynne's bereavement cast a spell of sadness over Dunloe. Eric was despatched to the Railway Booking Office to change their tickets and rebook Lynne's onward journey to Calcutta. She'd have to travel on her own from there to Dacca.

On the day of their departure, it was raining heavily. They had to take rickshaws down to the station. Verna thought Orlando was acting very strangely, running up and down the platform, talking animatedly to various railway personnel. The party made themselves comfortable in their First Class compartment—all except Orlando who was arguing with the railway guard. He bought a ticket for the pup but was then told that a dog would not be allowed to travel in their compartment. It would have to be put in the luggage van. For that, it would have to be in a cage. And there was no sign of a cage. So the dog would have to be left behind. Orlando had no option but to grease a few palms. He boarded the train two minutes before departure. He was breathless.

The toy train began descending on its tortuous journey down to the plains. Verna noticed a bulge in Orlando's jacket.

'What on earth have you got under your jacket?' she asked. 'What are you holding on to so…tenderly?'

'It's a present for you, my love.'

'Well, then, why don't you give it to me? I like presents. You have given me so few so far. Out with it!'

So Dorji was produced. The little ball of fur was fast asleep… And Verna fell in love for the second time in her life. She took charge of the pup and fed it warm, watered-down milk with tiny bits of bread soaked in it. Orlando had packed a thermos of milk in the food hamper. Then Dorji was put on the floor of the compartment where he kept producing little puddles, which had to be mopped up with pages of an old issue of the *Simla Times*. Orlando had thought of everything. The little dog took a shine to Eric O'Brien's shoelaces. Lynne cheered up momentarily.

When Verna, Orlando, Lynne and Eric reached Delhi, after changing to the broad-gauge train at Kalka, they found Gareth grieving for Horatio Ward. Allegro sensed his master's sadness and kept repeating a little speech he had composed.

'He was a fine soldier, a gentleman, and a steadfast friend. He was a devoted husband, father, and a visionary builder of modern Shillong.'

Rachel was impressed by this summary of fine qualities. She sketched out a design for a tombstone for Lynne's benefit and

Polly's approval. The pup kept nibbling at her toes, which were encased in open sandals.

~

During the month that the young people had been away to Simla, Gareth, Rachel and Blotto had toured the environs of Delhi in the new Model S. There were only dirt tracks in much of the region and their driver had to carry a shovel and pickaxe in the car. The roads had to be cleared of debris quite often. It was not safe to travel after sunset on account of bands of robbers.

Gareth was still searching for an appropriate site for the new city. There were monuments, ruins and small villages everywhere. The original location chosen by the government was around the Durbar site, north of the Old City. But Gareth ruled this out as being poorly drained and thus flood-prone. He felt sure that the new city would have to be in the south. It was at this point in his private deliberations that news of the Colonel's death reached him. Rachel and Blotto were due to leave for Calcutta a week after Lynne and company returned from Simla. Now it was decided that they would travel earlier: with Lynne as far as Calcutta, and then she would find an escort for her onward journey to Dacca. It was left to Orlando to confirm the necessary berths from Delhi. Lynne insisted on accompanying him to the railway station, claiming a lady's presence often opened doors. It did in this case. They were able to obtain a four-berth compartment at the last minute. An elderly German missionary would share the accommodation. So there would be Lynne, Rachel, Blotto and Olga.

As Lynne was doing the last of her packing in the morning, Rachel stopped by to admire her portfolio of paintings and drawings. She found them excellent and offered to buy the lot for two hundred rupees. Lynne was astonished at the offer. Emilio and Orlando advised Lynne against the transaction: the portfolio represented Lynne's identity, in a sense. Such artwork should never be for sale. Blotto, who was passing by, mumbled, 'They are worth only fifty.' So, in an outburst of emotion, Lynne gave a third of her works to Gareth, her real father, a third of them to

Rachel, her step-sister, and the remaining third to Orlando and Verna as a wedding present.

After the Calcutta-bound party left for the railway station, Orlando and Verna had an argument over Lynne. Hurtful things were said on both sides. Orlando could not understand why Verna was unwilling to have a child.

'I'm earning more than enough for both of us. So what if you lose your job at the convent? A baby will keep you busy enough. Dorji can play with it. Grandpa Gareth would be delighted—his first great-grandchild. And Allegro could teach it nursery rhymes in many different languages.'

Verna hit back. 'After your flirtation with Lynne I feel I hardly know you. I'm not sure what kind of father you'd make.'

'The child would help us settle down. It would cheer you up, just as little Dorji does. Why are you so suspicious? What you call my "flirtation" with Lynne meant nothing. I was just trying to be polite to a relative...'

'You call what you did "being polite"? Will you be so-called "polite" to every passing woman with good looks? Orlando, you promised me so much in the cemetery, and then in church. How can I have any faith in you?'

'Well, Lynne has gone,' Orlando said. 'She will find some dashing young captain to marry up in Shillong—good luck to her! Meanwhile, you and I must get on with our lives. The Braganzas, Pintos and Armstrongs all wish us to increase and multiply. I'd like at least four children. And two boys to take on Braganza & Sons from me..."Increase and multiply"—isn't that what the Church also teaches? You know we can't defy the Church.'

Verna softened a bit. Dorji was asleep on her lap. She made Orlando swear there would be no further flirtations. And she made him promise he would be back from work by six in the evening and accompany her for food shopping from six to seven. In short, she made him commit himself to the sort of regimented life to which she was accustomed from the days when she was just next-door Verna.

~

Verna was very suspicious of servants. She sacked three of them and engaged another three—one each for cooking, cleaning and washing. The household now consisted of Gareth, Allegro, Emilio (who drifted in and out), Orlando, Dorji and herself. The three Hindu men and the Muslim driver made up the domestic staff. Verna gradually took over the many managerial duties involved in keeping such a large household going. Much to Orlando's relief she admitted she had no time to teach music. When would the housework get done? It required minute-by-minute supervision. The servants were bone lazy, squatting on their haunches at every excuse and smoking those foul-smelling bidis.

Verna had taken to going to early-morning Mass with her mother. This way they could meet every day, a source of great comfort to Irene Pinto. When Verna moved over to the Braganza household, she found a good servant for the Pintos. So her absence was hardly missed. Unknown to everyone else, Orlando used to visit the Pintos on the first of every month and hand them two hundred rupees on the condition that it was not to be spent on liquor.

Orlando and Verna had now been on intimate terms for over three months, the heartache of their early days as man and wife mostly forgotten. She was sure she was expecting. When Orlando heard this, he rushed to inform Gareth and Emilio. Embraces, back-slapping, much shaking of hands. All within ear-shot of Allegro, who gave a snort and announced, 'You Goans breed like rabbits...Well, I'll welcome the little one when it arrives.'

~

The news from Shillong was troubling. Ka Paleimon was both unwell and in straitened circumstances. The Colonel, in a last impulsive gesture, had invested his entire savings in the jute industry. Due to large-scale supply disruptions, and strikes engineered by the nationalists, the Colonel lost all his money. Shocked and anxious, he had died of a stroke in Dacca. Lynne and Paleimon salvaged what they could, but it wasn't much. There was a widow's pension, which would take ages to materialize, a small Provident Fund, and a meagre amount from the distress sale of their household effects.

When they reached Shillong, the new army commander there very kindly allowed them the use of a small, fully-furnished cottage in the cantonment. They could stay for up to six months, on compassionate grounds. Reverend Miller, now middle-aged, sent across a basketful of fresh fruit and vegetables every week. Lurshai would bring it over. Paleimon noticed that he had lost most of his teeth due to his incessant chewing of tobacco.

Gareth acted swiftly. He instructed his bankers in Calcutta to despatch the rupee equivalent of fifteen thousand pounds to Lynne. This was the amount he was planning to leave her in his will. Half the money was to be spent acquiring a suitable house in lower Shillong. The other half was to be invested safely in, say, a railway company, so as to provide a steady monthly income. Lynne and Paleimon were overcome by Gareth's generosity and wrote him several letters of gratitude.

~

The construction of the new capital occupied most of Gareth's time. He and Mustafa, the driver, continued to explore the region to the south of the Old City. His friend Benoybabu would often accompany them when business at the chemists was slow. Benoybabu once remarked that the so-called new city should not be planned as a completely separate, self-sufficient entity, standing aloof from all the earlier cities which had served as India's capitals at various points in history. If this happened, you would get a segregated city all over again. Gareth and Benoybabu agreed completely on this point and communicated their views to the Town Planning Committee set up by Viceroy Hardinge.

A prominent member of the Committee was the famous architect, Edwin Lutyens. He was quite a celebrity but Gareth found him pompous, sarcastic and a bully. Only the Viceroy could deal with him. He was married to the daughter of an earlier Governor General and had powerful connections at Court. He was brilliant but nasty.

The plan that was eventually approved confirmed Gareth's worst fears. It provided only two road links to the Old City. It was to have its own railway station, markets, offices, and places of worship. There were no robust sinews that could have bound the old and the new together in an integrated whole.

Closer to home, Verna gave birth to a baby girl. Orlando and Emilio hid their disappointment as best they could. A boy would have ensured the continuity of Braganza & Sons. The Pintos and the Braganzas decided to name the child 'Isabella.' Soon they were calling her 'Bella,' unmindful of the fact that Benoybabu had a beloved tomcat named Billa. Verna's little dog, Dorji, took a keen interest in the baby and would bark whenever anyone approached Bella's crib. Allegro, who had little knowledge of human babies, sang out nursery rhymes at the top of his voice. Nobody knew where he had learnt them.

Emilio spent three or four months each year up in Simla. He returned to Delhi when the weather improved in September. Orlando had by now learnt all the theory and practice of piano-tuning that his father could teach him. He had his own list of regular clients. For best results, pianos had to be tuned at least twice a year, so Orlando was kept quite busy.

The European population of Civil Lines increased significantly after the transfer of the Capital was announced. A new complex of temporary secretariat buildings was being constructed there. The Viceroy lived in a sprawling bungalow at the foot of the Ridge Forest. While Orlando saw to the rapid increase of pianos needing to be tuned, Emilio spent a good part of his energies arranging for the shifting and installation of second-hand instruments from Calcutta. The piano shop was a hive of activity with a large range of merchandise for hire or sale. The various items that had been damaged in the monkey attack had been made good at considerable cost. Eric was kept very busy and allowed to retain a share of the profits. He felt well-off enough to have thoughts of marriage. If only Verna had a younger sister! Everything would then have been kept in the family.

Gareth, who by now had been appointed a non-official

member of the Town Planning Committee for New Delhi, couldn't stand the arch-imperialist Lutyens. He would communicate his advice through Delhi's other famous architect, Herbert Baker, whom he found far more modest and accommodating. Lutyens, on his part, would complain to Lord Hardinge about Gareth.

'Mr Armstrong wants my plan to provide roads that are wider than the famous boulevards of London, Paris and Washington. He assumes they will be crowded with buses and motorcars within a decade. He further wants each bungalow to be located on a plot measuring no more than a quarter of an acre...And he wants a modest house for the Viceroy! These are all important town-planning issues on which the interfering Mr Armstrong has no particular expertise.'

The World War was underway. Grandiose plans for the new capital had to be scaled back, much to Lutyens' distress. Lord Hardinge insisted on various austerity measures which pleased Gareth and Benoybabu. A slow but steady pace of construction was maintained. Up-to-date building equipment was employed. A million-odd trees were planted along the broad roads.

There was much discussion over what to do about the monkeys. Gareth had noticed they even roamed the various construction sites in large numbers, and were being fed chapatis and sabzi by the hordes of labourers. He suggested that millions of fruit trees and berry bushes be planted in the Ridge Forest. They'd take a few years to mature, no doubt, but they would eventually satisfy the simian buggers. But the notion of reforesting the Ridge was taken up only half-heartedly, and the monkey menace would continue for decades to come.

The citizens of the Old City would venture out in tongas to inspect the grand buildings under construction. They realized that something very special was happening, but they did not for a moment think that the new Capitol Complex was being built for them. It would be for the 'Fat Whites,' with the 'Thin Blacks' relegated to subordinate positions in the layout plan. These terms originated with Lutyens.

~

In Calcutta, Blotto's grandparents, Antonio and Flavia, were descending to the Braganza & Sons showroom one morning. They held on to each other tightly as they took one step at a time. Flavia slipped suddenly and both of them tumbled down the remainder of the stairs. Both suffered multiple injuries, including hip fractures. Rachel, Blotto and the servants carried them upstairs and summoned doctors as well as the compounder from Bagchi & Sons. X-ray facilities were not available. Plaster casts were applied based on guesswork. Rachel employed two private nurses to care for the couple in alternating day and night shifts. Blotto, who had a soft spot for his grandmother, would look in from time to time.

Construction work on the Victoria Memorial had picked up, so there were many demands on Blotto's time. Rachel, for her part, was distracted by her many duties. There were the invalid in-laws. There was her own gravestone business. The number of Europeans dying in Calcutta had begun to decline, and most native Christians could not afford her charges for designing and installing tombstones. Curating the folk art collection at the museum took up two mornings a week. Then, keeping an eye on business at Braganza & Sons took up more energy than she had bargained for. If only her truant husband Emilio had been in Calcutta to share in the work. She had never been enthusiastic about his migration to Delhi. And she missed his arms around her at night.

It had been Antonio's practice to tote up all cash receipts at the end of each day. Now Rachel had to do this and transfer the cash to the bank the next morning. She found that Derek Goff, now promoted to head piano tuner, had been systematically cheating the firm in a variety of ways. He had been with them for several years, ever since he and Eric O'Brien had been engaged by Antonio. Derek had learnt all the ropes. He could tune pianos, sell music scores, hire out or sell instruments. He thought he was indispensable. On discovering his cheating, Rachel was inclined to dismiss him but dared not. She started pestering Emilio to return to Calcutta to take full control of the piano business there.

She felt sure that their son Orlando was now mature enough to be left on his own in Delhi. He could also take care of the Simla end of the business by sending Eric up there each summer.

Emilio returned to Calcutta. The war years passed with news of sickening brutalities. The Great Powers played chess with national boundaries all over Europe. A very large contingent of Indian soldiers died on alien battlefields.

Emilio's parents passed away two weeks apart. Antonio and Flavia never recovered from their fall. They were buried side by side at Bandel and a grand tombstone was designed by Rachel and erected by Blotto. Emilio, an oldish man by now, settled into a carefully regulated regime of tuning no more than four pianos a week. Blotto, who had operated from a small office in one corner of the piano showroom, now demanded—and got—a larger space in Branganza & Sons. He was ambitious and aspired to become a big contractor sooner rather than later.

Blotto's calculations were straightforward. Emilio had been an only son. His two sisters were off the scene: one of them had married a Bandel boy and emigrated to Australia, and the other had become a nun. So no aunts, uncles or cousins to worry about. That left his twin brother, Orlando. And *he* had settled down in Delhi and gave every indication of remaining there for as long as the Empire lasted. So Blotto should be the sole inheritor of the Free School Street property. He planned to wind up the piano business and open a grand showroom of the latest building materials, plumbing fixtures, hardware, paints and varnishes. That was Blotto's dream. He had no feel for music.

~

In Delhi Gareth came to know through his membership of the Town Planning Committee that a large, crescent-shaped market was going to be built in the new capital, located midway between the old and new cities—a vast assemblage of big shops, showrooms, hotels and other civic amenities. This was planned essentially for Fat Whites who would then be spared the trouble of journeying to the Old City for daily necessities. Shopkeepers in the Old City, particularly the European ones, were encouraged to book commercial space in the crescent. Prices for plots were a bargain at one-and-a-half rupees per square yard.

The plots were almost wedge-shaped like slices of a pie. Benoybabu and Orlando put their names down for four adjacent plots overlooking what was to be the Central Park. They would go down in history as the first buyers of plots. Construction, subject to strict architectural controls, was still a few years away. Each plot stipulated commercial use on the ground floor and residential use on the first floor so that work and home could be together.

Benoybabu was a restless soul. His wealth, which was considerable, was systematically invested in property. Despite his advanced age he was constantly on the lookout for both vacant plots and built structures. He persuaded the now-thriving Orlando to invest in a large plot in the area of the new city reserved for private residences. This was in addition to the crescent market investments.

'Such properties will appreciate a hundred-fold in twenty years. I have seen other good plots too. Buy them up, my son. Bequeath your descendants, whenever they are born, one plot each. This would be much more valuable than cash. I plan to move out of the Kashmere Gate area once I have established a business in the crescent market.' This market was soon given a name: Connaught Place, after the Duke of Connaught who laid the foundation stone in 1919.

~

Meanwhile, the Braganza household increased in number. After years of fervent prayer, a son, Julio, was born to Verna and Orlando. A year later, another girl, Maria. The eldest child, Bella, was exceedingly jealous. Verna often told herself that the girl would have to be sent to a convent when she was older. Julio, who hardly ever cried, allowed himself to be kicked, pummelled and pinched in silence. He adored Bella and did not wish to get her into trouble by crying or complaining.

Allegro was quite attached to the little boy who, when he reached the toddler stage, would spend several spells each day visiting the bird's cage. They would talk baby babble and Allegro later claimed he had taught Julio the elements of English, Hindustani and Bengali. Verna, who remembered being taught a little Portuguese by her grandfather, also tried to teach little Julio some catchphrases in that tongue. As a consequence of all this instruction, Julio's sentences combined words and phrases from four different languages, with little thought to idiom or grammar. It took years to rectify this scramble.

In 1924, when Julio was five and Gareth was ninety-three, Gareth Armstrong finally made a will. Benoybabu's lawyer helped him with the niceties. Gareth had already taken care of his second daughter Lynne. He left an equal amount to Rachel, his first. The balance (some thirty thousand pounds) was to be equally divided between his grandsons Orlando and Blotto (whom he had never really liked), and his three great-grandchildren. That would be six thousand pounds each—a huge fortune in those days. He also set aside a handsome sum for the care and upkeep of Allegro who would surely outlive Orlando and possibly even the great-grandchildren and *their* grandchildren.

Gareth had two remaining ambitions. The first was to live to be a hundred and the second was to move into the new city as soon as feasible. Some people had started calling it New Delhi, thus cementing forever its remoteness, its separateness and its superiority complex. Others called it Imperial Delhi.

The authorities gave the green signal for the construction of Connaught Place. Each plot owner was responsible for his own construction. Benoybabu and Orlando rushed to complete their share of the crescent and were indeed the first to move in—true pioneers. All around the market and south of Central Vista, bungalows were being constructed and occupied at a furious pace. The grand vista linked the Viceroy's palace to the river, two miles to the east. The Fat Whites were moving in, abandoning Civil Lines, and the Thin Blacks were settled in clerks' quarters in the northwest. Schools, hospitals, places of worship, small markets, clubs and parks were gradually built and made operational. Indians hailing from the Old City had a problem. Their women folk were disinclined to leave their old haunts, their friends, and the narrow alleyways. Many of these ladies would take a tonga back to the Old City after their menfolk had left for work. They would spend their days there with friends and relatives and return to the 'new city' at sunset. Servants managed the housework while the women were away.

Gareth and the Braganzas were, again, the first to actually take up residence above their showroom in Connaught Place. Verna was unhappy with the move. It would be difficult to keep an eye on her parents and to go to Mass every morning. She would have to change churches, which would be traumatic. With three children to raise, her life was difficult enough. The only consolation was that Gareth had gifted his Model S to Orlando, so she had the occasional use of a car.

The old driver, Mustafa, had retired and gone back to his village in Moradabad, where the youngest of his wives was still alive and could look after him. The new driver, Krishan Lal, was very ambitious. He took a large loan from Orlando and quickly bought a sizeable plot off the service lane separating the Inner Circle and Outer Circle of Connaught Place. He set up a makeshift motor garage, hiring—at very low wages—young boys to do routine jobs while he put in two hours of repair work early mornings and two hours in the evenings, in addition to his nine-to-five duties with Orlando and family. Krishan Lal eventually built a thriving garage there, with a loft overlooking the parking yard. In that loft his wife gave birth to three children in a space of three years. As they grew up they all took a keen interest in auto-mechanics. Krishan Lal, like his employer, was a pioneer too.

~

Benoybabu would occasionally take the aged Gareth on drives through New Delhi. Many of the roads were yet to be named. White marble statues of colonial worthies were being installed on traffic roundabouts. The trees planted along the roads were only a few feet tall. There was hardly any traffic. You could travel the length of the longest road and barely spot a bicycle or two, or a bus after an hour.

The magnificent Capitol Complex—the Viceroy's House, the two Secretariats, and the circular Legislative Assembly—were almost completed and were being occupied. On one of these trips Allegro had come along for the ride. Gareth turned to Benoybabu with a question.

'Do you think all this will prove a waste? How long can the British hold on to India? Gandhi's freedom struggle is gathering force. You see how empty the streets are. Connaught Place is not even half constructed...When Independence comes, all this will be an anachronism...'

'The population will come,' said Benoybabu. 'Let the government move all its offices from Calcutta and some from Simla. The Viceroy, Lord Irwin, is making plans for a grand inauguration. It should happen soon.'

Gareth digressed slightly. 'You know I have been a severe critic of the New Delhi Layout Plan. That's why I resigned from the Town Planning Committee last year. In any case, my colleagues on the Committee felt I was too old to serve any useful purpose. The Viceroys, however, have always been courteous... Oh, yes, the land issue. Far too much land has been wasted. It should have been a much more compact city, a natural outgrowth of the Old City. That approach would have respected Indian urban traditions.'

'But, Garethbabu, you were the one arguing for wide roads. You were right there. In the future there will be thousands of motor cars and buses to deal with. And the Committee simply had to incorporate modern infrastructure for drainage, sewerage, lighting and water supply...The traditional Indian city lacks most of these facilities.'

'I suppose,' said Gareth, 'that the concept of a great Empire requires grand plans. The Viceroy's House is far grander than even Buckingham Palace, and rivals Versailles! It has hundreds of acres attached to it. The bungalows designed by Baker and mostly by Russell are huge, with several acres of gardens surrounding each. All these are going to be frightfully expensive to maintain in the future. Look at how compact Calcutta and Bombay are!'

Allegro was thoroughly enjoying the discussion. He had witnessed the rise and fall of many cities in his long life. He had seen the growth and decline of colonial powers—the Portuguese, French, Dutch, Danish, and now the British. He gave his considered opinion on the issues being discussed.

'Cities do not develop overnight. They take decades, sometimes generations, to achieve their full potential. Their populations ebb and flow with the advent of wars, epidemics and migrations. New Delhi too will be subject to such influences. From what I have seen today, I conclude that the buildings of the Capitol Complex will last at least three hundred years, which is well beyond the likely period of British rule. The bungalows will have to be replaced after a hundred years. The trees will have a limited lifespan, depending on the species...There will be many occasions when New Delhi will have to be reinvented. The city will become the heart of a great metropolis provided it is saved from haphazard construction, mindless expansion and thoughtless redevelopment...Master, I'm only repeating what you have taught me over the years—first in London, then Calcutta, and now in Delhi.'

The little lecture by Allegro was just like him. He loved to assume a professorial air and make grand assertions which were not particularly easy to rebut. They were full of gravitas and were often quite prophetic.

Gareth enjoyed living in Connaught Place. He, Allegro and Julio, his great-grandson, would sit on the various upper-storey verandas watching cars and tongas go by. Julio was quite an artist. He would sketch any and every thing—furniture, cars, the occasional aeroplane that flew overhead. He had a very fine sense of proportion and perspective. Gareth had told Julio he would inherit all of Gareth's scientific notebooks; they contained thousands of sketches from which Julio could benefit. Perhaps he would become an inventor too.

Julio was a devout child. He would accompany Verna to the just-completed Sacred Heart Cathedral every Sunday. He said the 'Our Father' several times a day and would urge the rest of the Braganza family to do likewise. His sisters teased him for being so 'holy-holy.' Orlando was not particularly religious. He claimed he said his prayers at night, and that was it. Verna's great ambition was that at least one of her children would become a priest or a nun. This was the teaching of the Church. She concluded the girls were too flighty. So Julio would have to become a priest, whether he liked it or not. She would send him to a seminary in Goa. Perhaps to Rachol—the name sounded close to his grandmother's, Rachel.

~

With every passing month Gareth felt the strength ebbing from his limbs. He could barely manage the stairs and needed assistance in many small ways. His hundredth birthday was coming up in January 1931. He wished he could meet his daughters just one last time, to say goodbye and explain the provisions of his will. Benoybabu, now in his mid-eighties himself, did not think Lynne would be able to travel alone all the way from Shillong. She had married a civilian employed by the army and had a sickly son, conceived late in life. Rachel might come if she felt well enough. She too was getting on in years. Benoybabu's lawyer was against Gareth discussing his will with anyone beforehand. Benoybabu would be the executor and he was very competent and a dear friend. All would go smoothly.

Rachel wrote from Calcutta to say she had broken her left leg on the treacherous stairs and was bedridden with a plaster cast. Emilio never wanted to visit Delhi again. He despised the heat and the dust. They made him ill. He wished his son Blotto would set aside some time each day to help him with the piano business as he was good at accounts. Ever since the Victoria Memorial had been completed, Blotto's services as a building contractor and supplier were much in demand; and he had become quite self-centred and arrogant. His aversion to matters musical had only grown.

Gareth's birthday came around. Orlando invited several friends for the lavish party. Verna wanted to invite her priest but Gareth was quite firmly against it. He said, 'I've lived to be a hundred not because of God's grace but because of my constitution and my scientific activities—in London, Calcutta, Shillong and, to a lesser degree, in Delhi.'

At the birthday party everyone looked very sober, as if Gareth would conk out any moment. Allegro decided to jolly things up. 'Bring out the brandy and I'll sing my London bar-room songs.' Verna was horrified.

'You'll do no such thing. I'll play something sober on the piano. Switch off the lights. I'll play by candlelight as they used to a hundred years ago.'

~

The festivities surrounding the Inauguration of New Delhi were spread over a two-week period in the latter half of February. An endless round of parties, polo matches, and arrogant speechifying from various platforms. Gareth and Orlando were invited to the Viceroy's garden party. Gareth had to be moved around in a wheel-chair as he had injured his knees in a minor fall in the bathroom. The moment came when they were presented to the Viceroy. One of Lord Irwin's aides whispered at length in his ear. The Viceroy nodded and smiled and shook Gareth's hand warmly.

'Ah, yes, you are the famous Mr Armstrong who took on Mr Lutyens! Your contributions to the planning and development of this Imperial City will go down in history. It's an honour to meet you in your hundredth year.' The Viceroy then turned to Orlando. 'And you are Mr Braganza of Braganza & Sons, I presume? I wish to record my appreciation for the exceptional services you have rendered to the British community. Our pianos have been kept in excellent shape thanks to you, your father and grandfather. It's a valued association that goes back several decades.'

~

Gareth's two outstanding wishes had been fulfilled and he felt the time had come to go. Several doctors and Benoybabu's medicines were keeping him alive. Benoybabu would console him from time to time.

'You are a philosopher and a scientist, my old friend. Philosophers know how to die. Just stop eating and taking medicines if you feel the time has come...You are my dearest friend, my guru. I'm going to miss you terribly. I vow to keep an eye on Orlando and the children. I don't know how much time I have left myself. Inspired by you, I may reach a century—if I go for a walk every day in Central Park!'

When all the excitement of the Inauguration had died down, Julio brought Gareth a unique present. Several special-issue stamps had been released in various denominations to commemorate the creation of the new capital. Each had a portrait of the King Emperor and a view of an important building. What Julio did was to design a unique stamp with Gareth's portrait on the right side and a bird's-eye view of Connaught Place on the left. The design occupied a full page of Julio's sketchbook. Gareth chuckled. He thanked his great-grandson and, laughing now, explained he had never fancied himself a king! The portrait should have been that of the irascible Edwin Lutyens or the much-neglected Herbert Baker, or of Robert Tor Russell who did much of the work but got little of the praise. Connaught Place was designed by Russell, and Julio should never forget that. Anyway, the stamp Julio had designed was a touching present.

That evening, Gareth wheeled himself to Allegro's cage. 'I have come to say goodbye, my immortal friend. Keep an eye on the family, particularly the children. Bella is good with languages but has a short temper. Do what you can to prevent Verna from packing Julio off to a seminary. He could become a fine artist. Maria is good at dancing and singing. These talents need to be nurtured. I know you have never liked Verna but you will have to make an effort to caution her from time to time...Orlando, my flesh and blood, has started working too hard. It is beginning to tell on his health. Persuade him to take on and train a couple of additional assistants to help Eric, who is too colourless and timid a character to shoulder large responsibilities...'

'Oh, Master,' Allegro sobbed. 'Why have you decided to

abandon us? You haven't eaten anything for five days. You could live another two decades if you had a mind to...I too have lived a long life, but have hopes of lasting at least another two centuries...Who will see to my modest needs? You never forget my shot of brandy at night...'

'Julio will take care of you. Or Verna. She likes birds, even if she is somewhat intimidated by you. Put her at ease. And Khansama has great respect for you. He's promised to serve your meals while Julio is away at school. I've made Orlando promise to take you around the capital city from time to time...They are putting finishing touches to all the construction...See how splendid Connaught Place looks? Though I wish the authorities didn't allow bullock carts and material-laden donkeys the run of the place. It's bad enough with the tongas. I sent a memo to the Municipal Commissioner suggesting that all the tonga horses be made to wear napkins. I even enclosed a sketch of the most appropriate pattern.'

Allegro noticed some unusual objects on the floor of his cage. 'Why have you left two bunches of keys in my cage, Master? I have no use for keys...'

'The larger bunch is for Orlando,' whispered Gareth. 'They open cupboards which contain my clothes and legal documents. I do *not* want Verna poking around in my papers and belongings... The smaller bunch—only four keys—is for Julio. They are to the trunks containing all my surviving notebooks and sketchpads. As he grows older, he will gain much from his great-grandfather's sketches. Ideas for fast aeroplanes, coloured moving pictures, spaceships, television, jet engines, submarines...Though Julio could easily become an artist, he might decide to be an inventor—or he could be both.'

Gareth then reached with difficulty into Allegro's cage and stroked the great bird's head. He had tears in his eyes. Allegro closed his eyes and muttered, 'The Lord is my shepherd, I shall not want...' That night Gareth passed away peacefully in his sleep.

~

Gareth had left clear instructions for his funeral. His body was to be cremated and the ashes were to be scattered in the forest on the Ridge. The forest was young—much of it only fifteen years old. Many flowering trees and monkeys grew wild there. Gareth's remains would not pollute the earth.

Verna, a staunch traditionalist, lobbied vociferously for a regular Christian burial, a priest, a funeral Mass, and so on. Orlando argued for his grandfather's wishes. Two days were wasted in the dispute. Allegro grew increasingly alarmed as Gareth's body began to decay and attract hundreds of flies. He shouted out:

'Enough! Enough! I have a compromise. We'll have a cremation first, then half the ashes can be scattered on the Ridge and the other half put in a casket and buried in the new cemetery. I have even determined what could be etched on the memorial plaque. There won't be much space:

Gareth Armstrong
Scientist and Friend of India
1831—1931.'

Verna reluctantly agreed to the formula. At a quiet moment she approached Allegro. 'Cemeteries are meant to help us remember the departed. Priests pray for the souls of the dead. Sometimes hymns are sung. Wreaths are laid. There is great beauty in the ceremony. How can we deprive the children of a memorial to their great-grandfather? It would be callous. This is why I compromised on a burial of the urn, if not the whole body. They can visit the plaque from time to time.'

Orlando wrote to his mother Rachel in Calcutta, giving details of Gareth's cremation and burial of half his ashes. Over-riding his objections, Verna had arranged for a Catholic priest to conduct a brief service at the cemetery. The Viceroy Lord Irwin, despite his many pre-occupations with the Indian freedom struggle, sent a wreath. Gareth's death was reported widely in the newspapers. Eulogies poured in. Julio collected these and pasted them into a large scrapbook. In the evenings, after his homework was done, he read them out to Allegro.

6

What Next, Julio?

Benoybabu did a very thorough job of implementing Gareth's last testament. He took his responsibilities as executor very seriously. One morning over coffee he advised Orlando that his share of Gareth's money and the shares of the three children should be invested in erecting four flats on the plot he had bought in New Delhi several years earlier.

'You will see how they appreciate in value. I have a young architect friend who will design them intelligently. The flats could have internal courtyards and be suitable for renting to wealthy Indian families. Four bedrooms in each flat. They should fetch two hundred and fifty rupees per month each in rent. It's a charming neighbourhood with an ancient stepwell—Ugrasen ki Baoli—down an alleyway. What do you think, Orlando? The children are too young to have money transferred to them. When they are adults, they will have a place to stay or rent out, as they please.'

Orlando thought about the proposition for a few days. He tried to discuss it with Verna. Her parents, the Pintos, were on their last legs. They had great difficulty managing the stairs in their Nicholson Road flat. Verna laid down some conditions.

'I'll support the idea provided my parents can shift into one of the ground floor flats, and provided you don't make a fuss over my going there for half a day. Every day. The children are old enough to take care of themselves. You must be back in time to have lunch with them and help Maria do her homework...Are you paying attention, Orlando? Are you aware that Sister Angela has complained three times about Maria this year? And Bella spends all her free time studying Portuguese dictionaries! Doesn't lift a finger over the housework! She'll be twenty next year—time she got married. Julio is the only one who behaves properly.'

Orlando had no idea how he would fulfil such complex conditions. Fortunately, Braganza & Sons was just downstairs. He could nip up to deal with Maria or she could come down to the showroom and study quietly in a corner. Anyway, the construction of the flats would take at least two years and a lot could happen between now and then. His in-laws may pass on as they were well into their eighties. More pertinently, they may refuse to relocate as they had lived happily in the Kashmere Gate area for over fifty years. All their friends lived in the Old City and they had a strong bond with St Mary's Church. Verna's notion that her parents would gladly move to New Delhi was somewhat bizarre. So Orlando felt quite safe agreeing to Verna's conditions.

Benoybabu was pleased that Orlando agreed to his proposal. It is always gratifying when one's advice is heeded. The young architect, one of the Blomfield brothers, drew up some beautiful plans, accompanied by watercolour renditions of elevations. Julio, now fourteen, was fascinated by the drawings and full of questions about what sort of gardens the ground floor flats would have, what species of trees would be planted...Where would the servants live? Where would the cars be parked? Young Blomfield was amused by the range of Julio's probing.

~

Julio studied at the Modern School which had outgrown its premises in Daryaganj in the Old City. A new campus was being developed near Connaught Place and Julio looked forward to the day they would shift. But Verna had always been uncomfortable with Modern School. Too many new-fangled ideas—now there was talk of enrolling girls as well. The school gave no religious instruction and her son would be growing up with Hindus, Muslims, Sikhs and only a handful of Catholic boys—few families could afford the fees—and they were either much older or much younger than Julio.

Verna was absolutely sure in her mind that the time had come to send Julio off to a seminary, preferably in Goa where she had distant relatives. She chose the Rachol Seminary as its name was reminiscent of Julio's grandmother Rachel. Julio was not consulted.

Orlando was appalled at the idea. Secretly he had always hoped that Julio would succeed him at Braganza & Sons. Unknown to Verna, he had been saving odd sums in a separate bank account over the past ten years. His plan was to send Julio to London for training to be a top-notch piano tuner. Just as his grandfather Antonio had done for his father Emilio...This seminary business was out of the question.

Verna became quite hysterical over the issue. Julio *must* go to Rachol and stay there until he became a priest. This would be according to the customs of the Church and the family tradition of the Pintos. Verna had been an only child and was thus exempted from becoming a nun. She often regretted this and was adamant that she would make up for it by having Julio take up Holy Orders. Orlando did not quite know how to handle the situation.

'What's to become of our business?' he asked. 'Our properties? My father would be horrified if he knew of your plans. And what about Julio's wishes in the matter?'

'Unlike the rest of you, Julio is a devout Catholic,' Verna almost screamed. 'You jolly well know he goes to early morning Mass with me before being dropped off at school. All while you are still snoring in bed...I'm sick and tired of the lot of you. Julio is the only one who actually loves and obeys me. I'm sure he'll have a calling sooner or later.'

'Verna, he's just fourteen, for heaven's sake. He has to explore other options. Grandpa Gareth always thought he had a mechanical aptitude, scientific curiosity and engineering skills...'

'Your grandfather corrupted the children, giving them fancy notions of their abilities! Look at Bella—Grandpa planted strange ideas in her head and she now wants to be a professional translator. Where's the money in that? She wants us to send her to Lisbon for training...'

'Why *not,* Verna? I'll find the money somehow. There's always Grandpa's bequest—'

'—and Maria has a fascination for Indian dancing! All that Butnutyam nonsense. She'll get into all sorts of trouble if she consorts with dancers, singers and actors. Have you no care for our reputation?'

This heated discussion occurred within earshot of Allegro. He now considered himself the patriarch of the family and occasionally felt obliged to intercede—but only when the time was right.

A couple of nights later, Verna made a real spectacle of herself at the dining table. She announced she was leaving the flat in Connaught Place and moving in with her parents at Nicholson Road. Her rationale was obscure.

'I'm just the housekeeper here in this ungrateful family. I'm not consulted on important issues. Grandpa—may his godless soul rest in peace—and your father have successfully alienated you children from me. May God forgive them...I leave tomorrow morning, taking a few of my *own* things...Don't try to dissuade me. My mind is made up...I'll take a tonga—I don't need your car and driver.'

~

The children were only dimly aware of the various issues involved in the conflict between their parents. For some years Bella had been troubled by her mother's propensity to flare up at the slightest excuse. But then Verna would simmer down and life would go on as before. Bella and Maria went to Allegro's cage one evening. They missed their mother despite all her faults.

Allegro had a coughing fit. When he regained his composure, he asked the girls to repeat what they had said. He listened carefully and promised to have a chat with Julio later in the evening. Allegro lowered his voice. 'We must determine what Julio wants to do with his life. Personally, I think it is too early to force a choice on him. Anyway, the decision on joining the church must be his and his alone.'

'Grandpa Allegro, if he goes off to the seminary will Mummy return home?' Maria asked anxiously.

'I should think so, little Maria. She would have made her point. Your father would just have to give in. Besides, a seminary is not like a jail where boys are imprisoned for life. They can always quit if they have sufficient grounds for doing so. That's my impression. They can always return home...Tell Julio to see me when he has finished his homework. And don't fret so much. Everything will be sorted out soon.'

Julio joined Allegro half an hour before dinnertime. The conversation confused Julio at first. He failed to grasp Allegro's meaning. He tried to make his own position clear. He enjoyed reading Grandpa Gareth's scientific notebooks at night. He enjoyed visiting the big showroom downstairs and looking at the shelves displaying musical scores. He loved the scent of freshly-waxed pianos and listening to the exhibition pieces Orlando played for prospective customers who came shopping for a new piano. He enjoyed going to church and participating in the Latin Mass. Going to confession always made him feel better—not that he had much to confess except for what the priest called 'self-abuse.' Julio explained all these joys to Allegro, who then asked him point-blank what he thought of going to a seminary. Julio answered carefully.

'Grandpa Allegro, I will do as Mummy wishes if it means so much to her. I won't break her heart...I want to see what the rest of the world looks like. I've never been anywhere, and Goa is the land of our forefathers. Grandpa Emilio once told me that we hail from a village named Saligao. I want to go there and to Bombay. I'm old enough to spend a few years away from Delhi. If I become a priest, I'll return here and serve in the Cathedral. What I want to say is that I can make a promise to Mummy to stay in the seminary till my interests change. That is, if they do...That is all I can think of for the moment. I'll fetch your nightcap now.'

The next day Allegro summoned Orlando and told him in

detail about his chat with Julio. Orlando was quite disappointed. He felt the Braganza dynasty was coming to an end. He had, in a strange way, rather enjoyed Verna's absence for a week. Now she would return and gloat over her victory...And make Orlando go to church every Sunday. If he resisted anything, she would run off to Nicholson Road in retaliation. How much of this behaviour could he put up with? Allegro spoke sternly.

'The boy's mind is made up. He is pragmatic. He has not made an everlasting commitment. Very sensible of him. Now concentrate on how we are to send him off to Goa. He's too young to travel alone. As for Verna, you and she hardly speak to each other at the best of times. No wonder there are so many misunderstandings between the two of you. You've got to learn how to communicate. I'll have a word with her over this Goa business when she returns, as no doubt she will.'

Eric O'Brien agreed to take Julio to the Rachol Seminary in Goa. The local priest in Delhi warned Julio he would be allowed only one trunk of personal possessions. Julio made a choice of Gareth's scientific notebooks—the ones concerning motorcars, jet engines, space travel and calculating machines. He also included some of his own drawings of buildings, motorcars, flowers and musical instruments. These were laid flat at the bottom of the trunk. Verna gave him a bunch of old photographs of various relatives on the Pinto side. He was to track them down in Goa. And new clothes: 'long pants,' white shirts, new underwear and two pairs of shoes. Julio had never worn long pants before.

It was a long journey to Goa. Eric and Julio first stopped for a week in Bombay. Eric had cousins there who played the violin in orchestras that provided background music for the fledgling Hindi film industry. The cousins took turns showing Julio the sights.

Then onto Miraj by broad-gauge and Vasco by narrow-gauge. Finally to Rachol by bus. Eric and Julio were awestruck by the immensity of the seminary building, the sheer width and height of the corridors and verandas, the beauty of the attached church and exquisiteness of the small chapel, the lush gardens, and the many frescos of saints and biblical characters.

Julio felt he could be happy here. To begin with he would be attending the school attached to the seminary. He was told there would be some Hindu boys from nearby villages attending as well. These were the charity cases. He was to have as little to do with them as possible: they were a rough bunch with very poor manners. Julio thought this was the precise reason they would make good friends. His best friends at the Modern School in Delhi had all been non-Christians.

Eric said his goodbyes that afternoon and set off for Saligao, the village from which the Braganzas were said to have emigrated to Bandel in the eighteenth century. He located Braganza House on the fringes of the village—a massive residence set within countless acres of coconut groves and fruit orchards. It was currently owned by a minor off-shoot of the Dempo family, one of the richest in Goa. The neighbours were not sure when it had passed into Hindu hands. But they let on that the house, full of antique furnishings, had been locked up for twenty years. The grounds were unkempt. There was a chowkidar who wilfully spent most of his time screwing his wife in his village about two miles away. He was useless as a watchman. Burglaries had been reported. Vilasrao Dempo, the principal owner, preferred the bright lights of Panjim and couldn't be bothered with maintaining the property.

Eric pieced together this information with great difficulty. The neighbours, for the most part, spoke only Konkani and/ or Portuguese. A few knew a smattering of English. Orlando had asked Eric to take photographs, loaning him a Leica for the purpose. But Eric did not know how to operate it. He was rescued by a ten-year-old boy who seemed to know all about cameras.

The child lived with his grandmother at the furthest end of the village. He invited Eric to meet his grandmother who was supposed to speak good English. Well, she spoke some English—enough to confirm the information that Eric had gleaned from other informants. Their house was plastered with drawings and paintings done by the precocious Francis.

'Francis thinks he is a good artist,' said Granny Souza, 'but

I cannot bear to look at his so-called modern art. It is grotesque and blasphemous...Did I say all that correctly...? And he plays mischief all the time. A bad student, very bad. He'll get thrown out of school one of these days. Imagine, he have a girl-friend already! Yes, you do: that slut Edna.'

Francis winked at Eric and, pointing at his grandmother, whispered, 'She has a screw loose—always finding fault. Edna is grand-daughter of next-door Macedos. We play a lot...I think I in love with Edna. She two years older and not like to play with girls. Anyway, I the only child on our street. Rest all old people waiting to die.'

When Eric returned to Delhi, he was the centre of attention for a few days. He took the camera to Mackinley Brothers to have it unloaded, the film developed and large prints made. Verna did not show much interest in the photos of Braganza House, likening it to a haunted castle. On the other hand, she was full of questions about the Rachol Seminary. Eric did not have answers to most of them. He did, however, have a telephone number and the names of the priests who would be in direct charge of Julio.

'I was at the seminary for only two hours and was shown around only parts of it. The priests there are a serious lot. They gave me lunch though. A very simple meal. Rice, a small piece of fish and some pickle. Julio will lose weight.'

The other members of the Delhi Braganzas were very impressed by the photographs of the ancestral house in Saligao. None more so than Bella. She lingered a long time over the views. That evening she showed Allegro some of the pictures and said, 'Grandpa Allegro, I'm going to live in that house one day.'

Allegro was puzzled. 'How do you propose to do that? It's not our property and it's not for rent as far as I can make out. And what would you do with yourself in that great big mansion? Anyway, I'm not one to disparage your dreams. It's good to have pleasant dreams. Some of them do come true, Bella. But you have to work to make that happen.'

So Bella set to work. With Julio's departure she no longer had to share a room with her sister Maria. She had privacy at last. A room of her own. Over the next three months she wrote off a dozen letters to various language academies in Lisbon and was accepted by one. She then presented Orlando with this fait accompli. She was determined to go to Lisbon, learn Portuguese thoroughly and become a professional translator.

Verna was, as usual, full of objections. Bella would have to travel alone, it would be extremely expensive, they did not know anyone in Lisbon—who would keep an eye on her? If she were to study in Goa, in Panjim, half these problems would not arise. The Pintos had friends, relatives, acquaintances there...If Orlando gave Bella the money to fund the foolish Lisbon enterprise, Verna would move to Nicholson Road to be with her parents in their last days.

Orlando had had enough of Verna's tantrums. 'Go, Verna, go! See if we care! You have no understanding of the dreams young people have. You have pushed—yes, *pushed*—one child of ours into a seminary and now you are determined to destroy Bella's hopes. I'll not have it...So start packing and be off with you and your vile temper! I can manage the house very well without you.'

Verna was so taken aback by the force of Orlando's counter-attack that she confined herself to her bedroom for three days. Maria saw to her needs of food and fresh drinking water. During this period Bella started her packing and Orlando began making travel arrangements for the complicated journey to the 'mother country.' By rail, ship and bus. He was confident that Bella—now a young adult—would be able to cope, provided she travelled light.

When Verna finally emerged from her room, she had only one question, 'Where will Bella stay in Lisbon? I only hope it will be in a convent. Hotels are full of undesirable types, don't you think?'

'Verna, you forget she is grown up now. Even so, I've arranged for Eric and his new bride Esme to take Bella down to Goa. You've met Esme before. She is a very mature woman. The trip to Goa will be a sort of honeymoon for the O'Briens. Eric will put Bella on the ship to Lisbon. Da Costa Travels Worldwide have made all the bookings. I would have taken Bella to Goa myself but dare not take the risk of Marquis Brothers stealing away some of my most valued customers in my absence. That firm has no sense of ethics. The owners think they're as good as us, even though I've heard their piano tuners are practically tone-deaf.'

~

When Bella and the O'Briens reached Goa some three weeks later, they first visited Saligao. Bella insisted on this. Because the village had no hotels they spent two nights in the home of Francis and his grandmother, who was glad to receive a generous compensation for her troubles.

The old lady had been thinking about Braganza House since Eric's previous visit and had several other bits and pieces of information to offer. She had done some research. Four courtyards, two Hindu temples, a grand Christian chapel, sixteen bedrooms, ten bathrooms, four reception halls, two dining rooms...The exterior of the vast house had not been painted for decades. The roof tiles were damaged here and there. When Bella peeked through the windows, all she could see were layers of dust covering everything. She told herself, 'I will restore this place to its former glory. I'll get a proper architect who will do research on what such mansions looked like two hundred years ago. But I must own the house first.'

The party then went to visit Julio at Rachol. He was cheerful enough and told Bella about the strict discipline to which the boys were subjected. She asked about his friends but he could not name a single Christian boy. The really big news was that the Fathers had discovered Julio's artistic talents and had promptly put them to good use. He was asked to touch up/repair/restore the many fresco paintings lining the wide verandas and corridors. Apostles, saints and biblical scenes. The Fathers were very satisfied with the results. It would take Julio up to two weeks to restore each painting. Very often he would change the colour of a garment or correct a perspective view. While his contemporaries were on their knees in the chapel, Julio would be happily busy with his paints and brushes. The other boys resented the exemption from prayers given to Julio. The Fathers said that painting too was a form of worship.

At other times, set aside for sports, Julio would sneak down to the village at the foot of the hill. He took his sketchbook along and made quick likenesses of the cars that passed by occasionally: Fords, Studebakers, Packards, Buicks…

When the visiting hour was ending Julio ran to his dormitory and fetched some recent sketches. Bella was charmed by what she saw as she turned the pages. For the first time in a long while, she doubted that her younger brother should join the priesthood. She told herself, 'I *will* rescue Julio if it's the last thing I do. For that, I'll need more evidence.'

~

The day came for Bella to board the ship, *Vasco da Gama*, that would convey her to Lisbon. Orlando had arranged for Bella to travel with a Goan family. Dr Da Cunha, his wife and two grown-up daughters were headed for Porto, the large town north of Lisbon. They were on holiday.

Eric, who had learned to operate the Leica by now, took several photographs, and his new wife presented bouquets to Mrs Da Cunha and Bella. The group photographs included a tall gentleman, handsome, with a cleft chin and a shock of luxuriant black hair. He was introduced as Marco Braganza, the Chief Police Commissioner of Goa. He was a close friend of the Da Cunha family and was going 'home' on six weeks leave.

As the ship neared Aden, Bella had seen enough of Marco to decide that he was the man she would marry. She was not quite in love with him but was definitely attracted. Marco's family had been settled in Goa for several generations and were clearly part of the local aristocracy. Marco spent his entire day helping Bella brush up her conversational Portuguese and Konkani. He found her very intelligent and extraordinarily quick on the uptake. By the time *Vasco da Gama* berthed in Lisbon, Bella was somewhat fluent in both languages.

Mrs Da Cunha had briefed Bella about Marco's background, hoping to discourage her apparent interest in him. Twenty years in the police, with a long stint in Macao. Married a Chinese girl early in life. Had a mentally handicapped son, Chico, who did nothing but dance all day. The wife died of meningitis a few years ago. Marco moved back to Goa and, it was said, was looking for a new wife to help him take care of his son. Bella was fascinated by this portrait and, far from being turned off, she felt sympathy for Marco and his idiot son.

Right in the centre of Lisbon there was a crowded locality known as Alfala. The winding lanes, the exposed electric cables, the many-storeyed houses all reminded Bella of Delhi's walled city, which she had visited frequently during her childhood. Alfala was where she took up lodgings. Many signs of Salazar's dictatorship were all around her: armed guards, soldiers on motorcycles, the absence of wall posters or other forms of protest. Bella started her classes at the language school, a mile from Alfala. Marco would wait for her at the school gates at the end of classes and walk her home. Then Bella would bathe and change and Marco would treat her to dinner at one or other of the quaint restaurants in the locality. On weekends they would hire a taxi for the day and see the sights of what was a rather drab city.

Bella amazed her teachers. Never in the sixty-year history of the language school had a pupil been able to achieve in three weeks what students were given six months to assimilate normally. Bella was a prodigy. The school decided to assign two teachers to work full-time with her in a secluded room. She had by now graduated to learning the finer techniques of simultaneous translation.

The time came for Marco Braganza to return to Goa. On the evening before his departure he bought Bella a magnificent bouquet of red roses. They had been eating regularly at Miranda's. Both Bella and Marco were somewhat sad. They reached the restaurant early; the regulars had yet to arrive. Marco took a ring out of his breast pocket and in an awkward gesture slipped the emerald-studded treasure on to her slender finger.

'Will you marry me, Bella?' he asked hesitantly, shyly. 'I can offer you my devoted attention for as long as we live.' Bella had half-expected something like this but felt some negotiations were in order.

'When I come to Goa, I'd love to live in Braganza House in my ancestral village, Saligao. The house is vacant now. Will you buy it for me?' she asked boldly.

'Of course I will—I don't think it is too far from the sea. I've told you how much I love swimming in the sea. I have a lot of land in South Goa that my brothers are too lazy to farm. I'll sell some of that and buy your house for you. Saligao—yes, I was there not long ago. We had a curious case of a ten-year-old boy who was accused of attempting to rape a twelve-year-old girl. I oversaw the investigation. It was a trumped-up charge.'

'Yes, I heard of it from Eric O'Brien, one of my father's employees. He was the one who took pictures of us at the dock... But there are other things to discuss. What about your son, Chico? I plan to work as a translator in Goa. I may even have to travel now and then. Will there be a governess for him? If he is the same age as my brother Julio, could they become friends? Julio is currently in Rachol. He is not too happy there.'

Marco's response was cautious. 'Chico keeps pretty much to himself. He does not crave company. His requirements are simple. Gramophone records, ballet music. He listens to them hour after hour. And dances in his room. People who don't know the tragic source of his affliction are always amused by Chico's dancing. He dances for about two hours in the morning, two in the afternoon and two at night. He has an endless supply of energy...I'll be frank. We need a house where Chico's room is a respectable distance from the other bedrooms. Will your Braganza House provide this? There is a limit to the number of times a day that one can listen to *Swan Lake*! I've bought several new ballet records for him on this trip. And an electric record player with volume control...Actually, Chico's no trouble once he gets to know you.'

Bella was a bit alarmed at the description of Chico. In her meticulously constructed plans, she had never provided for an encumbrance such as him. A Goan husband, yes. A fairly grown-up, ready-made son, no. Marco took out a photograph of Chico from his wallet. Bella examined it carefully. The boy was beautiful, with slanting eyes and a perfectly symmetrical triangular face. The muscles of his neck were strong and his shoulders broad. How could anyone not marvel at his good looks?

Bella held up her hand and admired the ring. She hadn't said 'Yes' yet. She had some further concerns. 'Will we be free to travel to British India? Don't forget I have parents and grandparents in Delhi and another set of grandparents in Calcutta. My sister Maria—a year younger than Julio—wants to become a dancer. I'd like to help her achieve that ambition. My maternal grandparents—the Pintos in Delhi—wanted me to establish contact with some of their distant relatives in Goa. I have their names but no addresses. I'll need your help to track them down. Pintos and D'Souzas—common names, aren't they! Braganza House will require extensive repairs to become habitable. Will you arrange these things?'

'I'll do anything you want, Bella, just give me a chance.' Marco had taken to talking in Portuguese now. 'Because of my position in Goa it is easy to get things done. The Dempo family you mentioned has often broken the law on a variety of matters. They can easily be persuaded to sell the house to me at a favourable price. Send me a list of the Pinto and D'Souza connections. I'll have my boys track them down in no time at all...When you return in four months, all your desires will have been fulfilled.'

Bella sighed deeply. A sigh of relief. 'Well, Marco, in that case I agree to be your wife...You are more attractive than I am—don't protest, you are extremely handsome. My fellow students at the language school consider you a good catch. Always remember that it was *you* who pursued me! Not the other way around. I suppose you may kiss me now that we're officially engaged.' Bella allowed herself to be kissed passionately, again and again. The other guests in the restaurant watched them and smiled indulgently. It was the first time Bella had been kissed by a handsome man.

Marco left the next day for the docks, an hour after he and Bella collected the photographs of themselves as a couple which had been taken in a studio the week before. At that time they had promised not to show the pictures to anyone. Now that they were engaged, Bella wrote to Orlando in Delhi.

My dear Daddy,

The most marvellous thing has happened since my last letter. I am to be married to a white Goan, Marco Braganza, when I return in four months. So we share a surname! Uncle Eric is bound to have shown you all the pictures of him taken when the Da Cunhas and I embarked for Lisboa, but I am enclosing a recent photograph of us taken together. He is so distinguished and handsome, don't you think?

Marco is the Chief Police Commissioner of Goa. A widower with a son the same age as Julio. Marco is forty-two years old but looks much younger, as you can see.

Send me news of Julio and Maria. Where is Mummy living these days—Connaught Place or Nicholson Road? I wish she were not so moody. She's going to throw a fit when she gets my news. You and Grandpa Allegro must stick up for me. Give my love to everyone.

Your affectionate daughter,
Bella

P.S. Marco is a devout Catholic and very wealthy. Tell Mummy this before you tell her the other details.

When Verna heard the news she was appalled that Bella was engaged to a man twice her age, and with a grown son. 'Orlando,' she screamed, 'you simply cannot permit it! This Marco character is bound to have bad habits—the wine, women and song thing. Policemen are given to violence and beat their wives...He'll die while our Bella is still in her prime. If they have children—and I hope they don't—there will be inheritance issues with the older son...We can't possibly give our permission for this match... Marco has probably already given her an expensive engagement ring. To show off his so-called wealth. Tell her to return it right away! I'll be the laughing stock of the Delhi Goan Association. Bella will be called a money chaser and *I* will be called a greedy money grubber...Oh, what have I done to deserve such children! Julio is the only pious one...'

'Verna, there's only one obstacle as far as I can see. Bella hasn't asked for our permission. So we have no say in the matter. She would appreciate receiving your blessings, I'm sure, but when all is said and done, she could probably do without them...I'm not going to interfere in any way and you mustn't either. You can't live Bella's life for her—you keep forgetting that she is an adult now.'

'All this is Grandpa Gareth's fault,' yelled Verna. 'First he persuaded Bella to become a translator. Then there were the Portuguese dictionaries and the escape to Lisbon. And now this most unsuitable liaison. We must persuade her to call it off.'

'I will do no such thing!' Orlando was quite irritated. 'Bella will be well provided for. And she will help us rediscover your distant relatives in Goa. I expect you will shift to Nicholson Road now. You are the most unreasonable person I have ever known, Verna. I often wish you'd move permanently to your parents' place so that we could have some peace and quiet here.'

~

Marco Braganza wrote at length to Bella in Lisbon. The freedom movement by Christian and Hindu Goans who wanted liberation from Portugal was picking up. This added enormously to the workload of the police force. Marco rarely slept for more than five hours each night. In compliance with the rules he had applied to the Governor for permission to marry Bella. The permission was denied on the grounds that she would be a security risk. She was a citizen of British India. She might even be a spy for the British. Marco was given a choice. He could continue in the service of the Estado da India if he gave up the idea of marrying an unsuitable woman. Or, if he insisted on the marriage, he would have to resign from the police. The Governor suggested that he resign. Marco gave in the mandatory three months' notice.

The matter of acquiring Braganza House posed its own problems. Marco had discovered through his junior officers that five offshoots of the Dempo family had claims on the house. Vilasrao, the patriarch, was disinclined to deal with the elaborate paperwork and court hearings involved in straightening out the legal tangle. Marco then passed orders that all police cases—old and new—against the Dempo clan be revived and pursued with vigour. The pressure worked. Their lawyers promised that the mansion would be handed over in three months at the latest. Marco negotiated for all the antique furniture to be included in the sale price. He sold off a good portion of his ancestral agricultural land in South Goa to finance the Braganza House purchase.

At the close of his fifteen-page letter he suggested that Bella postpone her return to Goa for a few months so that he could have the mansion fully repaired and ready to welcome her. Bella, though disappointed, saw wisdom in the suggestion. She signed up for another advanced translation course and thought often of Marco's kisses.

~

Meanwhile Julio was at a loose end at the Rachol Seminary. Prayers and studies took up only a part of the day. His assignment as art restorer was coming to an end. There were only three frescoes left requiring his attention. When these were finished he would have to spend three additional hours on his knees in the chapel. In silent meditation. One afternoon when he was working on a portrait of Saint Jerome, he was summoned downstairs to meet an unexpected visitor.

Marco Braganza, the Chief Commissioner of Police, had arrived with a security escort of four junior officers. Julio's mouth went dry when he saw them and he wondered what he had done to merit this interview. Marco put Julio at ease by suggesting that they take a stroll in the spacious gardens of the seminary. The junior officers waited in the reception hall which was furnished with ancient chests, benches and cupboards. Then Marco gave Julio the news: they were soon to become brothers-in-law. Julio was astonished at this turn of events. He had feared he would be questioned about his Hindu friends, some of whom were ardent admirers of Gandhi and the Indian freedom struggle. This matter was not raised. Julio did not have much to say because he had no idea what would be appropriate to talk about. Timidly he told Marco he wished to make him a drawing of his beautiful Packard car. He rushed up to his dormitory, brought down his sketchbook, hurried to the gleaming vehicle parked at the ornate entrance to the seminary, and within ten minutes had drawn a remarkable likeness. Marco was amazed.

'This is a work of genius, Julio. Would you mind if I sent it to Bella as a mark of our mutual friendship? She will be thrilled to receive it. I'll send it by airmail so that it reaches her in a fortnight...Are you happy here, Julio?'

'I'm training to be a priest, sir. Father Menezes says I have to develop the strength and courage of a saint—that a priest must be a saint...I'm not sure yet that I will ever fit that description. But I am trying, sir.'

Chief Commissioner Marco had a few words with the priests who had gathered in the reception hall to see him off. They were full of praise for Julio's artistic talents. Father Ribeiro was effusive.

'Goa is full of churches with exquisite paintings and altarpieces that require restoration. Julio could spend a very satisfying life attending to these masterpieces. He would, of course, be exempt from the routine duties of a Jesuit priest, but would leave his mark on the history of Christian art in Goa.'

When Marco and his police escort had departed, Father Menezes summoned Julio to his room, sat him down on his bed and questioned him closely on the visit of the Chief of Police. Father M, as the boys called him, sat down close to Julio and started stroking his thigh. This was the sort of thing other priests also did from time to time. The good-looking boys knew the routine. As they ate dinner there would be a tap on the shoulder. 'Father X wants to see you in his room after dinner.' Julio had been a victim of this stratagem on a number of occasions. Because of his good looks he was much in demand. The boys dared not protest or mention these sordid nocturnal encounters in confession. Julio was now seventeen and very handsome and well-built.

He toyed with the idea of quitting the seminary. He remembered Eric O'Brien telling him about the extraordinary modern art of the boy Francis in Saligao. Perhaps he could become an artist. Then there were the intriguing scientific notebooks of great-grandpa Gareth. Perhaps he could become a mechanical engineer and design wonderful machines. The least favoured option was to stick it out in the seminary and become a priest. But as a priest everyone would respect him. He could try earnestly to become a saint. His Hindu friends were puzzled by his indecision. Each of them knew what they would become: agricultural landowners, shopkeepers, petty bureaucrats, policemen, politicians or freedom fighters.

Marco was very kind to Julio. He would visit every ten days or so and bring Julio a big basket of assorted goodies to share with his friends. Marco too was at a crossroads. He wondered what he would do with himself after he retired. Perhaps the Dempos—whom he had got to know quite well by now—would give him a top job in one of their iron ore export ventures. Or perhaps he would just spend his days swimming in the sea. Regarding Braganza House, his official position meant that the various building contractors dared not drag their feet or make the excuses that contractors are prone to make. Marco wrote enthusiastic letters to Bella describing substantial progress.

~

In Delhi, Verna had calmed down. Her parents, the Pintos, did not die of old age but of malaria, within a fortnight of each other. They never got down to preparing the family tree, tracing the history of Pinto ancestors in Goa that would have gone back two centuries. In any case they had forgotten the bulk of their ancestors' names. Their Kashmere Gate landlord complained that the rent had not been paid for over seven months. Benoybabu let on that the Pintos had been buying their medicines on credit, but he had instructed his employees at the Kashmere Gate chemist to turn a blind eye. The joint will that the Pintos left was simplicity itself. All their possessions—furniture, knick-knacks, clothes, old books, and cooking utensils—were to be sold and the proceeds divided equally among their three grandchildren. Verna did what was expected of her and, after a huge effort, the various items were sold for a total of eight hundred and sixty-five rupees. Orlando bought the piano that Verna had grown up playing for two hundred and fifty rupees. It was in terrible shape and not worth more than a hundred. But Orlando fixed it up—new sounding board, strings, keyboard, etc. and made a present of the refurbished instrument to Verna.

Braganza & Sons were doing exceedingly well despite the strenuous efforts of their competitors, Marquis Brothers. A third music shop, Godin's, had opened in Regal Building. None of Godin's piano-tuners had been trained properly. They charged a mere fifty rupees for a shoddy tuning job. Orlando charged a hundred and fifty for tuning an upright and two fifty for a grand. Because of the sheer quality of his work he was way ahead of the competition. He expanded the business. He now sold Indian musical instruments as well: tablas, harmoniums, sitars and so on. There was a surprisingly large demand for these as the new city grew and tens of thousands of Indian civilians from all over the country settled into their new capital. Orlando maintained a roster of music teachers for both Indian and Western music and acted as an intermediary for those well-off enough to afford private lessons. A number of the teachers were Goans who played in the live bands in restaurants that had been established in Connaught Place.

The construction of Connaught Place—now affectionately

known as 'CP'—was practically complete. The last pieces of 'the crescent' had been put in place. Krishan Lal's motor garage was so successful that he could afford to send his eldest son to England to train with the Rolls Royce Company. The Braganzas' residential property now had a formal address: 8 Hailey Road. Construction of the four flats was almost complete, thanks to the competence of the architect and the efficiency of the chief contractor, a burly Sikh who had a love for opera, particularly Verdi. But Verna had, as usual, serious reservations.

'Don't expect me to move to Hailey Road. I don't know a soul in that god-forsaken place. What will I do stuck in the house all day? There are no shops there, no markets. It's also miles from the Cathedral. Here I'm just ten minutes' walk away from the Sacred Heart. While you are snoring I can get to church easily for the morning Mass every day. I enjoy the walk there and back. No, Orlando, *you* move if you want to, *I'm* staying put.'

Benoybabu's elder daughter-in-law Gauri and Verna had become fast friends. They would meet often and talk about the old days in Kashmere Gate when neighbours were not strangers. On the other hand, CP had its excitements—the cinemas, restaurants, band music in Central Park, shops of every description, all within easy strolling distance. The two women would gossip about the defects of their respective husbands while going window-shopping in this new commercial hub of Delhi.

~

In Calcutta, Emilio and Rachel were getting on in years. Emilio was too frail now to visit the homes of his clients. He only tuned the pianos in the showroom. He dreaded the day his wrists would become too weak for tuning. Rachel too would not give up. She now confined herself to designing tombstones on a drawing board in her home. No trips to distant cemeteries. She resigned from her committee work at the museum. She had the satisfaction of knowing that the folk arts and crafts galleries she had established were very popular and received hordes of visitors.

Blotto continued to flourish. His female friends concluded

he was too busy to think of marriage. He was rather lazy on this score. He would always maintain that at his age it would be difficult to find a bride. Rachel would point out that his grandfather Gareth had married a Khasi woman some decades his junior. And the significance of the newly-revealed fact that his niece Bella was about to marry a police officer twice her age could not be overlooked.

The Braganzas of Calcutta did not know what to make of the happenings in Goa. Now that his only grandson Julio was stuck in a seminary, Emilio hoped Bella would give birth to sons who could carry on the piano business. In spite of Blotto's material success, Emilio suspected he liked only men and would thus never produce a son and heir. Emilio kept his suspicions to himself as the rest of the family would be horrified if they knew. He often wondered what would happen to Braganza & Sons after he died.

~

At this point all hell broke loose at Rachol. One night in October—Diwali night—Julio slipped out of his dormitory and joined the village boys to celebrate the occasion with fireworks of every description: rockets, sparklers, crackers and what they called 'bombs.' Julio's friends prevailed on him to show them the small side-entrance to the famous Rachol church. The church was an integral part of the seminary. These friends wanted to appreciate its beauty by candlelight and offer prayers for the Hindu New Year. Julio was asked to stand guard at the side entrance, just in case some Father was on the prowl. These Goan Hindu boys had no business celebrating Diwali, which was chiefly an Indian Hindu festival.

After a few minutes, an extremely loud explosion was heard from within the church, and then the sound of falling plaster. The boys rushed out past Julio and escaped into the night. Julio was terrified. He hurried into the church and was pained by what he saw. There was smoke in the air and dust rising from large clumps of plaster that had fallen from the ceiling. He couldn't assess the full extent of damage because it was dark. He personally knew three of the seven boys who had been involved in this horrendous act of desecration. Within another couple of minutes several priests and Catholic boys from the dormitories had gathered around Julio. The priests had put on their cassocks over their pyjamas hastily and were cross to be woken up from their slumbers. The boys were shooed off and three priests—including Father Menezes—were deputed to conduct enquiries.

Father Menezes kept reiterating four points. Julio was fully dressed and had thus been absconding from his dormitory. The miscreants from the village had been let into the church while it was officially closed. Julio must have been a collaborator in the intrusion. Julio considered many Hindu boys his friends so he must be in a position to name them. The enquiry was adjourned after three exhausting hours and Julio was locked up in a cell. He hadn't spoken a word.

In the morning the priests decided to send for the police. But because Julio was the Chief Commissioner's brother-in-law-to-be they phoned Marco Braganza directly. Marco was busy dispersing a crowd of freedom fighters who had gathered in the hundreds in Panjim. He asked Father Menezes whether the suspects had confessed. Had Julio admitted his complicity? Father Menezes complained that Julio had remained silent throughout. That he wept from time to time and could be seen kneeling in prayer in his cell. Marco said he would come later that day and investigate the matter in a professional manner. Julio was not to be questioned in the meantime.

By the time Marco and his security personnel rolled into the Rachol compound at four in the afternoon, the priests were in a frightful temper. Several heated discussions were held in the verandas surrounding the grand courtyard. The priests wondered why Julio refused to speak. Who was he trying to protect? They led Marco to Julio's cell. Marco ordered that he be left alone with the young man so that he could interrogate young Julio without any distractions.

Two hours later Marco emerged from the cell and asked to meet the three-member enquiry committee. They met in a small study not far from the reception hall. Marco was tired after a strenuous day. He would have to patrol the streets of Panjim again after he had taken care of the Rachol business. He presented the committee with his definitive conclusions.

'Yes, the boy had joined the lads to celebrate Diwali. There were about a dozen of them. Julio knew only a few of their names because the majority had come from neighbouring villages. At about midnight, when Julio returned to the dormitory and was about to get undressed, he heard a loud explosion—a Diwali bomb. I must ban them...He did not know the explosion came from the church until he heard the sound of falling plaster. He ran to the side entrance of the church. The door was wide open. The miscreants had escaped. There was smoke inside and extensive damage to the ceiling and mouldings. This could be made out in the faint light of the votive candles. Then all of you, including Father Menezes in particular, came and roughed him up and questioned him for hours and locked him up...Julio can't be held responsible for what happened to the church. He is guilty only of leaving his dormitory without permission.'

Marco looked around him sternly as if daring anyone to contradict him. Then he drew Father Menezes aside and said he wanted a word in private. Marco was angry.

'Father, a distressing matter has come to my attention. A matter so grave that the Archbishop would call for the expulsion of a number of the priests here should he come to hear of it. Julio has testified that a number of you priests force yourselves on the boys at night. It's been going on for years...I understand that some of the boys are starved for affection, others hero-worship you priests. But these are not reasons to sexually molest the youngsters...Now when we return to the study, I want no further discussion of the falling plaster case. There are no witnesses. I have examined Julio thoroughly and see no grounds for further enquiry. The matter is closed from the point of view of the police. You too must treat the matter as closed. If I hear any more of it, I shall seek an audience with the Archbishop.'

When Marco and Father Menezes returned to the study, there

was a brief confabulation. It was noted by everyone—including Marco—that Julio no longer had any reverence for nor interest in the priesthood. The priests on their part thought that he was best suited to making a career in art. It would be best if Julio left the seminary that very night. Marco was rather surprised by the sudden decision. But he calmly used his walkie-talkie to instruct the Deputy Chief of Police to replace him on patrol duty that night, and make sure the two hundred or so political detainees in prison were well cared for. Then he rang up his house to instruct his domestic staff to prepare the guest bedroom, and enquired after Chico. He recognized the music in the background. In spite of the late hour Chico was dancing away to the *Nutcracker Suite*.

It took only an hour for Julio to gather and pack his things, and to wake up and say goodbye to his dormitory mates. Marco spent most of that time speaking into his walkie-talkie. Julio was made to sign some lengthy forms to the effect that he was leaving the seminary of his own free will and with the blessings of the Fathers. It was well after midnight when they headed to Marco's official residence in Panjim.

'Well,' said Marco, 'now we will have to get you back to Delhi in one piece. You will be safe with your own people. You could go to St Stephen's College, get a degree, study for the civil service exam...'

Julio shook his head from side to side. 'I can't return to Delhi. I have disgraced myself. If Mummy ever came to know what really happened, it would kill her. And my father would blackmail me into joining the family business...Isn't Bella returning from Lisbon one of these days? I could live with her until I'm clear what I want to do next.'

'Bella will be staying in Saligao with Francis and his grandmother, Mrs Souza, till Braganza House is fully ready for occupation. I've told you all about Braganza House on my previous visits. Bella and I have grand plans. Mr Claude Batley, a famous Bombay architect, is helping us. I've paid a huge advance for his services...I'll have to check if Mrs Souza has enough room for you as well. Otherwise you can stay with me and

Chico. You'll find him interesting. Unfortunately, not normal. You see, he doesn't talk. Only expresses himself through mime and dance. We have a fantastic collection of ballet music records that you might enjoy. And now's your chance to learn some proper Portuguese—better than the rustic Konkani you picked up in the bazaar at Rachol.'

Marco's car had reached the outskirts of Panjim. Not many lights were on at that hour. Julio and Marco were both exhausted. Marco had not slept for three nights because of the political troubles. Julio had been kept awake throughout the previous night celebrating Diwali and being interrogated. Julio shyly asked a question.

'When will your wedding be? Are Mummy, Daddy and Maria coming for it? If my parents come will you promise, sir, not to let me down by telling the truth about Diwali night? Don't even tell Bella. She was horrible to me as a child but now she behaves better and I feel is even growing fond of me. She has written thrice. Going to Portugal has been good for her. She has always wanted an important job. As a translator...Please tell me about your wedding. I'm looking forward to it.'

Marco wiped his forehead with a red handkerchief and yawned. 'We are to have a civil ceremony. No fuss, no grand reception. Church weddings can be so sentimental. If I were to host a reception I'd have to invite half the population of Panjim! And, what would be worse, scores of distant relatives and acquaintances from Canacona in South Goa. There is also the matter of being discreet. The Governor is against our marriage which is why I am obliged to retire in a week. He left me no choice. I had to choose between Bella and staying on in the police service...So, Julio, I just can't afford to make a big thing of marrying Bella...Whether your parents come or not is a matter best left to Bella. There would be no special function to attend. It would be a long way to travel from Delhi just to watch us signing a register. What would be the point?'

They reached Marco's house and the numerous guards snapped to attention. Julio's luggage was carried to the guest bedroom.

Marco's personal orderly brought in a tray of chicken sandwiches and two glasses of chilled coconut water. In the distance they heard Tchaikovsky being played on the gramophone. Chico was still dancing in the wee hours of the morning.

When he woke up late in the morning Julio was informed that the Chief Commissioner had been called away at dawn to deal with a fresh round of political protests in the port town of Vasco. Over a thousand Hindus and Christians had got together to demand, yet again, the departure of the Portuguese. The police inspector posted at Marco's residence had been given strict instructions not to allow Julio to wander around the neighbourhood. It was too dangerous. About three in the afternoon Marco phoned from Vasco to say that he hoped to be back for dinner. In the meanwhile, Julio should not attempt to meet Chico. They had to be introduced to each other very carefully. Julio may like to sketch the large bungalow and stroll in the well-tended gardens. There was also the library with novels by P.G. Wodehouse and Agatha Christie which might interest him.

Julio did some sketching—the handsome house, two big cars parked in the driveway, some unfamiliar trees, and a guard who stood to attention in a sentry booth. Then he toyed with the idea of writing to his parents to give his side of the story—Father Menezes was bound to have written to them by now. Julio was still confused over the rights and wrongs of the Rachol fiasco.

Marco returned at about eight in the evening, dog-tired and irritable. Fifty-four more arrests. That Gandhi was a real trouble-maker. His influence extended to all corners of British India and now even to Goa. There was talk of another war about to begin in Europe. He hoped Portugal would remain neutral...Marco consoled himself that he would retire in a few days and be done with all this bother. Bella's ship was due to arrive in two days. The thought cheered him up no end.

The next day began on a normal note. Julio and Marco ate breakfast at eight. Marco decided to tell Julio some things about Chico. He spent his entire day, and some nights too, dancing to ballet music. He could sing (la-la-la) but didn't talk. He used gestures to communicate his needs. He dressed in a bizarre fashion—pantaloons, Elizabethan doublets, sarongs, tunics, veils and so on. Chico was what some called 'weird'. This was what the American doctors labelled him when Marco had taken him to New York for medical investigations a few years ago. Lisbon's psychiatrists were equally confounded and unkind. They advised that his dancing be curtailed to two hours a day, that he be supplied with plenty of picture story-books, that he be taught to talk by a qualified speech therapist, and that he be made to interact with teenagers his own age.

Marco had tried out all these strategies but Chico refused to cooperate—sometimes reacting violently. He signalled again and again that he was happy as he was. He longed to be left alone with his music, singing and dancing.

Marco's eyes were moist at the end of his dismal description of his son. Julio scratched his head and looked acutely embarrassed. He wanted more details. The picture of Chico painted by Marco was too stark. He wanted to know about basics such as bathing, shitting and eating. Marco was rather surprised by Julio's questions.

'Chico bathes himself regularly—he works up quite a sweat with all his dancing. He has rarely given any trouble with the toilet, except for a few occasions when he forgot to wash himself... He has no fixed hours for eating. There is an electric bell in his room to the kitchen. Whenever he is hungry, he rings the bell and food is brought to him on a tray. He insists on eating alone. He's fond of pork dishes, Chinese food and fruit. I'd say he is a fairly finicky eater...Julio, I hope you understand that Chico is living in a prison of his own making. There is no cure for this. For years there has been no name even for his condition. Now, in America at any rate, some doctors are beginning to call it "autism". Chico seems to have a rare form of this malady. I'm in touch with the specialists in New York. I file regular reports on his behaviour... Have I told you enough to satisfy your curiosity?'

'Thank you, sir. I shouldn't have asked so many questions,' Julio said. 'In the seminary, the Fathers said that whenever we were troubled, we should pray and ask the Holy Virgin Mary to intercede for us.'

'I've tried that too. I've prayed in over a hundred churches in Goa—including some tiny chapels tucked away in coconut groves. I've even prayed at the great Hindu temples at Ponda... Yet I expect I have prayed without faith.'

'Does my sister know about Chico? Have you asked her to pray for him? I'll include him in my prayers from now on.'

'I've told her enough, when we were together in Lisbon. The rest she must discover for herself. She will be able to get to know him with fresh eyes and without any biases acquired from me...We will meet Chico tomorrow morning. I expect to be busy all day today. The Governor has called a series of meetings on the deteriorating law and order situation. I'll probably be reprimanded...An-y-way, I'll arrange for a car and driver and two security guards to take you around parts of the city. Avoid crowds and don't ever get out of the car. Go first to Cabo, the Governor's Palace, and then to Fontanhas and Altinho—you won't have enough time to visit Old Goa. Do you mean to say you are a complete stranger to Panjim?'

'We were brought here by the seminary Fathers on one occasion. To the Archbishop's Palace for a memorial Mass. And then taken to the Church of the Immaculate Conception. That was beautiful. The steps up the hill are fun to draw.'

Then Marco frowned. 'Julio, on second thoughts, I won't introduce you to Chico just yet. He's in a bad mood this morning. He accidentally broke a gramophone record and is upset. We'll meet him some time after Bella arrives and the two of you settle into Mrs Souza's house in Saligao. The old lady has confirmed she can fit you in. You'll be staying there for a few days.'

'Why can't Bella stay here in your house?' Julio asked innocently. Marco said, 'Because it would not be proper and because I'm in the middle of packing up my personal belongings. The place is in a mess. The ground floor of Braganza House—I've told you a lot about the house already—is now ready, except for the polishing of the marble floors. The contractor has promised me that the place will be ready for occupation in three days. But you never know with such fellows...Mr Batley, the architect, has extended his stay in Goa for another week so he can meet and discuss further plans with Bella...I'd like you to meet him. A wonderful, cultured gentleman. He practices in Bombay and also teaches architecture at the J.J. School there. He is an Englishman much in love with this part of the world...I'm really late this morning, so off you go on your expedition. Your car, an unmarked one, should be here any minute.'

The registry marriage was just five days away. Marco had seen to all the paperwork, the giving of notice, the lining up of the magistrate and witnesses. Despite the political troubles he attended three official send-offs, put in his pension papers, briefed his domestic staff and gave Inas, Chico's minder, instructions to pack his records and costumes carefully. Chico was bewildered by all the unaccustomed activity. He was fearful and wept often.

Marco's plans were upset by delays in getting Braganza House ready for Bella's arrival. The original idea was that Miss Bella Braganza would arrive in Panjim on the twelfth of November and stay for five days with Mrs Souza to recover from the journey. They would marry on the seventeenth, the official date of Marco's retirement. Then he would drive her to Braganza House, carry her over the threshold and hand over the house keys to her as a wedding present.

But Bella's ship too was delayed by three days. There were unseasonal rains. Chico was still out of sorts, fretting over his broken record and totally disoriented by all the noisy goings-on around him. The only thing that had gone right was the prompt arrival of Marco's brand-new personal car—a large green Studebaker.

At night Marco had nightmares about the political upheaval, about his unhappy love affair with a housemaid over two decades ago, about the illness of his Chinese wife, and about Chico. Always Chico.

7

Old Secrets

Some twenty-five years earlier, when Marco was still in his teens, two well-dressed ladies sat on the veranda of the smaller of two adjoining mansions, sipping tea and nibbling at assorted biscuits. Clara Braganza, the younger woman, was married to Francisco Braganza; and the older Octavia was married to Telo, Francisco's elder brother. Octavia and Telo Braganza were the proud parents of four sons. Clara and Francisco were childless, a source of great grief.

On this particularly sultry day Francisco had instructed Clara to give Octavia the big news. He and his brother Telo had decided to part ways. They had kept this secret till the sale and division of the family assets had been finalized.

Clara cleared her throat and leaned towards Octavia. 'It's not as if we were all happy here. Telo is good to you and you have your four handsome sons. What do I have? Francisco is drunk half the day. His only work—if you can call it work—is to spend hours at the distillery tasting the various flavours of feni being brewed. I tell you, that factory is a curse. So the men have sold it...'

'Sold the distillery?' Octavia was astonished. 'Why was all this kept secret from me? Surely I had a right to be part of such an important decision? If it goes, what will Francisco do with himself?'

'The distillery is only part of the decision. Fifty acres of coconut plantation will be parcelled off and form part of the deal.

And I believe the buyer, Pandurang Sardessai, has also managed to acquire some of our iron-ore mining rights in the southern borderlands. It appears Pandurang is a hard-nosed businessman. I met him once. He is fluent in Portuguese.'

'Clara, you haven't told me everything. Why all this selling? It seems so unnecessary. What is it in aid of?'

'You know very well I've hated this place ever since I came here as a bride, twelve years ago. Canacona has absolutely nothing to commend it. I've never understood why you put up with the lack of a proper market, the paucity of churches. We have to travel miles north to Margao for the simplest of necessities. I tell you, Octavia, I've had enough of this god-forsaken cultural and social wilderness...So Francisco and I are leaving. Within six months. With the money from the sales we'll go off to Lisbon and start life afresh there. I have a cousin in Almada, just south of the city. We'll stay with him at first while we look for a nice apartment in the centre of town. We'll have plenty of money. Telo has been most understanding...'

Octavia almost fainted. Her world had been turned topsy-turvy. She was suddenly filled with an acute anxiety. 'Clara, you were always a true European at heart. You have never had any love for Goa although you were born here. What will happen to your house? Marco turned only seventeen last month—he's too young to take it over...'

'Oh, I forgot to tell you. Sardessai has bought it along with the other assets. He plans to move in once we vacate. You will have some decent Hindu neighbours for a change. He wanted to buy the fort too. Claimed that Cabo de Rama had deep religious associations for him as it was the place where the Hindu deities Rama and Sita spent part of their exile. Telo had never heard such nonsense and declined to sell it. The fort grounds are on lease to the Braganzas and we have to hand them back to the government at the end of the ninety-nine year lease. I remember Telo saying the fort would be an ideal location to build a hotel someday. You know, it has fantastic views of the sea and several beaches. In my opinion it is the only handsome thing around here...Cheer up, Octavia! Sardessai is a decent man. His family made its fortune shipping iron ore up and down the coast. The only change you can anticipate is the small temple he plans to build in the garden separating our houses...There I go again. It's not my house anymore! The temple will be located between your house and *his* house. He has already lined up ten craftsmen from Ponda. You can always plant some flowering bushes to hide it if you don't like its looks. I'm pretty certain Sardessai won't mind.'

Octavia held back her tears and blew her nose. She didn't know what to say. After a minute spent gazing at a beautiful flower bed, she returned to the issue that had hurt her the most. 'But why wasn't *I* consulted? Why did *you* have to be deputed to inform me?'

'Because our husbands felt you would make a fearful fuss and put obstacles in their way. They told me something I didn't know. It seems that you have a greater share in the property. Our father-in-law's will made this quite clear. You could have had a legal basis for holding up the transactions. Well, anyway, it's all done now and I am off to Lisbon. Once there, I hope to get Francisco off the alcohol. And that great city is bound to have expert doctors who can help me conceive. I read all about the procedures in a magazine. I want a daughter. Judging by your sons, boys are a rough lot. With a daughter you can have a cozy intimate relationship.'

~

Octavia didn't say anything to Telo about her conversation with Clara. She didn't think any good would come of it. One afternoon she drew her eldest son Marco aside and led him to the veranda. In hushed tones she told him about the sale and its consequences.

'Everything will change here, son. Your father is bound to quarrel with the Sardessai family. Imagine, they intend to build a temple on the exact same spot that your father has vowed to build a new chapel. We will have Hindus crawling all over the place. And just one house left to be shared by the four of you brothers...'

'Three, Mother, not four,' Marco chipped in. 'I'm determined to join the police. I'll live in Panjim and wear a handsome uniform decorated with many medals and drive around in a black limousine. I don't know why Father does not agree with my ambition. I have no love for Canacona. As soon as I've finished with the parish school I want to join the police academy or—if my marks are good enough—go to Portugal for training.'

'Are you sure you want to be a police officer? Your father wants you here to look after the plantations and—it's a dream of his—to build and run a hotel up in the fort.'

'But Mother, I want no part of such dreams. I have no head for numbers. I could never run a business. If you, my parents, won't support me, I'll go—I'll go around with a begging bowl—that would embarrass you! My mind is completely made up, Mother.'

Octavia laid a finger on her lips. 'Hush, Marco! Talk softly. Not so loud, the servants will hear. Marcelena is dusting in the hallway. She takes an age. All that heavy furniture collected by your ancestors...As I was about to say, if you are adamant—though you are too young to be adamant—I'll see what I can do. I'll sell part of my share of the land and let you have a lump sum to go to Portugal. The next time your father sends you on an errand to Panjim, go to the police headquarters and find out the exact procedures for joining the police. There are bound to be many rules, fitness tests, entrance examinations, and so on. Take careful notes. Don't aggravate your father by letting him know. Let this be *our* secret. Leave it up to me to tell him at the appropriate time. He keeps secrets from me. Why shouldn't I do the same?'

~

Marcelena had a past. She had been orphaned many years earlier and taken in by the nuns of St Teresa's Convent at Pernem in North Goa. She was a bright child and by the age of ten became partially literate in Portuguese, English and, of course, Konkani, which had no script. But she suffered from a short attention span and was disinclined to join regular studies at the convent school for girls. The nuns wondered what they were going to do with Marcelena.

Sister Agnes, the head at St Teresa's, put Marcelena to work as a general purpose maid. She learnt to cook, swab floors, dust, make beds, decorate the chapel with fresh flowers every day, wash and iron clothes, and trudge to the village shops to make small purchases. The nuns of St Teresa's led a comfortable life and had five maids and a gardener to minister to their whims and fancies.

By the time Marcelena turned eighteen she had risen to the rank of Senior Maid and had other girls to boss over. But she had also formed an attachment to Ponciano Costa, the good-looking gardener. For some time she'd had, as one of her many duties, the task of collecting flowers daily from the gardens of the convent. This was the perfect excuse for lengthy flirtations with Ponciano. One thing led to another...They fell madly in love. Sister Agnes decided she must act.

Ponciano had grown into an exceptionally attractive young man right under their noses. Sister Agnes feared he might prove an unholy distraction for her nuns and the other maids. Marriage with Marcelena was out of the question as the nuns could not afford to lose their best maid. So the nuns decided that Ponciano must go.

Sister Agnes dismissed Ponciano at the end of the month. She gave him three months' pay in lieu of notice, and a glowing reference. She spoke to him sternly on his last day: 'You have betrayed our trust in you. But you are a good gardener and we must not allow your romantic escapade to ruin your life. Take my letter to Father Eduardo at the Mapusa seminary. If he can't employ you himself, he will help you find a good position. Now collect your things and catch the bus to Mapusa.'

Marcelena was heartbroken. She became very inattentive in her work and was scolded frequently by Sister Agnes. A week went by. Marcelena resolved that life at the convent had become insufferable. She counted up the coins she had squirrelled away from her daily shopping errands. They amounted to twenty-three rupees, a tidy sum in those days. She washed and ironed all her clothes and the next afternoon, when everybody else was resting, she ran off with a little suitcase containing her clothes, her Bible and a loaf of bread.

When she reached the seminary at Mapusa that evening, Father Eduardo told her that Ponciano had been engaged by a rich landowner in Canacona. The gardener had told him about Marcelena and the convent. The old priest was sympathetic.

'My child, your courtship will be sinful if you don't enter into holy matrimony. I'll send word to Senhor Telo Braganza to give Ponciano two days off. He can then come here and take you back to Canacona after you are married. I'll convince the parish priest to perform the marriage at short notice, without the reading of bans.'

'But Father, I never said I wanted to get married. That can come later. I just want to be with him, cook for him...do things for him. We must see how well we get on together. I've never lived in the company of men. He might get tired of my plain looks...'

'Oh my child, my child! I can have no part in your plans. What you propose is scandalous. It's against the teachings of the Church. Have you and he...?'

Marcelena was annoyed and embarrassed. 'Father, what do you mean? Have we what? Lain together as man and wife? No, not yet. When I join him and we have a place of our own, I expect we will do so.'

'So there is hope you will reconsider your rash action of running away from the convent? Sister Agnes will forgive you, I'm sure. You are educated and could even become a bride of Christ.'

'I will never go back to the convent. I'd rather take up domestic service in some rich household...You said you were going to send word to Senhor Braganza. Tell me his address and I'll trouble you no further.'

Father Eduardo hesitated for several seconds and then decided to tell her in a general sort of way.

'I believe he has large properties next to the old Cabo de

Rama in Canacona. Everybody there would know him. Search for your Ponciano there...I still think you are making a terrible mistake...Go now, if you must, and may God protect you.'

'Thank you, Father. I know I am bold for my age. The Sisters at the convent were constantly punishing me, even for minor mistakes. We servant girls were expected to be docile and modest and obedient at all times...The atmosphere there was claustro-claustro—oh whatever that word is...Can you tell me of a cheap place to have breakfast in the market? I find everything so dear and must make my money last until I find my Ponciano.'

~

Marcelena had to change buses four times to reach Canacona. On three occasions she was the victim of downright wrong directions given by old ladies—in Mapusa, then Panjim, and lastly Margao. At one point a college boy offered to put her up for the night in his hostel room. She quickly saw through that one and engaged a room in a cheap boarding house. All these experiences were new to her. She had never left the environs of St Teresa's Convent. Now she found herself at the other end of the State of Goa.

While she was waiting patiently at the bus depot in Margao she heard a familiar voice call out her name, 'Marcelena! Marcelena!' She looked over her shoulder—it was Ponciano, carrying two large shopping bags.

He hugged her and bent over to kiss her. She gently pushed him away. 'Not here, not now. It's too public.' She told him her news. That she had abandoned the convent and come in search of him. Ponciano was a bit rattled.

'I've come into Margao to buy provisions and seeds for my work. I can't be seen to be returning with a future wife! It's too sudden and looks suspicious. I'll tell you what. Once we reach the main gate you go ahead and meet Senhora Octavia. She is desperately looking for a senior maid—but the local girls are illiterate. She'll welcome you with open arms. She is a kind lady with four young sons. The other maid servants are all little more than children so you would have control over them. The Master does not interfere in domestic matters. I report directly to him... And—an important thing—we have to admit we know each other slightly—only by sight—from the convent. This would be wise in case the Braganzas check our backgrounds. I know the Master does not care but Senhora may wish to be cautious. And keep in mind she's a little deaf. So speak up when she interviews you.'

Octavia Braganza took to Marcelena right away. No awkward questions were asked. The newcomer was introduced to the other servants and it was made clear to them that Marcelena would be in overall charge. She was shown to her room at the back of the house. It was fully furnished. The other servants slept in dormitories. Ponciano's lodgings were a two-room cottage attached to a large garden some fifty yards away from the mansion. Its windows could be seen from Marcelena's room.

Three months passed with hardly a word spoken between them. They felt miserable at this self-imposed isolation. An exquisite pain. They loved each other deeply. One afternoon when Marcelena was feeding the chickens, Ponciano came up to her with an anguished expression.

'It's time now for you to come to my cottage. I can't stand this separation any more, my darling. Your room is next to the back staircase. You can slip in and out of the house easily. We can signal each other through candle light.'

Marcelena was scandalized by his suggestion. 'No, no...That cannot happen until after we're married. I've changed my mind about living together before marriage. It would be sinful *and* risky. If Senhor and Senhora found out, we would both lose our jobs. And it's nice here. We like the work and the two Braganza families are pleasant enough. And the four boys are energetic and adorable! Though I wish there was a little girl. A daughter. I'd care for her as if she were my own...The boys are so noisy. That Marco sets a bad example for his brothers.'

'Marcelena, oh my Marcelena! Why don't we get married right *now*?' Clearing a way through the thirty-five Braganza chickens, Ponciano dropped to his knees and kissed her hand. 'Will you marry me? We've known each other for ages. I can't stand being in a state of limbo any more… Will you marry me? I'll ask the Senhor for your hand tomorrow. I'm sure he'll agree. We can be man and wife within a month.'

Marcelena smiled sweetly. 'In all this time you've never asked me to marry you…' Then she burst into tears of happiness. 'Yes, yes, I will, my love. Go and make all the arrangements. I insist on meeting half the costs. I'm no gold-digger. I have savings from my wages. Unlike you, I get clothing, food and lodgings free. There is nothing here in Canacona to spend my money on. When we are married, I would like you to take me to Margao to see the sights and, perhaps, to buy a few small things…'

~

Nobody objected to the marriage. Marcelena moved into Ponciano's cottage and arranged to work part-time for Octavia. Eight to twelve in the mornings, three to seven in the evenings. But it was tough going. She also had her wifely responsibilities in the cottage. She was on her feet all day except for half-an-hour after she had cooked and fed Ponciano his lunch. At this time she dozed off and often dreamt of giving birth to a baby girl.

Seven years passed but there was still no sign of a baby. Ponciano's gardens flourished and were a delight to behold. The Braganza boys grew tall and strong. Marco, the eldest, was also the most athletic and carried away several sports prizes at the parish school. Marcelena grieved that she and Ponciano were unable to have a daughter, a fate shared by Senhora Clara Braganza, Senhora Octavia's sister-in-law. Marcelena felt her love for her husband was waning, though Ponciano remained as ardent as ever. They made love twice a day, even three times some days. This without any enthusiasm on Marcelena's part. But she tolerated all the sex in the hope it would result in a daughter. And she felt it was her duty to give her husband access to her body whenever he desired her. That was one of the teachings of the Church, wasn't it?

When the monsoon came around in the eighth year of their marriage, Ponciano was clearing some bramble up in the fort. His employer, Senhor Telo, wished to create a garden there and charge visitors a rupee each for viewing the beaches below from Cabo de Rama's battlements. One afternoon the hard-working gardener was bitten by a long snake and within minutes a poisonous paralysis spread through his body. He called out for help but knew fully well that there was no one else around.

After Marcelena had cooked and waited for more than an hour for her husband to return, she grew tense and hurried up to the fort. She found his body in a tangle of thorny bushes and was shocked into shedding some tears. She ran down to Senhora Octavia, woke her from her siesta and gave her the news. At that point she didn't know that Ponciano had died of snake bite. A group of servants from the plantations carried the body back to the mansion. Senhor Telo was summoned from a distant part of the properties. He examined the body and pronounced that the killer had probably been a king cobra. Death in this case would have been quick and relatively painless. There was, of course, the dimension of terror which lasted a few minutes as the paralysis set in. He turned to the servants.

'That snake must be caught and killed. It might have a mate. Find its nest. There may be eggs. Get the snake catcher from Margao. I want this done quickly so that work on the fort garden can resume. Have any snakes been reported from other parts of our properties? We can't have any more workers being killed this way. Ponciano was a good man, an excellent gardener and a good husband.'

Ponciano was buried in the portion of the Braganza cemetery set apart for servants. The more Marcelena thought about her dead husband, the more she regretted her indifference to his love-making. She now missed wrapping her limbs around his muscular body. She missed kissing him. She even missed his savage thrusts into her womanhood and his cries of ecstasy.

Senhora Octavia allowed Marcelena to continue living in Ponciano's cottage and the not-so-young widow invested in acquiring ten hens and two cocks as a strategy to combat loneliness. She also adopted a stray dog from the village. She named him Casimiro, an exalted name for a very plain mutt. Octavia's sons fell in love with him and within three weeks the dog had been renamed Cosmo. Marco and Cosmo were particularly close. They would play ball in the front lawns every evening and Marco trained him to be a good watchdog over Marcelena's cottage and chickens. Cosmo had one peculiar habit though. Every day he would take an hour off his watchdog duties and run down to the village to meet up with his old four-legged friends. He was always back by three.

~

Then the unexpected happened. Marcelena and Marco became deeply attached to one another. This turned into a powerful physical attraction. Marco would creep noiselessly down the back stairs and visit Marcelena in her cottage late at night. Cosmo would thump his tail by way of greeting. Soon the twenty-nine-year-old widow had taught the seventeen-year-old Marco all she knew of passionate love-making. In his eagerness to learn, Marco had been somewhat violent at the beginning and had to be taught tenderness.

Remembering Ponciano's brutal approaches, Marcelena scolded Marco quite often. 'Not so fast, my darling. You have to wait for me...You are hurting my breasts. Kiss gently, gently, my Marco...' After a few months of vigorous love-making Marcelena realized she was pregnant. She was torn between conflicting emotions. Would the child be the daughter she had yearned for? How could she hide her condition from the Braganzas? Senhora Octavia would never forgive her. Senhora Clara may be more understanding. The thing was never to let Marco and his extended family know that he was the father of the child-to-be. Anyway, Marco would soon go off to be trained as a police officer. Why burden him with the truth? He would be going to Lisbon in six weeks.

This left Marcelena in a quandary. She had to invent an explanation for how she was pregnant so many months after her husband's death; and she might later have to explain how the baby came to have a fair complexion.

But Marco guessed what had happened and was bewildered. What was the honourable thing to do? 'Marcelena, I'll quit my plans to join the police. I'll marry you. We'll have more children. I'll ask for my share of the property and we'll build a separate house. If I go off to Lisbon I'll certainly worry about both of you…'

Marcelena was tense. 'You are *not* the father, Marco. I should know. The father could be any one of three white senhors who raped me up at the fort one afternoon about three months ago. I kept quiet about it, hoping I would not get pregnant. I have been miserable. I recently consulted a midwife in the village. She offered to get rid of the baby—but then I thought, what if it is a baby girl? Could I murder a baby girl? No, Marco, all you are guilty of is making love to a widow. I will always remember your kindness…'

Marco started sobbing. 'What did they do to you? Oh, Marcelena, I can't abandon you now when you need me most. My mother will be most distressed when she hears of this. You've kept it secret for so long. I still want to marry you. My mind is made up, Marcelena.'

'Marco, my Marco. Don't fret so much. I'll manage somehow. I've learned that Senhora Clara and Senhor Francisco are about to move to Portugal. I'll offer to work for them. The baby can be born there. If it's a girl, I'll call her Carmen. I've always liked the name. Sister Carmen at the convent was always very kind to me. So, Carmen after Sister Carmen. You, Marco, get ready to go off to the academy in Lisbon. Be strong and brave.'

~

The two sisters-in-law were having an urgent conversation in the front veranda of Clara's mansion. Clara was feeling quite magnanimous.

'Marco can travel with us. We'll bear his expenses. You can repay me later when you've managed to liquidate your share of the property. As for Marcelena, I'm taking her on. I can't bear the thought of doing housework in Lisbon. She at any rate is a good cook and a maid with many talents. We plan to entertain a lot. I simply must have help. The child, I'm sure, will be a girl. She can keep me company while Marcelena works. I will more or less be looking after her in any case. It will be like having a daughter of my own, but without the bother of childbirth!...Tell me, Octavia, what was Marcelena doing up in the fort that afternoon? I often wonder about that.'

'She was watering the flowers that her husband Ponciano had planted. She had to fetch water from the well in the fort. Back-breaking work—it took up all her free time in the afternoons. After the snake-bite episode, Telo couldn't persuade any of the junior gardeners to take care of the garden. Wretched cowards! Telo has another, less charitable explanation. He suspects Marcelena of entertaining tourists in the bushes to make up for her loss of income after Ponciano's death. Anyway, he has scolded her for keeping quiet about the gang rape. He maintains the police should have been called in right away. Now Marcelena claims she can't recall what the senhors looked like.'

'Has Marco packed his things?' Clara asked. 'I've given Marcelena a number of my old frocks. We can't have her looking like a tramp. Francisco has got her travel documents ready—Marcelena Costa, widow of Ponciano Costa; daughter of unknown; profession: domestic service; employer: Senhora Clara Braganza; etcetera, etcetera. Presumably Marco's papers are in order?'

'Yes, Clara, yes. Why do you fret so much?' asked Octavia.

'It's not that I fret too much. I have a thousand things to see to. Pandurang Sardessai is coming tomorrow to take over the house. He's terrified of dogs. So tell Marcelena to keep Cosmo out of his way. You'll have to formally adopt Cosmo now and teach him to stay away from his bazaar friends. That's what the village looks like now—a wretched Hindu bazaar. The authorities should do something about it. God knows what diseases the dog will bring into your house. Your boys should avoid petting him.'

Octavia was rather tired of Clara's constant chatter. She changed the subject. 'Tell me about your cousin in Almada,' she said. 'Will you be staying with his family for long?'

'My cousin is some kind of historian. He specializes in the Moorish period of Almada and Lisbon. Who on earth would be interested in such a thing! Still, he is a devoted student of the subject. We'll stay with his family till we find a suitable place of our own. Marcelena will have to sleep on a carpet in the drawing-room. I've been warned of this. She doesn't seem to mind the prospect. She is as excited as I am to be going to Portugal. Francisco has mixed feelings. He will miss his so-called work at the distillery. But neither of us will miss Canacona. It's been such a boring life for me here. No decent shops, no genteel company...Well, you also know how dull life is here. I wonder what the Sardessai family will do with themselves. Rush off to the temples in Ponda at the slightest hint of anxiety? I wish Telo the best of luck with building the chapel. Telo and Pandurang will be in competition with each other. The Hindu temple versus the Christian church!'

~

Francisco, Clara, Marco and Marcelena boarded the *Lisboa Linda* at Vasco. The monsoon rains had arrived early and, as the ship headed out to the Arabian Sea, Clara felt increasingly sea-sick. Soon the nausea grew so severe that she confined herself to her First Class cabin. Her husband tried his best to persuade her to spend time on deck between spells of rain to get some fresh air.

'Oh, stop it, Francisco! If I go up to the deck there'll be twenty other souls vomiting over the rails. It will only make me feel worse. I can't bear the sight of the twenty-foot high waves. This ship is not heavy enough to plough smoothly through such rough waters.'

The only thing Clara would consume was three glasses of lemon-soda a day. With salt, no sugar. She couldn't eat a thing. Marcelena was faring no better down in steerage. Marco got permission to meet her in the large cabin she shared with some other women. There were occasions when Marcelena's co-passengers were away amusing themselves on the lower-most deck. Marco would then hold Marcelena's hand and she would reluctantly let him kiss her.

'Marco, my little Marco. We must stop now. I have to go to the toilet or I'll vomit all over you, my precious. You are such a naughty, romantic fellow...I'm afraid I'll have a miscarriage. Now be off with you or we'll be discovered.'

Francisco was at a loose end. He spent as little time with Clara as possible. He couldn't bear the stench in their cabin. He tried to make friends with other First Class passengers but they found him too unsophisticated. So he became a regular fixture under a deep awning on the upper deck. Francisco and his canvas bag filled with bottles of 80 proof cashew feni. He spent mornings and afternoons in a drunken stupor. Then, four days out at sea, he made a friend. A handsome man in his mid-fifties who went by the name of Benny Britto took to occupying the adjacent deckchair. He always carried a bottle of brandy with him.

Francisco took a liking to Benny. They had in common an addiction to the bottle and a gift for slurred conversation. Francisco told Benny about the rustic plantation life in Canacona and Benny told Francisco about his band. The Benny Britto Band, once based in Calcutta, now disbanded. Benny had been the lead singer and pianist, specializing in American numbers.

Francisco asked, 'What were the most popular numbers? We are so behind the times in Goa.'

'There was a woman singer, Pam Caine, who used to join us from time to time. What were the popular numbers? Both vocal and instrumental? That would be a long list:

In the Good Ol' Summertime
Sweet Adeline
I Wonder Who's Kissing Her Now
In the Shade of an Old Apple Tree
Because You're You
When You Were Sweet Sixteen
My Wild Irish Rose
By the Light of the Silvery Moon
Fascination
Auld Lang Syne

Senhor, I've only mentioned the very popular tunes—the American ones. There were also requests for waltzes and fox-trots. Customers would dance past midnight, on the strength of cocktails...Life is not very different on this ship. I'm the lead crooner and pianist with the resident orchestra. Our hours too are much the same. Twelve noon to three and seven-thirty to one in the evenings...In Calcutta we played in restaurants and the better class of hotels. This ship is a floating hotel, no? The Captain had the decency to allot me a second-class cabin. Made sure I have it all to myself...Senhor Braganza, I knew the Braganzas of Braganza & Sons in Calcutta. The music shop. They tuned most of the pianos I played. We used to meet often—you'd be surprised how frequently restaurant pianos have to be tuned! This ship has three pianos and they are tuned every three months...Are you related to those Braganzas? I think they moved to Calcutta from Bandel and originally came from some village in Goa.'

Francisco was intrigued by the possibility of a connection but couldn't even guess how this might be. Benny said, 'My Granny, a very old lady who lived in Calcutta, made an elaborate family tree of the Brittos going back two hundred and fifty years. I saw it when I was much younger. It featured a Braganza in the eighteenth century. The Branganza in question—I forget his first name—was a Lower Division Clerk at Fort William. Granny Britto, our conscientious chronicler of hatches, matches and despatches, had reached the mid-nineteenth century by the time she died. Now the family tree is with my sister...Tell your nephew Marco about the possible connection with the Braganzas of Calcutta...Oh, I think the Fort William Braganza was named Louis—it just came back to me!'

By the time the *Lisboa Linda* reached the Suez Canal, Clara's hair had turned completely white and she had lost twenty pounds. The ship's doctor had no explanation for the hair. He urged her to start eating solids to get her strength back. He reassured her that the Mediterranean was a calm sea. So Clara developed a liking for dates, abundantly available, and by the time the ship sailed past Crete she was eating a large cup full of these every day.

~

The Braganzas and Marcelena settled into Clara's cousin's flat. They were a bit cramped. Marco slept on a divan and Marcelena slept on the carpet in the living-room. This degree of intimacy lasted four days, after which Marco readied himself to report to the police academy in Lisbon. Clara gave him some spending money and his uncle and aunt wished him all the best. Marcelena looked deep into his eyes, convinced she would never see him again. She curtseyed as any polite maid would. There were tears in her eyes.

Francisco Braganza soon realized that they had better find a house of their own. He did a preliminary search but nothing was good enough for Clara. She wanted five bedrooms, two reception rooms and a maid's room for Marcelena. So Francisco found himself examining apartments in the poshest localities of Lisbon. These were well beyond his budget. But Clara kept reminding her husband that he would soon find a good job, advising the various distilleries that dotted the countryside. She finally selected a large first-floor apartment belonging to a retired Russian ballerina. This venerable lady proved a nuisance. She loved to talk—mostly about herself and her glittering career in Moscow, Paris and Rome. She also persuaded Clara to keep changing the colour of her hair.

Marcelena's child was born at home in the winter. She named her Carmen, and Clara took to her immediately. The child was allowed to be with Marcelena only at feeding times. Clara saw to all her other needs. Marcelena found this quite depressing but she had a lot to keep her busy.

Clara spent a large fortune on new clothes and weekly visits to her hairdresser. Francisco took to brandy once his stock of feni was exhausted. He drank at the rate of a large bottle of brandy a day, and was incapable of even the slightest of exertions. He was too unsteady in body and mind to go looking for work. Meanwhile, the money and bank deposits were dwindling rapidly. Lisbon was proving to be much more expensive than Goa. In his sober moments Francisco wondered why he had allowed Clara to talk him into moving to Portugal.

Marco was an exemplary cadet at the police academy. His fellow cadets looked up to him because he was the only one among them who claimed to have lost his virginity. As he grew older, he developed a fine physique. He had an above-average intelligence. He wished to grow a moustache but cadets were not allowed this privilege while under training. He thought now and then of Marcelena, the first and only love of his life, and resolved he would never see her again. It would be too painful. He would occasionally send a note to his Uncle Francisco telling him of his promotions and medals. Marco had a photograph of himself taken in a studio. He looked a bit like the movie star Clark Gable. Copies of this were sent to his parents in Canacona. Clara had their copy of Marco's portrait framed and put on the mantelpiece in the salon. Marcelena was thus forced to look at it each time she dusted the over-furnished room. And each time, tears would well up in her eyes.

~

The day came, a few years later, when Marco was ordered to proceed to Macao, half a world away. It was a field posting and he would have to learn some basic Chinese. At around the same time Clara discovered she was pregnant. She and Francisco had spent enormous sums of money on doctors of every description to make this possible. Clara, of course, transferred all her affections to the new child when he was born. Marcelena's daughter Carmen could not understand the situation. The sudden withdrawal of love left her perplexed.

Clara had made her plans. Carmen would be handed over to nuns who would train her in the domestic arts and send her to work in the home of a distinguished family. Marcelena would have none of this.

'Madame, I just cannot agree with the idea. I was taken over by nuns as an infant and have been miserable ever since. I will teach Carmen all I know—reading, writing, arithmetic. I will send her to school and pay the fees with my own money...'

'You stupid woman, Carmen was not born to be a lady,'

Clara said. 'Consider her parentage. An unknown father. A domestic servant as a mother. You must accept she is a bastard. If I am to feed and clothe her any more, she must do her fair share of housework. Such as scrubbing the floors and cleaning the bathrooms. She is six now and perfectly capable of assuming these responsibilities...And I can't think of any respectable school that would admit a child with Carmen's antecedents. She'll have to go to a convent sooner or later. Just resign yourself to that.'

Marcelena tried to reason with Clara and Francisco. He was only half drunk one evening. 'Marcelena, our money is almost finished. Very little left. Can't afford your wages. And two extra mouths to feed. It's too much. Can't pay for Carmen to go to private school...'

Clara cut in, 'We'll send you back to Goa if you're not careful. You've become increasingly cheeky over the years. If you were not such a good cook, I'd have thrown you out long ago. So concentrate on your cooking and cleaning if you want to continue working in my house. And teach your daughter what it means to be a good housemaid. You owe me at least that much.'

8

Saligao

Marco's new car, the green Studebaker, sped along the road between the port and Saligao village. There would be two breaks in the drive, when the car and its occupants would have to cross by ferry. Four police escorts on motorcycles preceded the car carrying the Chief Commissioner of Police and his bride-to-be.

Bella was excited. 'I never imagined the landscape of Goa could be as beautiful as what I am seeing now. Such a rich tapestry of villages, forests and paddy fields...Why are the villages so spread out?

'Simple, Bella. Each house has a large garden or a coconut grove. Land was never scarce. Practically every village has a chapel or a church, and the communidade oversees land use and land ownership...Judging by the sheer size of Braganza House, your ancestors must have been very influential people. The communidade records show the house was built in the early eighteenth century. There's an infant's grave on the grounds dated 1709. The earliest records were lost in a fire that took place in the early nineteenth century, some decades before the property passed into Hindu hands.'

'I can't wait to see it,' said Bella, 'why must I wait till after the marriage ceremony?'

'Because it's my wedding present to you.'

'You *are* getting sentimental in your old age!...Where is Chico? Surely I can meet him today?'

'Chico is unwell. Not at his best. The prospect of a major move has unsettled him. He cannot understand that he'll be much better off in Braganza House.' Marco changed the subject. 'Bella, I'm so sorry that everything is so rushed. My work has been very strenuous. There have been developments in the freedom struggle inspired by Gandhi and other troublemakers. The agitations are often violent. My police force has been kept busy day and night...'

'But what has Gandhi got to do with Goa?' Bella asked. 'His agitations are against British rule in India, aren't they?'

'The people of Goa should be grateful to Portugal. The local agitators don't appreciate the prosperity our government has brought them. There is a fringe element that opposes what they call "colonialism". It's all quite bothersome.'

'I was so looking forward to a grand church wedding. I'll be the first in my family to get married.'

'Don't fret, Bella. We'll have a grand ceremony on our twenty-fifth wedding anniversary. But for now you must understand that we can't get married until after I've handed over charge to my successor at eleven in the morning of the seventeenth. This was the arrangement communicated to the Governor. The marriage will be on the same day at four in the afternoon. It should not take more than half an hour. Julio will be the witness from your side.'

'Julio? Will he get permission to travel to Panjim on his own? I gather the Fathers of Rachol are very strict.'

'Yes, Julio—he will be part of our little family from now on. He has quit the seminary, for complex reasons that we can go into later. In brief, he was miserable there.'

As the ferry crossed the river, Bella watched the hills of Dona Paula come into view. Marco dared not put his arms around her. The ferry was crowded and as Chief Police Commissioner he had to behave with the utmost decorum.

Bella was distressed. 'When did this happen with Julio, Marco? Have my parents been informed? The development is going to kill my mother. She had set her heart on having a priest in the family...What will Julio do next? It's very kind of you to take him under your wing. Where is he now? Why didn't he come to Vasco to meet me?'

Marco did his best to calm Bella down. He was intentionally vague in his answers. The journey by car continued. They were just a few miles short of Saligao.

'When will I meet Julio? You must have worked out that moment in your detailed programme!...And who is this Mrs Souza I am supposed to stay with? Two nights, you said. There will be no time to get a special dress for me! I hope Saligao has a tailor who can take in a couple of frocks before the ceremony. You haven't noticed: I've lost some weight. You never notice such things!'

Marco rolled down the windows of the car and, nervous of Bella's questions, lit a cigarette.

'Old Mrs Souza is the only resident of Saligao who has bedrooms to spare. You can say she runs a modest boarding house. She's a dear old soul. She has a very gifted grandson. A real artist. Julio shifted to Mrs Souza's yesterday. He will be there to welcome you when we arrive.'

'Marco, you seem to be keeping everyone apart purposely.'

'It's not that at all. I have to juggle so many things in a three-day period. I've finally got some domestic staff in place at—I'll call it BH, for short. I'll shift Chico there tomorrow. Inas, who looks after him, and the cook will shift with him. As I said before, Chico is likely to react badly. I hope not violently. Anyway, Inas is used to his tantrums which never last more than a few minutes. Maximum twenty minutes...Don't be apprehensive about Chico. The American doctors hold out some hope...When you see him dance you will forgive everything.'

'I do not understand all this secrecy,' Bella said slowly. 'I can see you have put a lot of thought into making the arrangements. But I worry about Julio and Chico. You could have sent me a cable on the ship forewarning me of your complicated plans... Have we reached Mrs Souza's house?...It looks too small to have spare bedrooms. Stub out that cigarette, Marco...What a beautiful garden!'

Julio ran down the steps from the veranda and hugged his sister. Mrs Souza stood at the top of the short staircase with a welcoming and largely toothless smile. Young Francis went to the car to help unload the luggage. The police outriders shooed him off and carried the trunk and various boxes into the house and then into the small room where Bella was to stay.

'I had no idea you had grown so tall, Julio. You're almost unrecognizable...So handsome! If I were not your older sister, I'd fall for you.' Bella looked at Marco, chuckled and gave him a wink. Julio put an arm around her.

'Bella, I must wish you every happiness. Braganza Sir is a very kind man and has taken good care of me. He rescued me from Rachol where I had been unhappy for some time. Some of the Fathers there are not good men...But we can talk about that some other time.'

Bella frowned. 'But Mummy will want a detailed account of what went wrong. Don't forget, you were quite looking forward to life at the seminary. Your letters home gave no clue that you were facing problems.'

'I'll write to her once I'm clear on what to do next. I'm to meet Marco's architect soon. He will advise me on what my options are. The priesthood is certainly not one of them.'

Meanwhile Marco and Mrs Souza reviewed the arrangements. No, there was no tailor in the village. But the old lady had been the eldest of eight children, and had herself been the mother of four girls. So she had ample experience of altering clothes and would gladly help Bella out between her cooking and dusting. The young scamp Francis could nip up to Mapusa on the bus in case Bella needed anything to be bought. There would be an extra charge for the tailoring.

Just before Marco left, he was able to give Bella an ardent kiss when they were momentarily alone together in her room. 'Sleep well, my love. And rest as much as you can tomorrow. I'll be busy shifting Chico. And then there are three meetings scheduled. I have to brief my successor...Oh, I almost forgot. The last truckload of my personal belongings has to be dispatched to BH. My books, clothes, files, and odds and ends of furniture that I have accumulated as my personal effects...I'll need a whole room for my files alone. I look forward to having a study where I can sit quietly and write my memoirs. I saved every letter I ever received and kept a carbon copy of every letter I sent! My years of service in the police have been full of adventures—'

'How will I stay in touch with you, Marco? Your arrangements seem so complicated,' Bella asked anxiously.

'I'm not sure yet where I will spend tomorrow night. Our intelligence officers suspect some disturbances are being planned. If they materialize, I'll be on patrol duty all night. Mrs Souza says her telephone works sometimes. In that case I'll be in touch from time to time. Otherwise there's a police outpost down the road if you want to send me a message. There'll be a radio link from there...Mrs Souza says your dinner is ready any time you want it...I simply must rush off. The Governor wants a word with me tonight without fail.' With that, Marco and his security detail hurried off.

Bella was exhausted. She wanted to sleep. Mrs Souza wanted to chat. Julio wanted Francis to show Bella his bizarre drawings. The budgerigars in their cage on the veranda refused to shut up despite the lateness of the hour. It was well past their bedtime.

Mrs Souza went into a long description of Braganza House. Its massive size, the Hindu additions, the valuable collection of antiques, the flowing stream, the vast grounds—a hundred acres, she said. The details were often at variance with what she had told Eric O'Brien. Bella thought the old lady was exaggerating everything to do with Braganza House. An act of flattery. Finally, Bella managed to escape to her room, change and fall asleep.

~

When it was pitch dark outside, Julio and Francis discussed art. Julio was puzzled by Francis's views. 'This painting of Jesus. Why have you given him such big teeth? And you have shown multiple stab wounds all over his body. And there is a dove flying out of his heart. All this is not in the Bible. All your pictures are grotesque, Francis! Where do such ideas come from?'

'From a book I once read. We had a guest two years ago who showed me a little book with illustrations of the paintings of a madman named Picasso. That book opened my eyes and got me thinking. It was full of what you may say were dis-dis-distortions of reality. That's how I developed my own special style. Grandma showed some of my drawings to Father Afonso who said I should be sent to prison. But as I was too young for prison, Father said I should be deposited in a seminary where the priests would straighten me out.'

Julio told Francis about the unhappy time he had spent at Rachol. About the fresco restorations that he had enjoyed doing, about his Hindu friends, about the nightly horrors, and about the trauma of Diwali night. Francis, who was four years younger than Julio, suddenly had a brainwave. He hugged Julio, who was a good foot taller than him, and looked directly up into his eyes.

'Why don't you and I just run off to Bombay? We'll study art and do odd jobs to pay the fees. It will be great fun—'

'—Francis, what are the two of you up to, gossiping away? Now go to bed...I'm looking for my copy of Isidore Coelho's cookbook, have you seen it anywhere? I thought I'd cook a couple of dishes tonight because I have to help Miss Braganza with her dresses tomorrow. I'll have no time to cook then. Now find that book.'

Francis found the book next to the birdcage in the front veranda. He helped his grandmother cook a mango curry and some pork vindaloo. They did not get to sleep until two. Ever since Francis was kicked out of the local school for delinquency and alleged sexual assault, Mrs Souza had tried to reform him with love and by giving him things to do: the daily food shopping, chopping vegetables, fetching milk from Bernadette's dairy, washing up, and sweeping the house when the maid did not come...This still left Francis several hours in the day to draw and paint. His grandmother had given up criticizing his artwork. Occasionally she would say things like, 'I like the colours' or 'You need more sky there.'

The next morning, after a late breakfast of sannas and

chutney, Bella brought two dresses to Mrs Souza for alteration. A plain red silk one and a blue cotton one with an elaborate print of red roses. The old lady said she could manage only one—Bella should choose which one. She chose the red. Midway through Mrs Souza's labours Bella suddenly realized she didn't have the right shade of lipstick to go with it. She panicked over the little inconsistency.

'Don't worry, child. I'll send the two artists to DeMello's in Mapusa. He carries a full range of beauty products for ladies.... Francis! Francis!'

'*Now* what have I done? You are always yelling for me. We should get a bell. Julio was just showing me his great-grandfather's sketches. What do you want, Grandma?'

'Nip up to Mapusa, to DeMello's, and buy a shade of lipstick that *exactly* matches this sample. Take Julio with you. I hope I'm right in believing that you two artists can match colours. Here's five rupees. Take the express bus and eat something proper in the market for lunch. Something solid, not that Hindu pani-puri kind of rubbish. Now be off with you.'

Mrs Souza turned to Bella. 'That will keep the scoundrel out of my hair for three hours, depending on the bus service...I worry so much about him. He's so peculiar. I'm his only living relative and I think I'm eighty years old! Maybe older. All documents and many lives were lost in the big fire here a few years ago, it was terrible! I never talk about it, so don't ask me questions. It was due to an electrical problem. Francis, a baby then, and I—we were the only survivors.'

The phone rang. It was Marco. All was going as planned at his end. Chico had been transferred to BH and was fast asleep. Or at any rate Inas said his eyes were shut tight. He had refused lunch. The night before, the Governor had wanted Marco to list out the chief political troublemakers and their links to Gandhi and the Indian National Congress. He also wanted a list of spies and smugglers. The Governor took notes as Marco spoke. Marco did not elaborate over the phone as someone might be listening in. Bella told him about the lipstick. He found this quite amusing but dared not chuckle. His late Chinese wife had never worn lipstick.

The boys were embarrassed as they walked into DeMello's and asked for the lipstick counter. They showed the snippet of red cloth to the salesman who then brought out a large tray of red lipsticks. A dispute arose between Francis and Julio. They could not agree on any one shade. They ended up buying two lipsticks, one slightly darker than the other.

Mapusa's main market was a big place with a wide choice of places to eat. Julio was not hungry because of the late breakfast. Francis had four helpings of pani-puri and rubbed his stomach with satisfaction. He took a packet of cigarettes out from the pocket of his short-pants.

'Care for a smoke? Or are you a seminary innocent?'

'I don't smoke, Francis. My Hindu friends in the Rachol bazaar used to drink and smoke like crazy. They also used to visit the two loose women there. One rupee each time. I never knew where their money came from...Talking about money, how do you pay for your cigarettes and art supplies?'

'When I go shopping for Grandma, I give myself a five per cent commission on every item I buy.' Francis lowered his voice. 'This means I add five per cent to every purchase price and pocket it as my compensation. Shopping for her is hard work. She dithers a lot...but has the good sense never to question what I paid for this or that. I get the art supplies from this market. Smuggled paints and paper, charcoal sticks, canvas and picture frames. I think Grandma knows what's going on. She's not exactly blind yet. She is now resigned to the fact that I am determined to be a professional artist sooner rather than later.'

Instead of going home directly, Francis and Julio took a long bus detour via Candolim. Julio had never visited a beach before. They finally got home to Saligao at about seven in the evening. Mrs Souza was in a flap. The red dress was ready but quite crumpled. The electricity had gone off. She wondered how she would iron it. Bella rang up Marco who was quite exhausted after a full day of meetings and the tension of shifting Chico along with bag and baggage to BH. Bella asked him to use his last day of influence to get the power to the village restored quickly. He did so. The power came back at nine.

The two lipsticks were examined carefully under a bright table lamp. Bella announced that she would use them both. She did not wish to hurt either boy's feelings. The two Souzas and the two Braganzas went to bed early that night.

~

The marriage ceremony the next afternoon was quick. All involved were smartly dressed but looked somewhat tense. Marco was in civilian clothes. After handing over charge to his successor, he was no longer entitled to wear the police uniform. Both Bella and Mrs Souza wore hats. The old lady's straw sunhats had seen better days.

The magistrate was very efficient. After Bella and Marco had signed the register, he asked the witnesses to identify themselves.

'Witness number one? Name, sex, year of birth, occupation?'

'Bernardo Cabral, thirty-eight years old, born 1900, Chief Commissioner of Police as of today. I'm Mr Braganza's successor. But you know all this.'

The magistrate turned to Julio. 'Witness number two? Name, sex, year of birth, occupation?'

'Julio Braganza, nineteen, 1919, student, brother of the bride,' Julio replied.

The magistrate smiled, 'Nineteen, nineteen, nineteen. You'll be a lucky young man...Well, I congratulate you all, and my best wishes for the future.' He drew Francis Souza back to have a word with him privately.

'Aren't you the juvenile delinquent I saw in court a couple of years ago? The charge was sexual assault on a neighbour's daughter, if I remember rightly. I acquitted you because I felt you were being framed. Far too young to commit rape...Well, I hope you are staying out of trouble now. Next time the courts will not be so lenient. Now run along and catch up with the rest.'

It was a sunny afternoon. Bella and Marco kissed openly

on the steps of the courthouse. Photographs were taken. Some twenty or so of Marco's former subordinates lined up to offer congratulations. The five-member wedding party—if one could call it that—drove back in the Studebaker to Mrs Souza's house where she laid out a cake and the best Goan wine. She got Francis to write out an itemized bill for boarding, lodging, tailoring, lipsticks, etcetera. Francis added five per cent as service charges and pocketed the amount when Marco paid the bill.

The big moment then arrived for Bella. Her first view of the renovated Braganza House, a vast white mansion with blue cornices and blue trim around the windows and doorways. 'Oh, Marco, it's heavenly—and so large! Are you going to carry me over the threshold now?'

Marco took out a large bunch of shiny keys and handed them to Bella. 'The house is now yours. It's registered in your name. That is what you wanted...Now there...You look so beautiful. Since BH is your property perhaps you should carry *me* across the threshold!'

The Governor had passed strict instructions that Marco was to be guarded night and day by two security guards for at least six months. The guards were outfitted with guns, walkie-talkies and motorcycles. Bella resented this intrusion and asked Marco what danger he was in.

'Nothing specific,' he said, 'though it is well known that I arrested many troublemakers during my tenure as Chief Commissioner. I have a reputation of being tough on smugglers, brothel-keepers, bar-owners, drunkards, perpetrators of domestic violence, and those indulging in political agitations...I suppose I *do* have some enemies. What the Governor is most apprehensive about though is that I might be kidnapped and held for ransom—I'm afraid this applies to you as well, my love. Anyway, you will get used to the guards...Now let me show you around the house and explain all the improvements the architect has made.'

~

Braganza House included two large courtyards. One of them had a free-standing Hindu temple in it, a relic of the four generations of Dempos who had once owned the mansion. The other courtyard had a little gem of a chapel which the architect Batley had restored fully. Modern toilets attached to every bedroom, the very large bedrooms divided into two, the large reception room floor retiled, chandeliers electrified, kitchens remodelled, furniture repaired and restored...Bella was amazed at how much Marco had achieved in spite of his hectic official duties. She was thrilled by everything she saw, and kissed him again and again.

Julio had picked up a detective novel and planted himself in one corner of the smaller reception room. He had never seen his sister as animated as she was that evening. He tried to be as inconspicuous as possible. He wondered if he himself would ever marry.

When the tour was completed, Marco held Bella in his arms and kissed the top of her head. Bella disentangled herself and asked, 'Chico? What about Chico?'

'Chico is not well. Quite agitated all day. Inas had to give him a double dose of medicine to put him to sleep. The unfamiliar surroundings have disoriented him. We'll visit him in the morning...The cook says dinner is ready. Shall we eat our first proper meal together as husband and wife?'

Over dinner Marco told Bella and Julio about the British architect Claude Batley. He was famous in Bombay and had come to Goa in connection with designing office buildings for the Dempos and the Chowgules. Batley would come by the next morning to meet Bella and Julio. He had been informed of Julio's artistic talents.

~

The busy architect arrived at eleven sharp. He looked about fifty, and wore a cream-coloured linen suit and a Kashmiri silk cravat. Bella wore the same red bridal outfit because all her other dresses hung rather loose on her. She had never had the funds to have them altered while in Lisbon. Batley was friendly but to the point.

'I gather from my conversations with the Chief Commissioner that you plan to convert Braganza House into an exclusive hotel.

You can expect your guests to be largely Goans from Portugal, British India or the Far East. Such people normally come every two years, and many want a higher level of amenities than what is available in their ancestral villages. You can expect the average stay would be two to three weeks. Additional items of furniture will be required. Here's a list of establishments where those can be bought...The whole house is now termite- and weather-proof. Everything freshly painted. All rotting woodwork has been replaced. Living quarters for up to ten staff are under construction and should be ready in four months. The grounds around the house have been cleared of wild shrubs and weeds. You must start planting your gardens. I advise you to use only native species of flowers and trees. In my master plan for the entire property I have indicated preferred locations for various orchards: banana, cashew, mango, papaya and so on. I'm afraid the Dempos did not take much interest in horticulture or agriculture...Here's my number in Bombay. You may phone me any time you like. I'm at my office from nine to eight everyday including Sundays.'

Bella was somewhat intimidated by Claude Batley. He and Marco had thought of everything. She thanked him and sent for Julio who arrived with his sketchbooks featuring cars, churches, houses and people. Batley looked through them carefully and asked, 'Young man, have you ever thought of becoming an architect? You have a lot of talent in drawing. I'm the Principal of the Sir J.J. School of Architecture in Bombay and can admit you for a degree course on the spot. Today, in fact...But think about it overnight. I'm leaving for Bombay by the steamer tomorrow afternoon. You can travel with me and stay at my house till hostel arrangements are made. I'll arrange for a scholarship if you like... Mrs Braganza, what do you think?'

'This is all rather sudden, Mr Batley. We are all very proud of Julio's drawing abilities. If you see great promise in his art work—and you are the expert, your recommendations matter a lot—Julio, why are you so silent? Don't you want to become an architect? I'll ring Mummy and Daddy in Delhi and give them all our news. I'll book the call at lunch time. So what do you think, Julio?'

Julio gathered his sketchbooks and held them against his chest. 'I'm very grateful, sir. I promise to live up to your expectations. Bombay, I hear, is an exciting place. I have seen pictures of so many grand buildings there. Father Menezes at the seminary had many photographs he took himself. He was from Bombay...You have opened a new window for me, sir. I'll come with you tomorrow.'

Batley shook Julio's hand and said, 'I still feel you should think about it for a few hours—I'll tell you what, Mrs Braganza, *you* ring me at my hotel at ten tomorrow morning and let me know Julio's decision. I will have to get an additional ticket for the steamer, and alert my household in Bombay about a young man accompanying me...Now excuse me, I have a luncheon meeting in Panjim—I must flee. You never know how long it will take to get across the river.'

~

The three Braganzas sat in the huge veranda and thought their private thoughts. The cook brought out glasses of lemonade. Birds were calling all around. Marco eventually went inside and placed a trunk call to Delhi. Then he invited Bella and Julio to visit Chico in his room at the far end of an upstairs corridor. As they approached the room, they heard music.

'That's Prokofiev's *Romeo and Juliet*. A Russian composer. Chico has been playing that record again and again. I bought it in Lisbon. A very sad ballet. Chico may be dancing, in which case it is best not to disturb him.' Marco unlocked Chico's door and stepped into the room. Julio's and Bella's eyes gradually adjusted themselves to the darkness. All the curtains were drawn. Then they spotted Chico huddled on the floor in a corner. He was surrounded by piles of crumpled costumes. He looked up at them with tired and sad eyes. His body remained inert. The only part of his anatomy that moved were his eyes. They flicked from side to side examining his visitors. Bella noticed that his eyes were moist with tears. Marco drew aside the heavy curtains from the largest of the four windows in the room.

'Come on, son, cheer up! Start dancing to some happy music like the *Nutcracker Suite*. Bella is going to be your new mother, and Julio is her brother from Delhi...Shall I tell Inas to bring you some lunch? You must promise me you will eat it. I'm told you haven't eaten anything for two days. That won't do. Later, when you are feeling better, we'll show you around this wonderful house.'

Bella was most disturbed. She whispered so that Julio would not hear her, 'Marco, what have you got me into? You expect me to love that...that...*thing*?'

Marco protested. 'You should see how happy he is when he is dancing. It will melt your heart. And he is a beautiful young man. I have spent hours gazing at him, wondering how I deserved to have such a handsome son.'

Julio did not know how to react to Chico. He was disturbed by the thought of having to befriend this uncommunicative boy. How would he do it? In any case it was up to his sister Bella to win Chico's trust first. That would undoubtedly take time. So Julio did not comment. He was already pre-occupied with Mr Batley's proposition. When he was at Rachol the thought of studying architecture had crossed his mind off and on, but there was no one to discuss it with. He saw a link between his love for drawing cars and drawing churches, but had not quite understood the process of design that underlay each one...Julio was quite excited but dreaded the impact his news was likely to have on Verna and Orlando. He told Bella she should do the talking when the trunk call came through.

When they finally spoke that evening, Verna was predictably hysterical. She wanted a blow by blow account of the marriage ceremony. Where was it held? What did Bella wear? Who were present? What was Braganza House like? How many servants did it have? Did Julio manage to come from the seminary?

Verna practically shouted into the mouth-piece. 'I don't understand. What do you mean by saying Julio has left the seminary for good?...What?...How can he do such a thing?... Who gave him permission? I suspect Marco is behind all this...

I'm going to write to the Archbishop and the Fathers at Rachol... You children will be the death of me...Here, your father wants to talk to Julio...'

Orlando sounded grim. 'Julio, can you hear me?...Yes, I'm alright. Now listen. Sending you to the seminary was your mother's idea. I'm not surprised you were unhappy there. But why have you chosen architecture, an uncertain profession to say the least? You could return to Delhi and eventually take over Braganza & Sons from me. Everything laid on—premises, housing, a fully-stocked showroom, a long list of regular clients, the goodwill of very important people including Viceroy Linlithgow. You could carry on a family tradition that goes back two hundred years... I'm sorry, will you repeat what you said?...You are not interested in pianos? But you've grown up with them all your life...What?... Well, if you have made up your mind, I'll finance your studies. When you get to Bombay let me know how much you need and to whom I should send the money. Your Mr Batley must be a saint. Now say hello to your mother.'

'Julio?...Talk louder! I can hardly hear you. You have a sore throat? I'll pray God forgives you for what you have done. This is the worst betrayal possible. Who will keep an eye on you in Bombay? It's a wicked city. I have a distant cousin there, Sister Celia, who teaches in a convent. I'll contact her right away.'

Julio shuddered and handed the phone to Bella who repeated her account of the marriage ceremony and described the newly-renovated Braganza House in graphic detail. When she got to the subject of antique furniture the phone went dead. Marco was relieved that all the uncomfortable talk was over.

Julio rang Batley that very night and confirmed his desire to go to Bombay the next day. He told Batley that he had spoken to his parents in Delhi. His father would pay his expenses at the J.J. so there was no need for a scholarship.

'Well done, lad! You'll make a fine architect—but remember the education takes five years, followed by an apprenticeship of two to three years. And several years of struggle before you earn a decent living. It's something like preparing for the priesthood, a subject you know a good deal about. Have an early lunch tomorrow and get Mr Braganza to drop you off at my hotel at three. I'd pick you up from Saligao but I have an important conference at eleven...I'm not one for long teary farewells, so there is no need for Mrs Braganza to see you off at the dock. Don't forget your sketchbooks. They are your passport for admission to the J.J. So I'm looking forward to meeting you at three. Remember, three sharp. If by any chance I'm delayed, wait for me in the foyer. The steamer departs at five. We'll spend the night on it. Will this be your first experience of a boat? There's plenty to sketch...Give my regards to your sister and to Mr Braganza. Good night.'

The next day, Julio was all packed and ready to leave by noon. Marco handed him four hundred rupees to tide him over until Orlando worked out a regular system for transmitting funds to Bombay. They had lunch and went upstairs to check on Chico. He was dancing to music from the *Nutcracker Suite*. Chico had been transformed from an untidy bundle on the floor to a striking ballet dancer, swirling around the room. He waved at them. Bella's face relaxed at last.

She had decided that very morning that she would go into Panjim to have eight dresses altered and some new ones made at Couto's, the ladies' tailors. The plan was to drop Julio off at Mr Batley's hotel, proceed to Panjim's finest cloth shop Waglo and then to the tailors. While she was doing all this, Marco would visit Police Headquarters to chat with his erstwhile colleagues. Bella did not want him around her.

All went according to plan. Up to a point. Mr Batley was waiting in the hotel foyer when Julio arrived at 2.45 p.m. Hellos and goodbyes were said in a business-like manner. Julio's luggage was transferred from the Studebaker to Batley's waiting taxicab. The famous architect believed in punctuality. He and Julio drove off on the dot of three, heading for the port at Vasco. Marco's car departed from the hotel shortly after.

The traffic was quite heavy despite it being siesta time. Marco was driving, one security guard in front beside him. Another guard sat in the rear, next to Bella. Suddenly, some miscreant threw a brick into the car, hitting the guard who was sitting in front. Marco braked. A crowd gathered. The guard screamed, 'My eyes! My eyes!' Two traffic policemen rushed over and soon cleared a passage for the car to rush away to the hospital. The injured guard clutched his right eye and his right cheek which was cut wide open. His forehead on the right side had a long gash. He bled profusely. At the hospital, given Marco's former position, the guard received every possible attention but the doctors could not save his eye. He was stitched up and sedated heavily. The police from headquarters arrived in force. Bella and Marco and the second guard recorded statements.

In a typical case of over-reaction, the new Chief Commissioner, Bernardo Cabral, ordered two jeeps packed with policemen to accompany Marco and Bella home. The tailor was forgotten. Bella was quite shattered by the incident. Marco was silent. Midway through the journey she said, 'Say something for heaven's sake.' Marco turned to her and whispered, 'The brick was meant for me.'

'But Marco, how can you be so sure? The brick hit the guard, not you. Wasn't it something spontaneous?'

'Oh, I'm sure alright. What he—or they—had not bargained for is that our car is left-hand drive and I was driving in civilian clothes. The guard, in uniform, was sitting on the right side. They naturally mistook him for me, as most cars here in Goa are right-hand drive. It takes considerable strength and skill to lob a brick through the open window of a moving car...I think the attack was spontaneous. They could not have known the route I was going to take. I'm supposed to inform Headquarters each time I leave Saligao, giving details of my planned movements, but I forgot to do so this morning. The high level of security will last as long as the so-called "freedom movement" remains violent...As I've said before, we must put up with it. I have to accept that I'm a hated figure in certain circles. We'll go to the tailors tomorrow in a police car.'

The new Police Commissioner thought that the green

Studebaker was too conspicuous, too flashy, too one of a kind. He stationed an ordinary black Hillman at Braganza House to be used by Marco and family. A police driver came with it. In one corner of the back garden, six canvas tents went up to house additional guards. There they cooked and washed, and sang Konkani songs to while away the largely idle hours.

~

In the months that followed, four developments were important from Bella's point of view: she acquired a resuscitated wardrobe along with a dozen new dresses; her relationship with Chico improved to the point that he actually smiled at her and shook her hand; Julio had settled into a hostel room at the J.J. School and liked his roommate, a diminutive Parsi boy by the name of Russi Patel; and lastly, a world war had started. Portugal—and thus Goa—remained neutral. But imports were down to a trickle, and prices shot up.

Marco kept himself busy by being driven to the Candolim beach at seven every morning. He swam for a couple of hours and returned for a late breakfast. He loved swimming in the sea and would venture far beyond the breakers; he was strong enough to brave the most powerful of undercurrents. On one of these excursions he thought it would be a good idea to build a large swimming pool at Braganza House which was about three miles from the sea. The hotel guests would appreciate swimming closer. He noted this idea down on his list of issues to be discussed with Batley when they spoke next. Also the matter of additional permanent quarters for the guards. He feared that he and Bella would need heavy security for many years. When the police were no longer necessary, the quarters could be used by the hotel staff.

On the domestic front, Bella decided that Chico needed fresh air—that he should go for a walk in the beautiful grounds in the morning and evening. Marco refused to allow this at first.

'He will simply run away and get lost. How would we find him? He can run for ten miles at a stretch—you know how athletic his dancing has made him. No, Bella, it is out of the question.'

Over the next few days, Bella and Marco argued back and forth in their first ever tiff. Then Marco came up with an idea that addressed both their concerns.

'We could fit Inas and Chico out with handcuffs—the police kind. One locked around Inas's right wrist and the other on Chico's left. Running away won't be easy then. Inas is taller than Chico and sturdily built. I'll get one of the guards to accompany them as an added precaution.'

'Is there no other way, Marco? The poor boy—remember he is my stepson now—has a right to see gardens, flowers, trees, birds and clouds in the sky...What you suggest is quite cruel. But if it's the only way, let's try it. Make the arrangements and brief Inas carefully. No force should be used. I'll explain things to Chico, though I never know whether he has understood me clearly. Better me than you. Chico is afraid of you and trusts only Inas. The walks will also help him adjust to normal clothes. Please send for a tailor from Panjim. Chico shouldn't walk around in his ballerina costumes. We would be the laughing stock of the village!'

Chico took to all these ideas with enthusiasm. He thought the handcuffs were items of jewellery. The new clothes were not too much of an ordeal. The first walk went off well. A guard kept pace three yards behind. Bella and Marco followed at a discreet distance. It was a pleasant day. They satisfied themselves that the plan was working. Some mornings Marco, Chico and Inas were driven to the beach where the boy sang la-la-las into the sea breeze. He hoped his beloved Juliet would hear him all the way in Italy. The characters in the ballets he danced were his friends, lovers and enemies. Each one of them was fleshed out in his vivid imagination. Each story was his own invention.

Things were going so well that Marco decided the two handcuffs could be separated by an eight-foot long chain. This would permit greater flexibility and allow Chico to wander off the paths a bit. After about a month of such outings with Inas, Chico began to resent the handcuffs and the chain. He had observed young people walking free on the village roads and playing football on the school grounds. He signalled he did not want the guard to follow them. Marco removed the guard. But Chico had grown increasingly hostile towards Inas also. This created many difficulties as Inas was Chico's principal caregiver—in effect, his jailer.

One evening they walked to the Mae de Deus parish church which had been built in the Gothic style some seventy years earlier. When they passed the little porch, Chico wanted to go in but Inas refused to let him. There was a tug-of-war. Chico attacked Inas with heavy blows to his head. Inas fell down in a faint. Then Chico, in a rage, wrapped the chain around Inas's neck and strangled him with it. He then sat down on the floor and wept. Then howled. Then screamed.

He was found in that condition by Father Baretto, the parish priest who had come early to the church to prepare for the evening Mass. Mrs Souza, Francis's grandmother, was the next to arrive. She kindly offered to rush home and ring up Marco. Father Baretto satisfied himself that Inas was really dead. Other parishioners arrived and there were several cries of horror.

All this while Chico—who had stopped screaming—sat on the ground with his eyes closed. He was breathing heavily. He got up presently and searched Inas's clothes for the handcuff key. He knew it had to be on Inas's body somewhere. He couldn't find it in any of the pockets. Those gathered in the church were too afraid of Chico to prevent him from dragging the body to the open lawn in front of the church. He looked for the key again, found it and unlocked the handcuff on his left wrist. He had watched Inas do this every day since their walks began and so was sure of the procedure. Then Chico began to run. He had no particular destination in mind. Father Baretto tried to follow him but soon lost sight of the boy.

Marco arrived at the church with his usual complement of guards. He quickly summed up the situation: his son was a murderer. Marco dreaded what lay ahead. Detention, framing of charges, trial and punishment. He would need to use every loophole in the law to prevent Chico from being imprisoned. The main problem was that there were a large number of witnesses.

Marco had his police guards load Inas's body into his Jeep. He examined the church porch, looking for any possible useful evidence. He traced the path Chico had taken when dragging Inas's body out to the lawn. All this was done in a hurry. He left two policemen behind in the church compound. Marco had rarely been as alarmed as he was then. Chico had to be found. He asked his driver where he had driven Chico before.

'Sir, the beach at Candolim, sir. We have been there several times. So Chico knows the way. Perhaps, sir would like to check there first, sir.'

'That's a good idea. Radio headquarters for reinforcements. It's a long beach. We'll need several men to search it thoroughly. Just swing by Braganza House. It'll take a minute to unload Inas's body. Now hurry, and drive carefully.'

Marco as well as the police reinforcements reached the beach in ten minutes. They fanned out in both directions and began the search, calling out Chico's name. He could not be found. Then Marco noticed something large shimmering in the sea not too far away. He quickly stripped down to his underwear and swam out to the floating object. Then he cried out and was soon joined by two fully-dressed policemen.

Marco tried every technique he knew to resuscitate Chico. The boy had a smile on his lips. His left hand grasped something tightly. Marco prised his fingers open and found the key to the handcuffs.

The new Chief Commissioner was a stickler for rules and regulations. Two deaths under suspicious circumstances. The bodies were moved to the morgue at the hospital in Panjim. Post mortems were performed. Father Baretto, Mrs Souza and the various policemen involved were questioned. Marco was interrogated on three different occasions, embarrassing times for the new Commissioner. Lengthy reports were prepared. Chico's body was finally released and buried in Marco's ancestral graveyard in Canacona. This after much persuasion on Marco's part. His brothers were reluctant to allow a funeral Mass to be held in the chapel their father Telo had built twenty years earlier.

The three brothers were barely on speaking terms with Marco. They'd had to cough up one-quarter of the total value of their estate to finance Marco's purchase of Braganza House. Their parents, Octavia and Telo, had already made a big mistake selling half the original estate to fund Uncle Francisco's emigration to Lisbon...Marco's brothers did not even attend the funeral.

Inas's body lay in the mortuary for several days as no one knew his wife's address. The last Marco had heard of her was that she had run off with her children to Bombay along with a Hindu cook. This had happened some twelve years earlier. So Inacio Gomes was buried in Panjim and arrangements were made for a simple gravestone.

Ten days passed after the deaths. Marco and Bella had hardly spoken to one another, neither daring to be the first to complain or apportion blame. Then Marco fired the first salvo.

'I know you meant well, but those wretched walks were *your* idea. I warned you that Chico would run away.'

Bella bristled. 'The terrible handcuffs were *your* idea, Marco. Imagine treating your own son as you would a common criminal!'

'We agreed on the compromise,' said Marco, 'don't pretend otherwise. We both felt quite at ease with the arrangement at the time. Chico did not seem to mind very much.'

'Not mind? I could tell he felt very restricted. The long chain was also your idea. I would have felt more comfortable with a much shorter chain. One of your hefty policemen should have taken Chico for walks, not poor Inas.'

And so the bitter argument went on and on until Bella suddenly decided that enough was enough. She locked herself in the bedroom, went to the toilet and vomited into the water closet. Such episodes had occurred four or five times over the past two weeks. As she had also missed her period, Bella thought she might be pregnant. But she decided to keep the matter to herself.

Marco kept himself busy supervising the construction work at Braganza House. There was a lot left to do. He rang up Batley from time to time when the blueprints were not too clear on how certain materials were to be joined together. Batley reported that

Julio was doing very well in his classes. 'He's the brightest in his batch. He and his Parsi roommate Russi have become the best of friends. I do a lot of work for the Parsi community in Bombay. They are enlightened people. Forward thinking...Now to the main purpose of this chat. I'll send you some enlargements of drawing number eighteen. The details will be clear on those.'

One evening, a week after their arguments had stopped, Bella and Marco were discussing plans for the hotel they would run together. There would be twelve guest rooms. More if Bella agreed to reduce their private quarters. Bella smiled and said, 'We will need a nursery next to our bedroom, Marco.'

Like many men who had spent the greater portion of their lives in uniform, Marco was not blessed with a vivid imagination. He didn't get the hint. 'Why do you want a nursery there? Isn't that where you put babies?' Bella stepped across the room and placed his hands on her belly.

'Oh, you silly goat, we *are* going to have a baby! I've started playing Chico's records to it—I read somewhere that one should listen to music for an hour each day. It's supposed to be good for the baby in the womb. So Marco, dear Marco, we are going to be three again soon.'

Marco was still grieving for Chico. When it finally registered that he was to be a father again, he fell silent.

'Come on now, dear husband. Aren't you thrilled by my news? We'll have such fun teaching the little one how to play hide-and-seek in this big house of ours.'

Marco's face relaxed, though he kept staring at his notepad. Then he put his arms around Bella and simply said, 'I'm going to have to write a new will.'

9
Hailey Road

Orlando and Verna were sitting on the veranda of their Connaught Place flat in New Delhi. The gardens in the centre of the crescent were flourishing. Much of the construction work in the grand market had been completed. The arcades were bustling with activity. It was six o'clock in the evening. Orlando had completed his day's work at the showroom below. He had brought up a handful of letters to read. A few of them were thank-you notes from clients who expressed their deep appreciation of the excellent job he had done tuning their pianos. Then he recognized a letter from Goa—the stamps were distinctive.

'Verna, there's a letter from Bella. I hope it doesn't contain any bad news. Here, you read it first.'

'No, *you* go through it and tell me the main points. I've never been able to read that girl's handwriting...Come on, what are you waiting for!'

Orlando polished his spectacles with a handkerchief. 'Well, here goes. Darling Mummy and Daddy, etcetera, etcetera...She says she and Marco have had a bereavement: his son drowned on the beach at Candolim...Hmmm...She has had some new clothes made by a good ladies' tailor in Panjim...Braganza House is now in full repair and looks majestic...They plan to open a hotel there soon. You and I should visit. We would love the place and its extensive gardens and grounds—'

'—I hate trains,' Verna said. 'Couldn't we fly? When should we go? It's too bad about that boy of Marco's...I suppose it's just as well. He had no future that I could see. What's next?'

'It's all about Julio and his studies in Bombay. His teachers think very highly of him…He has a Parsi roommate in the hostel… He still hasn't told me whether I'm transferring enough money to him in Bombay…Oh, Verna, listen to this: Bella is expecting! The child is due in six months. She hopes the news will make us happy…Well, what do you think of that?! Our first grandchild! I'm thrilled. Aren't you?'

Verna frowned. 'Bella must come to Delhi for the confinement. I wouldn't trust the doctors in Goa. The Lady Hardinge Hospital here is quite dependable in simple cases. Orlando, you'd better inform the Calcutta people. I think this will be the first birth in the family for over two decades. Rachel and Emilio will be very happy. Their first great-grandchild…I wish Maria was with us. She'd be a great help with the birth and stitching baby clothes.'

'Not so fast, Verna. There is a long way to go. As for Maria, she is happy in Almora, studying contemporary dance with that Shankar fellow. Did I tell you there was a long piece on him in *The Statesman* the other day? He's considered a creative genius. Maria is in good hands. You must read her letters to us. She has two good friends, Zohra and Simki—who is some kind of European, I gather.'

'She should have become a nun, Orlando. One—at least one—of our children should have taken the vows. But you overruled me. Now we have lost all three. Will Julio come home for his holidays? He could at least do that…I'm not a monster, Orlando.'

That same evening Orlando placed a trunk-call to Bella in Saligao. It came through surprisingly quickly. Marco picked up the receiver. Orlando introduced himself and offered his condolences, followed by his congratulations. Then Marco handed the phone to Bella and Orlando handed his receiver to Verna. Mother and daughter had a long, reasonably amicable conversation. It was mostly about Braganza House, avoiding the lifting of heavy objects and preventing constipation. Bella then said she wanted a last word with her father.

'Daddy, I've located a Steinway grand for sale in Panjim.

They want six thousand for it. Is that reasonable? And I want you to come and tune it. The tuners here don't seem up to much…What?…I should wait till you come and not make any commitment to buy? But when will that be?…Everything except the gardens will be in ship-shape in four months. Marco works very hard at it—but then he has hardly anything else to do. The post-retirement job with the Dempos, who owned this place before us, has not come through. In the hot afternoons Marco retreats to his study and goes through his cartons of papers. His room is off-limits to everyone else…I need a posh piano in the grand reception hall to give the place some class. I will play it myself, and perhaps hold musical soirees from time to time. I miss the sound of pianos being played…Well, that's enough for now. This phone call will cost an arm and a leg. Goodbye. I love you both.'

The next day a long letter came from Maria. Her guru, Uday Shankar, was bringing his troupe of dancers to Delhi for three performances at the Regal Theatre in Connaught Place. Six young women and four young men constituted the troupe. Shankar would be dancing too. After Delhi the troupe would travel to Bombay, Madras and Calcutta.

Shankar was desperately short of funds. He was on the verge of closing down his dance academy in the hills of Almora. He was no longer young and could barely perform some of the modern dances he had choreographed. Amala, his wife, had just given birth to a son and so had taken a rest from dancing.

Some members of the troupe had drifted away. Maria, Simki, Zohra and Boris formed the core group of those who remained. Maria Braganza and Boris Benkovsky performed exquisite duets and were growing increasingly close to each other—closer than a professional relationship warranted.

Orlando bought tickets for the first show well in advance. He had no idea what to expect from what the newspapers advertised as 'Modern Creative Dance'. A blend of Indian classical dance forms and Western ballet techniques did not sound very promising to him. But *The Statesman* also referred to Uday Shankar as the creator of 'high dance', whatever that meant.

Then, while bombs were being dropped all over Europe, Delhi audiences were mesmerized by Uday Shankar's performances. There were a large number of American soldiers in the audiences who broke into wild applause, whistling and clapping and hooting at inappropriate moments. The three performances were completely sold out. Uday even made a neat profit because the troupe's hotel and other local expenses were entirely paid for by the wife of a prominent Delhi industrialist. She fancied herself a promoter of the arts. She had attended Bharatnatyam classes as a child of six and, as a consequence, claimed to be an expert in that dance form.

The day before the troupe's departure for Bombay, Maria brought Boris Benkovsky to meet Orlando and Verna. Orlando was struck by his daughter's beauty. Every one of her movements was graceful—from how she sat down in a chair to how she walked to the bar to pour drinks. Boris, originally from Poland, was tall and extremely well-built, with a handsome face and dimples when he smiled. He smiled a lot, for his English was not too fluent. You could tell he was a fine acrobat who had taken up ballet and now modern dance.

Verna was keen to offer the young couple something to eat. There seemed to be nothing in the flat that could be served as a snack. Not even what the Americans called 'peanuts.' She left the living-room and went to the kitchen, and ordered the young bearer to hurry to Pearey Lal's halwai and bring back a dozen deep-fried samosas. They had been Maria's favourite snack as a teenager. Verna yelled after the bearer, 'They should be fresh and crisp. No chillies. Have them fried in front of you.'

When Verna returned, she found Orlando telling Maria all about the property on Hailey Road. He reminded Maria she was the owner of one of the four flats. He had rented her flat to Krishan Lal, their old driver, whose motor garage in the middle circle of Connaught Place was prospering. Krishan Lal had wanted to rent a proper home in New Delhi for quite some time but landlords were snobbish and did not approve of his antecedents. He had turned to Orlando as a last resort and was relieved when Orlando agreed to rent him a ground floor flat for a hundred and fifty rupees a month.

~

The flat above Krishan Lal's was rented to the senior Maharani of Sandawa, a princely state in Rajasthan. She had been abandoned by the Maharaja in 1942, along with her three daughters. The Maharaja had run off to the French Riviera with a junior maharani, a tempestuous Hungarian opera singer. This left two other wives who were quite content to live in the fort palace in Sandawa. At least they hadn't been expelled—despite the fact that both had 'no issue,' as the expression goes.

On the other side of the driveway separating the two blocks of flats, there were two units, one above the other. The upper flat had been rented to a family in which the father was a Muslim named Muzaffar Imam and the mother a German lady by the name of Magda. She ran a small school named Ramniketan on the premises. They had a son and a troublesome daughter.

The ground floor of the unit was rented to a sardarji, Dalbir Singh, an electrical engineer who had made his pile during the construction of New Delhi. He had two wives, which was perfectly legal in those days. But the two sardarnis screamed at each other all day. The elder wife had a son but the younger wife was prettier.

Maria was fascinated by Orlando's account of the tenants but asked what the hurry had been to rent out the flats.

'The government has become very active in commandeering all vacant accommodation in New Delhi. The huge military and civilian presence in Delhi needs to be housed. The Americans arrived in droves after the U.S. joined the war. Several messes and barracks are being built in all the empty plots. Temporary construction, they call it. These include barracks on large plots left vacant by the maharajas who have dragged their feet over constructing their palaces…Barracks, barracks everywhere, and prices of everything have shot up…Maria, if anything were to happen to me, remember that your tenant is supposed to see to all repairs and maintenance—to be adjusted against rent payable. I'm too busy to go running after plumbers and electricians... Boris, do finish up that last samosa. Come and meet Allegro. He'd love to talk to you. His new cage is in the veranda and is large enough for him to exercise his arthritic wings. He loves to watch the traffic go by below. In summer he has an electric fan to himself. Talk loudly, as the old fellow is a bit hard of hearing.'

So Maria introduced Boris and told Allegro about her dancing career. She was full of praise for her guru Uday Shankar and his wife Amala.

Allegro cleared his throat. 'Ah, yes! Dancing. A good form of exercise. Never tried it myself. Involves fractures and sprains, I believe. Easy to injure yourself. You be careful, little Maria... Boris, you are a fine-looking young man with a nice name—'Benkovsky.' From the name I gather you're from Poland. From the way you and Maria look at each other, I conclude you have become intimate and are engaged to be married. Yes? You can tell me—I'm not a prude.'

Maria said, 'Shush, not so loud—Mummy will hear. We'll make firm plans after the war is over.'

Allegro continued. 'I've lived through dozens of small and big wars. They are a terrible waste of human and material resources. A terrible waste. The Germans and Japanese are asking for trouble. The Americans joining in will make a big difference...What? Can you please speak a little louder?...Yes, I'm well informed about the war because your father reads out the newspaper headlines to me every morning. *The Statesman* has a new office and printing press on the outer circle. I'm too stiff to be carted down to the car and driven around so I have no way of knowing what all the new buildings look like. Except when Orlando or Verna bother to describe them to me or show me photographs...A marvellous invention, that! I remember seeing the earliest versions of photo images about a hundred years ago. Put many portrait and landscape painters out of business. And I hear there is colour photography now! What will they think of next? A spaceship destined to carry on travelling indefinitely beyond the universe? Within it could be Hitler, Salazar, Franco, Tojo, Mussolini and all the other rascals from Europe and Japan! If only your great-grandfather were alive, he would think up a way to stop this awful war.'

Boris was struck dumb by the magnificent spectacle of Allegro. He could scarcely believe his eyes and ears. He had a sudden vision of Allegro perched on a throne in the centre of a stage. The giant bird was reciting poetry from many cultures while the Uday Shankar troupe danced a specially-composed ballet around the throne. There was no music. Just the voice of Allegro, rising and falling.

Verna came out to the veranda and called Maria inside. Meanwhile Boris made hesitant conversation with Allegro who told him the history of the Braganza family, going back to the Bandel days.

Verna told Maria about Julio in Bombay and gave her the news from Bella in Saligao. Maria exclaimed, 'So many strings, Mummy! Lynne in Shillong, the Calcutta clan, the Goa relatives, the Bombay connection, and all of you in Delhi. We seem to be typical Goans, spread out all over the country…I'll be travelling a lot with the troupe. We may even go to Europe if we find a generous sponsor. I'll send you postcards from all the interesting places.'

~

Bella and Marco finally opened their 'grand hotel.' It was a great success, with full occupancy throughout the year. The tariffs were quite steep—amongst the highest charged anywhere in Goa. They had a very competent Hindu manager, Giridhar, who lived on the premises and spoke fluent Portuguese. Bella's little son was now five years old. They had named him Caetano—Tonio for short. Marco taught him to swim at an early age. The child loved splashing around in the new swimming pool and was a great hit with the ladies.

The freedom struggle in Goa entered a non-violent phase. Intelligence sources assured Marco that it was now safe to move around in his Studebaker. So he would take groups of up to four on sight-seeing tours, mainly to the majestic churches in Velha Goa and Panjim. The guests who were interested in the sea would sometimes accompany Marco to Candolim on his early morning swims. No extra charge for this service. Life could not have been more pleasant.

Then, early one morning, a terrible thing happened. Marco was swimming far out beyond the breakers as usual. He developed multiple muscle cramps and waved frantically to the two guards and three hotel guests walking along the beach. They didn't notice him. He sank like a stone. Much later, after his body was towed ashore, efforts at resuscitation failed. Marco was dead. And Bella became the sole mistress of Braganza House.

The funeral in Marco's ancestral village of Canacona was widely attended. The Governor sent a wreath of white roses. There was strong representation of the police force. Tonio wept profusely when Bella told him he would not see Marco again for some time as he had gone to visit Heaven, which was far away. So far that it would take fifty years to get there and fifty years to get back. Tonio could only count to ten on his little fingers. Bella wore a black gown and a black veil borrowed from old Mrs Souza, relics of the days when she herself had been a slim young widow.

When things had settled down at Braganza House, Bella placed a trunk call to Orlando in Delhi. She gave her parents the sad news and reiterated what she had been telling them for years: she couldn't travel to Delhi now that there was a hotel to run. They should come to Saligao instead, in the mild winter season. This would get them away from the freezing temperatures of Delhi at that time of year. Orlando was doubtful whether it would be possible.

'Eric O'Brien has been called away to Calcutta by your grandfather. Emilio is ninety now and cannot continue to run Braganza & Sons. Eric is to help him wind up the business. The other option is for me to run it long distance from here and travel to and fro. At my age that might be difficult...I'll see if your mother can be persuaded to travel to Goa on her own. In any case, without Eric here it would be impossible for me to get away. It's a shame I have never been to the land of my forefathers... Here, say hello to your mother.'

The heated argument with Verna took place along predictable lines. Bella should never have married a man over twenty years her senior. Why did Marco have to swim in the sea when there was a large swimming pool at home? Why was Bella running a hotel when she was trained to be a translator? Why hadn't Bella sent recent photographs of Verna's only grandson? This was cruel of her. Why hadn't Bella reacted to news of Maria's scandalous relationship with a Polish dancer? They were roaming around the big cities of India, living together in sin...Verna complained that her children would send her to an early grave. She had given birth to a widow, a harlot, and a son who had been expelled from a seminary...No, she couldn't come to Goa on her own. She had been to Simla once and the train ride had made her nauseous.

~

In the meanwhile, things had not been going at all well on Hailey Road. The tenants had been complaining about each other almost every day. Krishan Lal felt really exploited by the Maharani living above him. She would summon him for every minor plumbing or electrical problem. Even to replace fused light bulbs. When Krishan Lal protested, she would scream in English: 'You bastard! Our landlord promised me you would attend to all repairs. *All* of them...Now see to them or I'll have you thrown out of your flat. Imagine having to live my days at the mercy of a greasy mechanic!'

On the other side of the driveway, Sardar Dalbir Singh complained bitterly about the Imams above him. The nursery school run by Magda was very noisy—from eight to one every day. Dalbir found the squealing of little children very tiresome. And then there was the thump-thump-thumpety-thump from the upstairs courtyard when the children stomped around during Kathak classes. And all the time there were the sounds of little chairs and tables being dragged along the floor...Dalbir tried to reason with Magda while her husband stood by.

'Perhaps you are not aware, Mrs Imam, that it is illegal to run a school in residential premises? You are having a full-fledged tamasha ghar up there. So much commotion, so much hulla-gulla.'

'Sardarji,' said Magda, 'perhaps you and I should exchange flats. *You* go upstairs and I'll come down...And what about the noises coming from *your* workshop—your good-for-nothing son seems to tinker around all day fabricating nonsense! At least the sounds my children make are sounds of joy and enthusiasm for all the creative activities I and my teachers arrange for them. Your son's noises are those of a bloody factory...My offer stands. We can exchange flats. I'm sure Mr Braganza won't object.'

Muzaffar Imam intervened. 'Sardarji got here first, Magda, four months before we moved from Daryaganj. His flat has two extra rooms and a garden, so the rent is much higher too. Just get the children to be less noisy. Avoid teaching them Kathak. And show them how to lift tables and chairs into place without scraping them along the floor...In these troubled times we have to learn to live in harmony.'

~

Mr Imam was a mechanical engineer trained in Germany. His brother, Jamal Imam, was an electrical engineer, also trained in Germany. Germany was the preferred location for studies in many fields: philosophy, sociology, archaeology, the sciences and, most popular of all, various branches of engineering. In the 'twenties and 'thirties, many Indian students went to Germany to study engineering. While studying in Munich, the two brothers had fallen in love with two sisters: Magda and Roma. Several Indians married local girls and brought them out to India. Some of the mixed couples emigrated to America and Canada.

Jamal and Roma went to New York, where they settled down in Queens. Muzaffar and Magda came to Delhi, where they moved into the family house in Daryaganj. Muzaffar got down to work right away. He invented what he called the 'Desert Cooler.' This was a metal cabinet with straw pads attached on three sides ventilated with slats. Water was pumped up and trickled down through the pads, cooling the air inside the cabinet—the cooling effect of evaporation. A powerful fan on the fourth side drew the cooled air and blew it into the room. Muzaffar's invention was an instant success with middle-class families who couldn't afford to get away to the hills in the summers. His family owned a large warehouse in Daryaganj. Muzaffar converted this into a Desert Cooler factory. He also manufactured slotted steel bookcases. He was happy.

But Magda wasn't. The Europeans and missionaries had moved out of Daryaganj to Civil Lines and some to New Delhi. Her children, Bilal and Laila, were bored with the place. The little school Magda ran in Daryaganj was a modest affair with just eleven children, including two of her own.

Muzaffar was a good father. He would take the children up to the ramparts of the walled city, the section that bordered Daryaganj on its eastern side. From there he would point out the river, trees, birds and boats. And they would watch dhobies wash and dry yards and yards of freshly-dyed cloth along the banks of the Jamuna. At other times, when the circus was in town, they would stroll across to the big maidan between the Red Fort and Jama Masjid. Muzaffar bought only the most expensive tickets, and the clowns sometimes clambered over the ring and sat the children on their laps, talking gibberish all the while. But Bilal and Laila soon tired of these outings. They wanted to experience Connaught Place, Central Vista, the Ridge Forest and other grand spaces in the new city. This is why the family had moved to Hailey Road.

~

Magda was very disappointed in her daughter Laila. From an early age she had stubbornly refused to learn how to spell. The child's logic was simple: you should spell it the way you heard it. Thus, for example, 'what' became 'wot,' 'you' was simply 'u,' and 'heard' was 'herd.' Laila was a great experimenter. She often spelled the same word three different ways. No Delhi school was willing to admit her.

Magda's sister Roma in New York had no children. She offered to care for Laila. She and her husband were sure they would find a school there for children with special needs. New York had everything. Laila's only pronounced gift was that she was a good painter of flowers and animals. In New York she could be sent to art classes. Roma promised to care for Laila as if she were her own child.

Muzaffar was not enthusiastic about losing his only daughter to his brother and sister-in-law. He raised several objections on the lines of: 'She can become an artist here in Delhi. Why go all the way to New York, a dangerous place?'

'Muzzi, you've been to art shows here. The artists are stuck in the nineteenth century. There are only a handful in Bombay who are aware of the modern movements in Europe and America. If Laila is to make a living as an artist, she must be exposed to the new currents in art. Paris and New York are the only places this can happen...I've arranged for Laila's travel to New York. Reverend Billy Smythe and his wife Doreen are going on home leave next month and will gladly take her. The Smythes have two children about Laila's age. They can play together on the ship. They are an American missionary family from Woodstock School in Mussoorie. He's the pastor there and thoroughly reliable. Now there is no time to be lost. Get a passport and the necessary travel documents ready...We mustn't miss this opportunity. Laila has already wasted too many years of her life here.'

When Magda and Muzaffar finally moved into the Hailey Road flat some years later, Laila was happily settled in New York, their son Bilal was thrilled to have a room all to himself, and Ramniketan (relocated from Daryaganj) had twenty children enrolled. All were children of parents who valued creativity over high marks in exams.

Modern School (also relocated from Daryaganj) was a short walk away from Hailey Road. Because of the good reputation of Magda's school, her older pupils were invariably admitted to Modern at the age of eight or nine (all except Laila).

In 1945 Magda decided her students needed contact with live animals. She acquired a dog, a cat, a spotted deer, a peacock and a monkey. They lived together harmoniously in the courtyard terrace, except that the monkey was impossible to discipline. He would crap all over the place. But he was very popular with the children, who called him Natkhat Singh.

That Christmas, Magda erected a real pine tree in her all-purpose living-room, and lit it with real wax candles. At the height of the Christmas party, the tree caught fire. There was a big commotion. Buckets of water were rushed from the two bathrooms. This was the last straw for Muzaffar. First the smelly animals and then the fire. He and Magda stopped talking to each other. For good. The silence between them was a puzzle to all their students, teachers and friends.

Muzaffar left the flat at seven every morning after making himself a cup of tea. He walked all the way to Daryaganj—some four miles—and spent the rest of the day in the Desert Cooler factory. He sent out for breakfast and lunch. His invention was widely copied by other fabricators in the Old City. He had seen no need to apply for a patent, and was wary of lawsuits. The competition was able to market their coolers at half his price. Muzaffar inserted notices in the local papers, warning prospective customers of being duped by counterfeit goods. He had a German-bred admiration for perfection and high quality. Muzaffar would not compromise on the quality of materials used in his Desert Coolers. As a result, his sales went down significantly.

At seven in the evening he took the bus back home and waited for Magda to ring the bell summoning him to dinner. Bread and soup were served. Always bread and soup. Not a word was spoken.

At around this time—though friends claimed it happened much earlier—Magda began to take a deep interest in things spiritual. The flat in Hailey Road became a gathering place for all species of Gurus, Saints and Holy Men (and a few Holy Women) of diverse faiths who came by in the evenings and chatted with her over tea and a prodigious quantity of biscuits. This activity peaked in the pleasant winter months. When the weather grew warmer, the visitors returned to their monasteries and ashrams in the cool hills of Kangra, Almora, Rishikesh, etcetera. The holy men and women were all 'characters in their own right', as Magda used to say occasionally. A few of them used to wander into Muzaffar's room at the end of the veranda and attempt to have spiritual conversations with him—without much luck, as Muzaffar was a staunch rationalist. He was polite but not receptive.

And then there were the Artists, Actors, Writers and Poets who were drawn to Magda. She ran a veritable salon from four-thirty to seven each evening. The spiritual friends interacted with the artistic types. College students often dropped in. It was all very interesting. Auntie Magda was a hit.

~

The Maharani next door, called Kitty by her social equals, was in the habit of dropping in on Magda unannounced. Her three daughters studied at the Mayo School for Girls in Ajmer. During vacations she would bring them over to Magda's to pet the animals. Delhi had no zoo then. Magda felt sorry for Kitty and suggested she learn to play the neglected dust-laden grand piano, the one Kitty had transported from the Sandawa Palace when her husband had sent her into exile. The piano would give her and her idle daughters something to do. Orlando came by and pronounced it would take several days and many hundreds of rupees to repair the out-of-tune instrument. Kitty agreed to the repairs but said she'd be able to pay only the next month when the Dewan of Sandawa deposited her measly allowance into her bank account.

Orlando arranged for a piano tutor to teach this offshoot of the Sandawa royal family how to play simple nursery rhymes. Orlando recalled the story of how his grandfather, Antonio, had arranged for a piano teacher for the three Begums and the Nawab of Ibrahimpur. That was a long, long time ago.

When peace was declared in Europe in 1945, the Maharaja of Sandawa decided to return to India. He sold his mansion in Nice because his beloved Hungarian Maharani had abandoned him and run off with a long-haired violinist from Budapest. His Highness saw no point in extending his stay in Europe. The Hungarian Maharani saw no point in living with a relatively impoverished Maharaja who once had very generous habits. Now he could not afford to give her even simple jewellery. The violinist came from an aristocratic background and was very rich. A Count, no less.

His Highness returned to Sandawa. His two junior maharanis tried desperately to become pregnant. After several months of trying and failing, the Maharaja thought he should try his luck with Kitty in New Delhi. They hadn't slept together for six years. He knew miracles sometimes happened. Kitty was still in her thirties. He instructed his Dewan to inform Kitty that he would be at the Imperial Hotel in Delhi for a week the following month. His Highness expected the estranged Maharani to have dinner with him on the seventh, eighth and ninth. There were business matters to be discussed. Their daughters had to be married off soon. All three of them were in their teens.

Kitty became quite jittery on receiving the summons. She went across to have a word with Magda. After hearing the background, Magda tried to excuse herself from any further involvement in the matter.

'But, Auntie, what am I supposed to do? You *must* advise me. I was married off to H.H. when I was only thirteen, and had my daughters by the age of twenty. So I am still young. People say I'm beautiful...I don't know what H.H. has in mind. A formal divorce? A reconciliation? How shall I prepare myself? We haven't even spoken all these years!'

Magda tried to calm her down. 'Three grand dinners at the Imperial sound rather nice. At least you will be spared the bother of entertaining him at Hailey Road. And the expense. As for the girls, you must put your foot down. No weddings until after college.'

Kitty looked worried. 'He'll never agree to that. The Dewan told me that H.H. has already started negotiations with various princely families of Rajasthan. I was told he has prepared a shortlist of twenty boys.'

'Kitty, the three dinners in a row must be because he has three different issues to discuss. It shows he is considerate and does not wish to overwhelm you with too many matters at one sitting.'

'Auntie, I'm convinced the Dewan has a spy among my servants. I think it's the ayah. Her husband is still with the Palace at Sandawa. They are a meddlesome couple who know everything, *everything* about us. The only thing I can say in their favour is that they haven't tried to blackmail us yet. The ayah cared for me first and then for my children. It's been almost twenty years. She knows absolutely everything.'

'Don't dread the future, Kitty. It can also be full of pleasant surprises. Unpleasant ones have to be taken in your stride...Don't drink his champagne: he is bound to offer you some! You have to keep your wits about you. And look your sophisticated best. Chiffon and pearls will do. None of that heavy brocade stuff you usually wear. Only light make-up. The idea must be to look modest, to invite his sympathy. Remember, less is more—a phrase coined by an architect friend of mine. We grew up together in a small town in Germany. Mies is now famous all over the world.'

'Auntie, how should I greet him when we first meet? Should we shake hands? Should I do pranam and touch his feet? Should I permit him to kiss me?...I'm so confused and nervous.'

'Kitty, Kitty, Kitty—why must you complicate simple matters?...Let me think. You need to say something charming...I saw an American film at Regal the other day. A Western, where the heroine just said, "Howdy, Stranger!" at one point. Try that. It may break the ice. H.H. will be impressed by your cosmopolitanism!...Be off with you now. I'm expecting Swami Sachithananda any minute. I've told you all I know about how to be a classy rani.'

Kitty showed up at the Imperial at seven o'clock on the seventh of July as instructed. His Highness was waiting in the entrance lobby. He had lost a lot of weight and looked quite sporty in a white lounge suit and an elaborately-tied red turban.

'Howdy, Stranger,' Kitty said timidly.

'We're not strangers, Kitty! Have you forgotten that you are my wife and Senior Maharani? You are looking lovely! I'd almost forgotten how beautiful you are...Come upstairs to my suite. We shall be dining there. In complete privacy.'

H.H. enquired after his daughters and the old retainers who had originally served in Sandawa and then moved to Delhi with the Maharani. They talked a bit about the difficult political situation. H.H. was worried sick about what would happen to the State of Sandawa once the British left India. The Maharaja was Hindu but the majority of his subjects were Muslim. Jinnah could make a lot of trouble for him with all this talk of a separate country. The British may even hand Sandawa over to Pakistan.

All this while Kitty had been addressing her husband as 'Your Highness' this, 'Your Highness' that. It irritated him.

'For heaven's sake just call me Bobby. You used to, you know. We are a modern couple, don't you think?' Suddenly he began to kiss her hand passionately.

Dinner over, they retired to the bedroom of the hotel suite. Bobby's love-making had become sophisticated and considerate. His several liaisons in Europe had obviously taught him a thing or two. Kitty was grateful and for the first time in her life actually enjoyed the act of sex. At eleven that night she declined a third round and insisted on getting back to Hailey Road. What would the servants think? Her daughters would be curious and worried.

On the eighth and ninth of July the routine of talk–dinner–sex was repeated. Kitty was a bit troubled, however, when she finally realized that Bobby's motive was not love but a desire to get her pregnant. (His astrologer had predicted it would be a son this time.) The dates Bobby had fixed for their meetings increased her chances of becoming pregnant. Rukmini, the old ayah, must have had a hand in this by passing on intimate information regarding

Kitty's monthlies. In the beginning—on that first night—Kitty had thought Bobby had fallen passionately in love with her all over again. Now that she had seen through Bobby's strategy, she did not want to have much to do with him. But he was keen on assuaging her.

'Come back to Sandawa. To the new palace by the lake, surrounded by the mango orchards you used to love visiting. I built it for Olga but she is gone and forgotten...Complete privacy and very modern facilities.'

'Bobby, it would be a jail for me. And your two other ranis would give me no peace once they noticed I was pregnant—*if* I get pregnant. They were always jealous of my looks. You know all this...No, Delhi is where I shall stay. It is beautiful and full of exciting places to visit. Markets, parks, monuments. The people here are so much more interesting...Why don't you build a palace here? You own a five-acre plot on Kingsway. The government will take it back if you're not careful. I might consider living in such a palace as long as you keep those two bitches away from me.'

Bobby pulled a long face. 'I've already lost the plot. I received a notice that barracks are to be built on it...I could rent a large bungalow for you on Aurangzeb Road. The Jodhpurs and Alwars live there. You'd be in good company.'

'That's too far away from Connaught Place. I'd be marooned.'

'But you have the car and driver to take you wherever you want. Besides, New Delhi—the new part—is quite small.'

'You know that petrol is still rationed these days,' said Kitty. 'I don't know why I pay Salman's salary every month. There's hardly any driving for him to do. I really can't afford to keep a car...Bobby, you haven't asked me how I'm coping financially. School fees, rent, clothing, electricity and phone bills, food and salaries—'

'I was coming to that,' said Bobby apologetically. 'My Dewan informs me he sends you five thousand a month. I'll increase it to seven right away, and to ten when a son is born. From what you tell me, you are short of funds and short of space. I drove past your compound on Hailey Road the other day. The flats look very small to me. Why not get your landlord to rent you the downstairs as well? We could build an inter-connecting staircase. That way you would get at least six bedrooms. If you like, I could stay with you on my business trips to Delhi. Not that the Imperial Hotel is bad. It's a new building. But it is not a home. Think about it. It's not such a bad idea.'

'I'll think about it, Bobby. The tenant downstairs—a dirty motor mechanic—is a rascal. How to get rid of him?...Think of my plight. Having to live above a mechanic! He always stinks of grease and grime. The only consolation is the German lady next door. We have become close friends.'

Kitty and Bobby parted on fairly amicable terms at the end of his brief visit to Delhi. Bobby even visited Hailey Road briefly to bestow traditional blessings on his daughters. They had very vague memories of him.

Two days later, Kitty dropped in at Braganza & Sons in Connaught Place. When she broached the idea of combining the flats, Orlando was incensed. 'Your Highness, the flats belong to my children. They are not to be tinkered with. Besides, where would Krishan Lal and his extended family go? They have a long lease on their flat. So what you propose is out of the question. You could find more spacious accommodation elsewhere—Barakhamba Road, Sikandra Road, Curzon Road, Ferozeshah Road and so on—you have many options. It should not be difficult to find a place that is available at a reasonable rent.'

Orlando found Kitty quite exasperating. If it was not her running feuds with Krishan Lal—'mend this', 'adjust that', 'replace this', 'change that'—then it was her constant complaints about the layout of the bathrooms, minor leakages from the roof during the monsoons, and so on and so forth. Matters requiring heavy expenditures for Orlando. He regretted several times taking her on as a tenant. Verna sniffed, 'After Independence, she'll just be plain Mrs Sandawa. Not a Maharani.'

~

Julio was in town those days. He had completed his architectural studies at the J.J. School and made a trip to Delhi to meet various architects. He hoped to show them his portfolio of drawings. He met Walter George, Medd, Russell, Shoosmith, and the few Indian architects who were then in private practice in the city. They all offered him jobs but Russell had some useful advice too.

'You have to see the world, young man. Great cities such as Rome, Paris, London and New York. I have a good friend in New York, Mr Antonin Raymond. He has done some excellent work in South India. Each project a modern masterpiece. He understands light and shade like no one else. Work with him for a couple of years. Then you will be ready to return here. If you join the government, you will be able to work on project after project. After Independence the government will have to build extensively. Such opportunities are not available in private practice. You have an excellent set of references. I'll add mine to them. If you like, I'll send a telegram to Mr Raymond enquiring whether he has a vacancy in his office.' This was done that very day. Antonin Raymond sent a telegram back:

> Your young man sounds very promising. Must be one of Batley's boys. Vacancy in two months. Warn him can't pay much.

Julio was thrilled by this offer. The anxiety he had been feeling in the pit of his stomach disappeared. He now knew where he was headed in life. After New York he would return and become a government architect.

Orlando took Julio across to the property on Hailey Road. He introduced him to some of the tenants. Kitty served them pound cake and tea, and announced she hoped to give birth to a son as handsome as Julio. Krishan Lal was at his garage, and Julio remembered him well from the days when he had been their driver. Sardar Dalbir Singh and the two sardarnis were most cordial and served lassi, which it would have been impolite to refuse. Auntie Magda Imam sat them down in her veranda and ordered her cook to make them coffee. This was accompanied by coconut macaroons from Wenger's. Julio and Orlando felt quite bloated by then. Orlando had to go to the toilet. Magda showed Julio around the premises and introduced him to the animals, all of whom had catchy names drawn from Hindu mythology. When Orlando returned, looking much relieved, Magda resumed charge of the conversation.

'Julio, did your father tell you that my daughter Laila is in New York? She is quite a character. She's been with my sister since she was twelve years old. Now she is a proper artist and once sold a water-colour in Central Park for five dollars! My husband, Uncle Imam, talks to her from time to time on the telephone. Her speech is normal but not her writing! Unfortunately, she and I don't speak to each other. We have never got along. Orlando must have told you that Uncle Muzaffar and I also do not speak to each other. This has been going on for some years. So, in a way, I'm cut off from my immediate family. Except for my son Bilal who is an airline pilot with Mr Tata. He stops by now and then, but prefers to stay in a hotel because of his odd hours. You will be sorry to hear that he too doesn't talk to his father. We are a strange family, each one very egocentric, I expect…

'Here, I've written down my sister Roma's address and phone number in New York. Do be in touch with them. It will be good for Laila to meet a normal human being. My sister Roma tells me that Laila's friends are all crazy bohemians who drink a lot and sleep around, but that Laila guards her virginity fiercely. I hope Roma's right. Bilal sees her occasionally and brings back photographs. Laila always looks so untidy in them. Unbrushed hair, crumpled clothes…She has always been weird.'

Julio was both appalled and intrigued by Magda's account of her family affairs. He made a mental note to avoid Laila when he reached New York. He had so little experience of girls that he felt he could not possibly handle someone like her. She would eat him alive.

~

Orlando's best friend, his oldest friend, Benoybabu of BBB & Sons, passed away while Julio was in Delhi. Orlando and Julio went to his cremation at Nigambodh Ghat. This was Julio's first Hindu cremation. He was amazed by the complexity of rituals and by the vast quantities of sandalwood consumed by the flames. Benoybabu's widow and his two daughters and grandchildren stayed behind and were comforted by Verna and several Bengali ladies from Karol Bagh. Verna promised she would offer prayers for the peace of his soul at the Sacred Heart Cathedral. When Orlando and Julio returned to Connaught Place, Orlando locked himself in his bedroom. Julio thought he could hear his father weeping.

Braganza & Sons was flourishing. Delhi was full of wealthy rajas, bureaucrats and businessmen who either wanted new pianos or wanted the services of an expert tuner. The competition—Marquis Brothers and Godin's—still could not match the quality of services provided by Orlando and his staff. He had lured away Ranjit Arora, a good tuner, from Godin's. The young man was the very first non-Christian to enter the profession. He had a fine ear and demonstrated a prodigious capacity for hard work: he could tune up to fifteen pianos a week, a record matched only by the patriarch, Emilio Braganza, in his best days in Calcutta.

~

Verna insisted that Julio acquire a completely new wardrobe. 'You can't go to New York shabbily dressed. Let's go shopping for nice fabrics and have some smart clothes tailored. Your rent money from the Imams is just lying there in the bank, doing nothing.'

Within a week Julio looked quite dapper in the latest fashions. He decided to grow a little moustache to make himself look somewhat older. Then, three days later, he shaved it off. He realized that as he was twenty-seven it would be best to look his age. Orlando was kept busy arranging Julio's passport, tickets and other travel documents. He had friends at various levels of government so everything was done swiftly and smoothly.

Bella used to phone from Goa once a fortnight. By sheer coincidence she rang a week or so before Julio was to travel to Bombay and sail from there to Europe. She persuaded—with some difficulty—Orlando and Julio to take a detour via Goa so that Orlando could see Braganza House, meet his grandson, Tonio, and visit the ancient churches in Velha Goa. Verna said she would go if they could travel by air, but this was before she saw the morning papers. A Dakota plane had skidded off the runway at Bombay airport the previous day. That put paid to Verna's notion that planes were safer than trains. She told Orlando that between herself and the new tuner, Ranjit, they would manage Braganza & Sons while he was away. He must be back in ten days—three days getting there, three days with Bella, and four days to see Julio off in Bombay and get back to Delhi. Verna would not tolerate a longer absence. There was a lot of political violence in Delhi. Looters had begun their work. So far, Connaught Place had remained peaceful. So far.

The long rail journey down to Goa was uneventful. Orlando had not seen Bella for several years, and Tonio only in photographs. He was enchanted by the countryside dotted with groves and churches. He was a bit intimidated by the sight and size of Braganza House, the plushness of the furnishings, the neatly-manicured gardens, and by the stern efficiency of Bella who ruled her domain with an iron hand. No velvet gloves for her. There were eight guests—two each from Bombay and Calcutta and the others from Lisbon.

Tonio treated his uncle Julio and his grandfather Orlando as he would have any other guests. He was polite and hardly smiled.

'Are you comfortable, sir? Is there anything you need? Are you enjoying your meals? Would you like to book a car for a tour of the sights?...Do you have children? What are their ages? I am almost six. You may call me Tonio. I am a Braganza. My ancestors originally built this house three hundred years ago. Now my mother owns it. She says I will own it when I am grown up. I will open a zoo then. Children will visit and I will have company to play with.'

At a quiet moment, Orlando and Bella went for a walk in the fruit orchards.

'Bella, my girl, are you happy running this hotel?'

'It keeps me busy...I really miss Marco. He and I formed such a good team. Now the entire responsibility—and the tasks grow each day—is on my shoulders. Tonio is a worry too. He needs a father. He wants me to start a zoo in the grounds. As if I didn't have enough on my plate! Sometimes guests bring their children, but they are usually a good bit older than Tonio. Do you think it would be a good idea to let him play with the Hindu children in the village?'

'Hindu, Christian, Muslim: they are children! What difference does it make? I'm surprised you haven't started him off in school yet. Do that and he will make friends on his own. And do something about getting translation assignments. That's what you trained for. View it as a hobby if you like. And get yourself a good—but not ostentatious—piano. Why do you need a Steinway grand when a second-hand Beckstein upright will do?'

'No, Daddy, it's got to be a grand. That's more classy. You are right about the translation, though. The Goa government must have to carry on a steady correspondence with British India. I'll offer it my services—for free, if necessary. I expect I'll have to get security clearance though...As for sending Tonio to school, there is only one school here in Saligao and I gather the children are mostly from rough backgrounds. There's a better school in Mapusa but that's a good distance away. Perhaps I should send him away to boarding school in Panjim. But he may be too young for that. I'm so worried about him, Daddy...Would you and Mummy consider taking him on in Delhi? St Columba's there is new but has an excellent reputation.'

'Send him to the local Saligao school, Bella,' Orlando said. 'Never mind the so-called rough backgrounds. He'll choose his friends with care. He's the son of a Police Commissioner. He'll look after himself. Why do you fret so much, my girl? Everything in life cannot be perfect. We must make compromises now and then.'

Bella had given Orlando and Julio the use of the green Studebaker. The driver gave them the standard tour lasting a full day: Velha Goa, Cabo Palace, Archbishop's House, the Panjim church, Fontanhas, and the beaches at Candolim and Calangute. While Julio was familiar with these destinations, everything was new for his father. Julio was now able to give knowledgeable descriptions of the architectural marvels they visited. Orlando asked to see the Rachol seminary but Julio said it was too far away to fit in. He had no wish to see Rachol again. Ever.

Goodbyes were a long-drawn-out affair. Tonio looked quite solemn. 'I hope you had a comfortable stay. Were all the services to your satisfaction? Do recommend Braganza House to your friends. It is always our wish to provide you with a home away from home. Até logo!'

Father and son left for Bombay. It had been decided that Julio's grand tour of Europe would be postponed to much later. Rome, Paris, London were all in a shambles after the war. Orlando had booked a berth for Julio on a ship to Genoa, and from there on another ship to New York. With his trunk full of new clothes, his sketchbooks, and three rolls of architectural drawings—his professional portfolio—Julio was impatient to depart.

Orlando was sad: Bella unhappy in Goa, Maria and Boris out of touch, and Julio setting off on a long journey into the unknown...Fatherhood was not easy. Verna wept frequently at the thought of her children wandering all over the place. She claimed motherhood was full of pain and disappointments.

Back to Delhi within ten days: Orlando kept his promise to Verna. He took his camera to the photographers and asked the assistant there to remove the film and make large prints from the negatives. Four days later he hurried back to collect his prints. The young assistant looked very apologetic and said, 'Just a minute, sir. I'll call Mr Mackinley.' Mr Mackinley emerged from the back-room. 'I'm sorry, Mr Braganza, the entire roll was blank. Something went wrong with your camera. There will be no charge.'

Verna was very disappointed. 'Now I'll have to wait for Bella to send some pictures. At least she has people on her staff who know how to handle a camera. You're useless in such matters. I can't rely on you for anything technical.' Orlando defended his position: 'Mr Mackinley himself—Delhi's most famous photographer—said it was the camera's fault. Why blame me? I'll have the wretched contraption mended.'

10
Laila

When Julio reached New York he headed straight for the YMCA. Orlando had written to them a month earlier to reserve a room in the hostel. But the letter never reached. The young man at the Reception was apologetic.

'Braganza? No booking by that name. No vacancy either. Sorry, sir, you'll have to try elsewhere.'

Julio was tired and felt feverish and it showed on his face. 'Can you recommend a hostel or hotel somewhere nearby? I need time to find more permanent accommodation. Can't you squeeze me in for three or four days? I am feeling positively ill.'

'Nope, sir. Try the Elysium around the corner. Turn left at the intersection. Five dollars a day. But I must warn you they also have hourly rates. Whores bring their clients there. It's that kinda place.'

Julio was horrified at the prospect. He felt his temperature rising. He collapsed onto a couch in the reception area and thought carefully about his options. Then he asked to use the telephone—'Tha'll be a nickel'—and called Roma Imam, Magda's sister.

Roma answered the call after several rings and proceeded to talk with a strong German accent. 'Yes, yes, Magda wrote me about you. You are welcome to come here right away. Take a cab. You have our address? Yes? Good. Meanwhile I will cook some tasty New York dish for you...Welcome to the greatest city in the world!'

She assured Julio he wouldn't get lost. The cab drivers of New York knew their way to every nook and cranny of the metropolis. Anyway, as she didn't drive herself, it was always difficult to give instructions on how to reach Albion Street. She often confused right with left. Her husband Jamal was practically blind and was of no use in the matter either.

When Julio arrived at the Imam home on Albion Street, the cab driver demanded eight dollars. It should not have been more than five, according to Roma. 'Must have been an Irish crook... You look completely washed out. I'll introduce you to Jamal and help you up the stairs to Laila's old room. Go to bed immediately. I'll look for the thermometer and bring you a bowl of soup. The special dinner I just cooked will keep in the ice-box for lunch tomorrow...Jamal has a favourite mixture for fevers. I'll ask him to look for the bottle. That will set you right.'

She came back after half-an-hour. 'Here's the soup. Cold cucumber. We couldn't find the thermometer or the fever mixture...Now I'm going to watch you drink up all the soup.' That night Julio had the chills.

The next afternoon Julio felt well enough to join the Imams for lunch. Roma was full of questions about India, Delhi and Number Eight Hailey Road, in particular. Jamal Imam listened to Julio's answers, head bent, trembling hands, and eyes magnified by very thick glasses. He asked about his brother Muzaffar and Daryaganj, where they grew up.

'Is our old house still standing?' Jamal wondered. 'We had a famous neighbour, Doctor Ansari. All this was before my brother and I went to Germany and fell in love with two vivacious sisters...Muzaffar hardly writes and I can barely see to write. Glaucoma. However, Roma and Magda are in touch. The mail takes so long to reach us, we are often three months out of date with regard to domestic and political developments.'

Roma changed the subject. She asked Julio about the job he had lined up.

'I think I've heard about Mr Antonin Raymond. Isn't he the Czech architect? There was a small piece on him in *The Times* not long ago. You had better call his office tomorrow and find out when you are to report for work. It's best to arrive when you have an appointment...Are you comfortable in the attic? It's actually Laila's studio. But she stopped using it when she moved out to the Village—which is where she claims all the art action is. Whatever that means.'

'Ah yes...Laila. Very troublesome, that girl,' Jamal muttered. 'I must tell you about the borough we live in—Queens. By coincidence it is named after Catherine of Braganza, who became Queen of England through marriage. Now that is interesting, is it not? And the King of England received the island of Bombay from the Portuguese as her dowry...May I call you "Julio?"... You look quite unwell. Do you have fever? Roma, look again for the thermometer. It's got to be somewhere in my room.'

The thermometer was found among Jamal's old pencils and pens. Julio's body felt as if it was burning. So he thought he owed the Imams some details. 'The fever comes and goes. I had it first on the ship coming over. I was determined to get through Immigration so I didn't seek any treatment. They would have barred my entry into the U.S...What is my temperature now? I feel quite weak...A hundred and three? It goes even higher every few hours.'

Roma put the thermometer away. 'It's too late in the day to take you to the hospital. We'll do that first thing in the morning, after you have had a good night's rest. Now eat something of the special dinner I cooked for you yesterday. Meanwhile, Jamal and I will look for his oriental fever mixture. He buys it from a Chinese doctor near the Bowery.'

At the Lutheran Medical Center the next morning, it was found that Julio's temperature had shot up to a hundred and five point five. He was delirious. The doctors wheeled him to a secluded room at the end of the Infectious Diseases floor. A nurse applied ice-packs to his head. Through the rest of the day, his temperature was taken every half-an-hour.

Jamal Imam was cross. He drew aside the attending physician and spoke sternly. 'The young man has malaria. I'm from India and have suffered two bouts of it myself. Start him on the medicine right away. In the old days it used to be quinine; there should be more modern treatment by now.'

The young doctor was defensive. 'We have to establish the pattern of fever first. Then there will be some blood tests. The medical team must have a conference—that'll be tomorrow, I guess—to decide the line of treatment. We have to be super-cautious about contagious diseases...'

'In the meanwhile, Julio might just die and his brains simply fry with the high temperature,' said Roma.

The medical bills started coming, payable daily. The Imams settled them dutifully. Various manuals on the principles of internal medicine were consulted and, four days after Julio had been admitted, a treatment for malaria was administered. A specialist had been called from the Center for Disease Control in Atlanta. The pills had to be obtained from the Veterans' Administration Hospital in the Bronx. It appeared that the VA Hospital was the only place in New York that had a semblance of expertise in tropical medicine.

The total payments for Julio's six-day stay in the Lutheran Medical Center came to almost two hundred dollars. Back in Albion Street Julio felt weak and lay in bed in the attic for most of the next two days. Roma was a superb nurse. Even Jamal climbed up the stairs slowly and carefully to check on him twice a day.

Julio insisted on paying the Imams back every cent they had spent on his behalf at the hospital. He did his accounts and found he would have exactly seventeen dollars and fifty cents left of the two hundred and fifty dollars with which he had started out in Bombay. Roma was shocked by the hospital expenses. 'They are supposed to be a Christian place. Julio, don't insist on paying us back right away. The money was just sitting in the bank. You can repay us in instalments once you start working.' But Julio was adamant and counted out a hundred and ninety-seven dollars to hand over to Roma, saying the rest would follow. She refused to accept the money.

~

Work. How to explain not contacting Mr Raymond's office for ten days? Julio would have to reveal that he had contracted malaria in Goa or Bombay. Malaria could have, as Jamal described, a long gestation period. Or would it be better to keep quiet about his illness and pretend that he had just arrived in New York? Jamal and Roma both felt that honesty would be the best policy.

Roma helped him locate the office telephone numbers. Julio dialled one morning, full of anxiety. A pleasant-sounding woman answered at the other end.

'Mr Raymond's office. This is Margo Weiner speaking. How can I help you?'

Julio explained who he was. Could he make an appointment to meet Mr Raymond?

'That won't be possible for a while, young man. He is down with malaria—caught when he was in India. He stopped in Pondicherry on his way back from Japan. I expect him back in office next Monday. Would you like to speak to his partner, Mr Rado? He is here now.'

'It will not be necessary to trouble him. Should you get a chance to speak to Mr Raymond, please remind him that Mr Russell of Delhi had telegraphed him about my coming over to New York to join as an apprentice. So here I am, awaiting his instructions. I'm staying with some friends in Queens—Woodhoven. Kindly note down their telephone number and address.'

Two days later Julio got a call from Mrs Weiner instructing him to bring his portfolio to Mr Raymond's office the following Monday. In the meanwhile, the celebrated architect wanted Julio to walk around Manhattan and familiarize himself with the streets, parks and landmark buildings.

Roma, who was quite fit, offered to show Julio around Manhattan. She also taught him about the subway system and the trains and bus services connecting Woodhoven to the central parts of 'the greatest city in the world'.

Julio was impressed by the skyscrapers of Manhattan, particularly the interplay of towers at the Rockefeller Center. But most of the island was occupied by five- or six-storeyed red-brick tenements with shops at ground level. North-south roads were called 'avenues' and east-west ones were known as 'streets.' It took Julio no time at all to get used to this geometry.

Roma told him that construction had picked up after the war. The tenements were being replaced by towers featuring expensive apartments. Some residents had moved on to barges on which they had built quaint little houses. The waterfronts on the east and west were an untidy mess of tugboats, ships and ferries. There was the smell of fish everywhere.

On another day Roma took Julio to see the Metropolitan, just one of New York's many great museums. After a few galleries she said, 'You'll have to see the rest on your own. There's too much to see in one day...Now that you understand the subway, you'll be alright...Would you like a couple of hotdogs?' She ordered three from a street vendor opposite the Met. 'The other good buy is a large slice of pizza from a Greek or Turkish shop. Twenty-five cents and quite filling.'

~

Roma wanted Julio to meet her niece. He was nervous at the prospect. Roma and Jamal considered Laila to be their own daughter. She was no longer a child: eighteen and fiercely independent. She lived in a large loft near Washington Square with two roommates, Barbra and Karina. They had six cats between them, and bedcovers were strung up across the large space to demarcate private territories.

Roma helped Julio overcome his shyness. They climbed five floors up to the loft door. There was a strong smell of cat piss. Roma rang the bell, and Julio and she waited...and waited... Eventually there was the sound of chains being unchained and locks being unlocked. The door opened a few inches and Laila took stock of the visitors.

'Oh, it's you, Roma. What do you want now? I'm in the middle of washing my hair. Karina and Barbra are still asleep. We had a party here last night. There's a lot of cleaning up to be done. The cats are still traumatized. The singing and shouting always upsets them. I would have thought they would be used to it by now. We have parties every week.'

Laila now reluctantly opened the door wider and let Roma and Julio in. Julio was introduced as Magda's landlord in Delhi. He couldn't take his eyes off Laila—high cheekbones, a fine nose, firm chin, generous bust and paint-stained fingers. Who would have thought she was only eighteen?

Laila was in a hurry. She looked suspiciously at Julio. 'Are you at all into art? In this loft, all three of us live and breathe art. We are painters. Call me if you want to visit other studios and galleries devoted to contemporary art and sculpture. We are all what the more-enlightened critics have begun to call "abstract expressionists." The old stuff is all fucking bullshit.'

Julio told Laila of his artistic experiences at Rachol, then of his sketching and the years spent at the J.J. School in Bombay. Laila grew increasingly impatient.

'I'm sorry, you guys, I simply have too much to do right now. I'm supposed to be at Jackson's this afternoon.' She looked at Julio with some pride. 'I'm Jackson's studio assistant. It's a long train ride to Long Island where he lives. His wife is very strict about my timings.'

Julio did not say much on the subway ride back to Queens. He was thinking of Laila—her striking good looks and grey eyes. It was a ten-minute walk from the station to Albion Street. Roma was in a talkative mood.

'Laila's been with Jackson Pollock for a little over a year. She cleans his studio, prepares canvases, mixes paints and cleans the brushes. It's strenuous work. She has to reach Long Island by two and leave at eight. Lee makes sure she doesn't stay too late.'

'Who is Lee?' Julio asked.

'Jackson's long-suffering wife. She's a good painter too, but totally overshadowed by her husband. I'm afraid he is a raging alcoholic. But gifted, very gifted. He'll be world-famous one day...Laila too may go down in history. She was stretching a large canvas one day and accidentally spilled three cans of paint on it. Lee came into the studio just then. Laila was afraid she would be fired on the spot. Silently, Lee walked across the studio and fetched more paint, of different colours, and proceeded to dribble it all over the ruined canvas. Laila watched anxiously and then, suddenly, Lee smiled at her and said, "What we now have is a drip canvas. Wait till Jackson wakes up. He'll be delighted." And Jackson *was* delighted. From then on he has concentrated almost entirely on drip painting—layer upon layer of squiggles and dashes and dots. I believe the critics call this kind of nonsense "action painting".'

Julio smiled. 'I look forward to seeing those paintings. In Bombay, artists are still painting in an academic style. Though I did have a good friend—Francis Souza—who is an exception. He calls himself a "modernist". He ran away to Bombay from Goa, from Saligao where my sister Bella has a big house. Francis once almost persuaded me to run off to Bombay with him. He was a very troubled teenager then. I was also filled with indecision—until the architect Claude Batley took me under his wing and made an architect of me. His buildings are most interesting. Not quite classical, not quite art deco, and not quite modernist. They are a masterful blend of all three styles.'

Roma stopped by a grocery store to pick up some cheese. Julio was very impressed by the layout of the store, the produce neatly arranged on racks, the clear labelling of prices. So unlike the shops in Delhi and Bombay. The Armenian grocer said they were out of that particular type of cheese but he had something very close to it in taste. He would fetch it from his store-room down the street. Give him a few minutes.

Roma sat down on a stool near the cash counter. Julio tried to be sociable. 'What does Mr Imam do in his room all day long? He is so quiet. I know *you* watch television. I had no idea a TV set could be so small; your screen couldn't be more than five inches by six inches! But the station logo seems to be on most of the time...When there are no programs you can stare at the logo for hours on end!'

'Oh, Julio, you must call us Roma and Jamal! Laila does. This is America. Traditions change fast here...What does Jamal do all day? He used to be an engineer at Bell Laboratories. He had to quit because of his eyes and the trembling in his hands. About six years ago. Since then he has become a poet and an amateur calligrapher. He has a large magnifying glass and slowly, very slowly, he writes out his poems in the Urdu script. Sometimes he copies the same page again and again until he achieves what he considers perfection…It's a harmless occupation. His brother Muzaffar has urged him to publish his poems in Delhi but Jamal is too modest.'

'What are his poems about, er—Roma?'

'Oh, the monuments of Delhi and Lahore, animals, parks and gardens, old friends, imaginary loves, the little children of Woodhoven, Laila, the bridges of New York…He never tells me much about his writing and I, of course, do not know the language. Laila is often very impatient with him. She wants him to do his own translation into English: "Poems are meant to be read or heard by others. There's no point in hiding them away in a cupboard," she says. She tends to bully everyone around her.'

Julio changed the subject. He did not relish hearing Laila being criticized. They had almost reached Albion Street. 'The houses in Woodhoven are so well maintained. The gardens are trim, the trees expertly pruned. Your house looks cute and "perky," as you Americans say.' Roma nodded in agreement.

'One street over is the house in which the famous filmstar Mae West lived as a child. Then we have Louis Armstrong and Ella Fitzgerald in other parts of Queens. In fact, the coloured population is increasing quite rapidly. I hate the way many white people still call them "niggers." I say, "So what? I'm married to one myself." Here we are. Home at last. I'm relieved we got the cheese. It's Jamal's favourite.'

Roma deposited her shopping bag on the patio floor and searched for the house keys in her purse. It took a full minute to find them. 'You know, Julio, you architects should always put a bench next to a front door. We would then have a place to put our shopping and sit down while we look for our keys. That would be considerate of you people. It's such a simple idea.'

The next evening Julio showed his portfolio to the Imams. It consisted mostly of coloured perspective drawings of various Bombay buildings he had worked on under the tutelage of Claude Batley. There were also sketches of Bombay's Indo-Gothic buildings and some Indo-Saracenic ones. Jamal's favourite was the perspective of the Bombay Central Station that Batley had designed in the 'thirties.

~

Julio had an eleven o'clock appointment on Monday morning to meet Antonin Raymond. The office was on Park Row, overlooking the City Hall gardens, just off Broadway. It had a clear view of the Woolworth Building and St Paul's Chapel. Julio managed the subway rides with some difficulty.

Mrs Weiner, the office secretary/receptionist, ushered Julio into the great man's presence at precisely eleven o'clock. Antonin looked up from his sketchbook and walked around his desk to shake Julio's hand. 'What a coincidence that we should both have got malaria at the same time. I hope you have been able to see something of our city this past week...Now let's take a look at your portfolio...What? Not a single modern building? But your drawing is excellent. You are certainly more talented than the other young fellas I've got. Much of our work was in Japan; and now, with the war over, I am working back there on incomplete projects. If you shape up, I'll send you there.'

'What will my duties be here, sir? Who will I report to?' Julio asked somewhat timidly.

'You'll be directly under Anthony Haas, one of my job captains. To avoid confusion with my name we call him Tony. He's from Hungary. I am Czech. We have had Germans, Swedes, Italians, French, British and five other nationalities. And now we will have a Goan. Or do you prefer to be called an Indian? A touchy subject, isn't it?'

'My ancestors left Goa centuries ago. We Braganzas are in the piano business—rentals, repairs, tuning—mainly in Calcutta and Delhi,' said Julio. Antonin nodded his head with sympathy.

'Your first assignment will be to put some order in the filing cabinets. Each drawer holds up to fifty drawings. Your job will be to familiarize yourself with each and every drawing, arrange them sequentially by project, and prepare a new register listing the drawer where each drawing can be located. Hunt out blueprint copies and file those under the original drawings. It's a very demanding, responsible job. And in the process, you will become acquainted with the kind of modern architecture we create in this office. Call it "immersion," if you will!'

'I'll do my best, sir. I look forward to it,' said Julio.

'A lot of my payments have been held up due to the war, so I can't afford to start you off on more than fifteen dollars a week. Tony Haas has been with us for twelve years and he started at ten. If business picks up, I'll increase all your salaries.'

Tony was quite cordial. He showed Julio around the drafting hall and pointed out where the large filing cabinets stood in a row, marked one to twenty. Julio's heart sank. The drawers would contain thousands of original drawings and tens of thousands of blueprints. Tony noticed the downcast expression on Julio's face. He said, 'Don't worry. This is how I had to start too. It's a very, very valuable experience.'

The working hours were strictly eight-thirty to five-thirty. Mrs Weiner took a dim view of late-comers. She would note the time of late arrivals in a special register. Julio was initially so terrified of her that he would arrive at eight and wait for her to come and open up the office. She was always dressed expensively and wore very high heels. She'd come into the drafting hall at eleven-thirty and announce it was time for the coffee break. The workers would all troop down to the Doughnut Café next door.

On one of these coffee breaks, Tony steered Julio to a quiet corner of the café. He lowered his voice and gave the young man some advice.

'You're working too hard. That just will not do. You have to learn how to take it easy, to spin things out. Of course, you must always give the impression you are working on something or other, even if it's just doodling. We are going through a bad patch. Things might improve as the boss has asked permission to work back in Japan where several old projects are in cold storage. If you just sit still on your stool and stare into space, you'll be fired...So I learnt how to make doughnuts. Do you know how to make doughnuts? Well, first you take a hole...' he paused for effect, '...then you wrap the dough around it...' He gesticulated with his hands. 'Get it? So much of the work in the office is making doughnuts. You have to learn the art, young man.'

Julio had not reached that stage. He kept himself very busy learning how Antonin used exposed concrete in his buildings. The detail sheets were fascinating...One evening he picked up the courage to broach a delicate subject to Antonin.

'Sir, my bout with malaria has left me completely broke. I owe a lot of money to my host family. Over two hundred dollars. They paid all my medical expenses and, now that I have a job with you, I wish to pay them back, and pay for my food and lodging. It's an embarrassing situation. Ideally, I'd like to get a room around here. I've heard the area around the Fulton fish market has low rents, though it's smelly...Could you kindly give me a raise of five dollars a week? I know it's a lot to ask but I am desperate to give back what I owe. The Imams have been so kind...'

'How many days were you in the hospital?' asked Antonin.

'Six days in an isolation room of the infectious diseases wing. They allowed my fever to rage for four days before starting the treatment for malaria. Meanwhile, I could barely sleep because of the ambulances and police sirens howling below.'

'Incompetent bastards! Charged you two hundred and fifty bucks! These private outfits are so greedy. I went to a public hospital—cost me nothing...Now about the raise you want: wait a while until you begin to draw and paint perspective views. I know you will be excellent. When the others see that you have special skills, they will be less resentful of a thirty per cent raise to a newcomer. That's all I can promise.'

~

Jamal and Roma Imam liked having Julio around, particularly on weekends. They wanted him to stay with them on a more permanent basis. Roma explained why.

'Laila finds Woodhoven too dull. There are no artists worth speaking of here. That's her unshakeable opinion. She and her girlfriends have been in the Village for three years. We rarely get to see her. She's stopped visiting us. So I have to travel to their loft now and then...We miss having a young person around. Jamal and I have been married so long we hardly have anything left to talk about. That's what I miss most. Someone to talk to. You came highly recommended by my sister Magda. I can see now why you made such a favourable impression on her...The attic is yours to decorate as you wish. You can pay us five dollars a week for food—you hardly eat any breakfast and are out for lunch. So there's only dinner to reckon with...Do agree to my proposal, Julio. I've grown quite fond of you. Jamal too holds you in high regard.'

At work the next day Julio consulted Tony Haas on the issue of staying with the Imams.

'It's a god-send, young man! Agree at once and plant roots there. Sounds like a very good deal—room and board laid on in exchange for a little talk. That should be damn easy. Piece of cake! If you want a night out on the town, you can crash in my apartment. I'm dating a cute airline stewardess but she's not in town too often.'

So Julio settled down to an easy domesticity. If asked, he would read out articles from *The Sunday Times* for Jamal's benefit. The old man was particularly keen on hearing about the political turmoil in India, talk of Independence, and the threatened creation of Pakistan. Julio would also go food shopping for Roma, mow the lawn occasionally and accompany her to Laila's loft off and on.

~

In the months that followed, Julio impressed Antonin greatly with the quality of his work. He had done a thorough job of settling the filing cabinets. Now he proved he had an exceptional ability to visualize the third dimension from two-dimensional drawings. His perspective drawings were thus exquisite. He was now familiar also with the Japanese architectural vocabulary beloved by Antonin. He therefore got to work on a few projects located in Japan. Long distance. His salary was increased to twenty dollars a week. Thanks to his arrangement with the Imams, he was able to save about half of that. A good portion of his initial savings had to be invested in winter clothing—boots, overcoat, jackets, caps, mufflers and so on.

The American media then became slightly more interested in news from India, though mention of Gandhi, Nehru, Jinnah and Mountbatten tended to be relegated to short items on the back pages. The fledgling TV news contained no images of the processions, fasts and carnage besetting the subcontinent. The partition of India was taken as inevitable. Jamal kept his ears glued to the radio. Nothing much there either. He thought that partition would have disastrous long-term consequences: conflicts that would last a century. Roma was more hopeful. She felt that once the British left, things would settle down after an initial spurt of blood-letting.

~

By the summer of 1947 Laila and Julio had become good friends. They'd go for long walks in Central Park and visit museums together. Laila had a wide circle of artist friends, a number of whom were surprisingly good cooks. So there were invitations to brunch and supper several times a month. However, Laila's roommates were not too keen on spending time with Julio. In fact, whenever he came to the loft they would avoid him and retreat behind their curtains. Julio would try to be friendly, often bringing the threesome bottles of Jack Daniel's or Southern Comfort which he could ill afford. They'd get drunk together but the banter and singing were somehow designed to exclude him. Laila made no effort to draw Julio into their tight circle. He asked Laila if there was anything he should be doing but wasn't. She looked at him directly.

'Don't you get it? Are you blind? The three of us are in love with each other. Call us lesbians, if you like...Though we like men too...Barbra and Karina are jealous: they think I'm sleeping with you, and that is betrayal. Silly girls. I've tried to explain my India connection. That you are my mother Magda's landlord. That my Uncle Jamal is my father Muzaffar's brother...They made the same kind of fuss over my employer and mentor, Jackson Pollock. They were initially convinced I was having it off with him. Don't worry, they'll get used to having you around.'

It took some time for Julio to digest the possibility that Laila could be a lesbian. He was determined that he'd cure her of this bizarre tendency. On their walks around town he would shyly reach out for her hand. She did not withdraw it. In Central Park he would place an arm around her shoulders. She did not remove it. He would often give her a quick kiss on the cheek. She did not protest. She viewed all his advances as tokens of friendship. Just friendship. On her part, Laila would often put an arm around Julio's waist or place her hand in the crook of his arm. In public, at any rate, they appeared to be an affectionate couple.

Then Julio's kisses got serious. Long and passionate. So passionate that Laila protested angrily. 'You're my friend, not my lover. Always remember that...It's high time I visited my folks in Queens. Tell Roma I'll come for lunch on Saturday. You'll be there, of course. Promise me you'll behave yourself...I picked up a second-hand copy of a translation of Ghalib's poems the other day. I'll bring it for Jamal...How I wish he'd translate his own stuff into English. He's so stubborn...I suppose I've inherited my stubbornness from my father's side of the family.'

'What makes you say you are stubborn, Laila?' Julio asked.

'Oh, you hardly know me. Kissing a girl does not reveal all her secrets. For example, I can't stand how regular English is spelled. I have my own phonetic system for writing. That is why I haven't had any formal education. No school would accept me. Then, I insisted on moving to the Village with only two dollars in my pocket. *That* caused quite a scandal as I was barely sixteen. Then, I was adamant I would work with Jackson although he lives so far away and has the reputation of being a womanizer. I said: what are trains for?'

On Saturday, Laila was late in coming. Jamal, who was a stickler for meal timings, shuffled into the kitchen at one o'clock and helped himself to lunch from the saucepans. He then returned to the living-room and sat up close to the little TV set and tried to focus on a programme on drug abuse. Laila arrived well after half-past-two, claiming her train had broken down. Julio and Roma had also eaten by then. Food for Laila had been kept warm in the oven. Laila was famished and helped herself to enormous quantities of pasta and beef stroganoff.

Jamal's mood improved when Laila presented him the volume of Ghalib's poems. 'Begum,' he said, 'kindly fetch the magnifying lens from my bedroom. It should be on the dressing-table. I used it when I trimmed my beard this morning.' Then he turned to Laila, 'I gather you and Julio have become good friends and are visiting museums and art galleries together. That is good. It's not safe for a young woman to walk on the streets alone these days. So much violence. Muggings and robberies. I heard on the radio that the consumption of narcotics—things like morphine, heroin and cocaine—is on the rise, and young people indulge in crime to finance their addictions...Laila, never walk in dark alleys. Never carry more than five dollars on you. The idea is to minimize your losses in case you are attacked. Never argue with a robber. Many of them have guns.'

Roma returned with the magnifying glass and switched on the table lamp beside Jamal's chair. He was soon completely absorbed in the book of poems. Roma, Laila and Julio moved to the dining-room where they got talking about art. Or at any rate, Julio and Laila did, and Roma tried her best to appear fascinated by Julio's description of the Willem de Kooning exhibition. She sat quietly, listening to the art talk, talk about Laila's cats, and news of Jackson's latest drip paintings. She noticed that Laila and Julio were completely at ease with one another...They sat next to each other at the dining table and their hands touched frequently. Whenever Julio said something funny, Laila would grasp his arm and laugh away. Roma was surprised at how tactile their relationship had become. She recalled how it had taken Jamal almost two years of a formal courtship in Germany before they dared even to hold hands. Roma's musings were stopped short by an exuberant gesture by Laila: she got up from her chair and wrapped her arms around Julio.

'Your imitation of Georgia O'Keeffe's paintings would bring the house down! You do amazing things with your lips. Where did you acquire your knowledge of female genitalia? Oh, you know what I mean. Her flowers are deeply erotic and you are able to mimic them with your mouth...Don't look so shocked, Roma. Nothing is taboo in art. Even three hundred years ago Titian painted reclining nudes. Sex has always been important in art. As has the depiction of sexual organs. Remember David's flaccid pecker in Florence? The female sex organs are equally beautiful and equally tasty. I think this was what Julio was trying to depict. Weren't you, Julio?'

Julio looked most embarrassed and tried to change the subject. But Roma had not understood what had just happened. She was confused by it all.

'I thought Georgia O'Keeffe was famous for her flowers. What is all this nonsense about private parts? I thought you were a good Catholic boy. I won't have such obscene things going on in my house.' Roma was very cross and, breathing heavily, she waited for Julio's answer. Laila stepped in to rescue him.

'We were talking about art and mime and theatre. Have you seen Julio's sketches? He is also an artist. He is therefore free to convey his impressions of anything he likes. And this includes Georgia's clear-cut realism of the folds and crevices, swelling forms and hidden hollows of what you call our private parts... Julio is a good actor with a very expressive face...Now I hope you get the point and we can forget this entire incident. It should never have taken place. I apologize for both of us. He was just trying to be funny.'

Julio felt miserable. He said in a soft voice, 'Yes, I'm sorry. I don't know what got into me.'

So Laila's visit home ended on a somewhat sour note. Roma led them back to the living-room where Jamal had fallen asleep in his chair. He had a slight smile on his face and was dreaming of Ghalib's Delhi. Roma woke him up. 'Laila's leaving now.' She turned to Laila. 'I need a nap before getting dinner ready. You'd better be off. Julio, here's a list of things I need from the store. You can pick them up on your way back from the station. You'll be seeing her off, won't you? Here's two dollars. That should cover everything...Laila, give Jamal a goodbye hug. You're lucky he didn't hear your discussion on art. He would have been outraged.'

Jamal was thoroughly awake by now. There was an urgency in his speech. 'You young people should remember that Pakistan becomes independent on the fourteenth and India on the fifteenth of August. I'm too old to celebrate India's Independence Day. But that's no reason you and Laila shouldn't have a party for your friends on the fifteenth.' Then Jamal added sadly, 'It's too bad about partition. Millions are dying to satisfy the egos of a few mischief-makers on both sides...Poets and novelists will write about this dark chapter. Ghalib would have wept...Goodbye, Laila. Thank you so much for the book. It was very thoughtful of you.'

The next day, Sunday, Julio realized he was very troubled, so he went to confession at the Catholic church around the corner. Father O'Toole heard his confession and gave him some practical advice. Julio's longing to spend time with Laila was not wholesome. She was a Muslim girl. At any rate, her father in India was Muslim. Only heartbreak lay ahead...There were a couple of Goan girls in the Bronx who would be more suitable, the D'Silva sisters...Julio should attend Mass every Sunday from now on. That alone would bring him some solace. But Julio could not get Laila out of his mind.

He did not tell Laila he had met a priest. She had contempt for all forms of organized religion. She had once told him why: 'Think of the hundreds of millions who have been killed in the name of religion throughout history. How on earth, then, could religion be a good thing? Your great-grandfather Gareth Armstrong eventually got the right idea about Christianity.' Julio had told her his family history.

~

Magda wrote from Delhi from time to time. She was, of course, keen to know how her daughter Laila and Julio were getting on. She also sent news of all the goings-on at Eight Hailey Road. The activities of Kitty, the Maharani of Sandawa, were a continuous source of gossip. She had given birth to a son, much to the delight of her husband Bobby. The baby would be the next Maharaja of Sandawa. He had been named Ravindra—Robin, for short.

Kitty's eldest daughter, Mia, had been married off to the Rajkumar of Rajgarh shortly before the birth. She was now very keen to get pregnant. Her lout of a husband beat her frequently and threatened to pack her off to her mother's house if she did not bear a son. So there was a sword dangling over Mia's head.

~

Julio's work at Antonin's office was proceeding extremely well. He was a quick worker, turning out perspectives and floor plans with equal competence. Tony Haas was a little apprehensive and somewhat jealous. Julio was violating Tony's recipe for making doughnuts. Antonin's partner, Mr Rado, wanted Julio to work for him but Antonin refused to give him up.

Lunch breaks were spent organizing the grand Independence Day party. Laila-Karina-Barbra were the chief organizers. They had a good friend, Benson Price III, who house-sat for his perpetually-travelling, wealthy aunt. He occupied the basement in her four-storey brownstone in Brooklyn Heights. The upper floors and attic contained five bedrooms. Benson liked only men and boys, and made no secret of it. He painted horribly inept paintings and was a drug addict. But he was generous to a fault. He gladly agreed to host the party on the condition that Laila-Karina-Barbra would see to the food and help clean up later. Benson would organize some booze. They invited fifty friends, knowing fully well that the numbers would swell to a hundred. It was to be a bring-your-own-bottle affair, but Benson knew that not everyone would do so. Free-loaders everywhere.

Julio undertook to cook a biryani, reasonably confident of the instructions contained in a Mughlai cookbook borrowed from Jamal. The appropriate spices could be had from an Armenian shop on Canal Street. The actual cooking would be done in batches in Benson's aunt's kitchen. The girls would prepare a pasta and order a few large pizzas. Other friends offered to prepare bacon quiche. Benson promised to supply the marijuana.

Julio got two days off from work. Laila got three days off from Jackson. The fourteenth of August was spent cooking and party-proofing the brownstone. All valuable works of art, porcelain and 'pinchable' knick-knacks were locked away in Aunt Tara's large bedroom. Tapestries and Buddhist thangkas were rolled up and also put away. Extra rolls of toilet paper were placed in the bathrooms. Large stacks of paper plates and plastic spoons and cups were kept ready. Guests started arriving at six and kept drifting in and out till the wee hours of the next morning.

There were about a dozen Indian men. Nobody quite knew who had invited them. They were among the first to get drunk on Benson's booze. They staggered to and from the bathrooms and were noisy, singing songs from Hindi movies. This encouraged the others to start singing. Smoke filled the rooms as a number lit up joints.

The food was laid out on the large ten-seater dining table. Most stayed clear of Julio's biryani because they found it too spicy and the rice half-cooked. Then some peddlers of narcotics made an appearance. Heroin and cocaine. Benson protested. He and one of the more-steady Indians pushed the offenders—two coloured guys and a Mexican woman—out the front door. The drug pushers stood on the pavement and screamed obscenities. The police arrived, arrested the peddlers, and warned Benson that the party was too noisy. Neighbours had complained. Benson was relieved that the cops did not insist on entering the house. Had they done so, the whole lot of them would have been arrested for possession of marijuana.

Things quietened down. There was a smell of sex in the air. Men and women, women and women, men and men formed twosomes, threesomes, and a few foursomes. Julio had never witnessed anything like it. He felt the excitement swell in his trousers and was embarrassed. Benson put his arm around Julio and shouted in his ear.

'I simply must ask you for some advice. You're an architect, so you should know. Let's get away from all this noise for a bit. I want to show you my plumbing situation on the second floor.'

Julio had just had his first experience of smoking pot. As he was in a benign mood, he allowed himself to be escorted up the stairs. Halfway up, they heard Laila call out from below.

'Benson, your police buddy Frank just arrived and is looking for you. Come and take charge of him. I'll take Julio to the loo.' She escorted Julio up to the attic, which was unoccupied. Benson was content to welcome Frank whom he kissed passionately. He lit up and shared his joint with the off-duty policeman.

The attic had been occupied by maids in the days when people had live-in maids. Laila and Julio flung themselves on the bed. They had both been smoking and drinking, and Julio in particular was feeling amorous. Very amorous. Laila was half asleep, not fully aware that Julio was gently undressing her. He then undressed himself and instinctively knew what to do next. Laila protested feebly, 'No, Julio, no.' But by then he was in her and had got into a rhythm. His orgasm came quickly and then he lay back panting. Laila had fallen asleep.

There was a knock on the door. Benson and Frank wanted to use the attic. 'Julio, your time is up. You've been there for over forty minutes. It's our turn now. All the other bedrooms are taken. Get dressed and rejoin the party downstairs.'

Laila looked angry. She dressed with a scowl on her face. Julio's feelings were more complex. A mixture of embarrassment, pride, guilt and remorse. Laila did not say a word. It had been the first time for both of them.

Downstairs, the party showed no sign of winding down. Guests were in various stages of undress. Music blared from the gramophone. Joints were still being passed around. The pizza, pasta and quiche had all been polished off. Julio's biryani lay largely uneaten. All except one of the dozen Indians lay asleep, spread on the floor, some in pools of vomit. The only survivor, Jogen Das, was mournfully singing 'Jana, gana, mana,' the anthem written by Rabindranath Tagore. This patriotic Indian was also swigging from a bottle of Jack Daniel's. He called Julio over to him.

'Come, you are also Indian, no? Shing the shpecial shong with me. "Jana, gana, mana..."' Julio knew only the first couple of lines. Jogen Das was dismayed and took a large gulp from the bottle, which he then handed to Julio.

~

A short while later, a telegram arrived for Benson. He tore the envelope open nervously. Laila stood at his elbow peering at the message:

> Darling Benson. Am returning home on the sixteenth. Probably around six. Do stock up on food. You know what I eat. Strictly vegetarian. And dust the house for god's sake. I will have been away for almost three months. Lots of love, Aunt Tara.

Benson and Laila were horrified. How to clean up the mess? They had exactly six hours to do it. Julio said it would be possible if they planned carefully. Benson's boyfriend Frank—the delinquent policeman—took charge and deployed the able-bodied on different floors. Frank said he would not be able to supervise more than fifteen. The rest should be woken up, told to get dressed and ordered to get lost. This was an emergency. Frank handled this part of operations himself.

Julio was assigned to the kitchen. Laila-Karina-Barbra were in charge of dusting out Aunt Tara's bedroom and restoring her precious objects to their rightful locations. Benson oversaw this operation as he was the only one who knew where things belonged. The soiled sheets in various bedrooms had to be changed, the bathrooms scrubbed clean, carpets put back in their original positions. But again, as Benson was the only one who knew the correct position of a hundred different things, he and Frank jointly gave instructions and answered the inevitable queries from the volunteers. Fortunately, there were enough clean sheets in the linen closet to go around. Mounds of garbage had been generated. This had to be stuffed into plastic bags and put out on the sidewalk. There was still a strong smell of dope and stale alcohol. Not to mention vomit. All windows and doors were flung open and four table fans were rigged up in the living-room windows to function as exhausts.

The brownstone gradually regained its interior dignity. Frank summoned all the forces to the living-room. 'You've done a swell job. Now promise me one thing. You are not to tell a soul I've been here. I'll get chucked out of NYPD if it came to be known I was partying with a bunch of stone-heads. We're not allowed to have a private life. I have to report for duty in an hour. Just enough time to shave, shit and get into my uniform...This has been the wildest party I've ever attended. Bye, folks. Now all of you just go home and sleep it off. Scram! Vamoose!'

After a while, the revellers actually left. Julio, Benson, Laila-Karina-Barbra sank into armchairs in the living-room. Then Benson remembered the need to pick up food for his aunt and drop off the pile of semen-stained bedsheets lying on the first-floor landing. He dashed to the neighbourhood Chinese laundry and the grocery store. Laila-Karina-Barbra chatted amongst themselves and conceded that things had gone too far. So what if India was independent now? Not a word was spoken to Julio. He was completely excluded. He tried to catch Laila's eye, but she kept looking away. She was determined to have nothing to do with him. Julio thought he deserved better. He knew he owed Laila an apology, but she should at least talk to him.

~

One of the first things Frank did when he was back in uniform was to arrange for the garbage bags on Willow Street to be removed. He had friends in the Sanitation Department. What could have been vital evidence against Benson was thus eliminated. Laila-Karina-Barbra left just before six o'clock, carrying four bottles of left-over Southern Comfort. They were exhausted. They made a point of not saying goodbye to Julio. Karina and Barbra fell asleep as soon as they reached the loft. Laila lay awake in her compartment regretting that she had inadvertently had sex with a man, something she had avoided till now like the plague.

Meanwhile Benson and Julio made themselves strong cups of coffee and popped analgesics. Benson then moved very close to Julio on the couch, their thighs touching.

'What were you and Laila doing up in the attic for almost an hour? Were you napping? Did you...?'

'Oh, no, nothing like that. She just wanted to get away from the smoke...I suppose we just talked a bit and maybe napped a little. I don't remember too clearly. We were pretty knackered, as you Americans say. I've never been to such a party. In fact, I've been to very few parties in my life. We mostly drank bottled lemonade at those events.'

'Do stay and meet Aunt Tara when she arrives. You'd like her. She's been to India, Tibet and China. Can't sit still. She's returning from a trip to Turkey, Egypt and Morocco.'

Julio shook his head. 'Benson, I have to catch up on my sleep. You forget I have to report for work at eight-thirty tomorrow. I also have the most dreadful headache. I would not be fit company for your aunt. I'll come some other day when I am at my best. See how grubby my clothes look? I've got food stains all over them from cleaning up the kitchen. Your aunt would want to know why I'm such a mess. That goes for you too. You'd better change before she arrives.'

Benson reconciled himself to Julio's departure for Queens. Another telegram arrived from Aunt Tara at seven that evening:

Missed my flight in London. Will arrive tomorrow evening. Have collected interesting recipes. Love, Aunt Tara

Benson was both relieved and irritated. He thought about Julio a long while, and then fell into a deep sleep on a couch in the living-room.

~

Julio gave the Imams a sanitized version of events at the party. 'There were over a hundred guests. Many Indians. We sang "Jana, gana, mana." Music and dancing. Scintillating conversations. The food was excellent—'

'How was the biryani? Did you get the ingredients right?' Jamal wanted to know.

'I'm afraid I overdid the spices and undercooked the rice. It was my very first experience of cooking. Here, I'm returning your recipe book. It says nothing about cooking for a hundred!'

'Well, now you'll know how to do it in future. Keep things subtle...How is Laila? I hope she didn't drink too much. We are alarmed at the company she keeps. All these years, and not a boyfriend in sight.'

'Laila and I got into a small argument. Nothing serious, but you know how stubborn she is. She isn't talking to me now. I'm sure it will blow over...Tell me, Roma, is she one to hold on to grudges? I'd hate to lose her as a friend. She has taught me so much about art, and life in the Village...Does she forgive easily?'

Roma looked up from her embroidery. 'She can be very, very stubborn, as you just said. She has strong opinions and we have found it almost impossible to make her change them. We find ourselves giving in on most matters. Moving to the Village at the age of sixteen was one of them.'

'She's fiercely independent,' said Jamal. 'Doesn't take a cent from us. It's been like this for three years. She relies on Roma and me to stay in touch with our people in Delhi. My brother Muzaffar writes to her occasionally. Sends her political news and accounts of the chaos in India. Her mother Magda—Roma's sister—and she are completely estranged. Roma, someday you must tell Julio how that happened…You look sleepy and exhausted, Julio. Drink some of Roma's soup and go to bed.'

At work the next day, Mrs Weiner drew Julio aside. 'You look simply awful, Julio. You're an hour late. I'm afraid I'll have to record that in my register. Go wash your face and splash some of this cologne over yourself.' She fished out a bottle of cheap English cologne from her purse and handed him the key to the washroom.

Antonin wanted to know whether Julio would agree to relocate to Japan. Not immediately but, say, in three or four months. A lot of work had piled up there. Meanwhile Julio could learn some Japanese in the evenings. Julio was alarmed by this offer. He had no wish to leave New York and abandon his one-sided wooing of Laila. He hesitantly declined and hoped Antonin wouldn't hold it against him.

'Give it a thought, Julio. In any case, I leave for Japan soon. You'd have to work with Mr Rado. You know he does not have an international practice. Designs only dreary office buildings on the fringes of Manhattan…Tony has agreed to shift. In Japan he'll have to work like a horse. That would be good for him.'

~

September and October came and went. Julio and Laila were now on talking terms again and resumed their visits to art galleries and museums. The girls in the loft got used to having Julio visit in the evenings and on weekends. He was popular with the cats who liked the way he stroked their throats.

Laila had imposed three conditions on Julio. 'No touching, no fondling, no kissing.' Julio was very careful not to breach any of these. He thought to himself, 'She'll agree eventually. I must not be in a hurry. The rest will follow.'

Then one evening as winter approached, they sat six inches apart on a bench in Central Park. Laila suddenly fell quiet. Then she wept silently. Julio longed to put his arms around her, but this was strictly forbidden. He was at a loss to know how she could be comforted. She began to sob. Julio asked what the matter was. Laila stood up facing him, now full of rage.

'Julio, I'm pregnant...I'm sure! I've just had the test. I'm broke. I have never had sex with a man before—or since—Don't interrupt me, you fucking bastard!—help me deal with it. The girls think you should be arrested for rape. But I say it's too late for that—Wait till I've finished!—I can't bear to think of that wretched party. It was a disaster for me...Now, I have a choice. I either deal with this on my own, or make you pay for your sins.'

Julio was shocked into incoherence. He felt as though a knife had been thrust into his guts. 'I...er...I never...just once...er... you agreed...must speak to Father O'Toole...I'm sorry...er...but I love you. You know that.'

He had tears in his eyes. But Laila was unrelenting. 'You took advantage of me, you swine! What do you mean by saying I agreed? We were both drunk and doped. I distinctly remember telling you to desist...But that's not the point. What do we do now? I don't want the child. I want to get rid of it as soon as possible. And what will Father O'Toole tell you that I can't? Think, Julio, think. You can't go running to a priest each time you're in trouble.'

Julio said, 'Let's not talk for a while. I'll walk you home. The long walk will do us both good. I don't know what to say just yet...I'll be guided by Father O'Toole's advice. Don't forget, I am still a Roman Catholic. The Holy Mother of God will see us through this catastrophe...We can't do anything illegal.'

'You are hardly a pious Christian, Julio...Anyway, let's not say any more. You always put your foot in it. Go, go and meet your priest. He'll give you an earful, I'm sure.'

When Julio went to see Father O'Toole, the good priest was scandalized by the happenings. The Father gave him an hour-long lecture about the sanctity of life, matrimony and parenthood. Julio's doubts gradually cleared up. He felt a new resolve to do the right thing.

He turned up at the Laila-Karina-Barbra loft on a Saturday

morning. Laila was grumpy. 'So what have you decided? Don't forget, I too am involved. More involved than you, in fact.'

Julio spoke hesitantly. 'An abortion is out of the question. I asked your Uncle Jamal in a roundabout fashion and he said Islam forbids it. You know the Church forbids it. My conscience forbids it. The right thing to do is to get married and then have the baby...We'll have a civil ceremony right away. City Hall is near my office on Park Row. I'll see to the paperwork on Monday... Oh Laila, we'll have a grand life together, the three of us.'

Laila was horrified at the prospect of marriage. 'Grand life? Where will we live? Who will take care of the brat while we are out at work?...I'll have to lug this—this thing around in my belly for another six months! And what about your income? Twenty dollars a week! You think that's enough to support us all? I haven't sold a painting in four months. Jackson pays me peanuts...As for marrying you, don't make me laugh. I think marriage is a totally outmoded institution. To hell with you and your bizarre ideas.'

But Julio was not one to give up easily. He met Laila several times a week and advanced his reasoning. As a Catholic he could not go against the teachings of the Church. The child was his too, and he had an equal say in its fate. He knew his responsibilities. He would be both father and mother to the child if need be.

Laila considered the offer carefully and discussed the matter with Karina-Barbra. The girls secretly rather looked forward to having a baby around. Something to cuddle and coo over—with none of the responsibility. They hoped it would be a girl. A baby would also liven up the atmosphere for the six cats who otherwise took turns staring blankly out of the two windows of the loft. They would find a baby more interesting.

After several rounds of heated arguments, Julio and Laila arrived at a compromise. They would get married to put a seal on Julio's legal responsibilities. Laila would have the baby, but after that, Julio would take over its entire care and upbringing. Laila would not ever be saddled with any of it. He would take the child with him to India or Japan or wherever his boss wanted him to move. Later, Laila would file for a divorce on grounds of desertion and child abduction. The talk of divorce made Julio uncomfortable but he had to agree. It might never come to that unless Laila wished to remarry.

~

The marriage ceremony took place in City Hall, conducted by a waspish Justice of the Peace who asked uncomfortable questions. Roma and Jamal, Mrs Weiner from the office, Karina and Barbra were present. Although puzzled by the speed with which the courtship had been conducted, the Imams were relieved that Laila would now lead a more settled life. They liked Julio very much and considered him a perfect gentleman. They assumed Laila would move back to her old room and the four of them would form a happy household. They were wrong.

As a concession to appearances, Julio spent the first three nights of his marriage on a couch in Laila's loft. Cat fur everywhere. Then he told the Imams a bit of the truth about his arrangement with Laila. They were scandalized. It would have been futile to hide the pregnancy, Julio thought. Laila would begin to show soon.

Roma was most concerned about Laila. An unwanted pregnancy, an unwanted marriage, no cohabitation, and barely concealed hostility towards her husband. What kind of future would the child have? Jamal was more understanding.

'I'm relieved they didn't follow the abortion route...Look Roma, you and I are fairly idle most of the day. We can take care of the baby for Laila. The doctors always said it was my fault we didn't have a child of our own. We can now make up for that. The experience of caring for an infant would be most gratifying, I think. Julio could do the night shift.'

The months rolled by. Laila went to Jackson's studio three times a week. Julio remained in touch with Antonin in Japan. Antonin kept asking Julio to join him there and even bring Laila, if she was the main impediment. Julio explained his awkward position several times. He was about to become a father, and

Laila had made it absolutely clear she would never move out of New York.

The child, a boy, was born in the loft in May. Laila had refused to go to a hospital. The delivery was attended by a close friend, a freelance midwife. After ten hours of labour and screaming and shouting curses, Laila told Julio she did not want him around. He should leave Roma in the loft and go back to Albion Street to keep Jamal company. Karina would ring them up in Queens when it was all over. The birth, a difficult one, took place after a total of eighteen hours of labour. Jamal was delighted by Karina's call and turned to Julio who, despite the unseasonal cold weather, had been perspiring with anxiety.

'Aren't you happy, Julio? I hope the child will bring about an era of forgiveness all round. If you like, we can call him Asif—which means forgiveness in Arabic. He would then have a Muslim first name and a Christian surname: Asif Braganza. Sounds quite poetic, don't you agree? I think Laila would accept it—but then you can never tell what she thinks.'

Laila, surprisingly, agreed to the name, but added a middle name. The baby was now Asif Jackson Braganza. But she refused to move out of the loft. So the baby had three mothers: Laila, Karina and Barbra. They shared the work involved, juggled timings, stayed up nights and gladly participated in all the messy things entailed in infant care.

Julio would stop by after office most evenings, except for the occasions when Mr Rado asked him to stay late. Mrs Weiner was full of unasked-for advice on baby care. 'Keep Asif warm at all times. Laila's loft isn't heated, you say. Keep adequate supplies of gripe water handy. The baby must be fed every two hours. Breast milk is best. Your wife can't go trotting off to Long Island for ten hours at a stretch...Who does the baby look like? Has he inherited your good looks? You can tell by the nose and the eyes. My own son looks like his ugly father—and is turning out to be a delinquent, too, like his father.'

Julio was getting along quite well with Mr Rado at the office. He had grown fond of Mrs Weiner and found his colleagues quite amusing. Tony had coached them well. They had evolved several strategies to give the impression they were working very hard. They fooled Mr Rado but not Mrs Weiner. She knew what they were up to each time they took off on what they claimed were construction-site visits—they were seriously into horse-racing, placing bets over the office telephone...

Roma and Jamal kept trying to persuade Laila to move back home with little Asif. Roma had heard of several instances of cats smothering babies. She was anxious on this score and also worried about the lack of hygiene in the loft. It was terribly dusty and the girls had no vacuum cleaner.

'Your cats are a menace and Asif is bound to pick up frightful infections. He has had four severe stomach upsets already. Bring him to Queens. We'll take good care of him. There are six grandmothers on our street. We'll get all the advice we need... What you are doing is inhuman, Laila.'

But Laila refused to shift the baby. She laid great store on the advice given by her midwife friend. Six months of breastfeeding were essential. The child could be handed over to his 'grandparents' after that. Laila made it clear that she would resume her work with Jackson after this period and get back to her own art. In order to do this, she had to continue in the loft. She would not on any account move to Queens. Ever. If she did, she'd get caught up in humdrum domesticity—regular meals at specified hours, taking the brat out in a perambulator at fixed times, shopping, cleaning, cooking and so on. She was not cut out for motherhood. Julio had to accept all this but he looked forward to the day when Asif could take up residence at the Imams'.

Julio had informed his parents about his marriage and the baby. He didn't know if Orlando and Verna had received his letters because there was no reaction from them to his news. This was puzzling. He shared his disappointment with Mrs Weiner.

'Look, Julio,' she said. 'Why are you moping? Just give me their phone number in Delhi and I'll place a long-distance call. I do this all the time when Mr Rado wants to talk to Mr Raymond in Japan. It might take a couple of days to materialize but should not be impossible. There's the time difference to reckon with. I'll aim for Wednesday morning. Your father is Orlando Braganza, isn't he? And your mother Verna Braganza? I'll ask to speak to either of them.'

When the call finally came through two days later, Julio learned from the cook that his parents had gone to Mussoorie, in the hills, to visit Maria-missy, Boris-sahib, and their new baby. They'd be gone for ten days. Yes, the cook would tell them to write to Julio. Yanek-baba was born two weeks ago.

Mrs Weiner did some rapid calculations on a scratch pad. 'That will be twelve dollars. Too bad your parents were not available. Write a long letter and I will see that it's safely and securely despatched this time. By Certified Post.'

~

On Thanksgiving Day, 1948, Asif was transferred, along with his baby things, to the care of the Imams. Julio had hired a taxi for the auspicious occasion. Laila had told him never to pester her again with baby matters. She had kept her side of the bargain and that was that. Karina and Barbra, though, promised to visit Queens from time to time. They had grown quite fond of the little boy, and marvelled at how rarely he cried and how regular he was with his bodily functions. Roma had nothing to fear.

Jamal gave up writing poetry and spent hours cradling Asif to sleep on a newly-acquired rocking-chair. Roma would often find that Jamal had rocked himself to sleep while Asif was wide awake in his arms, gurgling away happily.

As agreed, Julio did night duty, dealing with both input and output. He was often bleary-eyed and late for work. Mrs Weiner overlooked this, remembering the time she had walked out on her ruffian of a husband, taking her little son with her. Her aged father had cared for the baby while she went out to work. At night it was her turn, but the child kept crying for his grandfather. For over a year, she averaged only three hours of sleep a night. Oh yes, she well understood what Julio was going through.

Julio was now earning thirty dollars a week. With Roma's

consent, he hired a fifteen-year-old coloured girl to come in for four hours every morning to help out with the cooking, cleaning and washing. He was amazed at how much washing a baby could generate. The young girl, Terry, was cheerful and very enthusiastic about Asif. She had plenty of experience, being the eldest of six children.

A year passed. Asif could now walk around unsteadily. Julio thought he'd had enough practical training in America. Antonin had been an exemplary role model. Julio's parents urged him to come home. Roma's sister Magda, Asif's real grandmother on his mother's side, offered to take care of him. Verna, his paternal grandmother, did the same. Roma and Jamal were dismayed that Julio wanted to return to India. He was doing so well at the office, and Asif was very dear to them. If Julio stayed on in New York, perhaps Laila and he could bring about a rapprochement. Their presence there may awaken her maternal instincts. It was worth a try. In any case, Asif was too young to travel halfway across the world and have to adjust to a wretched climate. He was doing so well in Queens. The Imams had also grown very fond of Julio. If he and Asif left, the house would be bereft of conversation, laughter, and the hilarious antics of a toddler learning to walk and talk.

Magda made frantic phone calls from far-away Delhi. She emphasized that her school on Hailey Road would be good for Asif's growth and development. He needed the company of other small children and should be reared in an atmosphere that respected music, nature and theatre. Magda kept stressing she knew more about raising children than either Roma or Julio's mother Verna.

Orlando and Verna implored Julio to come home to Connaught Place. Verna's letters were almost hysterical. There was plenty of space in the CP flat and she had plenty of time on her hands. There was a full complement of staff in place and she would also engage an ayah to assist. Magda on the other hand was too busy running her school and entertaining heathen godmen to have time for Asif. If Julio decided on Magda's place,

Verna would never talk to him again. He should not trample on her rights as a god-fearing grandparent. With her, Asif would be given an authentic Catholic upbringing—Mass, catechism, confession and so on. Like Bella's son Tonio in Goa. Verna now had three grandchildren, all boys: Tonio, Maria's son Yanek in Mussoorie, and Asif. She'd have to do something about the child's name, though. 'Asif' was most inappropriate for a Catholic boy. He'd be the laughing stock of the Catholic community...Orlando was used to Verna's contorted reasoning. 'Oh, leave him alone,' he said. 'He'll soon be old enough to take his own decision. You must stop blackmailing everyone. Enough now, Verna.'

Laila had prevented herself from forming any attachment whatsoever to her child. When Julio went to the loft to get her signature on some papers that were required to get his travel documents, she just signed blindly and didn't say a word to him. She then busied herself with cleaning paint-brushes and called out to Karina. 'Offer Mr Braganza a cup of coffee and then show him out. I'm finished with him.'

Next, Julio had to mobilize funds to pay for the passage home. Jamal, despite his disappointment at the turn of events, advanced him the money. Julio was to transfer the rupee equivalent to his brother Muzaffar when he reached Delhi. Roma advised Julio on how to manage the child on the long journey: 'Make friends with families with young children. They'll help out.'

Julio wound up his affairs at the office. Tony Haas had returned from Japan. Both Tony and Mr Rado gave him glowing recommendations addressed 'To Whom It May Concern.' Antonin sent a similar but more effusive cable from Tokyo. He saw a great career ahead for Julio in Independent India. There was talk of a new capital being built for the state of Punjab. What an opportunity! Mrs Weiner presented Julio with a volume of humour by Mark Twain. 'Honey,' she said, 'if you ever get depressed just dip into that.' She also presented Asif with a cuddly, talking teddy-bear.

Terry was the most affected by their departure. 'Ma honey-chile, what-ah mah gonna do withou-tchya?' She'd lose her job and the prestige of working for 'white folks.' Well, almost white.

As the day of departure approached, Roma made a list of things that Asif would need on a daily basis on the ship. The first journey was to Genoa, the second to Bombay. Photographs were taken. Even Jamal had tears in his eyes. As the ship sailed out of the harbour, Julio and Asif were on deck. Julio pointed out the Statue of Liberty to Asif. The child gazed intently at the statue and said, 'Mama.' It was the first distinct word he spoke.

11
CPWD

'Cho chweet! Completely adorable! Come to Auntie Mantie Shireen...See, he's smiling at me!'

Shireen Patel took little Asif in her arms and, declaring the child needed to be changed, took him and his baby suitcase into her bedroom. Julio and Rustom Patel had a few minutes to themselves.

Russi, Julio's old hostel roommate, smiled. 'I couldn't get an earlier train booking to Delhi. So you are to be here for four days in Bombay. It will be a pleasure for Shireen and me. We'll take good care of you both. Just let us know what to feed the baby. As for you, I know you love Parsi food and Shireen loves cooking it for friends.'

Julio was perspiring profusely. 'God, it's hot here. But I've missed Bombay. I'd like to roam about a bit, visit some of our old haunts...Now don't keep asking me about Laila. She has chosen to stay on in New York because of her art, her work and her friends. Asif is my responsibility.'

'How did you manage the ship journey?'

'It was easy. We got a lot of attention because we were an odd sight. I survived because I learned to nap each time Asif slept. His New York Granny, Roma, had trained him to have fairly regular habits...Now if Shireen takes over for a while, and you take a couple of days leave from Mr Batley's office, we can go visiting here and there. I'd like that. Bombay is so much more interesting than New York. Not cleaner by a long shot, but definitely more interesting.'

'Julio, before I forget, there are a couple of letters waiting for you. They arrived last week. One is from your parents in Delhi and the other one from "Isabella Braganza" in Goa. That's your sister, I presume? I'll leave you to read them in peace, and go and firm up arrangements with Shireen.'

~

The long letter from his mother was full of dire warnings should Julio take the baby to Magda's on Hailey Road. Verna wrote that she had child-proofed the flat in Connaught Place and that Allegro was most excited at the prospect of having a little child to talk to. In the long history of the Braganza family, Allegro was the only one who had ever followed baby talk.

The letter from Bella was intriguing. She wanted Julio to postpone his journey to Delhi in order to track down a woman named Carmen Costa. Carmen had sent Bella a letter two months ago, claiming she was a relative and wanting to visit Goa. Could she stay with Bella for a month while she got her bearings? Bella had not replied to Carmen's letter. She was far too busy to attend to a possible impostor. Then a second letter arrived from Carmen, saying she was related to Marco Braganza. That she was, in fact, his daughter and was in dire straits.

Bella wanted Julio and Russi to visit Carmen and check out the facts of her life. Meanwhile Bella would start unpacking Marco's cartons of papers and go through the ones marked 'Private and Confidential.' Perhaps they would contain a clue to the origins of this mysterious woman. This would take weeks to do. Bella thought Russi would be a reliable witness for Julio's interview with Carmen. Her address was c/o Homi Satarawala, Flat No. 5, Seabird Mansions, Bandra Fort Road, South Bandra.

The next day Julio and Russi took the suburban train to Bandra station and then a taxi to Seabird Mansions. Julio told Russi the full contents of Bella's letter. Russi was surprised.

'Shireen and I know the Satarawalas. Homi died of a heart attack a few weeks ago. He led a scandalous life, changing mistresses every few months. That is why his wife Freny walked out on him a few years ago. They had no children. Could your Carmen have been one of his women?'

'It would be a huge coincidence if she was. Here's two rupees for the taxi. I seem to have forgotten how to speak Hindi—Bombay Hindi! Ask the driver if he can wait for a couple of hours and take us back to your house. I don't fancy taking the train again. It's too crowded and we'd have to take a taxi from Bombay Central to your place anyway. Besides, I'm a bit anxious about how Shireen and Asif are getting on.' The taxi driver refused to wait.

Seabird Mansions was a very posh assemblage of three blocks of flats. No. 5 was on the third floor. The friends took the lift up and rang the bell. There was no response. Then they knocked on the door. A woman's voice called out, 'Who's there?' Julio introduced himself. 'Julio Braganza, brother of Isabella Braganza of Goa. A friend and I have come to meet Miss Carmen Costa.'

'Just a minute while I make myself presentable.' Then she opened the door a fraction and peered out. Both the young architects were struck by her beauty and buxom figure, though her hair was a mess. Carmen let them into a very lavishly-furnished flat.

'I'm so relieved Senhora Braganza got my letters. Excuse my poor English pronunciation. I was born and grew up in Lisbon. My mother Marcelena was a housekeeper and I was packed off to a convent at an early age...I'd like to offer you some refreshments but have very little in the house. Half a loaf of bread and some black tea. No sugar or milk. I can go downstairs, if you like, and borrow some sugar and milk from the ayah in the flat below. Oh, I have a tin of sardines which I could spread on some toast. Do you agree to this simple fare? It would make me happy, something I've not been since Homi Sir died and his bitch of a wife Freny served me three months' notice to clear out of this flat.'

Julio was taken aback by Carmen's situation. He took notes and was full of sympathy for her. He and Russi nodded their heads as she told them the sad story of her life: her link to the Canacona Braganzas, her mother's long years of servitude in

Lisbon, the letters and visits from Marco after he joined the police. Marco would spend one month's vacation every year in Lisbon and visit her mother without fail. Then suddenly the letters and visits stopped. Mother and daughter assumed Marco had married or had died. Marcelena got a letter-writer at the post office to compose a very formal letter to the Chief of Police in Goa. She asked about Marco's whereabouts. A junior officer informed her of Marco's death by drowning and supplied his widow's address in Saligao.

Marcelena was heartbroken. Her health declined. In her weakened state she contracted consumption. The night before she died, she called out to Carmen. She could hardly breathe. 'Marco Braganza was your biological father. We fell in love when he was just seventeen—I was old enough to be his mother. Nobody knows this. Please, please forgive me. I had to pretend I had been raped by some Germans up at the fort in Canacona. I am not sure if even Marco knew that he—not the Germans—was responsible for my pregnancy.'

Marcelena was dying slowly. She had one more thing to tell Carmen. 'If you are ever in financial difficulty, contact Marco's widow, Isabella. She's bound to help you for Marco's sake. What happened between Marco and me was a very long time ago. Too long to hold any grudges. Write to Isabella if you are in trouble. If she has any children, remember they are your brothers and sisters...Please open the windows...' By the time Carmen had completed this task she found her mother had died.

Julio had remained silent through Carmen's tale of woe. He felt profoundly sorry for her. There was a pause in Carmen's narrative as she wiped her eyes with a not-too-clean handkerchief. Russi spoke up in a gentle tone.

'Miss Carmen, how did you meet the Satarawalas? My wife and I used to meet them at the Anjuman at New Year's Day celebrations. Freny dressed very well...Then she started to come alone—said Homi was abroad. Did you meet him in Portugal?'

'Yes, but that is a long story. My mother used to slave for a branch of the Braganza family that had settled down in Lisbon.

They were a spendthrift couple—Clara and Francisco. They were killed in a train crash in the French Riviera. This left my mother homeless and unemployed. She rented a room with her meagre savings and started cleaning house for other Goan families in the neighbourhood. She was quite old by then...I earned a pittance doing odd bits of secretarial work in Lisbon's smartest hat shop for men. The nuns had prepared me well. But I hated my job.'

'How did Homi come into the picture?' asked Julio.

'Mr Homi was in the import-export business. He used to come to the hat shop and try on various hats. He would ask for me—to help him decide among different styles. This was not my job but my boss insisted that I wait on the oriental gentleman from Bombay.

'One thing led to another. Mr Homi and I grew quite fond of each other and he offered me a job with him in Bombay. I could be his housekeeper and secretary rolled into one. There would be a handsome salary and full board and lodging. His wife had moved out so there would be no one to nag me. By this time my mother had died. I hated the cramped little room in which we had lived for six years! I despised the job in the hat shop. I had never seen India. And I had grown quite fond of Mr Homi—please don't embarrass me by asking any more about our relationship...I came to live in Bombay in No. 5 here.

'I was happy with Mr Homi. The work was light. There were two other servants to see to the heavy work—washing, cleaning, cooking, shopping for food. My duties were to supervise them and cook European food from time to time. Mr Homi adored western food, particularly French cuisine.

'Three times a week—Monday, Wednesday, Friday—I accompanied him to his office and dealt with all the business correspondence that was in Portuguese. I had to learn the names of various items that he traded in Gujarati, Marathi, Hindi and Konkani. Konkani, the language of my mother's birthplace...I want very much to see Goa and meet the relatives my mother mentioned before she died.

'Mr Homi had health problems. He drank like a fish—

reminded me of Senhor Francisco. That Senhor's capacity to drink three bottles of feni at one go was apparently well known in the Canacona region. I tried to persuade Mr Homi to cut down his drinking, but he refused, and told me it was none of my business.

'On one occasion he showed me the draft of a codicil to his will. If he died, I was to have the use of No. 5 for a full three months or until I found another place to live: "whichever was earlier". Then, a little over two months ago, he was found slumped over his desk in the office. Died of a heart attack.

'Mrs Freny has been vindictive. She had the telephone and electricity connections cut. Then a week ago she had the water supply stopped. I carry two buckets of water up every day from downstairs. My friend—the ayah—sometimes smuggles leftover food to me. So, Mr Julio, you can see what condition I'm in. Mrs Freny sent a note yesterday, ordering me out in six days. She says she has tried to find me a job but everyone has objections. One, I have no letter of recommendation; two, I have no record of being an office secretary; and three, I am not an Indian and have a very poor accent.'

Julio looked up from his notebook. 'Carmen, you have very little time left. The lack of a phone here is a nuisance. I'll ring up my sister in Goa tonight and tell her your story—Russi, I hope it's okay if I use your phone.'

'No problem. I can also give Bella my impressions. But there is one thing you and I can do before then. Here, Carmen, accept fifty rupees to tide you over for a week. That's all I have in my wallet right now. And give me Freny's address. I'll visit her tomorrow and ask for an extension of stay for you. We have to consult Julio's sister about your going to her place in Goa. Julio's train tickets to Delhi are booked. He'll leave in a couple of days. I'll take care of things once he's gone.'

~

Bella was astonished by Julio and Russi's accounts of Carmen's predicament. The records she had found of Marco's journeys to Lisbon, his correspondence with Marcelena and the references to her daughter, all corroborated Carmen's story. She asked Julio for another day to sift through Marco's last letters, written just before he drowned. The next day she rang Julio at Russi's.

'Julio, I'd feel much happier if you'd agree to bring the woman to Goa yourself. I feel rather awkward welcoming an adult step-daughter to Braganza House. Tonio will be puzzled to have a sister—so much older than him...Give it a thought, please. Nothing urgent awaits you in Delhi, except Mummy's nagging... Meanwhile, give Carmen a couple hundred rupees. I'll pay you back when we meet.'

'No, Bella. I can't take a week off to come to Goa. Some potential employers have invited me to meet them in Delhi. I can't miss those chances. Forgive me. Carmen is, I'm sure, fully capable of reaching Braganza House on her own. The steamer to Vasco and then two bus rides to Saligao. I'll be sure to give her detailed instructions. I'll even draw a map.'

'I'm disappointed. Oh well! Get Russi to ring me up when Carmen departs from Bombay. I'll have to get a room ready for her. Tell her she must never reveal her background to the people here. It would be most embarrassing for me. As she is fluent in Portuguese, I'll try to find her a job in Panjim. I'll do the best I can for her...'

~

The comings and goings over Carmen had taken up a lot of Julio's time. He had only a day and a half left to go roaming around Bombay.

Babies were a rare sight in Khushrow Bagh, the Parsi colony where the Patels lived. While Russi and Julio commuted between Russi's house and Seabird Mansions, neighbours kept dropping in on Shireen to coo over Asif. The child was on his best behaviour. Except that he kept reaching out to tug the scarves the women wore on their heads. Asif had had several mothers—Laila-Karina-Barbra, Roma and—after a fashion—Jamal, Benson and Julio. He was not intimidated by the many Parsi matrons who buzzed around him.

The first thing Julio noticed was how little Bombay had changed. Not a single skyscraper. And how drab the buildings looked. There was little maintenance. And how slums were coming up in every nook and cranny. There were few cars—outdated models, for the most part. Yet Julio found the whole assemblage interesting. There were many different rhythms in the morphology. This was not the case in New York.

Julio and Russi visited their alma mater, the J.J. School. They met old teachers and looked in on a couple of studios where perspiring students were bent over drawing-boards and T-squares.

Julio whispered to Russi. 'They know nothing about the modern movement in architecture. Makes me furious. It's all late art deco and revivalism. Mr Batley has cast a long shadow.'

'I thought you worshipped Batley,' said Russi. 'He's not been keeping too well. He's gone to Ahmedabad where we have some projects.'

'I used to worship him. He gave me my big break into the world of architecture. But he's a conservative when it comes to matters of style. I'll show you my New York portfolio. You'll understand then why my boss there, Antonin Raymond, was decades ahead of Mr Batley.'

That afternoon Russi took Julio to the Elephanta Caves, situated on an island a boat-ride across the harbour. Julio had actually never visited the caves before despite the years he had spent in Bombay. Russi was on his sixth visit, and ecstatic. 'Look at the vast spaces inside, the sculpture, the play of light and shade, the beautifully-proportioned courtyards. All conceived by master builders fifteen hundred years ago...Julio, don't scoff at what you call the "revivalists." We have a rich heritage of art and architecture to draw on. What does New York have?'

Julio had to admit he was impressed. 'But,' he said, 'you have to understand that the greatest modern masters are also inspired by tradition. You have Wright and Corbusier in addition to Antonin Raymond. Much of Raymond's work draws on traditional Japanese architecture. Like Corbusier, Raymond has experimented extensively with using rough concrete as an exterior finish. But enough of shop talk. Let's go to Madras Coffee House at Flora Fountain. We need to spend some hours there nursing a single cup of South Indian coffee, for old times' sake.'

~

Russi's face lit up as he turned to Julio. 'Don't stare, but two tables over, there are three modernist painters. The chap with the long black beard is Husain, to his left is Ara, and on his right, you have Raza. There are other artists too in the group. It included Souza—he's now pushed off to England. You told me you knew him when he was a child in Goa. Did you know he has the distinction of being kicked out of our J.J. School for participating in the Quit India Movement? Then he became a Communist. He helped found the Progressive Artists' Group. He's had a tough life—but I can't bear the little I've seen of his work.'

'Oh, Russi, you can't stand anything that smacks of modernism! There's so much happening in the world that is new. You've got to keep an open mind and get exposure to the new forms of expression in the arts, architecture, poetry, literature...'

The two friends then took a bus home and were greeted with glowing reports of Asif's behaviour. He was sleeping and Shireen looked quite exhausted. Russi had asked Shireen to track down Mrs Satarawala's phone number while he and Julio were away during the day. She handed Russi a slip of paper with the number. 'I'll rustle up some dinner. Haven't had a chance to cook anything decent. Read the paper while the two of you wait for your food. And Russi had better ring up Mrs Satarawala. The matter of Carmen must be settled once and for all.'

Mrs Satarawala's bearer picked up the phone. 'Madam is not available. She has guests in the drawing-room...Wait, she is arriving this minute.'

Russi introduced himself and described the Carmen situation, couching his words with the utmost delicacy. Freny Satarawala was not stirred.

'I will arrive at No. 5 day-after-tomorrow morning. I intend to move in there. I'll go with my carpenters and painters early in the morning. So that shameless whore had better vacate tomorrow itself. I never could understand what my husband saw in her, or what she saw in him...No, Mr Patel, an extension is out of the question. As you are an architect you should appreciate how difficult it is to assemble skilled workmen...I have guests so I must ring off. Good night.'

~

By an inexplicable coincidence an event took place on the last day of Julio's stay in Bombay that altered the course of his life. Early that morning Russi hurried into the spare bedroom, waving a copy of *The Times of India*.

'Julio, there's an ad for architectural positions in the CPWD—Central Public Works Department. There's even one for a Senior Architect, which you would qualify for...Julio, here's your chance! The last date for applications is a week from now. You always said you wanted to build, build, build—the CPWD builds innumerable buildings every year all over the country! Far, far more than the ten largest private architectural practices put together!'

Julio thought this development too good to be true. 'Let me see the ad...Yes, I'll have a couple of days in Delhi to get my application in order. My mother will gladly take Asif off my hands. You're an angel to have spotted the ad, Russi. I'm going to give it my best shot. I'm all packed now. Asif and I will take a taxi to Bombay Central in an hour. Don't want to miss the train to Delhi...Don't bother to see us off. It's more important to pick up Carmen and her luggage. It's saintly of you to have her stay here while you make her travel arrangements to Goa. Take Shireen with you to No. 5. She could help hurry Carmen up.'

'Julio, I'll do my best by Carmen. Freny Satarawala called this morning. She said her bearer would reach No. 5 by nine o'clock and take charge of the keys to the cupboards and the flat. That gives Shireen and me just an hour to reach Bandra.'

Shireen spoke up. She had Asif in her arms. 'Julio,' she said, 'why don't you leave the baby with me for six months—until he can run around on his own and is fully potty-trained? I think it's a brilliant idea, don't you? It would give you time to settle down to a job, and spare your aged mother a lot of strain. And it would give Russi and me great pleasure. What do you say, Russi?'

'Don't be ridiculous, Shiroo. Julio's mother must still be in her fifties—not aged at all. And she has raised three children, as I told you. What do you know about caring for babies?'

Julio, caught in the middle, tried to find a diplomatic way out. 'Thanks, Shireen, but I think we can manage for now. But should the need ever arise, I'll remember your kind offer. You never know what the future holds.'

Russi and Shireen dropped Julio and Asif off at Bombay Central with a twenty-four-hour supply of scented diapers and baby food. Then they instructed the taxi driver to take the shortest route to Seabird Mansions. Russi assured Shireen that Carmen was a very respectable lady, a good bit older than themselves. It's just that she had suffered more than her fair share of bad luck.

Freny Satarawala had given her bearer strict instructions to see that Carmen did not make off with any of Homi's belongings, particularly the valuable curios he had collected on his many travels to Europe, America and the Portuguese colonies across the globe. Forewarned, Carmen had done her packing the night before, so Shireen's presence was not strictly necessary. Russi explained his plan for the journey to Goa. Carmen listened attentively.

'I haven't had a chance to go to a travel agent yet. Steamer tickets to Goa are hard to get at short notice. But I'll try my best. Meanwhile, you can stay with us in Khushrow Bagh. So much has happened in the last few days that your head must be spinning. And Shireen must get Julio's baby out of *her* head. Your stay with us will do her good. And she is a very good cook, aren't you, Shiroo? We'll feed you up—you look starved, Carmen.'

The ticket to Goa was obtained for eight days later. By then Carmen had put on a little weight. At No. 5 she had had no money for soap those last few weeks. Now, with some of the money Julio had given her, she had bought soap and some inexpensive cosmetics. She wore clean clothes and applied some make-up. She began smiling.

~

Verna, mother and grandmother, took charge as soon as Julio and Asif arrived at New Delhi station. Asif reached out to a candyfloss-wala on the railway platform. Julio searched his wallet for a four anna coin. Verna smacked his hand.

'Put that away! Save it for the coolies. No grandchild of mine is going to eat that infection-filled rubbish. You have to be careful these days. Infection, infection everywhere. The child has come from New York—he has no immunity to our Indian diseases.'

Orlando smiled to himself. With Asif to care for, Verna might become less of a thorn in his flesh. That's what he hoped. Braganza & Sons was doing well. He had a competent staff that he had trained over several years. O'Brien had moved back to the parent shop in Calcutta, where Emilio and Rachel were on their last legs in their late nineties. They had finally managed to get rid of Derek Goff. Orlando had more or less given up tuning pianos except for his most loyal and insistent customers. He now had a bad back, developed by bending over the pegs of grand pianos.

Julio got his application together: biodata, testimonials, colour photographs of perspective drawings, pictures of projects he had worked on for Antonin Raymond and Mr Rado (no one in the New York office had known his first name). Julio submitted the application with supporting documents in person to the CPWD office located in the barracks north of the Central Secretariat. He obtained a receipt and decided he was relaxed enough to see a film with his father at the Rivoli—Charlie Chaplin's *Modern Times*.

Then the visit with Asif to his biological grandparents, Magda and Muzaffar, on Hailey Road. Magda was of the long-held view that Asif would be best off staying with her.

'He would have other small children to play with. What's the point of him being cooped up in a flat in Connaught Place? You must have noticed the increase in traffic and the smelly petrol fumes. Here I have two ayahs, several pets and flowering shrubs in the courtyard...Trust Laila to leave you holding the baby. She was always stubborn and arrogant...You had better go to Uncle's room and introduce the child to his grandfather.'

Muzaffar was napping. He woke up at the sound of Asif laughing. He had difficulty recognizing Julio. 'You are...? And the child...?'

'Julio Braganza, Uncle. Your landlord. And this is my son—Laila's son—formally known as Asif Jackson Braganza.'

Muzaffar reached behind his headrest and produced a jar of Marie biscuits. 'Here you are. A biscuit from your Nana...But why "Jackson?" Strange name for an Indian.'

So Julio explained about Jackson, the famous painter. He also told Muzaffar about the money he owed him on account of the loan from Jamal. Two hundred and fifty dollars.

Muzaffar looked puzzled. 'That's about twelve hundred rupees. Just set it off against the rent we would pay you for the next eight months. That's a tidy arrangement and I won't have to declare it for income tax. Jamal should have written to me and clarified what the money is for. I always found him so absent-minded. Didn't you? But he's a real gentleman. He's wasting his time in Queens. He's a poet now and should keep the company of other Urdu poets. Here in India. After Independence we are seeing a flowering of the arts. The winds of modernism are blowing here and there. There is some good art being done even in Delhi. Of course, the financial returns are painfully meagre. But that too will change in time. Practically every artist or writer I have met has to have a day job to make ends meet...Asif, visit me every week. I'll teach you some Hindi nursery rhymes. The ones they sing in Nani's school. Your other grandma, Verna, is bound to teach you only English ones.'

On his way out Julio found Magda deep in conversation with a Swami Shivananda in the living-room. They did not appreciate the interruption. Magda smiled stiffly. 'So you're off, the two of you? Swamiji, please bless my grandson. Let us pray he has a happy, creative childhood.'

The swami produced a small tin from somewhere in the folds of his saffron-coloured robes. He dabbed a little of its contents on his right forefinger and applied a tika on Asif's forehead. He recited some mantras in a high-pitched voice, and then farted loudly. Asif was terrified. He began to cry. Magda shooed them off.

~

Russi rang the next night with news of Carmen and Bella. 'It seems Carmen has reached Goa safe but not too sound—she was upset by the lurching of the steamer. Bella was standing on the dock, displaying a placard—"Carmen Costa," as she and Carmen would not have been able to recognize one another.'

Julio was puzzled. 'Carmen could have travelled to Saligao on her own. I'd given her detailed instructions. It's a shame Bella troubled herself. By the way, why didn't she ring *me* up?'

'Well, Julio, she wanted to thank us for the Carmen business and, as she put it, would have had to talk to your mother had she called Delhi. Then there would have been thousands of questions. Bella is not prepared to be quizzed about Carmen. Not yet. She wanted to thank Shireen and me anyway. It's the least we could have done for the poor woman. Have you submitted your application for the CPWD job? I have a feeling you will get a good position. Keep me informed about developments on that front.'

'Yes, Russi, all is in order. I expect it will be an age before they call me for an interview...Give my love to Shireen. If Freny Satarawala calls, don't tell her where Carmen has gone. She would only create mischief.'

~

Asif was fascinated by Allegro, now widely reputed to be the oldest bird that had ever lived. A short write-up on him was included in every guidebook on Delhi. Tourists often came to visit him, to chat a while about life in the various cities in which he had lived—a hundred, two hundred, three hundred years ago. Although Orlando and Verna were quite well off, Verna couldn't resist passing around an old biscuit tin, asking for 'contributions' from visitors at the end of every visit. She would say, 'It's for founding a bird hospital when Allegro finally leaves us. It will be called, "The Allegro Armstrong Braganza Memorial Charitable Hospital for Birds".' A Swedish visitor once suggested the hospital simply be called 'Wings.'

Remembering his own childhood friendship with Allegro, Julio would hold Asif up against Allegro's 'house'—Allegro had always disliked the word 'cage' and insisted that it be called his 'house'—and the old bird would sing to him the music-hall ditties (la-la-la) learned at The Lazy Duck and The Black Bull in Victorian London. Verna had expressly forbidden Allegro from teaching Asif the naughty words of such songs.

~

After three weeks of anxious waiting, Julio received a letter from the CPWD summoning him to an interview. He prepared a portfolio of original drawings and presented himself at ten o'clock sharp. There were seven other short-listed candidates, some of whom had foreign degrees—from London, Liverpool and the U.S. When Julio's turn came at two o'clock he was full of anxiety. He answered questions hesitantly. No one had had lunch. The examiners wished to hurry things up.

The CPWD bigwigs were divided on his candidature. Two of the senior architects on the interview panel had been students of Batley's at the J.J. School and supported Julio out of a sense of loyalty to the great teacher. Others, the majority, found the work Julio had done with Antonin Raymond grotesque and too modern for their taste. Too much exposed concrete. The Director General of the CPWD, a civil engineer, cast the deciding vote. 'His perspective drawings are excellent, and his architectural work is forward-looking. As good as Le Corbusier's plans for Chandigarh. Batley has had his day. On my last study tour of Europe, I saw a lot of the new architecture. And the PM supports a new beginning in the style of our public buildings. I'd put

Mr Braganza at the top of the panel. He has just returned from New York and is willing to join immediately. The other candidates are all from State PWDs and it would take ages to arrange transfers and deputations to the Centre.'

'But sir,' the Chief Architect protested, 'he is too junior. Only thirty-one. We should consider him for a post of Deputy Architect only, not Senior Architect. Others in the Department would resent such a young man being posted over their heads.'

'No, Sharmaji, Mr Braganza's work is brilliant. We must reward merit and not mere seniority. He has the potential to become the most accomplished architect in government service... Enough of all this quibbling. My mind is made up. I have to go to the Prime Minister's office at five. Let's sign all the papers right away. I may get Cabinet clearance this very evening. I'll take Mr Braganza's portfolio with me. He can join in a couple of weeks, after he clears his medical exam at Willingdon Hospital. Sharmaji, as Chief Architect you must expedite everything.'

The offer of appointment reached Julio in six days. He promptly accepted and submitted his joining report the day the new Constitution of India was adopted by Parliament. 26th January 1950. Chief Architect Sharma reluctantly gave Julio a large room to himself in the barracks, the first time Julio had been so privileged.

He bought a Raleigh bicycle. Only the Director General had use of an official car. Julio reckoned the bike-ride to office would take about ten minutes from Connaught Place. The bus journey would take forty-five minutes if one included waiting time. Orlando offered him the use of the family car and driver, but Julio declined. 'I don't want to encourage envy in the office. Most of my colleagues use bicycles. There's a secure stand to which we can chain them.'

~

Julio soon realized that the civil engineers in the CPWD had the upper hand in most matters. He resolved to befriend them in every way possible. The architects were a small minority in the staff and were great grumblers. Julio soon made friends with everyone. He made a charming suggestion to the Chief Architect.

'Sir, may I have your permission to host lunch-hour in my room? We all bring tiffin boxes but have nowhere to sit and eat, except at our drawing-boards. I have a large desk. It can easily seat ten. We could share our lunches—dishes from different parts of India—and talk about our families and current affairs. This would promote cordial relations among the staff and help reduce hierarchical stratification.'

'Haikal...what? Such big words you use, Braganza. The rules permit you to have only five chairs in your room. Now you want ten! If I permit feasting in your room, who will clean up afterwards? And you would all talk office politics and undermine my authority. I'll have to present your proposal to the Director General. Only he has the power to permit such unconventional things.'

The Director General, DG for short, agreed to Julio's plan right away and said he would join the group for lunch from time to time. He had a Master's degree in Civil Engineering from Cornell and rather liked Julio's idea of bringing about a more egalitarian atmosphere in the office.

Julio was assigned to work on several projects simultaneously: hospital, airport, railway station, numerous office buildings, housing, defence installations, buildings for All India Radio and the Post and Telegraph Department. Julio tried his best to introduce the modern idiom in his sketches and perspectives but was usually over-ruled by his seniors. He thought of appealing to the DG but this would antagonize his colleagues. They wanted a profusion of chajja awnings and pavilions decorating government buildings as a means of asserting an Indian identity.

Julio would arrive home dog-tired at around eight in the evening. Asif would be asleep and Verna impatient to start dinner. Some days the pressure of work would be so intense that Julio would spend the night at the office. His salary was only six hundred rupees a month.

~

Allegro now had a slice of toast, a fried egg and some bacon for breakfast. This was enough to carry him through the day until five o'clock when he would have his dinner of dal and rice and an apple. And then the peg of brandy at eight. At first he rather enjoyed his visitors. They asked such silly questions: Do you remember the day you were hatched? Can you read books? How do you like Connaught Place? Can you fly? What do you think of Winston Churchill? Do you support the creation of Pakistan? Allegro had witty answers ready for all.

Verna had taken to suggesting how much of a contribution the visitors should make: five rupees for Indians and ten rupees for white people. Orlando disapproved of Verna's exploitative scheme to collect funds. He thought the urge to collect and hoard money was due to her lower-middle class background. He also feared the income tax department would get after her. No trust had been set up and registered yet. He appreciated his wife's charitable motives but deplored her tactics. For example, she would write to the publishers of various guidebooks making outrageous claims: Allegro was three hundred and fifty-six years old, the longest-living bird in recorded history; he spoke eighteen different languages; he knew all the holy books of ten different religions by heart; and he could tell the future.

News of the wondrous bird soon reached the staff in Julio's office. His colleagues, their spouses, and sundry children and in-laws would visit Orlando's flat on Saturday afternoons for 'darshan.' They declared Allegro was a sacred bird and insisted on performing puja before him. Verna had the good sense not to shake her biscuit tin in the face of these 'official' pilgrims. Admission was free for them. Allegro found the smoke from the incense sticks a real trial. He choked often.

The sacred angle was good for Verna's business. Visitors dropped in at all times of the day. She had a sign painted and installed at the foot of the stairs leading up to their flat.

For Darshan of the SACRED BIRD
Pilgrims and Tourists
may Kindly Respect the following Timings
10 a.m. to 12.30 p.m.
4 p.m. to 6 p.m. ONLY.
Sundays and National Holidays Closed.

Little Asif was quite bewildered by all the strangers trooping in and out. He detested being chucked under the chin, by women in particular. He would often burst into tears. His ayah, a Bengali widow named Agnes, would be summoned to take him away.

Agnes had a history. She had looked after the aged Emilio and Rachel in Calcutta until the task of carrying them from bedroom to bathroom and dining-room had become too much for her. Her place had been taken by two strapping young nurses from a private nurses' bureau on Park Street. Agnes had been seduced by an American soldier in 1943. This scoundrel had decamped two months before their child was born. The baby, a daughter, died of malaria six months later. Agnes carried the burden of those memories stoically. She herself had been an orphan, raised by nuns. Thus she was completely fluent in Bengali and English and went to confession and Mass regularly. The Braganzas were the only family she had now. When the decision to shift her to Delhi to take care of Asif was taken, she took the train from Calcutta on her own. Verna resented her at first. She complained to Orlando.

'Agnes speaks English. Don't you remember? Now we will have no privacy. She'll understand all our conversations. I refuse to speak to her directly in English...She'll have to learn my version of kitchen Hindustani. She's a servant after all. You can try out your rusty Bengali. She has a terrible accent when she speaks English. I don't want Asif to pick up her dreadful pronunciation.'

Allegro's fame had continued to grow. Verna had to organize queues, particularly when the special pujas were held on Tuesdays at the Hanuman Mandir down the road. People would pray there and then make a beeline for the Sacred Bird. Sometimes busloads of school children would arrive, shepherded by harassed teachers.

Foreign tourists were keen on questioning Allegro about the past. Indians, on the other hand, wanted to hear predictions of the future. Some wanted their fortunes told. Now Allegro had no means of doing this. He would therefore size up the age of the supplicant and offer safe advice:

- If you don't eat scientifically you will suffer from gas.
- If you study hard you may become a doctor.
- If you don't practice birth control you will have too many children.
- There will be discord in your family.
- You are thrifty, so will become rich after twenty years.

Allegro knew he was pulling fast ones but he hated to disappoint the pilgrims. They were, after all, satisfied with his predictions. It was a matter of faith and they had faith in this miraculous Sacred Bird. Agnes, though, took a dim view of these tamashas. She grew tired of going down the stairs dozens of times a day to let in the curious and the devout.

After a couple of years of being on constant display Allegro declared he'd had enough of being a Sacred Bird. He longed to return to the old days when the Braganzas allowed him plenty of peace and quiet and he interacted only with members of his own family. Verna was forced to put up a new sign downstairs:

The Sacred Bird has taken a five-year vow of complete silence.
He will therefore NOT give any interviews.
Inconvenience is regretted.

But Verna had the satisfaction of having collected a little short of sixty thousand rupees for the charitable bird hospital. Now she constantly nagged Orlando to lease some roof-top premises in Connaught Place where a large enclosure could be erected for the birds. Orlando was unenthusiastic.

'Constructing large wire-mesh enclosures will not be enough. You will not only need a bird doctor, but also funds to pay for attendants and medicines and food. At a conservative guess you will need three thousand rupees a month.'

'Oh, faithless husband! Just set up the trust and donations will start pouring in. My Hindu friends will be generous, just you wait. Put up the netted enclosures and build two rooms, and leave the rest to me. Allegro likes the idea of a hospital named after him. He says it would give a larger purpose to his life, and we should not wait until he dies because he may live another hundred years.'

Orlando clutched at a straw. 'A bird hospital would be against municipal by-laws. They'd come and demolish it.'

Orlando consulted Allegro, who didn't see what the fuss was about. 'Build the enclosure above our own building. We can surely get Benoybabu's descendants to agree to a few honourable encroachments on their terrace rights. That will create a vast enclosure for the ailing pigeons, crows, parrots and sparrows who are likely to be our patients. You will need to partition the enclosure because not all bird species get along with each other. I learnt this to my cost in Shillong.'

Orlando was rather ashamed that this simple arrangement had not occurred either to Verna or to him. Benoybabu's grandson readily agreed and promptly made a donation of five thousand rupees, which was really a lot of money in those days. The Allegro Braganza Charitable Hospital for Birds came into existence when the trust was registered. The roof-top rooms and netted enclosures were designed by Julio and looked quite handsome. He arranged to get a licence from the Municipal Committee through his CPWD contacts. Verna was thrilled by all the progress but began to worry about getting the right staff. Also, the vast facility was ready but there were no birds in it as yet.

Agnes had watched all these preparations. She told Verna one day that she knew something about caring for birds. She had helped the nuns treat injured creatures at the orphanage in which she had grown up. Calcutta was full of such birds, especially in the kite-flying season when they got entangled in kite strings. So Agnes volunteered her services to get things started.

Against her better judgement and at Agnes's urging, Verna agreed to launch the bird hospital and infirmary with no staff except for the part-time services of Agnes. Verna contacted Ashok Kumar who ran a thriving advertising business from a hole in the wall in B Block of Connaught Place. Her idea was to prepare slides inviting members of the cinema-going public to bring injured birds in to the Allegro Braganza, etcetera, etcetera. Such slides were to be shown before the commencement of films, during intervals, and at the end of film screenings.

Ashok prepared the slides according to Verna's instructions. At the top of the slide was a rough rendition of a bird of indeterminate species dragging an injured wing. Below that was the message inviting the public to avail—Free of Charge—of the Hospital at No. 2, A Block Terrace, Connaught Place. Timings: 10 am to 1 p.m., 4 p.m. to 6 p.m. The slides were shown at every show in the four local cinema halls for a week. All this set back the trust some eight hundred rupees. But it was worth it. Patients were brought in at the rate of eight to ten a day.

The routine was as follows. The patient was first interviewed by Allegro in Birdy Hindustani. Allegro would then communicate his preliminary diagnosis to Verna and Agnes, who would take the bird up to the first-aid room on the roof. After treatment, the bird would be placed in the appropriate enclosure. Once there, it would convalesce for as long as required. Then it would be released into the wild. This was the theory.

In practice it was rather different. Many members of the public brought in ailing pet birds: budgerigars, parrots, mynahs, even chickens. Verna had intended to treat only wild birds. But she was blackmailed into treating pets—and that too for free. The pet-owners complained that the cinema ads they'd seen made no reference to wild birds only. Why should pet birds be discriminated against? They would complain to the police if Verna turned them away.

So it was back to the biscuit tin, soliciting a flat contribution of five rupees per private patient per visit. Verna reverted to this strategy as a way of cross-subsidizing treatment for the wild birds.

Also as a means to fund the salary of a sincere young doctor, Nitin Dhar, who Verna had lured away from the Jain Mandir Bird Hospital in Chandni Chowk. Agnes, who for some time had felt out of her depth, was relieved when Dr Nitin signed on. Her duties were now largely confined to feeding the patients and ensuring the sweeper cleaned and washed the terrace enclosures every day to prevent an accumulation of droppings. Agnes could only spare about three hours in the mornings for her hospital work. Asif returned from Magda's school by one and Agnes had to take care of him after that.

~

Magda Imam ran her school with a mixture of humour, kindness and sternness in an unlikely combination of virtues. It was a very creative environment. The little children were encouraged to act out all their lessons. This developed self-confidence and a love of theatre, music and dance. Asif loved every minute he spent there and was thoroughly bored on weekends in Connaught Place. He called Magda 'Nani' and not 'Aunty Magda' as did all the other children. Asif hardly ever got to meet his 'Nana,' his grandfather Muzaffar. On some Sundays Julio would take Asif to meet the old man after church. On these occasions Magda would shut herself up in her room, deep in meditation.

Sometimes on Julio and Asif's visits, they would run into Kitty who had started to bring two little children to Magda's whether the school was in session or not. Kitty was always exhausted, as at forty-something she had to care for her young son Robin as well as a toddler, Bubbles. This was her granddaughter, whose mother Mia had died in childbirth. The child's father, the Rajkumar of Rajgarh, refused to take responsibility for the baby girl and insisted that her maternal grandparents, the Sandawas, take over. And so Bubbles had been unceremoniously deposited at Eight Hailey Road.

Asif was now five and talked nineteen to the dozen. Julio had to work long hours at the CPWD. He regretted that he spent so little time with his son, and hoped the child's extensive interactions with Verna, Orlando, Allegro, Agnes and the other servants made up for this. He prayed they would give sensible answers to the five hundred questions Asif asked every day.

The Braganza clan were not great letter-writers. From time to time Julio's sisters would write to Orlando and Verna giving bare-bones accounts of their lives. Bella was very pleased with Carmen, now her manager. Carmen had taken over the day-to-day supervision of the staff and was a wizard at keeping accounts. Bella's son, Tonio, was now a teenager and went to school in Panjim. Bella's guest house had become a landmark in Saligao, with visitors coming just to admire the architecture of Braganza House and have a cup of coffee. With Carmen in charge, Bella had the leisure to take up some translation work from time to time. The Portuguese administration gave no indication of quitting the territory. 'We've been here for four hundred years and we are here to stay a thousand,' was a common assertion.

Maria, Boris and their son, Yanek, spent nine months of the year in rented accommodation up in the hills of Mussoorie. They were cabaret artistes at Hackman's Grand Hotel and also at the Savoy. Maria had a new stage name: Kashmirabai Benkovsky. She had always loved to dance and loved her work. Boris called himself Bravo Benkovsky. When the weather turned cold they shifted base to Fonseca's Hotel in New Delhi, travelling to the Taj Hotel in Bombay or the Park Hotel in Calcutta from time to time. They'd go wherever they could get bookings for their exotic floor shows. These included modern dance duets learned at Uday Shankar's erstwhile dance academy in Almora, and several 'exhibition' dance numbers of different schools of ballroom dancing. At Hackman's in Mussoorie they were occasionally accompanied by a live band. The rest of the time they had to make do with a temperamental Grundig tape-recorder, their most prized possession.

Yanek got used to spending several hours on his own each evening and night. His parents rarely returned home before two o'clock in the morning. Yanek would wake up at seven, get dressed on his own, eat cornflakes, and sprint off to the Hampton

Court School down the hill. It was a convent school that also admitted small boys. A simple lunch would be served by the nuns at noon. Yanek would be home by three, when his parents were to be found cooking, bathing and doing strenuous exercises to keep their bodies in beautiful and supple shape.

Maria was not a good cook. So Yanek was raised on a diet of boiled potatoes, plain dal and rice, and various dishes of boiled cabbage hastily put together by his Polish father. Yanek's parents, on the other hand, had sumptuous dinners at the hotels where they performed. Yanek never complained about the Benkovskys' gypsy lifestyle. He was a bit afraid of his father, who hardly ever spoke to him, but he loved Maria. He never tired of combing her 'long, long, long' black hair. She would sit on a stool in front of a low dressing- table, and Yanek would comb her straight luxuriant hair from the top of her head down its entire length—which stopped just short of the floor. Maria never failed to hug and kiss him after this.

Asif and Yanek would meet at Magda's school in the winter months when Hampton Court was shut. They had great fun banging away together on Magda's ancient German piano. She had long given up trying to keep it in tune.

On their occasional visits to Connaught Place, Boris and Maria would feel most uncomfortable. Each time, Verna would say or do something to remind them that she did not approve of their liaison. Verna was convinced that they had never gone through a proper marriage ceremony, which made them mortal sinners and Yanek an illegitimate child. In private moments Verna would bemoan her fate to Orlando.

'What have I done to deserve this family? Tonio has no father and it is now too late for Bella to marry again. Asif has a selfish mother who prefers to dabble in art and who-knows-what-else. And Yanek is a bastard. Tell me, Orlando, did I not bring up my children properly?'

~

The bird hospital had taken off successfully. Dr Nitin Dhar, a Kashmiri, found the workload much less than he was used to at his old hospital in Chandni Chowk. In free moments he would chat with Allegro, marvelling at the old bird's defiance of aging, evolution and biology. Science had no ready explanation for Allegro's unique characteristics. Dr Dhar secretly wondered what an autopsy on Allegro would reveal. What was the magic of his seeming immortality?

Julio was now busy designing housing for government servants and for refugees from Pakistan. The many colonies were located all over New Delhi and its suburbs. Chief Architect Sharma would praise him for his industriousness and turn to him for advice on major and minor issues. He would even occasionally drop in for Julio's lunch-hour conclaves, eating ham sandwiches and not saying much. He promised his young architects that he would get government flats allotted to them on a seniority basis. Julio's turn would come up in four years.

The Chief Architect was an unhappy man in his private life. His Scottish wife, Alison, had run off with an Austrian violinist. She had closed up her dress shop in Khan Market and escaped the heat and grime of Delhi. She was somewhere in Europe. Alison had, more pertinently to Sharma's sense of misery, abandoned a daughter and a son. These details were revealed to Julio only gradually.

Sharma would grumble, 'We are both the fathers of motherless children. We have a lot in common and must stick together. My boy, Rana, is at St Columba's and the girl, Lekha, is at the convent next door—on the other side of the cathedral. You must send your son to Columba's—how old is he?...Going to be eight? Then next year he must shift from that school run by the lunatic German lady. I would not recommend Modern School. It's full of rowdy children from rich business families. Bad role models for children of middle-class government servants like us. At Catholic schools, at any rate, they inculcate frugal habits and enforce strict discipline.'

Julio was embarrassed. He had already signed up for Modern School. According to Magda it was the only school in Delhi that had the resources to fund a creative environment for young children. It had a little zoo, a pottery studio, a photo laboratory, playing fields for sports of several kinds, a swimming pool, and even arrangements for horse-riding. Magda felt that the transition from her Ramniketan to Modern would be smooth and not traumatic for 'Auntie Magda's babies.'

Orlando and Verna were keen that Asif learn to play the piano properly. With years of piano-teaching experience behind her, Verna undertook to introduce him to five-finger exercises, scales and the correct posture of the back, arms and hands. She had a special adjustable high-stool made for him. Orlando did not approve of her approach to teaching.

'For heaven's sake, playing the piano should be fun and a joy. Your approach is too grim and painful. You'll turn him off. Teach him some simple tunes first. How about Mozart's "Twinkle, twinkle, little star?" That's classical music, isn't it? When my father Emilio taught me to play, I was never burdened with scales or elaborate theory.'

Verna did not like being ticked off. She lost her temper. 'Alright, *you* teach him then. I will not—WILL NOT—dilute my principles. In any case you have much more time than me. What with supervising the household and the bird hospital I'm worn out. Your whole world centres on Braganza & Sons. You don't even lift a finger with the food shopping. The driver, not you, takes Asif to Magda's and back. It's time you took Asif off my hands. Agnes can barely cope with him. Why don't you take him for a walk around CP in the evenings? Show him around our locality and the city. You have a car and your knees are still good. *You* run after him for a change.'

Orlando agreed to give Asif piano lessons and take him for walks around CP. He had been preoccupied with a bold idea for some months. He thought it would be in the fitness of family tradition if Asif were to be called 'Asifio.' He broached the subject to Julio, who raised an immediate objection.

'But Daddy, his legal name is Asif Jackson Braganza. It's on the birth certificate issued in New York. It's there on his passport. It can only be amended by applying to the City Hall there. God knows what that would involve. Laila too would have to agree...'

'Well, do look into the legalities, for my sake,' said Orlando. 'I'm sure we have a consulate in New York—they should help out in this matter. In the meanwhile, do you mind if *I* called him Asifio? It would mean so much to me. For now, it would be what we Bengali Goans call a "dak naam," a pet name...Never forget our family traditions: Antonio, Emilio, yours truly Orlando, Julio and now, hopefully, Asifio. All our first names have ended in the letter O! You know this very well. That would make it five generations of O's. You should never forget we are a dynasty of piano tuners. You have stepped out of line. Perhaps you and your son will return to the fold someday in the not too distant future.'

~

The population of Delhi was growing very fast. There had been the refugee influx after Partition and now there was the migration of business and government personnel from all over India. The demand for land and housing was tremendous. It was the CPWD's finest hour and Julio felt privileged to be working on a wide variety of projects in Delhi. Director-General Verma was often peeved by the way Prime Minister Nehru allotted land to individuals and institutions. Totally ad hoc and arbitrary. The PM would say, 'Come, ask, and take the land.' As a result of all the feverish building activity, Delhi was becoming an unplanned mess.

Chief Architect Sharma's wife, the delectable and delinquent Alison, wrote him a letter from Glasgow. Her lover, Carl, had died of a heart attack while playing the violin in a Tchaikovsky concerto. Alison begged to be taken back. Her letter was full of apologies and contained a memorable phrase that she must have lifted from a book on spirituality: 'Forgiveness frees the forgiver.' Sharma was touched by this. He called Julio to his spacious office, bolted the door, and instructed his secretary that he was not to be disturbed under any circumstances. He was tormented by doubt and needed to talk to Julio, whose integrity was beyond question.

'Tell me, Braganza, what would you do in my place? The children have missed their mother—it has been four years since she disappeared. Four years of complete silence, and now this.' He showed Julio Alison's pathetic letter asking for forgiveness.

'Sir, as you know, my son is named Asif, which means forgiveness in Arabic. Christianity also preaches the virtues of forgiveness. Sharma Ma'am would probably like to return to her dress-making business. Your children are at a vulnerable age...'

'But Braganza, I'll be the laughing stock of Delhi if I take her back. Unpleasant criticism will be made. Insinuations of all kinds. I will be called a cuck-cuck-cuckold!'

'Sir, you remember what people used to say when Ma'am first left? It all died down soon enough. You must have heard the saying, "Sticks and stones may break my bones, but words will never hurt me." I would not worry about what people say. It's none of their business anyway.'

'I can always trust you, Braganza, to give me good advice. Especially on confidential issues. I will now tell Rana and Lekha about this development. They will be thrilled to have their mother back and we will carry on as a complete family. I can't thank you enough. You Christians have a clear code of conduct that is always reassuring. No grey areas...Now let's take another look at the Diplomatic Enclave plans. The Ministry of External Affairs has still not indicated how much land is to be allotted to each embassy. I expect our DG will have to take it up with the PM's office. The Soviets, China and the U.S. are making extravagant claims, I hear. Politics in everything, Braganza. Politics everywhere. The three countries are vying with each other to see who gets the largest plot.'

Chief Architect Sharma had his government flat painted—interiors and exteriors—by the maintenance wing of the CPWD. The garden was spruced up, trees pruned, hedges clipped. New curtains were tailored for the living-room and the master bedroom. Though he could scarcely afford it, he bought a slightly-used Hillman car so that Alison could drive on her own to Khan Market and the homes of expatriate ladies who formed the bulk of her clientele. Her talents as a dress-maker had been sorely missed.

These arrangements had taken about three months to complete and Chief Architect Sharma was now worried that there had been no response from Alison to his conciliatory letters inviting her back to Delhi. Had she given him the wrong address? Like a good bureaucrat, he had retained handwritten copies of his three letters to her. Blushing, Sharma showed these to Julio, who advised Sharma to send another set of copies by registered post to Glasgow. And then Sharma waited. As the weeks went by, his newly-awakened love for Alison grew even more ardent.

Then he received a legal notice from a Glasgow lawyer. Alison intended to file for divorce. She wished to remarry and demanded custody of the children. Her intended was a Mr Percival Parker-Hayes. A cellist with the Glasgow Symphony Orchestra. Alison had always loved classical music. The plan was that Mr Parker-Hayes would legally adopt the children. The Glasgow lawyer assured Sharma that the children would be well taken care of as Mr Parker-Hayes had ample inherited wealth and properties.

Julio was summoned to Sharma's room, the door bolted, etcetera, etcetera. They discussed the unhappy developments thread-bare. The upshot was that the Chief Architect would consent to a divorce on condition that he retain custody of Lekha and Rana. That was to be his bargaining chip. Julio had advised this.

The Sharma children could barely follow what was happening to their family. Sharma tried to explain matters to them in simple words and as gentle a manner as possible. They did not like the idea of a new father and had grown used to Alison's absence. Besides, they were deeply attached to Tulsi, their ayah, who had been with the family for over nine years.

Julio often wondered why his boss shared so many secrets with him. He was so many steps down the office hierarchy. He supposed it was a matter of trust. He never spoke a word about the Chief Architect's agonies to his colleagues. Sharma was grateful for this. Besides, Julio had problems of his own.

~

Asifio—everyone at home called him that now—had developed a patch on his lungs and his eyesight was poor. He had to wear glasses. The doctors at Willingdon Hospital had advised Julio to send the child to the hills for a year. This would be good for his condition. Julio wrote to his sister Maria and asked whether it would be convenient to care for Asifio up in Mussoorie. She and Boris agreed readily. This took a big load off Julio's mind.

Asifio was admitted to St George's College, way down the hill slopes from Mussoorie proper. Nobody knew why it was called a college and not a school. Yanek was also a student there and the two of them sprinted up and down the hills to attend classes. Yanek was much tougher than his cousin and would stop every now and then to allow Asifio to catch his breath. Gradually, Asifio's legs developed strong muscles.

Julio missed Asifio a lot and would look forward to Sundays when he could place a trunk-call to Mussoorie and have a brief chat with the family there. In Delhi, Sharma placed huge demands on Julio's time and emotions. The procedures for obtaining a divorce were tortuous, particularly when one party was in Scotland and the other in Delhi. The Delhi lawyer, Khubchand, was rather lazy and tardy with paperwork. He would repeatedly tell Sharma, 'Find yourself another lawyer who can hurry things up better than I can. Then you'll go back to point zero.'

One morning Sharma summoned Julio, bolted his office door, etcetera, etcetera, and presented Julio with the surprise of his life. Sharma, despite his troubles, looked very pleased with himself.

'I have just sent your name to the Ministry to be deputed to work on the ruins of Angkor Wat in Cambodia. You will work with a team of French archaeologists. Your engineering colleague Ramachandran is my other nominee. DG has approved in principle. The two of you will make a very competent team. A foreign posting is the dream of a lifetime. I owe you this much, this is the least I can do for you. Your son is safely residing with your sister in Mussoorie? Don't mention the posting to anyone just yet. Formal approval of the government has to be obtained first.'

Julio was astonished. 'But why me, sir? I know nothing about archaeology.'

Sharma shot back. 'And archaeologists know very little about architecture. That is the basic issue. When the two disciplines work together great things are possible. This is the DG's view. I agree completely. The French have asked for someone who can draw realistic reconstructions of the great temples there. There is no one better than you. And Ramachandran is a wizard with structural analysis. You've worked with him on various projects. You get on well. The great temples in Cambodia are inspired by Buddhist and Hindu architecture. The French team there know nothing about these styles of building and sculpture. So, you see, you will be much valued there.'

Verna and Allegro were a bit sad that first Asifio had left for Mussoorie, and now Julio would be off to an unknown country. Allegro was philosophical.

'The tribes who live in the Khasi Hills where I was born are descended from the Cambodian people. This was one of Master Gareth's discoveries. So Cambodians could not be a bad sort. Somewhat quarrelsome but very artistic. As for the temples, there are both Buddhist and Hindu ones. Your boss has told you this? Good. Alexander Cunningham told me about them—must be a hundred years ago. They were completely covered by overgrown roots. The weather is hot and humid for most of the year.'

Verna wished to know when Julio would be back. Asifio's year in Mussoorie would be up at Christmas and he would have to change schools in Delhi. 'Modern School refused to admit him to Class Three. What cheek! Good riddance to bad rubbish. Anyway, the standard of Hindi taught there is too high for Asifio. The vast majority of students there come from Hindi-speaking homes and barely speak English, and that too with atrocious accents...Julio, you simply must send him to St Columba's where there are Irish Brothers and decent Anglo-Indian teachers. He would get a Christian upbringing. And when he is older, Asifio can easily walk to school. Or use a bicycle like you...Go speak to the Brothers. I'll come with you.'

And so it was fixed. St Columba's would take Asifio into Class Three in January. Julio warned his mother Verna that he might be in Cambodia for three years. She was quite happy at the prospect.

Julio cleared his desk at the office, handed over charge of various projects to his juniors, went to Mass three days in a row with his mother, bought a supply of stationery (reimbursable), had his teeth checked, bought a stock of malaria pills, packed, picked up Ramachandran in a taxi and drove to the airport. The civil engineer was very nervous.

'I have never been in an aircraft before. And the journey will entail *three* flights. One to Calcutta, then Singapore, then Phnom Penh. I hope I don't vomit. That would be most embarrassing, sir. My mother has performed several pujas on my behalf. She hopes I will save money from this foreign posting. You know my father is no more. My sister, who is married in Madras, also performed pujas for me. My brother-in-law works for the State Bank of India and is well regarded. I have no wife and children to worry about. Should there be a fatal accident, my mother should receive my Provident Fund. You will see to this, sir?'

'Oh, don't be so morbid, Rama,' said Julio.

'What is the meaning of "morbid," sir?'

'Pre-occupied with illness and death. It's very unhealthy.'

'But sir, we have to make arrangements to satisfy every contingency.'

Julio grunted. The two of them boarded a bus and eventually reached Siem Reap, the large village a few miles from the great temple of Angkor Wat. They located a cheap boarding-house a stone's throw away from the Grand Hotel where their French colleagues were lodged. Julio and Rama were on a very modest 'Travel and Dearness Allowance', known all over India as 'TA/DA.' They had to count every riel, the local currency. Their landlord advised them to buy two cycles.

~

Madame Simone, their trilingual interpreter, introduced Julio and Rama to the French and Cambodian project-team members.

Typically, the French spoke no English and the better class of Cambodians spoke only French. To be effective, everything had to be translated into the native Khmer. Julio and Rama were horrified by their predicament. Simone, a trained archaeologist, did her best to ease communication but she could hardly be expected to accompany the Indian innocents everywhere. However, when she learnt that Rama was single, she began to take a special interest in him. She found his dark skin and deep-set, long-lashed eyes most attractive. His lips were full and with his high cheekbones and cleft chin, she found him irresistible. Rama was dimly aware of Simone's feelings for him and asked Julio for advice on how to handle those feelings.

'Tell her you are betrothed to a young lady in Madras. That you will marry this lady when you return home from Cambodia. Tell her everything is pukka, fixed up, final.' Julio did not know what else to suggest. Rama protested.

'But that would be lying, sir. I think Madame Simone is very kind and generous and beautiful. She makes me feel manly, and you and I have to spend much time with her. We can't avoid her. You are good with languages, sir. You are picking up the French quickly because you know Portuguese. I am helpless without her…I'm growing to like her very much also. In a manly way.'

Julio was impatient. 'You sound as if you are headed for an affair with Simone. I will not permit that. News of such goings-on would reach Delhi and even your sister in Madras in no time at all. Remember our Chief Architect would be very sensitive about that sort of thing.'

~

Work at the Angkor Wat site was strenuous: removing blocks of stone that had tumbled down from upper storeys and numbering them according to Julio's visualizations of where they had fallen from. Rama gave expert advice on the structural soundness of various lintels, beams, columns, staircases and towers. Bas-relief depictions of mythological stories in the long temple corridors had to be cleaned and restored. And everywhere there were giant tree-roots choking the stone work, extending their tentacles in every direction. These had to be removed, the trees felled, and the structures restored according to Julio's beautiful sketches of the largest Hindu temple in the world. He and Rama cycled to about twenty other temples in the micro-region to learn about various Khmer building styles spanning eight centuries.

Their French colleagues could not bear the midday heat and humidity. They napped for two hours in their hotel every afternoon. Julio thought they were a lazy, quarrelsome lot. Apart from a few professional matters, he had as little as possible to do with them. There was no socializing. Simone was the only one who invited Rama and Julio to the Grand Hotel for dinner off and on. But then she had her private reasons.

Julio and Rama resented the stand-offish behaviour of the French members of the team. Julio was never quite clear what their contributions were. They did so little. The Frenchmen would drink vast quantities of chilled beer on site, joke amongst themselves and occasionally make jottings in their pink notebooks. At one point Julio concluded that a grand city had existed *within* the vast moat of Angkor Wat. When he shared this hunch with the Frenchmen, they started digging at various places to uncover its foundations. Julio did not tell them that the city had probably been built of mud and not of stone, and that all traces of it would therefore have been covered by the wild forest. He was glad to be rid of them for a while. Then, suddenly, they were informed by telegram that there would be a royal visit.

The Crown Prince of Cambodia, Prince Norodom Sihanouk, visited the temple on his tour of the province. He was, for understandable reasons, not particularly enamoured of the French government or of its agents in Cambodia. The French colonists had quit the country a few years previously. The Prince insisted that Julio and Rama show him around. He spoke a passable English and was enchanted by Julio's sketches and perspectives. Later he summoned the Frenchies and asked about their work.

'Your Royal Highness, we have discovered a magnificent city adjacent to the great temple. We will be submitting a report to your government within four years. We are also recording the history of Angkor from the tenth to the twentieth centuries. The role that Hinduism and Buddhism played. It is painstaking work and we need two more Khmer-to-French translators to cope with the many tasks involved. We have only one translator but she is kept busy by the Indians. She has little time for us. So we are helpless.'

The Prince turned to his Inspector General of Antiquities. He drew him aside and whispered in Khmer. 'It seems these jokers have not produced anything worthwhile. The Indians are doing all the work. Remind me to send a letter of appreciation to Indian Prime Minister Nehru. I want you to conduct an enquiry. Prepare a draft of the letter to Nehru. I also want some land allotted to us to construct an embassy in New Delhi. The letter should serve both purposes. After I've left, shake up the French slackers. They have ruined our country once before. How did we end up with such incompetents? Who took the decision to employ such a lazy lot?'

After the royal visit the Frenchies were a subdued bunch. They stopped returning to the Grand Hotel for eight-course lunches and two-hour naps. A couple of them even started to talk some broken English. They were hesitantly resigned to learning the finer points of architectural conservation, the properties of sandstone, and the wonders of mortar-less stone construction. The architect, engineer and archaeologists had at last begun to interact.

When Julio had been abroad for several months, he received a letter from his mother Verna, the dragon lady. It contained two pieces of distressing news. Emilio and Rachel (his English grandmother) had died of typhoid within a month of each other. Orlando had flown twice to Calcutta to attend the funerals. Blotto, his twin brother, had decided to fold up the Calcutta branch of Braganza & Sons. It had ceased to be profitable now that three other music shops had opened in central Calcutta. Indian musical instruments had become popular. So the interest in pianos was fast declining in the post-colonial city. Most British families had left. The Bengali babus were now more interested in transistor radios and tape-recorders.

The other bad news concerned Asifio and Yanek. Verna had taken Asifio up to Mussoorie to escape the heat during his summer holidays. In the busy tourist season Yanek's parents, the dazzling Kashmirabai and Bravo, worked triple shifts, with a floor-show at noon as well. They had little time for the boys who were left largely to their own devices. A time came in June when the priest at their church asked for parishioners to help organize the annual church fete. Yanek and Asifio volunteered and were deputed to work for the 'White Elephant Sale.' They were put under the supervision of fifteen-year-old Albert Chand.

The three of them fanned out over the hills collecting old clothes, shoes and hats, all donated for a good cause. The hill-station was full of old missionaries and upper-class Indian families who came up from the plains for the season each year. They were glad to off-load old stuff. Albert was put in charge of pinning price-tags on each item, according to some mysterious system of pricing.

The fete day came and went. The crowded White Elephant stall was a grand success. Everything was sold out by three o'clock...But it was later discovered that there was a discrepancy between the cumulative value of what had been sold and what Albert handed over at the end of the day. He had slyly skimmed off one hundred and sixty rupees. Yanek and Asifio had watched him do this from their vantage point behind the counter. Realizing he had been discovered, Albert handed Yanek forty rupees and Asifio twenty rupees when no one was looking. He told them to push off and spend the money at other stalls: games of skill, games of chance, and many types of food stalls. Albert thought this was very ethical of him. He kept a hundred rupees for himself—a lot of money in those days.

The long and the short of this escapade was that the Benkovskys had to pay sixty rupees back to the church, and Albert's parents forced him to cough up the hundred rupees. They were too embarrassed to go to that church ever again.

In Verna's long letter she asked Julio whether he thought

Yanek had been a bad influence on Asifio. Or was it the effect of having sent him to that weird woman Magda's school?

~

After a couple of years Julio received a letter from Chief Architect Sharma, written in his personal capacity. The Chief wanted Julio to wind up his work at Angkor and return to Delhi to take up another challenge: work on a new Master Plan for the city. He would be working with a team of Indian and American planners sponsored by the Ford Foundation. It would be a great opportunity.

Rama was downcast when he learned of this development. He could not bear to be parted from Simone. She took the lead and decided she would go to India with Rama, meet his mother, and definitely, positively marry him. She went to the capital Phnom Penh and met the Inspector General of Antiquities. She tendered her resignation, giving one month's notice. He was full of concern and half-inclined not to release her.

'You are infatuated with Ramachandran. You will get over it. Delhi has an impossible climate and many diseases. What will you do with yourself after you are married? Have a lot of dark-skinned babies? You will come to hate the country and will long for France. This is the fate of most mixed marriages. Your work here has been excellent. Your translations from English to French are outstanding. The work of the Indians—their reports and sketches—must be completed without delay. I intend to publish a couple of papers based on them. If you stay, I will give you joint authorship.'

Simone shook her head from side to side. 'No sir, it will not be possible to stay. I've been here six years and have done all I can for Cambodia. Now I must do something for myself...Here is a letter from the "Indians"—as you call them—giving two months' notice of their departure...I'm sorry sir, but I must follow my heart. Rama is a true gentleman, sensitive and gallant. He will take good care of me. The climate in Delhi could not be any worse than in Siem Reap...'

~

Julio hurried up his work on the documentation of the ruins. He and Rama hired a hot-air balloon and took photographs at every conceivable height, light and angle. These pictures were printed in the capital. It was the first time such vivid pictures had been taken. Rama put forward a theory that Angkor Wat had been constructed from the top downwards, starting with a huge pyramid of mud in the middle and then building in stages up and down the slopes. This was a plausible hypothesis as there could be no other way to achieve the great heights of the temple complex.

Julio tidied up the site office, obtaining drawers for all his blueprints and sketches. He catalogued every one of these in a big register. Then he made a copy of the register to take back with him to show Chief Architect Sharma. He also had duplicates made—at his own expense—of a number of photographs to show to officers at the Archaeological Survey of India. There were also snaps of the Cambodian labourers, of the Frenchies napping, and of Simone and Rama. He included photographs of the colonial part of Siem Reap and the markets along the muddy little river that passed through the settlement.

The Frenchies were dreading the departure of the Indians. Now they would have to get down to some real work or the big boss in the capital would have them by the balls. Simone was another matter. The Frenchies pitied her for her decision to go off to India.

Julio and Rama's last month among the ruins of Angkor Wat—in their view the most splendid temple in the world—was spent in close but uneasy contact with the Frenchies. Julio and Rama explained patiently what had to be done over the next ten years. The temple had taken over forty years to build. The sculptures, bas-reliefs and other carvings on lintels and columns would require skilled craftsmen to repair and restore. Such men would have to be trained. Rama handed over several notebooks containing recommendations on the priorities for structural repairs. These would have to be translated into Khmer and French. A trilingual translator would have to be engaged to replace Simone.

Rama and Simone spent the last month at his boarding house. She had quit the Grand Hotel when her notice period was over. While Julio and her husband-to-be were hard at work she kept busy replenishing her wardrobe, getting her hair cut and permed, and having four pairs of shoes custom-made in the market. In the evenings she started teaching Rama some elementary French and he would try to teach her some useful Tamil phrases. At night they would kiss each other passionately. There were no flights going out of Phnom Penh because of terrorist activities. They had to take a ship to Singapore. They prevailed on the captain to marry them at sea. They could not wait to make love.

12

Great Expectations

Karol Bagh, in the west of Delhi, had a large concentration of South Indians—retired clerks and their descendants, government servants whose forefathers had migrated to Delhi along with the transfer of the capital. This is where Rama and his widowed mother lived in rented accommodation.

Mrs Ramachandran had just come back from her jewellers when Rama landed up with his luggage and his bride. Mrs Ramachandran was one of those rare Tamil Brahmin women of her generation who spoke fairly fluent English. She had been educated at Stella Maris College in Madras. Her father had been a professor of botany at the university. But Mrs R was a staunch traditionalist when it came to religion and rituals. She maintained a puja room and spent two hours there every morning after her bath.

When Rama presented Simone as his bride, Mrs R was too shocked to say anything at first. She then thought back to the moment, thirty-five years ago, when she first saw the face of Mr R at their wedding. He had one good eye and no chin to speak of. She had been very disappointed. But she was reassured by her father that their horoscopes matched. All said and done, it had been a happy marriage.

This woman, Simone, was six inches taller than Rama. She wore far too much make-up and, quite frankly, looked rather silly in the poorly-draped saree and very tight-fitting blouse she had worn for the momentous occasion. The tailor at Siem Reap had no idea of how to stitch an Indian saree blouse. The cheap saree had been picked up near the railway station.

'Miss Simone, I am glad to make your acquaintance, but in my eyes you are not married yet—not without a Hindu ceremony. I'm sorry to be so blunt and to have got to the point directly. This ship wedding is just not acceptable. It violates our traditional sentiments. It simply will not do. My son, my only son, should have known better. His father, if he had been alive, would have disowned him on the spot. I am somewhat more broad-minded. I will only insist on a proper Hindu ceremony.'

Rama spoke sharply to his mother, 'But Amma, our marriage is perfectly legal and will be recognized all over the world. There is only some registration work to be done at the local courts. I'll see to it immediately.'

Mrs R was, however, adamant. 'The next time Simone steps into my house will be as a properly-married daughter-in-law. She is not welcome until then.'

'But Amma, where will she stay? She doesn't know anyone in this city. We can't afford a hotel. You have put us in an awkward situation. To live apart at this stage would be a cruel predicament.'

Mrs R shook her head. 'I will welcome her as my daughter if you do as I say. Where are her parents? We must have a proper kanyadaan. I will contact the pundit on your behalf and pick an auspicious date. Send her to the YWCA on Ashoka Road. She should get a room there. Or she could stay with Mr Julio Braganza in Connaught Place. What is clear is that she cannot stay here.'

'But Amma, the YWCA does not admit married women. They are sure to refuse Simone. And the hostel is reserved for young working women. Simone is not a working woman—not here.'

'Listen, my son, you are *not* married yet. No need to mention the ship. That was all bogus.'

Rama did not like the idea of Simone being holed up in the YWCA. He rang up Julio at his parents' CP number and asked if they would put up Simone for a few days until the Tamil wedding could be organized. Julio, who was suffering from lack of sleep because of the long train journey from Calcutta, said he would consult his parents and call back.

After the circumstances had been explained to him, Orlando was quite agreeable. Verna was ambivalent. 'You say she is French? If it was an Indian she wished to marry, why not a good Catholic boy? All this marriage across communities and nationalities is not good for family or spiritual life. Look at you, Julio. Wifeless now. And Maria married a Pole. Bella married a policeman. And he's dead now. All of you made unsuitable matches. You ignored the teachings of the Church. And now your colleague Mr Rama is about to make the same mistake...She is a translator? Same as Bella. Well, I expect she will get plenty of work here. There seems to be an international conference every week or so. Wait a minute—I'll consult Allegro.'

The Great (once Holy) Bird said, 'Right on!'—an expression he had picked up from some visiting Americans in his days of fame. 'There's no harm in being kind, Verna. The quality of charity, etcetera, etcetera. Mr Rama is a close friend and colleague of Julio's. The trouble with you, Verna, is that you are too suspicious. I would agree to host Miss Simone if I were you.'

So Verna succumbed and Julio called Rama to say his family would be delighted to have Simone stay with them for a few days. Simone and her luggage were safely installed in the Braganza home within two hours.

~

Mrs R was disappointed by the local Tamil priests. They said a traditional wedding was out of the question. Who would give the daughter away? Which of her relatives would participate in the various rituals? The closest auspicious date was five months away, in any case. No, a Brahmin wedding was simply out of the question.

With great reluctance Mrs R agreed to have an Arya Samaj ceremony, a relatively simple, ritual-free affair. Simone's parents in Lyon were informed. They knew nothing about Rama and the courtship and were too puzzled to respond, except for a curt telegram asking, 'Why, oh why?' Simone was saddened by this sparsest of reactions. She resolved to send them a set of wedding photographs to prove that Rama was handsome, elegant, and employed in a secure job with the government.

The Arya Samaj wedding went off without a hitch. Mrs R had invited only the most liberal-minded among her numerous Karol Bagh friends to the reception. Julio and Orlando attended, as did several of Rama's CPWD colleagues. Chief Architect Sharma put in a brief appearance and presented the couple with a framed photograph of the barracks where they all worked. A not-too-subtle reminder that Rama's attention should now turn to work. Enough of romance, the barracks seemed to say.

While all this marriage business was going on, Julio briefed his seniors about Angkor Wat and his work there. He let slip that his task was left unfinished. If only he had another two years in Cambodia. He had hoped to leave a lasting impact on the conservation of the great temple...Now his sketchbooks and notebooks were in the hands of incompetent Frenchmen who were in Angkor only to have a good time.

Sharma told Julio about the Master Plan assignment. He would be involved—for the most part—in two tasks: to evolve an open-space plan for the landscaping of Delhi, and to work out what to do with the city's numerous uncared-for monuments. This would be a great challenge, and his work could leave a lasting legacy for the city's quality of life.

Julio asked if Rama could also be deputed to work on the Master Plan. There would be many drainage issues, river-front conservation issues, etcetera, apart from the analysis required of the structural soundness of decrepit monuments. Sharma referred Julio's request to the DG who, in his typical magnanimous fashion, readily acceded: 'I'm sure Bonnie, Syed and Edgar would welcome his talents. His work was especially commended by Prince Sihanouk of Cambodia. The PMO sent me a copy of the letter of appreciation that His Royal Highness wrote to Pandit Nehru. He also praised you to the skies, Braganza...Just make sure the new Master Plan is not too American a document. If it turns out to be that, no one here will understand it...Our country has great expectations of this Plan. It might even serve as a model for initiating master planning exercises in the rest of India. Our CPWD must be thoroughly involved in the process. We know this city better than any other organization does. Just think of how much we have built here over the past century.'

One afternoon a few days later, Sharma sat staring out of a window in his office. He was uneasy at the rate he was losing his senior staff. Manickam had resigned to set up a School of Town and Country Planning. Kulshreshtha had gone on a teaching assignment to Nigeria. Ansari and Banerji followed. Sharma was desperately short of experienced officers. He was left with Rahman, Rana and Benjamin. Julio's talents would be sorely missed. He'd be gone a couple of years, and would return even more thoroughly indoctrinated in the American way of thinking about city planning: segregated land-use planning, low residential densities leading to a colossal waste of urban land, and high-rise commercial centres dotted inconveniently over the urban landscape. Sharma shuddered. He rang for his peon. He needed a strong cup of coffee.

~

Sharma's divorce case was getting nowhere. Alison wanted a divorce *and* the children. She maintained that Lekha had reached a delicate age—she had female needs. Both children deserved a top-notch education in Britain. None of this 'shuddup-you-dam-fool' stuff that teachers in India indulged in. Besides, the schools in Delhi did not foster creativity. The teachers were not trained for that. And, to top it all, there was corporal punishment. If the children went to England, they would have a nanny *and* a competent governess to take care of every need. Alison wanted to marry Percival Parker-Hayes as soon as possible, but she equally wanted the children. Meanwhile she had, thanks to Percival's great wealth, opened a grand dress shop in Glasgow and had twenty women working for her.

As was usual in his moments of domestic crisis, Sharma summoned Julio, bolted the door, etcetera, etcetera. What should he do? Should he give custody of the children to Alison? Could he trust her to take good care of them? Would she dump this chap, Percival, one day and run off with another musician? This time maybe an indigent trumpet player?

Julio had second thoughts about the Sharma children who were teenagers now. They'd be ready for college in no time at all. The few intervening years might just as well be spent in Scotland with their mother. The education would certainly be better. What Sharma should insist on were visitation rights. The children should visit Delhi once every year during their holidays. They were grown-up enough to travel by air on their own. In any case, air-hostesses were trained to care for unaccompanied youngsters. For his part, Sharma should be free to visit the children in Glasgow whenever a conference or meeting took him to Europe.

Sharma had his doubts. 'You propose a very American kind of solution. The courts here and in Glasgow may not agree to such an arrangement. My instinct is to let Alison stew in her own juice. It's not as if *I* intend to remarry. Why doesn't *she* do the American thing—simply live with Mr Parker-Hayes. Has she forgotten that she and I lived together for almost a year before *we* got married? I really don't understand what this remarriage fuss is all about. Religious beliefs? She was never a religious woman. So the urgency must be on *his* side. Maybe the chap has scruples. Maybe his family is insisting on a legal marriage. I wish I knew the truth of the matter...Forgive me, Julio, for burdening you with my troubles.'

Julio pointed out a major issue. 'Sir, think of the impact all this uncertainty is having on the children. I'm sure they would be thrilled at the prospect of going to Scotland. Teenagers these days are quite curious about the West. All the books and comics they read are set squarely in England or America. If you don't believe me, sir, just go to Fakir Chand's bookshop in Khan Market. Not a single children's book written by an Indian! Since the children are half-Scottish anyway, they have a right to claim the other half of their social inheritance.'

Sharma thought for a while as he munched a Marie biscuit and sipped a little of his coffee. 'Alright, young fellow. I expect you are right. I'll let them go. But who will accompany them? I'll think about that while I'm processing passport applications and so on.'

It took several months to finalize the terms of the divorce. Mr Percival Parker-Hayes swore an affidavit that he would bear all expenses in connection with the children's education and travel. Alison agreed to the rather unconventional arrangements for visitation rights. Meanwhile, Julio and Rama cycled daily to Ferozeshah Road to work on the complex Master Plan for Delhi.

This was Julio's first experience of town planning, and he was witness to several heated arguments between the Americans and Indians on the team. Rama helped finalize the alignments for major arterial roads, documented the course of natural drainage channels, and helped Julio lay out a system of parks serving the entire city.

A major problem surfaced. They could not locate authentic detailed maps of the vast area. There were a few produced by the Survey of India, but these did not show true contour lines. Without such lines it would be impossible to calculate slopes and gradients. The Ford Foundation team made hectic enquiries. They found some old registers that listed hundreds of maps and drawings left behind by the British. But no one would tell where those drawings were stored. The only solution was to obtain copies from London, where the Royal Institute of British Architects was custodian of a large archive connected with the making of New Delhi. The matter was most urgent.

This was how Julio and Rama were sent to London for three weeks, to obtain blueprints of pertinent drawings. Sharma was particularly keen that Julio be put in charge of this operation. The Americans at the Ford Foundation would have preferred someone more senior, a qualified town planner. But Sharma was insistent it had to be Julio and Rama. He told the Americans that His Royal Highness Prince Norodom Sihanouk and the PM had praised this couple's excellent work in Cambodia. (This was a bit beside the point.) The Americans finally agreed and Sharma's expectations were fulfilled. Julio and Rama took charge of the Sharma children and flew off to London. Simone, unwilling to be parted from Rama for even a day, went along for the ride at her own expense. She secretly hoped to introduce Rama to her parents in Lyon, but was not clear how she would manage this. A fleeting weekend visit perhaps?

The contingent of three adults and two teenagers arrived in London on a day the weather was particularly wretched. They had very little money and took up lodgings in a cheap boarding-house run by a Pakistani couple on Brick Lane. Alison was contacted by phone. The next day the children and their luggage were handed over to her and Mr Parker-Hayes. He shook their hands and said, 'Welcome to England, your new home.'

Alison was distinctly unfriendly. She hugged the children dutifully and then said, 'But look how shabby your clothes are. Your father obviously does not care a fig for how you dress. I'll soon set that right. Come along now, children. We've got a taxi waiting and the train for Glasgow leaves at half past four. I'll get you out of this hell-hole.'

Julio produced a large parcel wrapped in brown paper and tied with red string. 'I almost forgot, ma'am. This is for you from Mr Sharma.'

'What does it contain?' Alison asked suspiciously.

'I believe it is their birth certificates, medical records, school records, and some letters.'

'That's unusually thoughtful of the old sod. I have no time to check them now. I'll have my lawyers do that.'

Percival spoke up. 'It's awfully decent of you chaps to bring the children over. We can't thank you enough. I'll make sure the children write to their father once a month.'

'Stop referring to that wimp as their father, Percy. *We'll* give them a new life, you and I. Mr Braganza, keep an eye on Sharma. He tends to eat and drink too much, and has frequent stomach upsets. Farts all the time. I still can't understand why I put up with him all those years in Delhi. He's just an old drunkard...

We'll be off now. Say goodbye, children. Didn't the old fart teach you any manners?'

When Alison and her entourage left, Julio and Rama went upstairs and collapsed on their beds. Julio was inclined to burst out laughing, but Rama looked quite solemn.

'Sir,' he said, 'she is a very disagreeable lady. But the gentleman seemed courteous. At least he thanked us for our trouble. It's good Simone was not here to witness all the unpleasantness. She would have ticked off ma'am. Simone told me she would spend the day at the British Museum. She will join us for dinner and I am to request the landlady not to put so much chilli in the curry.'

The two emissaries of the Ford Foundation then began to concentrate on their primary mission to London. The librarians at the RIBA archive were most cooperative, and the Indians soon obtained blueprints of over a hundred drawings dealing with the planning and building of New Delhi and its environs. Julio also took the precaution of obtaining three hundred and fifty blueprints of the original 'as built' drawings of Government House, the Secretariats and Parliament. One never knew when they might be needed. He also got photographs of the correspondence between the principal architects, Lutyens and Baker. Theirs was not a happy relationship.

The rolls of blueprints were packed in large, four-foot long metal tubes. They needed special permission from British Customs to carry these on the flight to New Delhi. Julio had to pay BOAC close to two hundred pounds for excess baggage.

Simone was not on the return flight. She had decided to make a short trip to Lyon to visit her sceptical parents. She had the album of wedding pictures to show them. Rama would have gone to Lyon too, but he was unable to get a French visa at such short notice. He was disappointed.

'Just as well, Rama,' Julio said. 'A side trip to Lyon was not on your official itinerary. If discovered, you would have been charged with indiscipline, dereliction of duty, fraud and god-knows-what-else. Not worth it. You've seen photographs of Simone's parents. You know what they look like. And Simone is carrying photos of you. That's enough for now. Don't fret. She'll be back in no time.'

~

Julio's chief contribution to the Master Plan in-the-making was the delineation of large open areas and gardens across the city. The majority of these parks were laid out around monuments, spanning several centuries of architectural heritage. Many open spaces were created around old villages that dotted the countryside. Some of these villages contained priceless gems of historic architecture.

Rama worked on drainage and water supply and assessed the structural soundness of the many monuments located in Julio's parks. The Archaeological Survey of India officials were deeply resentful of his activities. The ASI-walas felt that this 'bunch of foreigners' had no business interfering with their priorities—which were to keep in repair only those monuments that were on the government-notified 'Protected List.' The other monuments could go to hell as far as the ASI was concerned.

The final Master Plan document consisted of several volumes of text and drawings, and was published and notified in 1962, a year after the liberation of Goa from Portuguese rule. It was a path-breaking plan, and its authors hoped that the document would guide the basic physical structure of the capital for decades to come. Vast tracts of agricultural land had been acquired for urbanization. The Americans departed. The Indians returned to their parent organizations. All concerned were full of hope, and Delhi's citizens had great expectations that an era of planned orderly growth would follow.

~

Julio and his father Orlando learned that a five-acre plot—actually a mango orchard—was up for sale in the southern outskirts of the city. Orlando was looking for a safe investment, having been swindled by the Hailey Road tenants, three of whom were still paying pitiful pre-war rents. The fourth, Kitty, the Maharani of

Sandawa, had not paid a single rupee of rent for several years, claiming that Orlando neglected even routine repairs. This was in violation of the Rent Control Act. All four tenants, including Magda Imam, behaved as if they owned their flats.

Orlando promptly bought the orchard, erected a high boundary wall of stone along the perimeter at considerable expense, and dreamed of building a grand farm-house there for his retirement. He engaged a full-time chowkidar and looked forward to harvesting a luscious mango crop each summer.

Meanwhile, the New Delhi Municipal Committee served Orlando a sternly-worded notice. He was ordered to dismantle the monstrous netted enclosures housing the bird hospital on the roof of his CP premises. These eye-sores marred the skyline and were a non-conforming use, according to the new Master Plan. He was given one month to get rid of the hospital and to make alternative arrangements. Verna was outraged.

'The charitable hospital is doing so well. We are providing a much-needed medical facility. Do something, Julio! Get an exemption—redemption—whatever. Those babus have no feeling for birds and animals. The fat cats in the NDMC eat chicken every day and go out to shoot pigeons and doves on weekends. Many of my patients have been shot in their wings and it takes months to rehabilitate them...Should I get my pet owners to sign a petition to the Chief Commissioner?'

Allegro came up with the obvious solution. 'Why not re-erect the cages in the mango orchard in Mehrauli? The city is growing southward. Many new housing colonies have come up or are being planned. Pet owners will get used to the extra distance. You can allow them to have picnics under the mango trees. Julio can design a small cottage hospital. Separate toilets for Ladies and Gents. The extra expenditure on all these items can be offset by an enhancement in fees. That is how you planning types talk, Julio, isn't it? But Verna, don't ever let the business angle overtake the charitable one. I simply will not let my name be associated with a money-making enterprise...Now, I've given you my advice. Just get on with it.'

So the Allegro Braganza Charitable Bird Hospital (ABC BH) was hastily relocated to Mehrauli. A good portion of the wire mesh, steel pipes and perches were recycled. Even so, the total out-of-pocket expenditure came to almost five thousand rupees. The young Dr Dhar insisted that Orlando and Julio also construct an independent four-room cottage in the orchard. Dhar had said, 'Otherwise it will take me two hours by bus and three changes to get from my ancestral home in Daryaganj to Mehrauli. Four hours of my time would be wasted everyday...If accommodation for me and my family cannot be provided in the orchard, I shall have to resign. The Jain Hospital in Chandni Chowk would welcome me back any day.'

Julio visited the NDMC office and explained the need for a six-month extension. This was grudgingly granted. The logistics of shifting a fully-operational bird hospital were complex. Temporary quarters had to be provided. Clients had to be informed. A fresh lot of cinema ads had to be prepared and screened in the South Delhi cinema halls. A replacement had to be found for Agnes. She refused to move to the mango orchard.

'What will I do there alone?' she said. 'My head will go crazy. The shops in Mehrauli village are over a mile away. If I have to care for birds all day, when will I shop, cook and eat? There is no Catholic church nearby...All my friends are here in Kannat Pless. And how can I be separated from my chota baba, Asifio, and *you*, madam, and Allegro...It is impossible!'

The issue before the Braganzas was that if Agnes were to continue in the CP flat, with the bird hospital gone there would be nothing much for her to do. Asifio was all grown up at fifteen, and certainly did not need an ayah. Allegro's needs were simple and could easily be met by one of the other servants. He loved talking in Bengali with Agnes, of course. Her cooking was not great. What to do with Agnes?

The problem was solved in a fortuitous way. Sharma called Julio to his room one November morning. He announced that Julio's turn to be allotted a government flat had come at last. He had been assigned a flat in Shan Nagar, not far from Khan Market, adjacent to Golf Links. Verna was heartbroken.

'You will abandon us? It would be miles from Asifio's school. He'd have to take a school bus. Valuable time wasted. Too much time taken away from homework. And what about his piano lessons? He's up for his Grade Five exams now. I often think he's good enough to become a concert pianist. We can send him to London for further training...And Julio, you will have to buy all new furniture and kitchen things, and bed-linen and crockery-cutlery and curtains and...everything. Who will cook and clean?'

Julio was looking forward to having a place of his own where the air was less polluted than in CP. Shan Nagar was ideal. He'd persuade Allegro to move with him. It would be so much better for the great bird's lungs. And he'd take over Agnes, who was a reasonably good cook, contrary to what his mother maintained. In Shan Nagar Asifio would have a chance to make friends with boys his own age. Play football and cricket and hockey, none of which were possible in the over-planted central park of CP. As Julio had recently received a promotion, he even thought he would buy a second-hand Baby Hindustan car. One could be had for three or four thousand. With re-treaded tyres and a fresh coat of paint it would look as good as new.

~

After Julio, Asifio, Allegro and Agnes moved to Shan Nagar, they discovered their upstairs neighbour had a pet leopard who was kept on the roof. He was so fierce that no one could touch him except the old grandmother who was in charge of feeding him a kilo of raw beef twice a day. The animal's name was Badshah, and he spent most of his day either sharpening his claws on an old log or sitting on the parapet wall with his long tail dangling over the edge. The beast's instincts told him that this was not where he belonged. At night he would sigh and weep. The grandmother, originally German, tried to persuade her family to give Badshah to the zoo—where he would at least have other animals to talk to, to roar at, to commiserate with. But two generations of the Dhindsa family refused to give Badshah up. He had become a status symbol.

Micky Dhindsa, the old lady's grandson, was also at St Columba's. Same class as Asifio, but different section. He was a bad influence, and taught Asifio to smoke hash and masturbate in bathrooms. They naturally took the same school bus to Columba's, which they found an exceedingly boring place. They would sit and stare out of the classroom windows, unmindful of the lessons being taught. And so they were sent to the sadistic Brother Crease frequently for caning.

Then Micky had a brilliant idea. He and Asifio would take the bus to school each morning as usual, then get off the bus and slink away to sample the adventures the city had to offer. They would walk back slowly, sometimes taking in a film show at the Rivoli. Or they would go to Bengali Market for snacks, or take a nap under the great jamun trees along Central Vista, or catch tadpoles in the ponds there, or go to the National Museum to view the many ancient sculptures of bare-breasted women...The two adolescents even trudged to the red-light district on three occasions and lost their virginity to the cheapest of whores. This made them feel quite grown up. The girls had been very considerate, teaching them how to prolong their ecstasy...Asifio and Micky would return home from these jaunts at precisely the same time as the school bus reached. That is, three p.m.

Needless to say, they were soon discovered. The Principal wrote identical letters to Julio and Colonel Dhindsa. He noted grimly that their wards had been observed taking the bus to school each morning but not attending classes. Could the parents offer any explanation for these acts of truancy?

Micky's father, the Colonel, gave him a sound thrashing, breaking some minor bones. Julio, angry, asked his son what he had done with his time during these absences, and then, where had he got the money to pay for unhygienic snacks and adult pictures?

'I'm sorry, Daddy...but we learnt so much about so many things...Micky got the money from his grandmother...Actually, from her cupboard when she wasn't looking...It was never more than five chips a day. She can't see or count too well. My pocket-money all goes in buying P.G. Wodehouses and Agatha Christies—one book a month.'

'Saying sorry is not enough, son,' said Julio. 'I forbid you to have any further dealings with that rascal. He'll have you drinking rum and visiting brothels next. Micky is wild and obviously has criminal instincts. Unlike the Colonel, I'm not going to thrash you. I don't believe in beating children. I have never slapped you even once...Now go and borrow notebooks from your brighter friends and copy all the lessons you have missed. I'll go and see your principal tomorrow. You'll be lucky if he doesn't expel the two of you...I had such great expectations of you. Don't ever disappoint me again.'

Micky was expelled. Asifio was let off with a warning. After Micky's minor fractures healed and he could climb the stairs, he decided he would not let go of his buddy so easily. He would come downstairs after tea and chat with Asifio about their great adventures, including getting pissed on Sikkim XXX Rum and screwing whores.

In Asifio's home, Micky noticed a fragment of exquisite sculpture, an apsara's head, placed on a cabinet. It was something Julio had been presented as a memento of Angkor Wat. Tenth century, Buddhist. The delinquent reckoned it was very valuable. Must be at least ten thousand. Probably much more. Early one evening, when Asifio was away visiting his grandparents in CP, Micky stole the apsara head, packed it carefully in some clothes, and disappeared.

Julio supplied a photograph of the sculpture to the police, and was told that such a head had been sold to an American tourist a month after its theft. This information was obtained from the Jaipur Art Palace behind Delhi's Jama Masjid. It seems that the tourist and Micky brought the head there for authentication before a deal was struck. The Art Palace owner had valued the head at thirty-two thousand rupees and charged the tourist another three thousand for his services. Micky was never seen after that.

The Dhindsas moved heaven and earth to locate him. The

most recent photograph of him had been taken when he was twelve years old, before his body filled out and he grew a fuzzy moustache. This was not much help to the police. Nevertheless, they found traces of him in Udaipur, Pushkar, Srinagar and Kathmandu. But they always reached these places after the boy had left. There were rumours that he was part of a roving gang of hippies who were into smuggling drugs. As he was never found, the police labelled him a 'juvenile absconder' and soon forgot about him.

In Shan Nagar, Badshah, the leopard, fell ill with grief after Micky's disappearance. They used to play football on the terrace. It was the only exercise the leopard got. There were other games played as well, but Badshah would never let Micky stroke him. That privilege was reserved for Granny. Then one day, the beast stopped eating and stopped drinking water. The vet from the zoo was summoned. He advised that Badshah be shifted to the zoo hospital. He had to be put in intensive care, strapped down, administered glucose drip, and so on. The zoo ambulance was sent for. Expert handlers muzzled Badshah and carried him down to the smelly vehicle. Badshah died on the way to the zoo.

~

Asifio's music lessons were continued with an energetic Goan piano teacher who lived next door. Her husband was a dam engineer of some sort who was away much of the time. They had a teenage daughter, Christine, who loved to visit Allegro. In fact, the giant bird was quite a hit with the children of the locality. He would tell them adventure and ghost stories.

Asifio was now sixteen, and was supposed to be studying hard for his Senior Cambridge examinations. Christine was fourteen, and it was her mother's ambition that she become a concert pianist. She and Asifio would often play duets on his piano. They would sit very close together, sharing the two-foot long adjustable stool. Their thighs and arms would touch often, and Christine was soon convinced that she was in love with her handsome neighbour. Asifio, for his part, treated her as the sister he never had. He valued her friendship and there was no more to it than that. Though he had to admit she was very attractive. It was an awkward situation for him.

Asifio took his problem to Allegro, who promised to straighten the matter out with Christine on her next visit. He persuaded her that she was too young to know what romantic love was. She should concentrate on her music and on finishing school. And then there would be Vienna to look forward to, a city full of music, orchestras and concerts. The best piano teachers in the world. She could get a scholarship if she worked hard at her music.

As a result of Allegro's intervention, Christine stopped visiting the Braganza household altogether, and could be heard practising Mozart and Scarlatti into the wee hours of the morning...Julio had to complain to her mother.

'Mrs Rodrigues, like you, I work hard all day long. I need some peace and quiet to sleep at night. I must say I admire you. You give ten or twelve piano lessons every day and then have to see to Christine's practising half the night...Oh, she's very good—she plays the same pieces very well, over and over again. Can we agree on a curfew at ten?'

'Mr Braganza, you surely know how much homework these children have. She has to complete that before sitting down to the piano. That reminds me, Asifio has the potential to do well in both academics and music. But he doesn't practise enough. Now that the Dhindsa boy has disappeared, Asifio has no major distractions. He needs to practise at least an hour a day. If he can't do that—for whatever reason—I have no wish to be his teacher.'

From then on, Asifio was diligent in his piano practice. He was proficient at reading music and would often tackle the major Beethoven sonatas on his own, even playing for the likes of Chief Architect Sharma, Rama and Simone. Julio felt the young man might have a career in music. At the very least, he could become a piano teacher like Mrs Rodrigues. She charged twenty-five rupees for a half-hour lesson, so made a pile each day. But Julio was firm that Asifio should first obtain a college degree. And that's how

Asif Jackson Braganza was enrolled in St Stephen's College in North Delhi. Despite his improbable name, he gained admission on the Christian quota. Also due to the fact that his grandfather tuned the two ancient college pianos. This was a relief for his father and grandparents.

Asifio opted for the B.A. Honours course in history and did reasonably well, getting a second class. Over the course of the three years he spent in college, he often wondered what he would do with a history degree. Allegro warned him that he should 'catch the right train' or else he'd land up at the wrong destination.

Asifio shared his confusion with Allegro. 'But I don't know my destination,' he said. 'My friends in college are mostly thinking of the civil services exam. Some have gone in for Master's degrees, some to work on tea plantations in Darjeeling. That would be a lonely life...I think I'd like to be a civil servant—which means doing the competitive exams. I can do them after I'm twenty-one.'

'What rubbish, Asifio. You want to be a file pusher for the rest of your life? Attend six meetings every day? Get transferred often? You might end up in the Police Service or in the Income Tax Department! It would all depend on how well you did in the exams. If you came in the top five, you could get into the Foreign Service. There you would have to lie for your country day in and day out, attend boring receptions every evening, and run the risk of becoming an alcoholic. Besides, you're no good at foreign languages...As you can see, I do not think much of government service.'

Asifio had a counter-argument. 'But there's security. You can't get chucked out so easily. That's what my friends say. Security, prestige and a pension. You have a lot of power also. The civil services are the "steel frame" holding the country together.'

Allegro responded: 'Steel, maybe. But steel corrodes easily. The babus of today are certainly not made of stainless steel!' Then Allegro changed the topic and steered it in the most obvious direction.

'Why not think of taking over Braganza & Sons? It's your

birth-right. You've grown up with pianos and music. And Connaught Place. Your father Julio took another path and is now a government servant, worrying how he will make his salary stretch to the end of the month. Every month. Oh, I know how financially strapped he is, with little rent coming in. That Hailey Road property is a white elephant. Even your grandparents, the Imams, are guilty of defaulting on the pittance of rent stipulated in their lease.'

But Asifio was adamant. He had, by now, made up his mind to become an officer in the Indian Administrative Service. He signed up for coaching classes at Rao's Study Circle. He had to memorize eighteen books on History, General Knowledge, Geography and so on. Julio was not too supportive of Asifio's ambitions. But he recalled how stubborn he himself had been at Asifio's age. He held his peace and paid all his son's expenses.

~

The two years spent doing his Master's degree and preparing for the civil service exams passed quickly. Asifio missed his visits to the Cellar, the discotheque located in Connaught Place. He cut himself off from his Cellar friends: Barry, Meena, Rajiv, Anup and others too numerous to mention. He missed the hash-and-rum routine of college and the film shows in various cinemas. But he showed a remarkable sense of discipline, giving up all pleasures of the flesh. So it came as a shock to him when he learnt that he had failed the preliminary exams. The rules permitted him to take them again and again, but he almost lost heart.

Julio was somewhat embarrassed to tell his colleagues the bad news. They all said the young chap must try, try again. It seemed each one of them had a near or distant relative who had sat for the exams, believing that the life of an IAS officer would be prestigious and glamorous. Such officers could attract beautiful brides and handsome dowries from 'good families.' Not a single one of these relatives had cleared the exam in one go. Some had succeeded only after three tries.

Allegro was not one to say 'I told you so.' He just praised the self-employed life of numerous family acquaintances. All were doing very well financially, with the freedom to come and go as they pleased. They worked hard but they got to keep the entire profits from their labour: doctors, lawyers, accountants, shop-owners, contractors, architects in private practice and, of course, piano-tuners.

Asifio decided he'd give the exam one more try. If he failed again, he promised Allegro he would join the family business. Meanwhile, he would accompany his grandfather Orlando on his piano-tuning expeditions, but only twice a week. He had to study even harder now than the first time around.

Orlando found Asifio a quick learner, able to handle the tuning apparatus with dexterity and a firm grip. He had an uncanny ear for the stock-in-trade of piano-tuners: tuning with sequential octaves. When the tuning was done, Asifio would play two or three pieces for the benefit of clients: Bach, Schubert, Mozart, and the eighteenth-century Italians. He was by now a better pianist than Orlando, who had become slightly arthritic. The old man hoped against hope that Asifio would take over the shop and adopt the tuning vocation. But he would have to fail in the IAS nonsense first.

Verna watched from the sidelines with bated breath. She hoped that Asifio *would* pass the next time around. There had never been a civil servant in the family. Julio was a government architect but not a 'civil servant.' Not like the ICS, IAS and so on. If Asifio became an IAS officer he would be in a position to help the family in many ways. He would be influential.

Verna rarely looked beyond five years. She didn't think of what would happen to Braganza & Sons once Orlando couldn't work anymore, or when he died. She sort of assumed her husband would go on forever and ever like Allegro. She also assumed Julio would take on the shop after he retired from the CPWD at the age of fifty-eight. Run it like a business. Do it up, repair all that needed repair, leaving the piano-tuning side to hired employees... Why entangle poor Asifio in all these matters? He had not shown any sign of having a head for business. If he was an IAS officer, people would be falling over themselves to give him gifts and inducements and to do him favours. All above board, of course. There were well-established mechanisms that regulated such transactions.

~

Asifio sat for the preliminaries a second time and waited impatiently for the results. He resumed his visits to the Cellar and caught up with his friends. Bubbles, who had been just a pretty girl a year ago, was now ravishingly beautiful. She wore make-up and looked most elegant in her tight slacks and high heels. She was an excellent dancer and many boys were keen to partner her. Asifio knew that she was off-limits as far as he was concerned. She was the grand-daughter of Kitty, the Maharani of Sandawa, the most troublesome tenant at Hailey Road. But Bubbles—whose official name was Hina Devi—took a great shine to Asifio. She would grab his hand and drag him on to the dance floor. She would kiss him often (on the lips) and pay for the endless cups of coffee he consumed (like the rest of the Cellar crowd). Gradually, very gradually, Asifio couldn't help but fall in love with her. She was escorted to the Cellar by her Uncle Robin, Kitty's late-born son, who also fell in love with Asifio quickly and passionately. It was an awkward situation when Robin would cut in and insist on dancing with Asifio. Everyone in the Cellar knew that Robin was queer. Robin made no secret of it.

The Maharaja of Sandawa—who visited Delhi once in three months to inspect his children and quarrel with Kitty—knew about his son, and reserved judgement. He now also had two other sons by his junior Maharanis. So he had a choice of heir. Although Robin was the eldest son, it was unlikely that he would ever marry and carry on the line. The second Maharani nagged the Maharaja to name *her* son the rightful heir. There were silver mines, vast land-holdings, seven palaces, jewellery, and company shares at stake. The loss of his privy purse had not made much of a difference to the Maharaja's income though he hated Prime Minister Indira Gandhi for having abolished this and other privileges of the princes.

Bubbles did not seem to mind that she and her uncle were both in love with the same man, Asifio. A few years earlier, Robin had been in love with *her*. And they had fondled one another each time Kitty was away socializing or at the hairdresser's, which is to say, quite frequently. Bubbles was not a virgin. There had been Krishan Lal's son Ashok, who lived downstairs. And Helmut, the Finnish diplomat's son.

In those days it was not advisable for boys and girls to hold hands while walking on the streets of Delhi. One day Asifio and Bubbles were out for a walk along Central Vista. It was a beautiful autumn evening. They held hands and talked of inconsequential things, as young lovers often do. Suddenly they saw two uniformed policemen approaching from the opposite direction. Bubbles thought quickly.

'Put your left hand on my right shoulder. Shut your eyes and pretend to be blind. Remember, I'm your cousin sister taking you for a walk. Say nothing. Act all helpless. I'll do the talking.' And she did.

The sceptical policemen escorted them on the short drive to Shan Nagar and demanded to meet the boy's father. Bubbles asked them to wait while she checked if Mr Braganza had returned from office. Julio was tired but listened with growing distaste to what this beauty had to say. He was expected to testify that his niece and blind son were out in Central Vista with his full knowledge and consent. Julio met the policemen in his living-room and did the unpleasant needful. He was deeply embarrassed and asked the guardians of morality to stay for a cup of tea. They declined, saying they had to get back to their beat. The taller of the two said, 'No need for tea, sir. We must go. You must pay the fine for indecent exposure. Hundred rupees.' This was the first time in his life that Julio paid a bribe.

Now that Asifio's affair was out in the open, Julio did not know what to do. Should he complain to Kitty? Should he reveal all to Allegro and ask his advice? He spoke to his son.

'Listen, sonny, I know what it means to be in love. But even my love for your mother did not last long. Remember that next-door girl Christine who was all over you when you had hardly crossed puberty? Well, you know she's in Australia now, married to a golf champion. You've not given her a second thought. It will be the same with this silly Bubble girl. Besides, you know our family can't stand her grandmother.'

Asifio was defiant. 'You're being unfair, Daddy. When I get into the IAS, she has promised to move with me wherever I'm posted. She doesn't want to live with her grandmother any more. It seems there is constant friction between them. Her uncle Robin says he will move in with us too. All that remains is to fix a date for the wedding. Bubbles says it should take place in Sandawa, in the main palace there.'

'But look, sonny, such a wedding could never take place without the agreement of her family and us Braganzas. You must be mad to hope for such a thing. Mad, or just blind to the realities...By the way, what happened to your exam results? They should be out by now...'

'They will be out in the newspapers very soon. Perhaps five or six days. In time for my birthday. The suspense is killing me. But I'm quite confident this time. I'll be eligible for the finals, just you see...I'm rather enjoying the piano-tuning sessions with Grandpa. He is a good teacher. I could always tune pianos as a hobby.'

Now that Asifio was at a loose end, he spent more and more time with Bubbles. They would spend hours chatting in the fourteenth century step-well located just off Hailey Road. They didn't mind the occasional presence of other couples who surreptitiously held hands, the girls looking down at their feet. The police left them alone. On hot days, urchin boys dived into the well for fun. Bubbles and he decided they would hold a wild party at Ugrasen-ki-Baoli on his twenty-fourth birthday which was just around the corner.

The party was a grand success with food, drink, music and dancing. Their Cellar and college friends brought huge quantities of food of every description. Asifio even remembered to bring extra sets of batteries for his portable record-player. The maximum volume on the player was quite low, so neighbours were not disturbed. There was guitar-playing and singing—mostly the Beatles and protest songs of the 'sixties. The boys had promised not to be noisy despite the rum. A few of the guests ended up thoroughly stoned…Asifio was rather quiet throughout. He had told nobody, not even Bubbles, that he had failed the exam. Again.

The next day Asifio slept late and woke up with a splitting cheap-rum headache. He rang Bubbles with the bad news. Then he rang his father at work, gave him the news, and said they could discuss it when Julio returned from his office in the evening. Julio, in turn, rang his parents. Orlando was relieved, Verna was livid.

'How could they do this to the poor boy? He's so brilliant. He would make an outstanding officer. I'll write to the Union Public Services' Commission. There must be a mistake…Are the rascals asking for a bribe? I'll expose the lot of them. Meanwhile Asifio must prepare to sit again next year and not go fooling around with girls of dubious character!'

'Mummy,' said Julio, 'he's just not cut out for taking exams of this nature. Don't, please, stir him up. He has to reconcile himself to his dismal results. Daddy will know how to handle him. He has a ready-made career waiting for him at Braganza & Sons…I have to go now. We'll talk later.'

Over the next week, Asifio talked at length with Julio, Orlando and Allegro. All three said that his failure in the exams was for the best, a clear signal that he should avoid the civil services. Allegro threw in a red herring: if Asifio wanted, he could do another Master's—in Business Administration?—or become a college lecturer at St Stephen's. Orlando repeated himself again and again: taking over Braganza & Sons would be an exciting challenge. Orlando was thinking of opening a new department to sell records, cassette tapes, tape-recorders and electronic record-players. The shop had enough space. Something like this new department had become inevitable now that the sale of pianos had declined significantly. People mostly wanted to hire pianos rather than buy them. Allegro reminded Asifio of his promise to join Braganza & Sons should he fail to clear the exam.

Verna and Bubbles were the only ones to be acutely disappointed. Bubbles had rather looked forward to being an IAS officer's wife. In the district postings she would have been queen of all she surveyed. In the city postings she could have ordered around the wives of junior officers. Post-retirement there would be governorships to look forward to. And there was money to be made in such a career, provided one didn't have an over-developed conscience. Now her dreams had crashed. She'd have to look for someone else. A marriage to a mere piano-tuner was out of the question.

So Bubbles let Asifio down rapidly over the course of three days. First, she and Robin avoided the Cellar. Then she refused to take Asifio's phone calls. Finally, *she* rang *him* and said she could not marry a failure and they must stop seeing each other. When he showed up unannounced at Hailey Road, she was furious and shouted at him: her grandfather, the Maharaja of Sandawa, had fixed up a match with the Oxford-returned son of the Maharaja of Neemtala. The young Rajkumar was a star cricketer. Bubbles, crying now, sobbed that she had other offers too.

When it was clear that Bubbles had no intention of changing her mind, Asifio went into a slump. He stayed locked up in his room for a week, talking only to Agnes, who had little experience of how to mend a broken heart. He ate hardly anything and was too depressed even to read P.G. Wodehouse.

Orlando came visiting. He had a proposition for Asifio. Would he like to accompany him to Simla for ten days? There were a number of pianos he wished to inspect, maybe even buy, on behalf of Braganza & Sons. Do them up for hire. These instruments were not played at all. The first generation of owners had long since died; the second generation failed to have them tuned regularly; the third generation had simply ignored them, often just dumping them in storerooms or garages.

'Come on, Asifio,' said Orlando. 'You are no longer a child. You have to steel yourself for the real tragedies to come. Life, as you go on, will have many of them...The trip to Simla will do you good. I don't think you have been there before. Your great-grandfather Emilio was a frequent visitor...There's a fine grand piano at the Viceregal Lodge that I used to tune when I was a young man. We could have some fun getting it back into shape. I gather it requires re-felting. I'll let you tune it all by yourself. It would be a baptism of sorts.'

So Orlando and his grandson went to Simla and were there for a fortnight. Asifio cheered up considerably. He hardly ever thought of Bubbles and resolved to make a success of the piano business.

Julio suggested that his son move back to Connaught Place so that he could spend time with Orlando and Verna and be close to work at Braganza & Sons downstairs. Asifio agreed readily, mainly because he could then watch adult movies freely. He would go to hear jazz bands in CP restaurants and visit the Cellar where, if he saw Bubbles or Robin, he would cut them dead. This thought cheered him considerably. He'd find a new girlfriend. Her Exalted Highness Hina Devi could go watch cricket all day for all he cared.

Orlando was of course delighted by the turn of events. Asifio had always been his favourite grandchild and would now be his successor. Orlando's only worry was how to get Verna to take a more positive view of Asifio's failure to make it to the civil services. She had the bad habit of raking it up at mealtimes, and of taking up the issue again and again with Allegro at Shan Nagar. She would drop in on the great bird on her way to the bird hospital several times a week. Allegro was quite irritated by her visits. Fed up, he told her off one day: 'Enough of your ranting and raving. Can't you see how happy the child is now? What more could we want? Now buzz off. It's my nap time.'

13
Transitions

'So what do you think, Braganza? It's a newly-created post: Chief Architect of the Archaeological Survey of India. It's in a small building located next to the National Museum on Janpath.' Habib Rahman, the new Chief Architect of the CPWD, looked up from his desk and smiled at Julio before adding, 'I have noticed your waxing and waning interest in modern architecture. In your work you seem to be reverting to the Batley School of Revivalism. As I grow older, my respect for Batley grows. But, still, I remain a staunch modernist.'

'Sir, I am also a modernist. But why can't contemporary Indian architecture also respect the past? I'm a great fan of your Rabindra Bhavan. That building has more than a touch of India's built heritage in it. Why can't we have more buildings like that?'

Rahman was not too pleased by what he considered Julio's flattery. He let it pass and returned to discussing the ASI job. 'Your background in Cambodia and work on the monuments in the Master Plan have been widely appreciated. The ASI post appears to be tailored to your talents. You will get to design many site museums all over the country, and to supervise the designing of state museums in the provincial capitals. The work will not be too demanding. You will have more free time to spend with your family...So, what's it to be, Braganza?'

'Sir, I would also like to work on setting up the Delhi Urban Arts Commission. Could I do both? The DUAC and the ASI would have many interests in common.'

Rahman had a slight frown on his face. 'I'll see what I can arrange. Staying on in the CPWD, you would never acquire the designation of Chief Architect. Consider how many of our colleagues are ahead of you in seniority: Benjamin, Rana, Laroya, Saxena...You will have long retired before your turn came. At the ASI you could be Chief Architect for seven whole years. That's nothing to scoff at. You could frame new policies and have enough time to actually implement them. I am confident you will be superbly successful. You are not like Sharma, my predecessor. He achieved very little despite being the longest-serving Chief Architect in the history of the CPWD. He thrived on domestic crises...I know you were close to him, so I will not say anything more...He resented the Padma awards I received from the President of India.'

'Sir, every office has its politics,' said Julio. 'What if I can't get on with the ultra-conservative archaeologists? I met a few of them when I was working on the Master Plan.'

'Braganza, I'll tell you what I can do. I can send you to the ASI on deputation for five years. You may return to our department after that. That's the best I can do...Would that suit you? The selection committee for the ASI post meets on Monday. I am on it. So prepare a handsome portfolio of your work, particularly your drawings of Angkor Wat. I intend to ensure that you are selected.'

~

The problem with Julio's new job was that there was so little money to implement construction projects that most of his ideas remained on paper. The ASI, which should have been one of the most important departments of the government, was amongst the worst funded. Its Director General was a lady IAS officer who held the post as an additional charge. Her main job was in the Ministry of Civil Aviation and Animal Husbandry, jokingly referred to as the 'Ministry of Cows in the Sky.'

But Julio was happy. Mrs Bhowmick (DG-Acting) would come to the ASI for two hours every Friday afternoon. She would sign papers, 'take' meetings, and instruct Julio to prepare large budgets for forwarding to the Minister. Beyond this, she left Julio alone. Sometimes weeks would pass before he met Mrs Bhowmick, as Julio travelled a lot. He was often out of Delhi for three weeks in a month. It was his ambition to visit each and every important centrally-protected monument in the country. This was next to impossible as there were thousands of them.

Verna was very proud of Julio. He was now officially a *Chief* Architect. She would preface her comments to friends with, 'My son, the *Chief* Architect,' this..., 'My son, *Chief Architect* Julio,' that..., so Julio had to remind her that he was only a tiny cog in the mammoth machinery of the Government of India.

Julio knew from experience that monuments required breathing space. They should, if possible, be surrounded by gardens and parks. They should have attractively-designed boundary walls. The frequently-visited ones should be ticketed to raise revenues for their upkeep. Building regulations in the immediate environs of monuments should be framed to restrict heights and preserve sightlines and skylines. Julio knew all these things from his Master Plan experience. But his office was hopelessly understaffed. He had just three young assistant architects working under him. Six posts at a more senior level were vacant. The common excuse was that suitably qualified architects were just not available.

Julio explained all these shortcomings to Verna. She simply reiterated her standard line. 'But you are a *Chief Architect*. They can't take that away from you.'

Allegro was lonely in the Shan Nagar flat. Julio was away most of the time. Asifio was in CP. That left only Agnes for company. She had very little interest in history and geography, so there was not much to talk about except the prices of vegetables and cereals, and her bus rides to and from church.

The condition of Allegro's lungs had improved in the clean air of Shan Nagar. But he felt a general weakness in his wings and legs. This problem occurred every fifty years or so, and each time it happened he would pull out of it in a few months. He felt well enough now to return to CP, to his 'house' in the upstairs veranda from where he could watch the crowds go by. Allegro persuaded Julio to take him back. Even sharp-tongued Verna was glad to have him at home. She needed Allegro's sage advice on the running of the bird hospital. The original vet, Dr Dhar, had felt very isolated in the mango orchard. He and his family preferred the hustle and bustle of Chandni Chowk. He was replaced by a young lady doctor with one good eye and a caring heart.

Meanwhile, Asifio decided that everyone around him—his family, the employees of Braganza & Sons, and his clients—should call him by his legal name, Asif, now that he was largely in charge of a big shop, making out bills and receipts, dealing with many clients each day, signing cheques, and so on. (He had often found himself signing 'Asifio' instead of his proper name. This was not legally acceptable.) He was twenty-four now and felt he did not need a pet name. It took a while for those around him to adapt to 'Asif,' but all concerned made a sincere effort. All except his grandfather, Orlando.

'Would you mind if I—and only I—continue to call you "Asifio?"' Orlando asked. 'It has a ring to it. It is poetic sounding. So what if it defies convention. I promise not to use it in the shop or when we go visiting clients. I've called you Asifio for over fifteen years now—it's too late for an old man to change his habits. Besides, "Asif" is so...so...un-Christian. Are you sure your other grandfather, Muzaffar, hasn't put you up to this? He still owes us thousands in back rent.'

'Oh, Grandpa, I haven't visited Hailey Road for years—ever since...that...girl...that girl...Well, I don't want to talk about *that*. If only you would try a little harder, my real name would come to you easily. Don't, please, get all emotional about it.'

So from late 1972 onwards, young Braganza was known as Asif J. Braganza. When asked what the letter 'J' stood for, Asif would say it was what a great American artist was called. Simply 'J.' Or it was what his friends at St Stephen's called him. Simply 'J.'

Braganza & Sons quickly became a favourite hangout for young students and older business types. It was the only place in Delhi where there was a truly wide selection of records and tapes: classical, semi-classical, pop, Hindi film hits...Under one roof you could buy Western and Indian musical instruments, tape-recorders, gramophones, 'two-in-ones'—any and everything connected with music. The prices were reasonable, and behind the showroom was a large workshop where repairs/tuning took place.

~

Julio enjoyed his work at the ASI. He quickly mastered the various styles of Buddhist, Hindu and Islamic architecture. This was essential for rendering reconstructions of various edifices. For example, he identified twenty different styles of Islamic arches belonging to the Sultanate period, and seventy-two different shapes of Hindu temple shikaras. The basic forms of the arches and shikara towers remained the same, but it was the subtle variations that made them interesting. Julio did not involve himself too deeply in the ASI's major pre-occupation: several excavation projects going on across the country. These, he felt, took decades to complete and were best left to what he called the 'hard-core archaeologists.'

One winter morning he was accompanying Sir Arnold Armstrong, the famous expert on Islamic architecture, around the monuments of Delhi. Sir Arnold was a distinguished historian from Cambridge University. In the course of conversation, he happened to mention that he had a family link with India. His great-grandfather had a cousin who came out to India in the nineteenth century, but had not been heard of since. Sir Arnold believed his name was Gareth Armstrong. Had Julio heard of him?

Julio was startled by the coincidence. He was excited.

'Why, yes. He was *my* great-grandfather. Father of my English grandmother Rachel. He was a missionary and well-known inventor. You must meet my father, Orlando Braganza. He will tell you more about him.'

Sir Arnold was astonished. 'If that is so, you would be my

cousin—several times removed, of course...I say, what luck! What an incredible surprise! When can I meet your father? I have so many appointments...Could I invite you and your parents for dinner at the Imperial Hotel over the weekend?'

They were at the Hauz Khas group of monuments. Sir Arnold was taking pictures with his Asahi Pentax. He wanted to take a shot of Julio against the backdrop of the Islamic madrassa located alongside the vast reservoir constructed in the fourteenth century. Sir Arnold framed his shot but was not satisfied with it.

'Would you kindly step back a bit, Mr Braganza? I'd say three steps, if you don't mind...There, that is almost perfect...Just one more step, please...A smile now...'

Julio did as requested—and fell off the platform. He crashed down some thirty feet to the terrace below. Sir Arnold and a few stray tourists clambered down steep staircases to reach the unconscious Julio. One of the ASI guards rushed out of the narrow gate to fetch the driver of the official ASI vehicle they had come in. He, in turn, ran to the only phone in Hauz Khas village. He called the head office and reported the accident. He spoke to the personal assistant to the DG, who said he should rush the Chief Architect to Safdarjung Hospital. There was no time to organize an ambulance. The driver should drive carefully and avoid the many potholes on the roads.

All this happened on a Thursday, when Mrs Bhowmick (DG-Acting) was busy in her main office at the Ministry of Civil Aviation and Animal Husbandry. To give her credit, she acted swiftly as soon as she learned of the mishap. She arrived at Safdarjung Hospital and, holding the rank of Joint Secretary to the Government of India, began to throw her weight around to ensure that Julio got prompt and competent medical attention. At the end of a long day of many x-rays and tests, it was found that Julio had multiple fractures in both legs, complete loss of sensation in his left leg, and a fractured left wrist.

Orlando, Verna and Asif hovered around, too shocked to say or do very much. Sir Arnold was guilt-stricken. He offered to pay for everything, including private day and night nurses.

He resolved to bring up the issue of visitor safety at Indian monuments at a more appropriate moment. His encounters with Verna were intimidating. She was dripping with venom.

'Oh! My Julio! What has this man done to you? He almost killed you with his wretched little camera...' She turned to Sir Arnold. 'You'd better leave India before you kill us all. I thought we had got rid of your kind when we won Independence.'

Sir Arnold had only four days left in Delhi. He cancelled several appointments and insisted on transferring a large sum of rupees to Asif—enough to pay for special nursing care round the clock for six months. Other expenses would be met by the government-run Safdarjung Hospital. The guilty scholar of history would sit quietly on a bench outside Julio's room and talk to other visitors.

There were many of them. The CPWD Chief Architect Rahman came daily. Rama and Simone, ASI colleagues, Mrs Bhowmick and other DGs all stopped by to enquire after Julio's condition. He was unconscious for two days. The doctors had almost given up hope. They feared damage to the brain.

When Julio came to, on the third day after the accident, he asked for Sir Arnold. When told he was sitting on a bench in the veranda, Julio asked to meet him. Sir Arnold, perspiring profusely, came to Julio's bedside and clasped his right hand. Julio looked at him with half-closed eyes and muttered, 'Don't fret, Sir Arnold. It...was...just...an...accident.' Nothing further was said by either of them.

Sir Arnold met Orlando several times at the hospital, and they would discuss—in snatches—their respective professions. The historian and the piano-tuner also gradually unravelled the history of the Braganzas and the remarkable story of Gareth Armstrong. His years as a brothel-keeper, then a missionary, inventor, town-planner and philanthropist. The marriage of Emilio and Rachel, Orlando's parents. Orlando was less clear about Gareth's days in the Northeast. There had been a Khasi daughter, but the Braganzas of Calcutta had lost touch with her. Then Orlando talked about Allegro, and said the great white bird would be able to tell Sir Arnold further details. But he didn't see how this could be arranged in the time available. He knew that Verna was full of hostility. She would never welcome the Englishman to the flat in CP.

All through these sporadic conversations, Sir Arnold took notes. He promised to stay in touch and write in detail about his side of the Armstrong clan. Orlando, who was not much of a letter-writer, said he would send further information about Gareth as and when Allegro parted with it. Allegro had a superb memory.

Julio's government flat in Shan Nagar now had a single occupant—Agnes. Verna would stop by twice a week on her way to the bird hospital at Mehrauli. She would upbraid Agnes for not dusting the rooms properly and for not keeping a strict eye on the gardener. A family of mongoose was causing havoc in the garden, and it was the gardener's job to get rid of it. Agnes, on her part, would complain that Verna did not give her enough housekeeping money. Was she expected to survive on only plain boiled rice and salt?

~

After three months of being bedridden, Julio requested the DG (still Acting) to arrange to send files and sketching materials to the hospital. He felt he could resume work. Several projects were stuck in the pipeline due to his absence. His father-in-law Muzaffar and his mother-in-law Magda endorsed this resolve whole-heartedly. Although they visited quite often, the matter of the overdue rent was never mentioned. Muzaffar, now an old man, gave Julio news of Laila. She was contemplating a trip to Delhi but was at a loss to know where she would stay. Muzaffar knew Laila would never agree to stay with Magda at Hailey Road, and hotels were so expensive. Laila wanted to spend a lot of time with her father. His brother Jamal had died, and Roma had turned over several volumes of his handwritten poetry to Laila. Laila wished Muzaffar to decipher the calligraphy and provide her with translations that she could transform into visual images for her art. She hadn't found anyone in New York who would readily undertake this. The only person who showed some interest demanded five dollars a page, which was well beyond her limited means.

Letters to and fro followed in quick succession. Julio had been thinking. After agonizing over Laila's predicament for over two months, he wrote inviting her to stay at his Shan Nagar flat, in the bedroom that Asif used to occupy. She wrote back in her inimitable style.

> Thanx J. But no tuching. No hankipanki. I wil pay for my own food. I wud like to see sumthin of Asif. You axed about my mentor Jaxon. He died in a kar krash in Long Iland yers ago. 1956, if I remember ritely.

Four months after his accident, Julio was put on an exhausting regimen of physiotherapy, morning and evening. He was clinically depressed and was being treated for it. Sometimes at night he would sob quietly, alarming the night nurse. There was a huge backlog of work that he couldn't catch up with. Laila had given no indication of when she would arrive. Muzaffar said she was hoping to raise funds for the trip by participating in a group show. She also had to invest in a large assortment of art materials which she planned to bring to India. All this would take time. She also had to find a tenant to whom she could sublet her share of the loft. It was all very complicated.

~

Late one morning, Magda appeared at the hospital in an exceptionally cheerful mood. She bent over Julio and whispered, 'You have a surprise visitor. Make yourself respectable. I'll hide the bedpan and urine bottle under the bed.' Then she walked out to the veranda and called out, 'Indu, you can come in now. Doctor Paintal, you please wait outside. We won't be long.'

'But Madam, I'm the Medical Superintendent. It is my official duty to accompany the Prime Minister.'

The Prime Minister turned to Dr Paintal. 'Why don't you clear the corridors instead? Everyone and their uncle seem to have learned of my presence here. I thought my office had given you clear instructions that my visit was to be a *strictly private* one.'

Magda led Indira Gandhi into Julio's room. The PM was carrying a large bouquet of gladioli. She had been fully briefed on the details of Julio's accident and his medical treatment. So she wasted little time on such matters. Within five minutes, she came to the point of her visit.

'Mr Braganza, cheer up and start moving about. The chair of the Chief Architect of CPWD is waiting for you. It will fall vacant once Mr Rahman retires in a few weeks.'

Julio was astonished. 'But Madam, I lack the seniority for the post. There are others ahead of me in years of service...I...I...feel very honoured. Thank you, Madam...Thank you for your kind visit.' Julio's head was spinning. He had never visualized himself in such a position.

The PM smiled at Julio. 'Well, I've said what I came to say. You think about it carefully. The CPWD deserves a worthy successor to Rahman. The seniority business is a non-issue. Goodness knows why you government officers make such a big thing of it...Come, Auntie...I mean, Magda. Forgive me for calling you "Auntie," but that's what Rajiv and Sanjay used to call you. How they loved your little school!...We must hurry or I'll be late for Parliament. I'll have the car drop you off at Hailey Road. Give Uncle Muzaffar my love.'

Magda came again that evening. Julio was transformed. He joked and laughed. His depression seemed to have lifted completely. Julio asked Magda how the PM's visit had come about.

'Indu has always been interested in the arts. She told me she admired certain government buildings in Delhi and detested many others. I pointed out the ones you had worked on and she said she would like to meet you. I then told her about your accident, and your current position with the ASI. This was maybe a month ago. Then I received a phone call to say a car would come to pick me up at ten the next morning for an appointment with the PM. We had coffee at her residence on Safdarjung Road—the rest you know.'

Julio made rapid progress after the PM's visit. Over the next three weeks he learnt to move around his room with the help of a walker. He could use the toilet but still needed help bathing and changing his clothes. He recovered full sensation in his limbs and applied himself more seriously than before to his physiotherapy. After Indira Gandhi's visit, his doctors—led by Dr Paintal—took good care of him. A team of three Registrars visited him three times a day. Much to Julio's irritation they would ask repeatedly, 'How are you feeling this morning/afternoon/evening?'

Sir Arnold Armstrong stayed in close touch with Orlando. There were several long-distance phone calls from him, and a few letters from Orlando to Cambridge. Allegro had proved a goldmine of information on the early life of Gareth Armstrong, and Sir Arnold decided he would write a little book on the extraordinary life of a man the historian called his 'Indian relative.' Sir Arnold sent a further sum of money to help defray the expenses of physiotherapy at home and to meet the salary of a full-time driver for Julio's car. The old Hindustan required extensive refurbishing as it had been in storage in the garage behind Julio's flat.

Verna was disappointed that Julio insisted on returning to his own government accommodation. She wished him to move into her CP establishment. Asif—formerly Asifio—tried his best to convince his grandmother that his father wished to be self-sufficient and valued his independence. Verna just could not understand this attitude. She viewed Julio as a handicapped invalid.

~

Julio thought long and hard about returning to the CPWD as its Chief Architect. The more he thought, the more convinced he became that it would not be a good idea. He would have to spend hours each day reading dozens of files rather than sketching and designing at the drawing-board. He concluded that the ASI job would be more satisfying as he could actually get deeply immersed in the designing of buildings. At the CPWD he would spend more than half his working day attending meetings and the rest on files...So he put in a request that the term of his deputation to the ASI be extended to the date of his retirement. The DG CPWD graciously agreed, and sent the PM's office a note to this effect.

Julio felt somewhat bad that he had let the PM down. Using Magda's good offices, he sent her a separate letter of apology, explaining the rationale for his decision. He thanked her for the confidence she had shown in him and assured her that his work at the ASI would be of the highest quality. He would ensure that his slight disability would not hamper his tours and his designing. At least he would not have to face a mountain of files each morning.

Parliament had debated the Bill setting up the Delhi Urban Arts Commission. Julio and Chief Architect Rahman had worked hard on this. The Bill had become an Act and, post-retirement, Rahman was appointed the Commission's first Secretary. Julio was made a Member, ex-officio, representing the ASI. The Union Minister of Works and Housing was sceptical of this legislation: 'Yeh art-shart kya hai?' He had no understanding of why Delhi needed to become a beautiful city. To him, a city was merely a place to make money.

The day finally came when Mrs Bhowmick (DG-Acting) told Julio that she was reverting to her state cadre, Maharashtra. She shrugged her shoulders. She would be Secretary, Department of Inland Fisheries there. It was considered a promotion. She would have to rush through writing the Annual Confidential Reports of fifteen senior officers of the ASI, including one on Julio. He reminded her that, though he had been on long medical leave, he had continued to sketch plans and turn these over to his subordinates for translation into scaled drawings. Mrs Bhowmick gave him an 'Outstanding' rating. It was rumoured in ASI circles that the widowed Mrs Bhowmick was half in love with Julio. Why else had she visited the hospital every week without fail?

Half an hour of physiotherapy, morning and evening, restored some strength to Julio's legs. And then there were the dumbbells for the upper part of his body. The evening nurse helped with his bath. His appetite was healthy, bowel movements regular and, thanks to exercising with the weights, his torso swelled to a muscular configuration it had not had before. Agnes too put on some weight, now that she could cook and eat nutritious meals.

But still no news of Laila. Julio would ring her father Muzaffar frequently. All the latter could tell Julio was that Laila was busy making arrangements for the group show, and she needed to sell at least twelve paintings before she could afford to travel to India. Muzaffar thought she would come in two or three months. He did not keep too well and was anxious to meet his daughter before he died.

Julio wrote a long letter to Laila. She would be his honoured guest, with a room to herself and a separate studio with plenty of light. Agnes would cook whatever food Laila liked. The car and driver would drop him off at the office and pick up Muzaffar from Hailey Road and bring him to Shan Nagar by ten-thirty. Then he and Laila could work on the poems for a couple of hours, have lunch and, in case Muzaffar wanted a nap, there was always Julio's bedroom. Or, after lunch, the car could drop Muzaffar home, and the driver would be at Laila's disposal until six o'clock. Then he would fetch Julio home from the ASI.

Julio was rather pleased with his plan. He shared it with Muzaffar, who regretted that mother and daughter still did not wish to be under the same roof for even an instant.

'You know, Julio, I can't even remember what their original quarrels were about. Magda will not even utter Laila's name. It's as if she didn't exist...Do you think I could bring about some semblance of peace between them? I'd like to do that before I go. My late brother and Roma tried and failed. Laila never mentioned her mother even once...Send your letter, and let's wait for her reaction. She was always a proud and stubborn child.'

So Julio waited. He couldn't help think back to his many outings with Laila in New York. They were such good friends then. She taught him all he knew about art, particularly the abstract expressionists. Then he thought of that passionate night when he had spoiled it all.

Asif had seen a photograph of his mother, taken just after World War II ended. A fierce expression—a frown—on her face. A perky hat on her head. Hands gloved. This was the only memento Julio had of Laila. One would never have thought this severe girl would become a professional artist one day. At that time, she was certainly no Bohemian. He wondered what Laila looked like now.

~

Julio enjoyed his weekly visits to the Delhi Urban Arts Commission. His views on proposed urban projects were listened to with respect. But he privately deplored the poor quality of much of the architecture that came up for scrutiny and approval. He often felt the Commission was running remedial classes for architecture students. Government projects were the worst offenders. Government bodies rarely presented their designs for scrutiny and, if they did, they largely ignored the DUAC's recommendations for improvement. Rahman, Secretary, was a frustrated man.

Julio's own work at the ASI was greatly appreciated by the new DG (Acting, once again), a Sikh gentleman who had the unlikely name of Sonny Singh Lovely. His substantive posting was as Joint Secretary in the Ministry of Space and Sanitation. When Julio had to go on tour, Mr Lovely would approve arrangements for him to be accompanied by a personal attendant at government expense. He also sanctioned spacious cars to await him at every destination. All these favours and concessions were a source of some embarrassment for Julio. But he felt he would offend the DG-Acting if he turned them down.

The flat at Shan Nagar was painted. The twenty-year-old bathroom fixtures were replaced with new ones. The kitchen garden at the back was planted with a variety of vegetables as Julio suspected Laila would eat only organically-grown produce because of all the new-age ecology-environment stuff going on in America. Julio even had much of the old-fashioned CPWD furniture replaced by items of his own design. He hoped Laila would arrive by March when the front garden and vegetables would be at their best.

She did. Asif and Julio were at the airport to receive her. Customs held her up for over two hours while she tried to explain that the fifteen kilos of art materials she was carrying—sixty dollars in excess baggage—were for her own use, and not for trade and commerce. She had to pay a hundred and forty-five dollars in customs duties, all the same. She was in a foul mood after this, and sat on a bench inside the terminal, quivering with anger. She emerged after forty minutes of deep breathing exercises. Julio and Asif were about to leave the airport, assuming she had missed her flight or something.

They were the only people standing in the outdoor reception area apart from the touts representing taxi-walas or seedy hotels, and pimps of various persuasions. Then they saw a tall woman, jean-clad, pushing an overladen luggage cart. She came to a halt in front of the barricade. She looked over the small waiting crowd and winced at the raucous chorus of the touts: 'Taxi, madam? Hotel, madam? Best jewellery in Delhi. Massage, madam?'...She couldn't recognize anyone. Then Julio called out to her.

'Laila Imam? I'm Julio,' he said. 'And this is Asif. We can't blame you for not recognizing us. It's been over twenty-five years since we last saw each other in New York. Asif, go fetch your grandfather's car while I chat with Laila. My car has a very small trunk. I've been standing for over two hours. I need to sit down.'

Laila was exhausted from the flights to London and then Delhi. The encounter with the Customs' officers had depressed her. She had intended to convey a bright, chirpy presence to Julio. She had wished to show him how happy she was in New York, how fulfilling life as an artist was. She wanted to justify the decisions she had made in 1948 that she would never be a housewife or a mother.

'It's good of you to come all the way to the airport. Everything looks different from what I remember. People are taller and better dressed...I'm so tired, Julio. I've got to crash. Sleep for two days. The Customs business was the last straw.'

On the drive to Shan Nagar, Laila kept remarking how the city had changed. But so had Brooklyn. So had Manhattan. The trees in New Delhi had grown tall, the streets had been widened, and the traffic on them had increased many times over. At Julio's flat, she was introduced to Agnes, who welcomed Laila in her broken English and led her to the room she was to occupy. Julio had invested in a second-hand air-conditioner for her. He turned it on while she did a bit of unpacking, perspiration streaming down her face. Then Julio took out a little case from his pocket.

'Laila, here is the wedding ring you returned to me in New York. I've kept it safe ever since. If you don't mind very much, I'd like you to wear it while you are in Delhi. I will have to introduce you as my wife. Otherwise your presence here will give rise to needless speculation. Is it too much to ask? We are, after all, still legally married.'

Laila was too tired to protest. She held out her ring finger and Julio struggled to slide the ring on. She had put on a good deal of weight. She said, 'I've never cared much for appearances...Well, if you insist, Julio. As far as I go on this issue, don't ever think it means anything more...Now scram. I've got to sleep. I'll talk to Asif later. I guess I have a lot of explaining to do. I can't believe I have a twenty-seven-year-old son.'

When Julio returned from office the next day, Laila was still asleep. Muzaffar had called several times, only to be told by Agnes that she was still 'slipping.' On the following day, Asif told his father that Laila must be on drugs or something. They should wake her up, give her some breakfast. Julio did not agree. It would be best to let her be. They should wait until the following morning. She'd said she needed to sleep for two whole days, hadn't she?

The next morning, Julio was woken up very early by clattering sounds from the kitchen. Agnes and Laila were making an American breakfast of pancakes and maple syrup. Laila had

brought the syrup with her. She wore make-up: extensive black mascara around her eyes, like a racoon, and white lipstick. Julio was startled by the ghoulish effect. But he noticed she was still wearing the ring. That was a blessing. It was then decided that his driver would pick up Muzaffar after dropping Julio off at the ASI. Laila wished the reunion with her real father to be a private affair. Even Agnes should make herself scarce. Perhaps go off to Lodi Colony Market to buy a couple of chickens.

No one was told what happened when Muzaffar was driven to Shan Nagar. Presumably there were hugs, tears and reminiscences. Talk of calligraphy, poetry and symbolism in art. And no mention of Magda by either one. She was too touchy a subject to be broached at this stage. Muzaffar took three volumes of his brother's poetry back to Hailey Road. He needed to determine whether his Urdu was good enough to translate the poems.

Laila set up a small studio in the enclosed veranda next to her bedroom. There was excellent natural light. She bought a large easel, stretched some canvases, and cleaned her paint brushes with turpentine bought from a paint shop in Khan Market. She was ready to paint. Anxious to paint.

Muzaffar had difficulty deciphering his brother's calligraphy. It took him a week to understand the erotic images in a poem entitled, 'Monsoons.' When he explained it to Laila, she took notes in her own brand of shorthand and was quite excited. The next day she started to paint. She painted day and night for three days and then, exhausted, declared to Julio that the work was done. This set a pattern. The old man would explain a poem, his daughter would take notes, and some days later a fresh painting would appear.

Laila would explain her paintings to Asif, who was gradually drawn into his grand-uncle's world of a vanished India recollected in exile. Sometimes Laila would talk of Jackson Pollock and the other great abstract expressionists of New York. She told Asif about Jackson, his many lovers, his long-suffering wife, his heavy drinking, his love of fast cars—and his genius as a painter. She

had chosen 'Jackson' as Asif's middle name because she hoped Asif would have a creative life, the only kind of life worth living.

~

Julio had not been directly in touch with Bella for several months. News of his health was relayed to her by Verna and Orlando. But the developments over Laila required a personal explanation. He feared Verna would paint a very unflattering portrait of the brilliant Laila. Verna had always held her responsible for the breakdown of Julio's marriage and abandonment of her child. On one angry occasion, Verna had even called her a whore.

So Julio called Bella one Sunday morning, when the phone rates to Goa were at their lowest. He told her all about Laila the great artist, showing off his newly-acquired knowledge of New York abstractionists. He described a few of her paintings and something of the poetry that had inspired them. He told her about the wedding ring, and then turned to more routine pleasantries.

'And how is Braganza House doing as a business venture? It's due for white-washing, isn't it? The sea air must cause havoc with the exterior. And have you been keeping an eye on the plumbing? It's old. How is Tonio doing? Has he decided what to do with his privileged young life? And Carmen? How is she shaping up?' A barrage of questions. Bella replied to them as best she could. But when it came to the matter of Carmen, there was a long pause before she answered.

'...Well, Carmen is a bit bored with our village. She had got used to the bright city lights of Lisbon and Bombay. Nothing much happens in Saligao. It seems that old lecher Satarawala used to take her dancing in Bombay. They went to private parties to avoid prohibition in clubs and restaurants.'

'But that was years ago,' Julio cut in. 'Isn't she working now—as your Manager? That must keep her busy. There's so much to do, running a hotel like yours.'

Bella said, 'Yes, there's a lot to do. Did I ever tell you she is sorting out Marco's papers? Boxes and boxes of them. Mostly copies of his office correspondence. Marco had planned to write

his memoirs someday. There is also personal stuff: letters to his Canacona relatives, letters to Marcelena, Carmen's mother. Her replies—in Konkani written in the Roman script—her letters were full of concern for Marco's safety.

'Carmen has strict instructions to catalogue all the official documents and keep the personal correspondence aside. She is doing the work meticulously...But I find it disheartening to learn so much about Marco's time in the police. So much shady stuff... violence...anti-Hinduism. When the ledgers are complete, I plan to donate Marco's papers to the Inspector General of Police. He is an amateur historian, I believe.'

Julio asked, 'Would that be wise? The papers must implicate many people in atrocities committed by both sides. The liberation struggle was not too long ago...'

Bella sounded somewhat impatient. 'Well, Carmen's got fourteen more boxes to go. She's slowed down a bit. She goes off to Panjim for several hours every Saturday. Takes the car and driver. I have to apologize to our guests that the car is not available for sight-seeing on Saturdays. You should see how she togs up for these visits to the big city. Make-up, high heels, short skirts...She buys copies of some popular magazines—*Illustrated Weekly*, *Femina*, *Eve's Weekly*, and *Shanker's Weekly* for those interested in Indian political doings. Carmen goes through them before setting them out on the rack in the reception hall. For the benefit of our guests.

'When I asked her why she took so long to buy a few magazines, she said she enjoys window-shopping and exploring the old localities of Panjim on foot. She can't remain cut off from city life...The driver says he parks in front of Vishnu Naik's bookshop and goes to sleep on the backseat. Miss Carmen wakes him up around three-thirty for the drive back home. I tell you, Julio, her behaviour is so strange. If it weren't for the fact that she's Marco's daughter, I would have broken off with her.'

Julio spoke at last. 'But, Bella, you have said often that her work as Manager is excellent. I reckon she relieves you of a lot of tension. I'm sure she helps out by keeping Tonio out of

mischief at the hotel! He's a young man now and must have many girlfriends...'

'That's enough about Carmen now. I want to know how Allegro is.' She was told that the great bird wished to 'write' an autobiography in ten volumes before his memory began to fade. He had asked for a tape-recorder into which he could dictate the thousands of adventures he had had over the centuries. He would also require the services of a pretty young secretary to transcribe the words into printable text—and then a publisher who could make a fortune for the family.

Bella did not know that Carmen was living a sort of double life, and that the trips to Vishnu Naik's bookshop served a triple purpose. There was the legitimate act of buying magazines. Then there were the secret meetings of the Marxist Study Circle which were held in Vishnu's living-room above the shop. Carmen would reveal all sorts of juicy bits of information gleaned from Marco's cardboard boxes. Her companions in the study circle were keen to know which Goans had collaborated with the Portuguese during the freedom struggle. They deserved to be named and ostracized. Why should the Indian state forgive them? The third purpose was a romantic one. Carmen was fairly in love with Vishnu Naik. At least they enjoyed the sex they had in his bedroom, which led off the living-room. The study circle meetings started at twelve noon sharp and ended by one-thirty. Vishnu served samosas and chicken puffs. Then Carmen and he would lock themselves in the bedroom from one-thirty to three.

14

Braganza House

Bella began taking an interest in Goan politics and now subscribed to a daily newspaper—*The Times of India*. She keenly followed national news as well and was aware of the court case against Indira Gandhi. The PM was accused of electoral malpractices and was threatened with imprisonment. There were violent protests against her regime. There was turmoil in the country.

Then in June 1975, the PM imposed a state of Internal Emergency to save her neck. Press censorship, incarceration of her political opponents, suspension of fundamental rights, mass sterilization camps as a means to enforce population control, cringing bureaucrats...Bella found her newspaper full of blacked-out or blank pages. She called Julio in Delhi, thanking God her phone still worked.

Julio was equally disturbed. He could not associate the now-dictatorial Indira Gandhi with the gracious lady who had visited him in hospital. He could not believe Sanjay, her thuggish son, had once been a pupil at Magda's school. Now Sanjay and his violent friends were busy organizing forced vasectomies, even of teenagers and old men. Apologists for such draconian measures claimed that order had been restored in the country, trains ran on time, prices had come down. They also claimed that petty corruption had ceased. There were no industrial strikes, hoarders were jailed, and industrial output increased noticeably. Political troublemakers were in jail for their own good.

Laila was disgusted. Muzaffar told her how rowdy Sanjay had been as a child. Magda had warned his mother that he would grow up to be a bully. And that prediction had turned out to be true. Asif told Laila that one of Sanjay's goons had barged into Braganza & Sons one day and made off with twenty-two long-playing records without paying a single paisa. Orlando registered a complaint with the police but, as Asif had failed to ask the goon his name and address and failed to take his photograph, nothing came of it. A month later, another young man marched into the shop. Asif recognized him immediately. It was Robin Sandawa, Bubbles's young uncle. He too was now part of the Sanjay brigade: white kurta pajama, Gandhi cap, sandals. Robin embraced Asif enthusiastically and kissed him on the lips.

'Arre, Asif bhai, why don't we meet more often? I think of you every night.' They were talking in a quiet corner of the shop. And then Robin whispered: 'Bubbles wants you back and...*I* want you, too. She realizes she made a mistake breaking off with you. She says you are more intelligent and better looking than all the chaps Mummy has been parading before her. I've come all the way from the PM's house to tell you that you'll have only yourself to blame if your shop gets ransacked. My friends are very thorough at that sort of thing. Difficult to restrain. I have only to give a nod and they will be here in minutes. So do we have a deal? You save your shop and *we* get you? Remember, I could always have you sterilized.'

As Robin had broken no law, Asif saw little point in complaining to the police. They would dismiss it as a private matter between two individuals. Even if it weren't, they would never register a case against one of Sanjay's supporters. Asif was in a bind. Should he spend a couple of hours with Robin in a hotel room and get it over with? Did he really want to resume relations with Her Highness, the Princess of Rajgarh?

Asif had become quite close to Laila. They had begun to confide in one another. Laila even told him about her many lovers—including the amorous sessions with Jackson Pollock. It was all part of the New York art scene. Asif told her about

Bubbles and Robin, and the attempt at blackmailing him. The shop was at stake. Braganza & Sons would never recover if all the merchandise were looted: the large stock of records and tapes, the diverse musical instruments, the pianos...The hooligans might even set fire to the place. If they did that, Orlando's flat above would also go up in flames.

Laila was amused by Asif's anxiety. 'Why don't you strike a bargain with this odious character? Agree to spend one whole day with him at the Imperial Hotel. What's the harm in a little clumsy sex between consenting adults? Believe me, Asif, I've had to do this kind of thing with gallery owners...Good-looking actors and actresses call it the "casting couch"...This Robin will soon realize you are as straight as an arrow. Tell him you will do this only once and provided he stops threatening the shop...As for Bubbles, meet her a couple of times but act aloof and cold and uncommunicative. To complete the image of a lout, dress sloppily and blow smoke rings in her face.'

A week later, Asif and Robin spent the day in Room 202 of the Imperial Hotel. Food was ordered through room service. They ate, they talked, they tried to have sex three times. Asif was shy and as cold as a dead fish. Nothing much happened because Asif was inhibited and could not manage a single erection. In between attempts at arousing Asif, Robin talked of Sanjay Gandhi's great leadership qualities and of how the PM's son and his friends were running the country efficiently. They were instilling a sense of discipline in all sections of society...Asif, for his part, concentrated on listening to the sound of traffic hurtling by on Janpath. When they checked out late in the evening, the receptionist bowed and scraped. 'You have no charges, Robin-ji. You have always been our honoured guest.'

Asif and Robin walked the short distance to Braganza & Sons. At the foot of the staircase that led up to Orlando's flat, Robin whispered, 'You're not my type. That's obvious now. But don't forget the other part of our deal—Bubbles. She's waiting for a call from you. You'd better make a success of that. If not, you can kiss your shop goodbye. Oh, by the way, you are a lousy kisser. And you had better visit the Sablok Sex Clinic. There's something wrong with your fucking apparatus.'

Asif stopped shaving. He stopped combing his hair. He didn't bathe for three days. He dressed in the loosest clothes he could find in Orlando's old cupboard. The one that hadn't been opened for decades. He looked at himself in a full-length mirror and was reassured that he looked positively disgusting. He told his bewildered grandparents that he was auditioning for a play and so dressing for the part of a tramp. He wore a moth-eaten cap that had once belonged to his great-great-grandfather, Gareth Armstrong. Before he set out for his rendezvous with Bubbles at the Laguna, he drank—with great distaste—a quarter bottle of Sikkim XXX Rum, smoked four Charminar cigarettes and practised blowing smoke rings. He then felt ready to face the girl he had once loved.

Bubbles couldn't recognize him at first. Asif went up to where she was sitting in a dark corner of the restaurant and introduced himself.

'So here I am...Asif...Asifio? Asif Braganza. You are Hina Devi? Bubbles?...I hardly remember you.' He sat down, hiccupped, lit a Charminar and started blowing smoke rings in her face. This was all from Laila's script. What he was unprepared for was Bubbles's reaction.

'Oh, you look so manly! Rugged, in a casual sort of way. I love *everything* about your new image...Yum, yum. So sexy! You smell so masculine...strong—you look so strong!'

'But Bubbles,' said Asif. 'It was all over between us ages ago. Remember? *You* broke it off. I'm a confirmed bachelor now.'

Bubbles reached across the table to take his hand. 'Don't talk rubbish, darling. I'm sorry I was mean to you. I was just confused, as I was meeting other boys too. The fat pompous princelings. But you are the *only* guy I've ever loved. My Sandawa grandfather has arranged to marry me off to a plump arsehole from Jaisalmer. Who wants to live in an ancient, crumbling fort-town in the middle of a desert? So, so far away from the places we love in Delhi...If I marry you, we can build a nice house in

Golf Links, you'll have your shop, and I'll have my gang of old friends. We'll summer in Europe every year and send our children to the best schools...I might add, I'll have the income from five hundred and sixty acres of land in Rajgarh—my share of the ancestral property. That will be my dowry. We'll be rich, Asif, rich...Meanwhile, if my grandfather makes a fuss, I'll get Uncle Robin to report him to dear old Sanjay. Granddaddy has evaded paying income tax for years...They'll send him to jail. This threat will scare the shit out of him. He'll agree to anything I want.'

Asif sat there, shell-shocked. Bubbles had made no secret of her plans for them. He remained silent, aloof and uncommunicative, as advised by Laila. This only increased his attractiveness in Bubbles's eyes. She started sobbing and raised her voice.

'You have *no idea* how much I love you. I always have. Uncle Robin knows this and wants to make me happy...You...you used to kiss me *so-o-o* passionately. And we...we did all those... those...things! together. I *never* let other boys even *touch* me. Believe me, I'm telling the truth...We'll get your father to design our house in Golf Links. I'll buy us a grand piano from your shop...Kleinway & Sons is the best, no?...Grandma—remember Kitty?—has given me several piano lessons over the years. I can play Chopsticks in *six* variations. Both hands. You can teach me Beat-hoven—and all those classical guys. I'd like to be good enough someday to play—what's his name?—Paga-ninny...Oh, do say yes. You *must* love me, or I'll die.'

Asif realized that Bubbles was even more beautiful than he remembered. She was still slim, dressed elegantly, and had learned good table manners. She ate one small pastry very delicately while she waited for a response from him. He had to think quickly. His strong silent act was clearly not working. He had to do or say something that turned her off completely.

'Look, Bubbles, it's only fair that I tell you something serious. Strictly confidential. I'm in the habit of visiting prostitutes on G.B. Road every Saturday. Going to the fifty-rupee variety. Can't afford any better. I have a venereal disease that cannot be cured.'

Bubbles broke into a sob, collected her purse, and ran out on to the street. Asif ran after her, and caught her by the wrist. 'Do you understand what I mean? I'll continue to visit such women because I like...variety. No girl will ever marry me because I'm covered with blisters everywhere. That's why I don't shave often. I have white patches on my neck where I have no sensation—a sure sign I have contracted leprosy also...'

All this was said in the parking lot in front of Laguna. A scraggly long-haired fortune-teller sidled up to them: 'Madam is a princess. She will marry a prince and live in a grand house like a palace. I am right? I'll tell you more. I charge only seventy-five rupees per session...I can say much about sir also. Only fifty for second telling.'

The fortune-teller was the last straw. Bubbles shook herself free from Asif, blew her nose and powdered it using a compact from her purse. She touched up her cheeks and looked Asif straight in the eye.

'You are the most—disgusting—bastard—I've ever met! To think I ever loved you! You are *worse* than disgusting. You're a large pile of dog shit. I hope I never set eyes on you again.'

The next morning, Bubbles sat, red-eyed, at the gleaming dining table in the Sandawas' flat on Hailey Road. Robin sat across from her, eating a second banana. Bubbles stared at her dish of Quaker oats.

'So how did your date with Asif go?' Robin asked. Bubbles glared at her uncle.

'He's a shitty arsehole. Thoroughly disgusting. I'm through with him. I don't want you to ever mention him again.'

Robin nodded, 'I think so too. He's not my type...I think we can forget the Braganzas. Mr Orlando has had the cheek to send a legal notice to Mummy for the rent. I've told her to ignore it. What can the courts do? Judges are easily intimidated. I'll get Sanjay to take care of the matter...As for that bum, Asif, let's just forget him. If you like, I can arrange a sound thrashing.'

Both Bubbles and Robin were relieved that intimate details of their unsavoury encounters with Asif were neither sought nor offered. Asif and the shop were safe. Orlando and Verna were spared news of the sordid happenings.

~

Orlando and Verna had a lot on their minds, what with the various court cases Orlando was embroiled in. And then there were Maria's problems. No one wanted to see a middle-aged husband and wife team dance. They had lost their looks. Bookings were few and far between. Money was tight. Orlando gave them an allowance of two thousand a month, and urged them to quit trying to perform their old routines and start teaching. He even offered to build them a studio-cum-residence in the mango orchard at Mehrauli, provided they agreed to keep an eye on the bird hospital. Verna had stopped her regular visits there. The heavy traffic on the Delhi-Mehrauli road vexed her no end. Maria should take over. She'd always had a feel for birds.

Bella wrote from Goa. The Emergency had resulted in a large number of Goans being put in jail. Carmen had gone missing. The driver returned from Panjim one Saturday evening to say that there was no sign of her in the bookshop. Even Vishnu Naik was not there. Bella drove to the Police Headquarters the following Monday, sick with worry. She was told that twelve members of the Marxist Study Circle had been arrested and put in jail. Further arrests were anticipated, based on interrogation of those who had been imprisoned.

Four days later, Tonio wrote to his grandparents in Delhi. (The events he recounted had taken place before Bella's letter had reached Verna and Orlando.) Bella had been picked up. Someone low down in the police hierarchy had informed him that Bella had been implicated in spreading Communist propaganda, and of retaining unlawful possession of Marco Braganza's secret papers. All copies of confidential correspondence. Totally unauthorized. The new Inspector General would not tolerate it. All Marco's boxes were confiscated at the time of Bella's arrest.

Verna and Orlando were horrified by Tonio's letter, which had somehow escaped the censors. Months went by. Bella, their eldest child, born in the year the First World War erupted, had had her share of misery—and now jail. Bella's son Tonio was running Braganza House, but Verna heard gossip that he had become an alcoholic. This from a tourist who was passing through Delhi. Verna nagged Orlando, who was now well over eighty.

'Why did Bella have to go and meddle in politics? I'm sure that woman Carmen is behind it all. Tonio said she was a Communist. Can't you do something to get Bella out of jail? What about Kitty's son, Robin? The whole city knows him. He's influential these days. Bubbles—that vixen—doesn't have to be involved... *Do* something, Orlando. Otherwise *I* will! We must be careful because it's easy to make enemies these days. What a country this has become!...I don't know why Julio continues to design buildings for a bunch of fascists!'

Orlando looked up from his heavily-censored copy of *The Indian Express*—blackouts on every page. 'Verna, I've tried again and again to teach you that we are all very small people. Why would that thug Robin care a fig about us? He even coerces men my age and young boys to undergo vasectomies...I'll tell you what. I'll ask Julio to write to the PM. She was impressed by him. She'd remember him. Julio can get Magda to carry the letter in person to Mrs Gandhi. It would never reach her otherwise... Anyway, it's worth a try.'

Verna sounded doubtful. 'And when will all this happen? Julio is away somewhere, supervising the construction of a museum. While that so-called wife of his is luxuriating in his flat, eating him out of house and home. She is "painting poems," if you please. Whoever heard of poems being painted? They are written and printed in books...Julio says I don't understand what artists are up to these days...That Souza fellow paints ugly rubbish, as far as I am concerned. A good Goan boy corrupted by western ideas! And he is famous for that?'

'Verna, I'll see to it once Julio returns. It's more complicated than you think. Julio would have to approach Magda personally. Magda would have to be persuaded to take the letter to Indira Gandhi. Don't forget we have the court case against the Imams...

She is bound to be hesitant. Besides, I can't remember whether she's ever met Bella.'

Verna had a strong practical streak. She said, 'I expect we can kiss the four Hailey Road flats goodbye. The construction of Maria's studio cottage in the mango orchard is almost complete, you say. Julio should build himself a cottage too. There is more than enough land. He and Maria can look after the bird hospital once I'm gone...Asif will inherit the shop and this flat. Bella is well-provided for, so we won't have to worry about her—once she's out of jail. Tonio will get Braganza House...What do you think, darling?'

'I'll think about it, Verna. I must say you often come up with good ideas...The orchard hasn't produced any mangoes for seven years. The only things flourishing there are weeds and encroachers...And the bird hospital—the hospital was one of your excellent ideas! I'll talk it over with Julio...I don't know what plans he and Laila have. Maybe she'd welcome a large, bright studio where she can paint her poems or whatever...But I wonder if this is the right time to be making long-term plans. The political situation is most uncertain.'

'Oh, Orlando, I don't agree. The Emergency has generated some opportunities also. Julio would be a fool to wait till he retires to build his cottage. He, of all people, should realize that construction costs have come down dramatically. Contractors are behaving themselves and bureaucratic delays have reduced. Julio can take a loan from his Provident Fund. We can also help with finances...The old lady next door told me that her grandson has built a huge mansion in Vasant Vihar for under two hundred thousand rupees. That's cheap.'

The crucial letter to the PM was written by Julio as soon as he returned from Sanchi. In it he thanked Mrs Gandhi once again for her kindness to him and her appreciation of his work. He assured her that his sister, Isabella Braganza, was innocent of all charges and was not a politician. (He knew nothing of her secret life.) Julio suggested some mistake must have been made. He begged for her release from prison.

The letter was handed by Laila to her father, Muzaffar, who left it discreetly propped up against the salt cellar on the dining table for Magda to see. Three weeks later, Bella was out of jail. She was warned not to engage in subversive activities or her licence to run the hotel in Saligao would be revoked. She had spent several months behind bars. Her crime? She had been making hefty donations to the Communist Party of India which supported the rights of workers to strike. Industrial workers, teachers' unions, transport employees, utility company workers...Bella had been donating twenty per cent of hotel profits every month for some time—maybe three years. The priests at the local church resented this. The money should have come to the church, they felt. They had even spotted Bella in a procession organized by the Communist Party in Panjim. They could not understand why the wealthy woman kept such bad company. Bella's reason was quite straightforward. She felt she should share her undeserved good fortune. Braganza House was a gift from Marco. In his career in the police, Marco had often come down hard on the Leftists. Now it was the turn of his widow to compensate for that. In absolute terms, the money was not much, but her donations helped ease Bella's conscience.

Carmen and her lover, Vishnu Naik, continued in separate jails. There was no one to intercede for them. Bella thought it best to maintain a discreet distance. But she found that in her and Carmen's absence, Tonio had mismanaged the hotel. Bookings were down to a trickle. The staff sat around idle and had become insolent. Several guest rooms had cobwebs. The cooks had been pilfering supplies. The gardens had been neglected, the gardeners absconding for long spells. Bella asked the receptionist why things had been allowed to deteriorate to this extent. She requested the spritely old Mrs Esme Dias to be frank.

'Madam, I will tell you my opinion. So much work I had to do. Madam and Manager in jail. No help from anyone. Up and down, up and down, all the time. Going to the kitchen every hour. And only a receptionist's salary. The servants were so cheeky. They did not obey most of my instructions...The big trouble started when Master Tonio met this girl, Imelda Vaz. Soon after you...Imelda lives in Panjim with her father. He runs a shoe shop. Tonio has been going to see her every day. They watch fillums and eat lunch at expensive restaurants...Tonio has been spending money from the safe like water. And he has started drinking also. Most expensive feni. A full bottle a day. Imelda's father says nothing—I hear all this from my cousin who lives next door to the Vaz family...I tell you, Madam, Tonio is sinning with this girl. How to tell you all these things when you were in jail? Everything censored. I'm so tired, and my feet are aching from all the up and down I've had to do. I am seventy now and my body is old...No one to help...I think I will retire now that you are back.'

Bella calmed her down and promised her a hefty pay increase if she stayed on. Bella talked to Tonio that very night. He was half-drunk.

'Has this girlfriend of yours been staying in Braganza House?' she asked.

Tonio nodded assent. He looked defiant. 'But I love her, Ma. We'll get married this year. As soon as she finishes her secretarial course. We need a good secretary here. Mrs Dias is practically blind and your eyes are not what they used to be...My mind is made up. I've proposed and Imelda has accepted...So there. That is that.'

Bella felt trapped. She could not afford to alienate her son. Who would take over after she died? She was over sixty herself and could not go on forever. On the other hand, Imelda was obviously not a virtuous girl. Imagine—films and restaurants and hanky-panky every day. The girl had no mother, and a father who dealt with smelly feet all day...But then, Bella reminded herself that Tonio was no aristocrat either: mother, the daughter of a music-shop owner; and father, a policeman, son of a cashew farmer in distant Canacona. And Bella herself was, after all, a champion of the working classes.

Over the next few weeks she went painstakingly over the account books filled with Mrs Dias's spidery handwriting.

Bella reviewed the investments she had made in the years when Braganza House was a flourishing business. Now that bookings had resumed under her management, she took stock of potential revenues. She concluded she could afford a reasonably decent wedding for her only child.

General elections had been announced. The Congress Party was bound to be trounced. Indira Gandhi was certain to be defeated, and that alone would be cause for celebration. She made careful calculations and fixed a date for the wedding. It would be in 1977, the centenary of the year that Victoria was proclaimed Empress of India. Nineteen seventy-seven would, Bella was sure, mark the downfall of the latter-day empress, Indira Gandhi.

By her calculations Bella had five months to get Braganza House in order. A few months to persuade all her Braganza relatives to attend the celebrations. They must not forget that 1977 also marked the centenary of the year their legendary ancestor, Gareth Armstrong, almost drowned in a bathtub in London and then decided to come out to India.

But first things first. She had to get Father Sebastian on her side. This was easily done by a promise to pay for the entire white-washing of the Madre de Deus church, Saligao's most prominent. She would use the same contractor to paint Braganza House—exterior and interiors. She spent a small fortune refurbishing the rooms, polishing the antique furniture, and replacing broken tiles. Tonio and Imelda were now enthusiastic assistants. Bella began to take a liking to Imelda. Though not much to look at, she was an extremely intelligent girl. Hector Vaz, her father, was of tremendous help in getting discounts on building materials and locating competent workers.

Julio and Orlando were the only Braganzas who had been to Goa before. They had seen and admired Braganza House and could be counted on to persuade any reluctant relatives to make the journey. Bella made a list of members of the extended family, with question marks against the names of those she was unsure would come.

Allegro (?)
Uncle Blotto and Personal Assistant (2 rooms)
Orlando and Verna (2 rooms because Daddy snores loudly)
Asif (1 room; has he got a girl-friend?)
Julio and Laila (?) (2 rooms?)
Maria and Boris (1 room)
Yanek (1 room, but can share with Asif maybe)
Muzaffar and Magda (2 rooms; must make up with Laila)

Bella included Muzaffar and Magda on her list because they were Asif's grandparents on his mother's side, and there was a lot of damage to be repaired. Besides, Bella was deeply grateful for the part they had played in securing her release from prison. If Laila came to Goa, there was some chance she would patch things up with her mother.

Bella could not do much about the gardens in the time available. She hired extra help on daily wages. Bushes were trimmed, lawns weeded and mowed, the swimming pool emptied out, scrubbed and refilled, pathways repaired. Bella was hyperactive those days. Tonio felt ashamed that he was the chief reason his mother had to exert herself so much at the age of sixty-three.

Imelda undertook the job of organizing the grand reception that was to follow the church ceremony. Her father, Hector Vaz, was a shrewd businessman. He proposed they host a joint reception with invitees from both the girl's and boy's side. Bella took the precaution of inviting several senior police officials, two of whom still remembered her late husband, Chief Police Commissioner Marco Braganza. These were the officers who had ensured, for Marco's sake, that her time in prison was not altogether too ghastly.

~

'So you've turned up at last! You're all skin and bones. When did you get out of prison?'

Carmen Costa looked down at her mud-caked shoes. 'Only yesterday, Miss Bella.'

'And what brings you here? You've done a lot of damage already.' Bella's face was flushed.

'I had only twenty rupees in my purse. So I walked from the jail to Vishnu's bookshop. It had large padlocks on the doors. I made enquiries at the neighbouring shops and was told the bookshop has remained closed all these months. Vishnu's cousin has the keys. I don't even know this cousin's name, let alone his address. The neighbours didn't know either. So I sat in the bus depot all night...'

'That was a foolish thing to do. Anything might have happened.'

'I had no choice. With Vishnu still in jail, I had nowhere to spend the night. His so-called Marxist friends would never have given me shelter.'

'Why is Vishnu still in jail? He should have been let out by now...'

'He is recovering from typhoid—and the serious injuries he received at the hands of the prison guards. They kept thrashing him for his political beliefs—beat him regularly two or three times a week. One of the assistant wardens in the women's section told me that Vishnu would be discharged only when his bruises disappear...Maybe in a week. Meanwhile, I have nowhere to stay...unless you...'

'Look here, Carmen, you've brought me a lot of bad luck so far. What you did with your father Marco's papers was completely unforgivable...I'm wary of having you around...Still, I expect I might have some responsibilities towards you. Your clothes and things are here...Go up and make yourself presentable. A touch of make-up will bring some colour to your cheeks. At present you look like a scarecrow.'

'Oh, thank you, Miss Bella. Thank you! I won't stay long. Once Vishnu is out of jail and the bookshop is back on its feet, we should get married. It would be a simple wedding—something like your marriage to my father. We'll do it under the Special Marriages' Act. That's some new law...'

Bella was caught off guard. 'But...but...that will take weeks, if not months. You will have to give a month's notice at the court. Then, who knows how long it will take for Vishnu's bookshop to be a going concern again...Carmen, it's not for me to give you advice, even though I'm your late father's widow. Have you thought through all this carefully?...Also, I must tell you, Tonio is getting married in a few days. My relatives are coming from Delhi and Calcutta. I'll have to explain your presence here. It's going to be embarrassing—both for you and for us...Marco's love child.'

'I promise to make myself inconspicuous, if that's what you wish,' said Carmen.

'I'll think of some plausible explanation,' said Bella. 'Meanwhile, you can help Imelda, Tonio's fiancée, to get the catering organized. There's a lot to do. A menu has to be planned. Crockery has to be hired, tables, chairs, tablecloths...I have not had the time to take stock of what we already have here. We should make full use of that before paying exorbitant sums hiring stuff.'

'I'll be happy to help arrange Tonio's wedding. I know Braganza House like the back of my hand...And, if it's your wish, I could lock myself in my bedroom and stay out of the way at the wedding time. Though I rather look forward to meeting everyone...If Vishnu gets out of jail before then, may I invite him too? I'd like you to meet him. Then you will see for yourself what a fine man he is. And handsome, too.'

~

All the Braganzas were thrilled at the prospect of a grand family reunion in Goa. Asif wrote to say Allegro was most enthusiastic, and that the two of them would leave Delhi a few days earlier and take the train to Bombay, and then to Vasco. Orlando and Verna would fly, even though Verna had a deep distrust of planes. Laila thanked Bella for the invitation and said she looked forward to visiting the village in which her dear friend, the famous artist Francis Souza, had grown up. She also looked forward to visiting the numerous, jewel-like churches that dotted Goa's landscape. Blotto wrote from distant Calcutta that he and Peter, his ever-so-attractive twenty-eight-year-old male companion, would stay a month or so. It was the first admission to his family that he was gay—to use the new American term. They would, of course, share a bedroom, so not to worry. Maria, Boris and Yanek would come by train as they could not afford to fly. Yanek would stay only a week as he had cabaret commitments he could not get out of.

Julio requested a ground floor bedroom as he still had trouble navigating stairs. He would try to coordinate with Laila as he would need help to get on and off the airplane. If they got adjacent seats on the plane, he would tell her stories of the Goa he once knew. Magda tried to say that Muzaffar was too unwell to travel. She, however, would come to scout for land to set up an ashram. A few days later, Muzaffar called to say he was quite fit and would definitely come. He said this would probably be the last journey he would ever make.

The great day approached. Asif and Allegro were the first to arrive. The journey to Bombay had been difficult, particularly for Allegro, who had been forced to travel in a small cage in a noisy brake van along with unwashed cattle and goats. Allegro tried to strike up conversations with these fellow passengers but could make little sense of their mooing and bleating. Asif and Allegro had stayed for two days with Russi Patel, Julio's architect friend in Bombay. Russi's wife Shireen had died in childbirth some years earlier. Russi took Asif and the famous bird around Bombay in an ancient convertible. For Allegro the city had changed beyond recognition, apart from a few famous Indo-Gothic buildings... Then the pair took a steamer to Goa because Allegro could not bear the thought of another train journey just yet.

Bella, Tonio—and Mrs Dias, Imelda and Carmen—made a great and affectionate fuss over Allegro. It was decided that his cage would be installed alongside the reception desk, from which vantage point he would be able to keep an eye on all the comings and goings.

~

Bella had to do some quick thinking on the subject of Carmen. She had to make up a believable story. On quizzing Asif, she satisfied herself that he knew nothing about Carmen. Julio was the only one who had met her many years ago in Bombay and knew of her links to Mr Satarawala and Marco. But he had clearly been discreet and not mentioned her name even to the family in Delhi. So Bella, along with Carmen, invented some facts:

1. Carmen was Marco's daughter by his first marriage to Marcelena. They were both very young, barely out of their teens, when Carmen was born.
2. When Carmen was only three months old, Marcelena died of snake-bite. Marco's uncle and aunt, taking pity on the child, adopted her and took her to Lisbon when they migrated to Portugal.
3. Carmen grew up in Lisbon but was treated no better than a servant. When she was eighteen, she ran off with a neighbour's son, Edgar Costa. She married him and, as he was very poor, she began to work in a hat shop. He died some years later and Carmen began to save every penny she could to travel to Bombay, from where she hoped to work her way to Goa. It was her ambition to establish contact with her real father, Marco Braganza.
4. In Bombay she heard he had married again and had a son by his new wife. Then she heard he had drowned. So she continued living and working in Bombay. She worked as an accountant and part-time typist.
5. She grew tired of the hectic life in Bombay, of living in a single room with no balcony, and moved to Goa.
6. Once here, she established contact with Bella, her father Marco's second wife, and started working as the Manager of Braganza House.

Bella and Carmen rehearsed these facts many times and satisfied themselves that they contained enough truthful details to make a plausible life story. They tried out the fiction on Allegro, who said, 'I think it will do. Carmen has to be very careful, and Julio must be alerted as soon as he arrives. Or else he may inadvertently spill the beans. Verna is the one to be wary of. She can find flaws in anything...Oh, by the way, how many guests do you have here at present? Only three? The place looks so empty...Tonio said I must try some top quality feni. It costs about the same as a bottle of brandy. I think I'll try some tonight. Would you kindly issue the necessary instructions?'

~

Other relatives trickled in. If Bella knew their time of arrival, she would send a car to meet them at the airport/train station/harbour. The Imams arrived two days apart. Laila and Julio were surprised when Magda and then Muzaffar showed up. Laila had not been told that her parents had been invited. Bella purposely wanted to keep their inclusion a surprise. Had Magda known that Laila and Muzaffar were coming, she probably would have opted out. Anyway, the deed was done—husband, wife and daughter were all under one roof. Together after a gap of almost fifty years.

Two days before the wedding, Magda tripped while descending the main staircase, and would have tumbled down the steps and broken her neck if Laila had not caught her just in time. The old lady looked up at Laila and said, 'Thank you so much. You saved my life. What is your name? Have we met before?' Just then Muzaffar appeared, a bit unsteady on his legs. 'Shall I send for a doctor?' It was the first time all three of them had spoken to each other. Magda was badly bruised, and Muzaffar and Laila were full of guarded concern. Not much was said but the ice had been broken.

The arrival of Uncle Blotto, leaning on Peter's arm, caused quite a stir. There must have been a sixty-year age-gap between them. Peter was stunningly attractive: tall, broad-shouldered, a perfectly symmetrical face, large long-lashed eyes...He was, in addition to being Blotto's live-in lover, his secretary, nurse and general Man Friday. They had been together for eight years, and it was rumoured that Blotto would leave the young Adonis his vast fortune in construction companies. Wealth that Verna had hoped would be left to *her* three children. That would be the right thing for Blotto—who had no children—to do.

Orlando was delighted to have all three of his children together after a gap of several decades. Three children and three grandsons.

Verna wasn't the only one to be overwhelmed by the grandeur of Braganza House. Everyone was impressed by its immense size, its grand antique furniture and old paintings (salvaged from sales at sundry flea-markets). Three of the paintings were showing signs of indeterminate damage, and Bella made a mental note to ask Julio to restore them when he came to Goa next.

At the family dinner the day before the wedding, Bella came up with a generous offer: 'Braganza House was built by Braganzas, and lived in by six generations of our family before it passed into Hindu hands. Now it's ours again. Our ancestral home...Feel free to come and holiday here whenever you like. After I go, Tonio will welcome you—Tonio, please pay attention. Did you hear what I said?...Now that we are governed by Indian laws, I'm thinking of setting up a trust to ensure that Braganza House remains open to all branches of our family in perpetuity. The idea will work only if the hotel keeps running and some of the income from it is ploughed back into the trust. The trust must also donate generously to the worthy leftist causes for which I went to jail.'

The assembled Braganzas all thought it was a noble idea. Muzaffar and Magda refrained from commenting as they were not Braganzas. Muzaffar turned to Magda and whispered, 'It will never work beyond one generation. They'll all start squabbling, mark my words.' Magda looked thoughtful, inclined her head towards Muzaffar and whispered back. 'This house would be ideal as an ashram. Swamis from all over India could come here for meditation and discourse. Devotees would also find it comfortable. It would attract many foreigners.'

Rather than risk an argument at this early stage of their rapprochement, Muzaffar changed the topic. Shouldn't the Imams pay some of the back rent that was due for the flat on Hailey Road? The Braganzas were being so hospitable...Orlando might withdraw the court case against them if they owed him somewhat less. Muzaffar had not touched the money he had received from his brother Jamal through Julio...

The next morning, the big day, Bella rose early and consulted her list of 'Things to Do.' The most critical one was to buy exotic flowers in the Mapusa market and decorate the church. She left Tonio and Mrs Dias to look after the relatives and the handful of paying guests (who were thrilled to be part of an almost authentic Goan wedding.) She also had to travel to Panjim to check personally on Imelda's arrangements with the caterers. She left instructions with the household staff on how to sweep, swab and dust Braganza House thoroughly in her absence. No time for chit-chat. Carmen insisted on helping out with the flowers and the caterers. Allegro, anticipating a hectic day, dozed in his cage to build up his stores of energy.

During the car ride to Mapusa, Carmen raised a most awkward subject in a manner that was totally lacking tact. 'Mummy, last night when we were told of your long-term plans for Braganza House, there was no mention of me. What's to become of me? The house was purchased with my father's money. He cared deeply for my mother and me. There are copies of the letters he wrote to us in Lisbon. Don't I have a share in his legacy? When you pass on, Tonio and I should get equal shares. For that to happen, Braganza House would have to be sold and the proceeds divided fifty-fifty.'

Bella was shocked by this audacity. She tried to control herself. '"Mummy?" *When* did I become your "mummy?" I'm not old enough to be your mother—in fact, you are older than me! Remember, always, that I am "Miss Bella" to you...As for a legacy, your father's will makes no mention of you. So that is that. I can show you the will if you don't believe me. You are an illegitimate child.'

Carmen raised her voice. 'But that's not what you made me tell your relatives. They would be surprised if I got nothing. It wouldn't be fair. Vishnu's bookshop will not make much money. We have resolved to donate half of whatever we make to the Party. That leaves hardly enough to keep body and soul together. You and I went to jail for similar causes. We must...stand together...'

The car was about to reach the big market in Mapusa. Then it had to stop because an overladen truck had overturned on the road and other vehicles had to find an alternative route. Bella remained silent for the duration of the detour. Then she spoke. She had mellowed a bit.

'Look, Carmen, this is not the time or place to be debating such matters. Not today of all days. I'll talk to Tonio and my lawyer, and see what can be worked out in the long-term interests of Braganza House.'

~

Magda and Muzaffar made their peace over a series of often-heated conversations that night. Neither slept a wink. Magda was full of bruises and sprains. Yet she insisted on attending the ceremonies. 'What is the use of sitting in my bedroom while all you people have fun? I paid an arm and a leg for the air ticket to Goa. How far is the church? A five minute walk? So it will take me twenty minutes. Laila or one of the staff can help me get there. I was told that the motorable road to the church means a long bumpy ride. Full of potholes, I believe. It would be painful to be jolted every few yards...No, I will walk in my own fashion.'

Laila and one of the servants supported her as she hobbled down the path to the church which was just beyond the coconut groves. Muzaffar followed meekly. He wore his old grey suit and a red tie—something he hadn't done since 1961 when he had been invited to the President's garden party in honour of Queen Elizabeth. Magda, who normally wore slacks, was now dressed in a red Conjeevaram saree and a beautiful diamond brooch. The brooch had been a gift from Muzaffar when they got engaged in Germany. Magda had never asked him how much it had cost for fear it would turn out to be a cheap item of costume jewellery.

When everyone was assembled in the church, the bride's father rushed up to Bella.

'The organist has fallen ill and can't come. What should we do, Mrs Braganza? We must have the music! The Wedding March and so on...'

'Relax, Mr Vaz. I'll find someone. So many of us musical Braganzas here! Someone is bound to agree to play.' So this is how Asif got to play the organ at his cousin's wedding. It was the first time he had touched an organ, and it took him a few minutes to get used to the many stops and pedals. But this also meant he could not be Tonio's best man. Yanek had to be roped in to fulfil that function, but he neglected to take charge of the ring from Asif. There were several tense moments later when the music had to be stopped and the ring passed from organ to altar...

Archbishop Claudio Vaz, a second cousin of Hector Vaz on his father's side, was slated to conduct the nuptials, but was half-an-hour late in coming. Imelda, looking pretty in her wedding finery, broke into tears, and had to be administered smelling salts when she fainted a few minutes later. The confusion can be imagined. It was Bella's job to move from crisis to crisis, dowsing fires, placating irate in-laws, thankful that she had only one son and so only one wedding to organize.

Carmen had stayed behind at Braganza House on the pretext that she had to supervise the catering arrangements and take care of any guests who arrived early. Truth was that she and Vishnu had vowed never to have any dealings with churches and temples. Such institutions dispensed only opium to the masses.

After the much-delayed service ended, the congregation strolled in ones and twos and family groups towards the big lawn of Braganza House, the venue for the reception. Archbishop Claudio invited Magda and Muzaffar to ride with him in his car. Bella decided she would accompany the Archbishop as a matter of courtesy. She was grateful, in a way, that Carmen was at the house to hold the fort. When all was said and done, Carmen was a sensible woman, a good manager.

Bella instructed the driver to proceed slowly and avoid potholes. The Archbishop and Muzaffar dozed off. Magda looked out at the landscape, appreciating its beauty. After a few minutes she cried out.

'Stop! I see a hillock rising above the coconut trees. It doesn't have a church on it. Bella, who does that land belong to?'

Bella was surprised at the question. 'I suppose it belongs to me, Aunty Magda. It's part of the Braganza House estate. Why do you ask?'

'Remember I told you I was coming to scout around for a suitable site to build Swami-ji's Inter-Faith Ashram? That hillock would be an ideal location. Would you be agreeable to selling us some of the land? We'd pay the market price, of course.'

'How much land would you need?' asked Bella. 'I was wondering how to raise funds to pay off a special kind of debt. I need a large lump sum. Don't ask me for further details. I'd have to consult Tonio and the lawyers, and the village functionaries.'

'I don't know off-hand how much land. I'd have to sit down with your architect brother Julio and work out what our requirements would be. I'm excited at the prospect of a beautiful complex coming up on that hillock. Maybe Julio could design it. He's an expert at blending motifs from the architecture of different faiths.'

'Auntie Magda, please let's keep all this to ourselves for now. Once Julio works out the area requirements, I'll get the land parcel surveyed and demarcated. Not a word to Carmen. She will be the major beneficiary if the deal works out. But we mustn't get her hopes up. There's many a slip...I'll brief Julio. Before he returns to Delhi, he and I will walk across to get a hang of the contours of the site. The rest you can work out in Delhi after you have consulted your swami friends. There's no great rush. At this end, I fear the village council will raise objections. They want to have the final say on all land transactions. And then there is the church...'

~

The wedding reception was to start at six o'clock. Carmen gave the signal for all the outdoor lighting to be switched on. Braganza House was itself festooned with bright strings of twinkling lights. The total effect was magical. The guests sat on chairs arranged in groups of six. The children were restless and hungry. Nothing could start before the guest of honour, the Archbishop, arrived. He reached eventually, late by almost an hour, due to the treacherous condition of the road from the church. Bella apologized to the guests. Magda and Muzaffar collapsed on to a sofa placed next to Allegro's cage. They were exhausted for lack of sleep and the excessive bumping.

The Archbishop had long had his eyes on Braganza House for use as a small seminary. He hoped Mrs Braganza would will it to the Church. It was the vast grounds he was after. Plenty of room for expansion. On the way over to the reception he thought—drowsy as he was—that he had overheard the good lady discussing the sale of some of her land to a Hindu ashram. He wasn't quite sure if that was what she said...If so, it was a disturbing prospect. Meanwhile, now that he was fully awake, he was determined to have a good time, and indicated his desire to have a drink.

Archbishop Claudio was a talented man. He was quick to imbibe vast quantities of rum-laced cherry punch. On this occasion, the cherry pips had not been removed. Empty cut-glass bowls had been provided on the low tables for guests to discard the pips discreetly. But in the Archbishop's case, the nearest bowl was five feet away from where he sat. Undeterred, he remained seated on the comfortable sofa and spat the pips into the bowl with unerring aim. The children among the guests watched this superb display of skill with fascination. They regretted they were too young to be served the rum punch.

Grand-uncle Blotto was supposed to make a speech and raise a toast to the newly-weds. But he was found to be quite tipsy when the moment arrived. So the next most senior Braganza, Orlando, was requested to step in. (He was born twenty minutes after his twin brother Blotto.) But as he was totally unprepared, he pointed to Allegro: 'He'll make a much better speech than I ever could.' So Allegro's cage was moved to the centre of the lawn, and he made a twenty-minute speech on the history of the Braganza dynasty, on its ups and downs, on the joys and responsibilities of the married state, and on his hopes that Braganza House would remain a beacon of traditional hospitality. There was wild applause and Allegro was the centre of everyone's attention for a while. Particularly the children's, as they were fascinated by the miraculous bird.

Bella had engaged Panjim's best band to play throughout the evening. At seven-thirty, the serious drinking started. Groups formed here and there, and there was much singing of Goan mandos. Mostly in Konkani, but some in Portuguese. At one end of the large garden, a dance floor had been erected, and all age groups danced to old and new favourites. Bella had to chide the band frequently for playing too loud, particularly the wind instruments which were invariably off-key. Throughout, uniformed waiters plied guests with drinks and small eats of many different varieties. This was Mr Vaz's idea. No need to serve dinner after all that.

Muzaffar took a keen interest in the eats, asking the bearers for the names of the different items and English translations where possible:

- Sonhos de Camarao (Dreamy prawn puffs)
- Duck, Bacon or Tomato sandwiches
- Patolleo (Rice, coconut and jaggery steamed in a turmeric leaf)
- Chouriço do Reino (Royal sausages)
- Empadinhas (Small pies with pork or chicken)
- Fish Fingers

These were the eats that Muzaffar helped himself to. There were several others. Carmen and Imelda had outdone themselves. They had literally provided a banquet, and Bella was apprehensive of what the reception would cost.

The celebrations were slated to end with Maria and Boris performing two salon tangos to tunes the band knew. Maria had changed into an elaborate costume after the church ceremony, but as she was emerging for the performance she tripped on the stairs and sprained her right ankle. The pain was excruciating. So they begged off. Bella was disappointed as this item would have added a touch of class to the festivities.

When she informed Mr Vaz, he and one of his little nieces went up to the band leader and shouted something in his ear. Benny da Costa nodded, and there was a quiet moment before he spoke into the mike.

'And now, a request from a lovely young lady. I'm going to sing "I Want to Hold Your Hand." Come on girls and boys! Onto the dance floor!' Benny and his band gave a spirited rendition of the Beatles' classic. The children jerked and hopped and waved their hands enthusiastically and asked Benny to sing it again. Benny obliged and then turned to Mr Vaz.

'And now, to end this lovely evening we have a request from our generous host, Mr Hector Vaz, the father of the bride! Will the newly-weds and Mr Vaz and Mrs Isabella Braganza kindly step forward...We are going to perform a classic, sung originally by our very own, Madras-born Englebert! We...give...you..."The Last Waltz!"'

The band started to play. Benny crooned out the lyrics (which were not entirely appropriate for the occasion). The two couples glided across the floor. Hector held Bella very, very close (which was not entirely appropriate for a waltz). Although moderately drunk, he was an expert dancer. Midway through the number, he mumbled something in Bella's ear. She couldn't quite make out what he was saying. His speech was quite slurred.

'Yes, Mr Vaz? I couldn't catch what you said.' Hector mumbled some more. She tried to lip-read. It seemed he was asking her to marry him.

'Oh, Mr Vaz! At our age?...We hardly know each other! Let me see, I think we have met on only five occasions...I promise to think about it. We'd have to know each other really well before I consider your proposal...Now pull yourself together...Come on. We have to say goodbye to our guests—and carry all the gifts indoors before they are spirited away by the waiters...Haven't you noticed the song is over? The music has stopped.'

The children gathered around Allegro, wanting to say goodbye to him. He asked for all their names and cracked a few jokes aimed at several ten-year-olds. As the last of the children left, he called out, 'Send your great-grandchildren to see me and I'll tell them some more stories.'

Tonio, Imelda, Bella and an unsteady Hector stood at the gate. There were many 'Congratulations,' 'Long/Happy married life,' 'Thanks for the lovely evening,' 'You danced beautifully,' etcetera. The Archbishop had slept through the music and the dancing and had to be shaken quite energetically to wake up. As he was escorted to his car he kept repeating 'God blesh you, my children.' He had had a good time.

~

Just as the arrivals of the Braganzas had been staggered, so too were their departures. Blotto and Peter decided to stay on in Braganza House for an indefinite period as the fresh air did wonders for Blotto's old lungs. Julio spent a day getting the measure of the tentative site for Magda's inter-faith ashram. Bella was too busy to accompany him. After this was done, he spent two days driving Laila around in a taxi to various churches which they both sketched.

Magda and Muzaffar were on easy terms now and chatted amiably with the paying guests. Mrs Dias went to Panjim to re-book their tickets on Indian Airlines so that they could travel back to Delhi with Laila and Julio. Orlando, Verna and Asif also asked for tickets on the same flight. Verna had been uncharacteristically quiet during the wedding. She was upset by all the expenditure on flying to and from Goa, on Orlando's wedding gift of an expensive reel-to-reel tape recorder, and on the lavish reception. Although she was a fairly rich man's wife, she was after all the daughter of a railway clerk and thereby very frugal in her habits.

Allegro declared his intention to settle down in Braganza House. This surprised everyone, particularly his favourite great-great-grand-nephew Asif who wanted the bird to attract customers to his music shop. Bella, Tonio and Imelda welcomed the idea, as the famous bird would be a great tourist attraction for the resort and had no bad habits except for drinking a full cup of feni after his evening meal. The alcohol helped him sleep, he said. He wished to live in a village-like atmosphere for the next hundred years. Saligao was ideal.

Maria, Boris and Yanek left early because of Yanek's cabaret bookings. The train journey to Delhi would take three days. They looked forward to moving into the dance-studio-cum-residence that Julio had designed for them in the mango orchard. They would be eternally grateful to Orlando for financing its construction. They were the poor relatives.

Julio's own cottage next door was much larger. It contained two studios: one for Laila and one for himself. This too was ready for occupation. When Julio retired from the ASI in a few weeks, he planned to set up an architectural conservation practice. Because Laila had said nothing about returning to New York, it seemed to Julio that she had come to stay in Delhi for good. He had grown rather fond of her. Again. She continued to wear the wedding ring.

Acknowledgements

I shall be eternally grateful to Meera, my partner in life, for her unflagging support and inspiration throughout the writing and publication of this book. I wish to thank Sambuddha Sen for information on 19th century Calcutta; Albert Tham for material on 19th century Shillong; Ravi Singh, my publisher, and Yauvanika Chopra, my enthusiastic editor, for their expert advice during publication.